THE REBELS

THE REBELS

THE NORTHWEST UPRISING: BOOK ONE

NADYA SIAPIN

SKU: 2370001684904

The Rebels/Nadya Siapin—2nd ed.

The Travelling Storyteller Press

Cover art by MIBLArt (https://www.miblart.com)

Maps by @Saumyasvision/Inkarnate

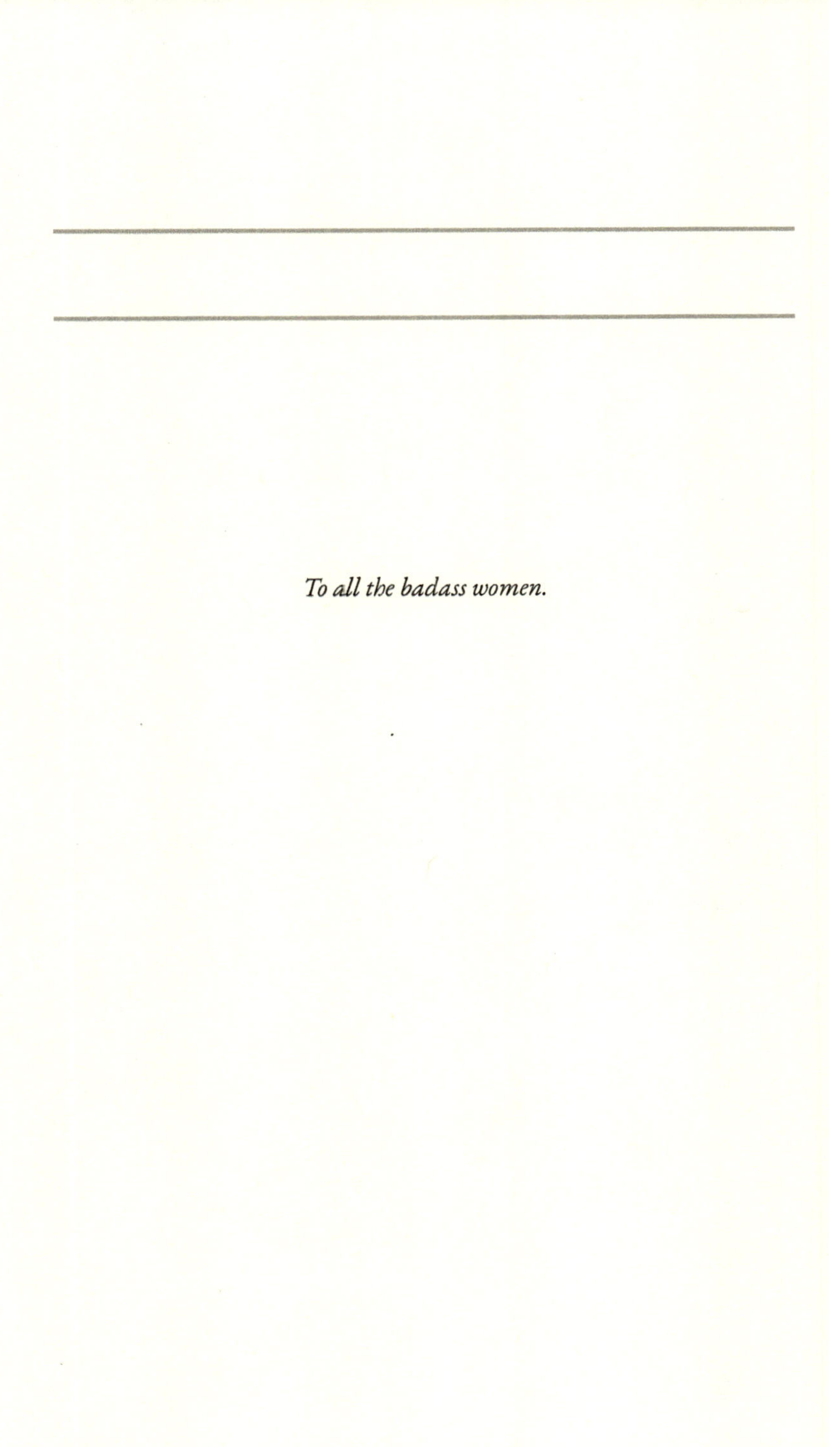

To all the badass women.

CONTENT

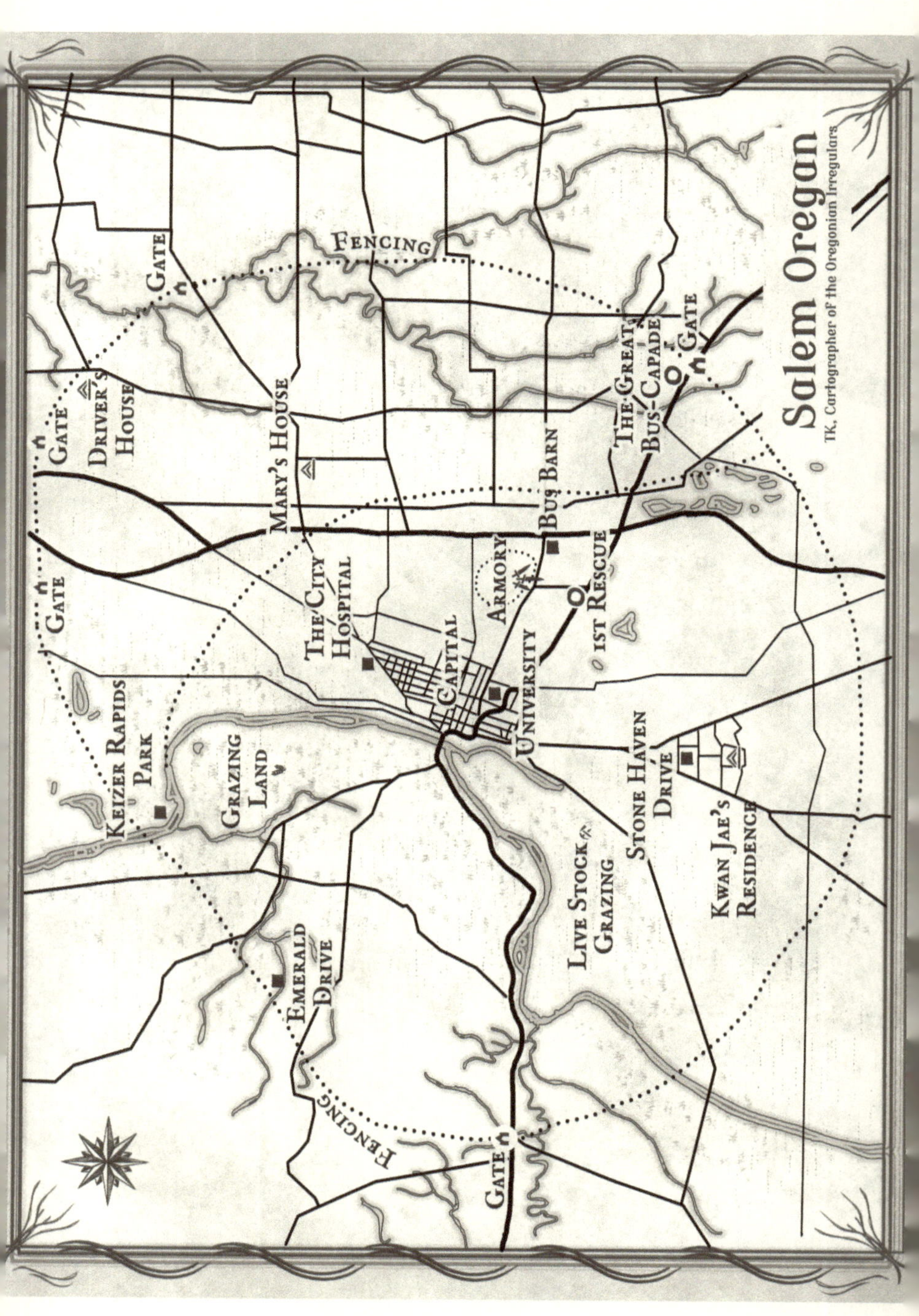
Salem Oregon
TK, Cartographer of the Oregonian Irregulars
FENCING
GATE
DRIVER'S HOUSE
GATE
MARY'S HOUSE
THE GREAT BUS-CAPADE
GATE
BUG BARN
ARMORY
THE CITY HOSPITAL
1ST RESCUE
CAPITAL
UNIVERSITY
KEIZER RAPIDS PARK
GRAZING LAND
STONE HAVEN DRIVE
LIVE STOCK GRAZING
KWAN JAE'S RESIDENCE
EMERALD DRIVE
FENCING
GATE

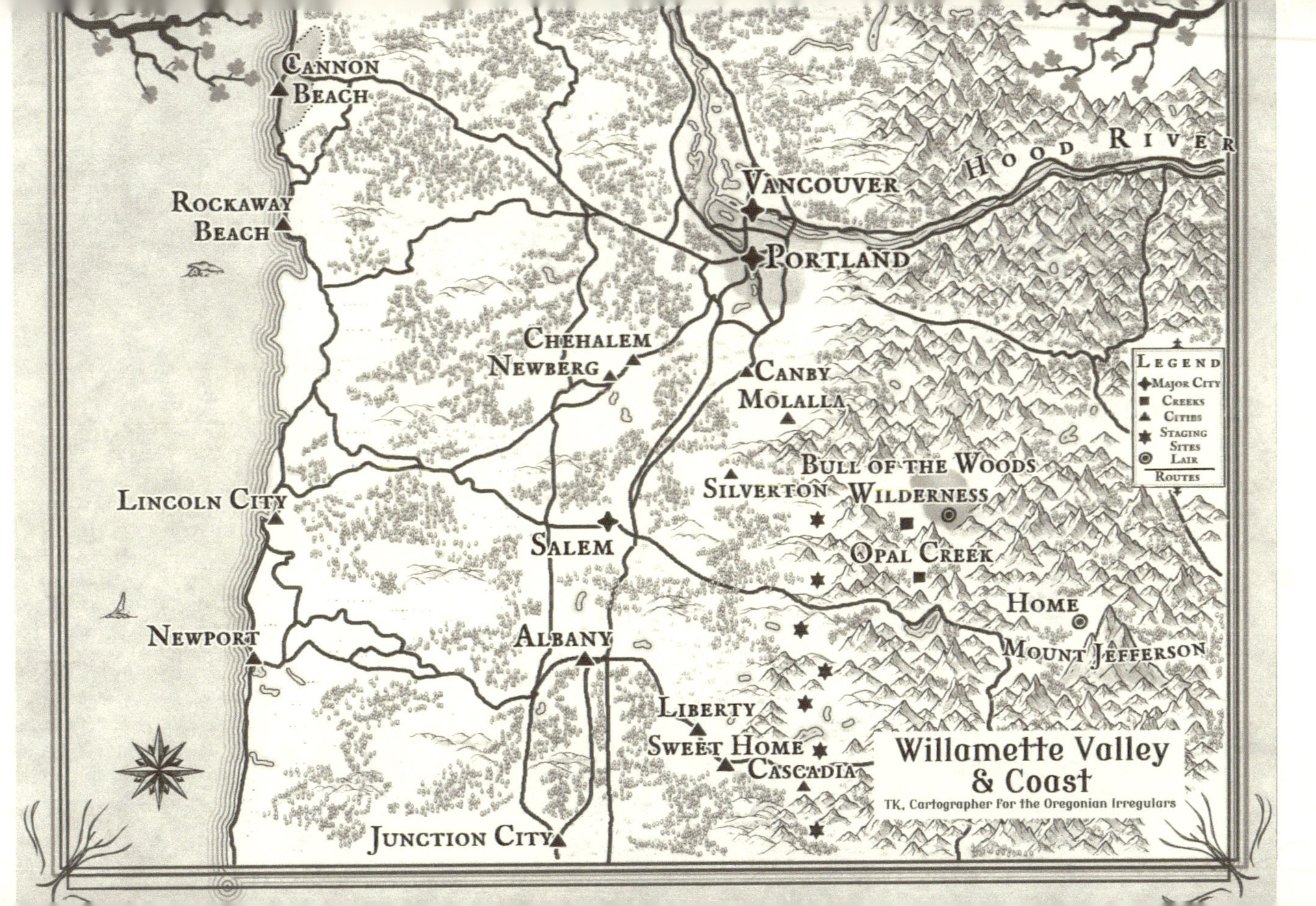
Willamette Valley
& Coast
TK, Cartographer for the Oregonian Irregulars
LEGEND
Major City
Creeks
Cities
Staging
Sites
Lair
Routes
HOOD RIVER
Cannon Beach
Rockaway Beach
Vancouver
Portland
Chehalem
Newberg
Canby
Molalla
Bull of the Woods
Silverton
Wilderness
Lincoln City
Opal Creek
Salem
Home
Newport
Albany
Mount Jefferson
Liberty
Sweet Home
Cascadia
Junction City

Prologue: The Present

The intern loitered a dozen feet away from the event's speaker, watching the woman as she waited backstage to be called out. People rushed around, techs, crews, and plain old busybodies, but they all avoided the woman. Middle aged, she wore clothing the intern considered horribly unstylish and plain. There's no way cargo pants, moccasins, or a patched leather jacket would ever have been trendy.

"I can't decide if the rumors are true," a young sound tech whispered behind the intern. "On the one hand, her weaponry is impressive, but I was expecting...more."

The intern agreed. The speaker was tall, but the stories always made her out to be a giant. Oh, and everybody assumed the person known as Captain was a man. The intern wasn't sure how the rest of the Irregulars had managed to keep that quiet all these years.

In her right hand, the speaker held a rifle with a casual negligence that spoke of long familiarity, and through her open jacket the intern caught a glimpse of some kind of harnessing. Was that the butt of a pistol? There was no mistaking the two handguns on each thigh, however. The worn handle of a machete jutted above her left shoulder.

Weapons and clothing displayed a level of wear and tear the intern had never seen before.

"She's really a rebel leader?" the intern whispered to the tech. "I mean, you'd expect someone with better looks or charisma or something. She's not even trying to hide the gray in her hair! So what if she's blonde. She should still do *something.* Instead, she's been standing like a statue for the last five minutes. I'm not even sure if she's blinked."

Indeed, the speaker stood, a rock of calm in the ocean of chaos around her, the rush of people intimidated by her stillness.

On stage, Mrs. Price, the local high school's principal, who'd found the woman, passionately gave her introduction. The intern privately wondered if Mrs. Price would ever stop talking. Just as the intern decided to be witty and offer another opinion to the sound tech, the woman turned her head, and the intern found herself speared by cold blue eyes.

I can hear you, the speaker mouthed, pointing to her ear.

The intern blushed and hurriedly found somewhere she desperately needed to be, dragging the sound tech with her.

***

The speaker, Hope Sanders, smirked, then settled back into waiting, staring into space and letting the tide of humanity wash around her. Now that she didn't have two kids to distract her, she wasn't really sure if she could get up on that stage and tell these strangers about the most amazing and horrifying years of her life.

Onstage, the principal continued enthusiastically about the high school's history curriculum. It was that damn curriculum and an old photo the twins had shared in class that had shone the spotlight on Hope and her family. Now here she stood, waiting to be the guest of honor at an event called—of all things—Recent History: Heroism on the Front. Heroism had been the farthest thing from anybody's mind during the war.

"Hope?" A gentle hand touched the speaker's shoulder. "Are you all right?"

Hope turned, recognizing the voice. "Alex," she said gratefully. "Damned if I know." She gave the smaller woman a quick hug.

"Still scaring kids, huh?" Alex gestured towards the departed intern.

"Some habits are hard to break." The tiny smile returned. "Besides, it's fun."

Alex rolled her eyes but continued watching her friend carefully. "Could you actually hear them?"

Hope's smile widened. "Of course not! Though I won't tell if you won't."

"Nope." Alex shook her head, then changed the subject. "Did you tell the boys anything beforehand?"

Hope's slight smile vanished. "The usual, when you and Tom were there. Details? No. I'm still not sure I can get through it once. Tell it twice? Not a snowball's chance in hell."

Hope's twin teenaged sons, Michael and Gabriel, had asked her to take the offer to speak about the war years. Hope closed her eyes. The boys wanted to know the truth about their parents, and why everyone of her generation was so...serious. Sad. She'd bet they were about to get more than they bargained for.

"Look at that sky." Alexandra peeked through the curtains blocking off the backstage and changed the subject. "What a beautiful day. Thank God it isn't raining. Would've been typical if it was," she added wryly.

Hope followed and stood behind the shorter woman, peering over her head. The stage had been built in just over twenty-four hours, inside the Silverton football stadium out on the western edge of town. One could call it drafty, hastily crafted, or even Mickey Moused. Hope preferred to think of it as spacious and reassuring. She got anxious if she couldn't see outside or smell fresh air.

The trees had begun to change colors, their fiery foliage standing out against the deep green of the fir trees marching up the flanks of the Cascade foothills. Above everything, the sky was a heartbreaking, familiar blue, decorated with long, feathery wisps of cloud that looked like an outstretched angel's wing. Her heart twisted in her chest, and she rested a hand lightly there, feeling it pound.

"Excuse me, Ms. Sanders?" Hope turned from the sliver of light to see the intern right behind her, shifting nervously from one foot to another. "They're ready for you." The girl looked ready to bolt.

"All right, kiddo." Hope mustered up a smile. "It's okay. I won't eat you."

"Though next time maybe you shouldn't be so quick to judge," Alex interjected. The intern's eyes widened, and Alexandra smiled slowly. "*I* heard you. We survived. In order to do that, we had to learn a thing or two. You should try it sometime."

The intern ran, and Hope gave her friend a reproving look. "Now who's scaring the children?" Alex grinned back, unrepentant.

"Ma'am, ma'am, you must take your seat—oh, it's *you*, Mrs. Carrington!" The event coordinator arrived, giving Alex an ingratiating smile. "Will you be remaining backstage?"

"No," Alex assured her. "I'll be joining my husband." Then to Hope, she added, "We're in the front, next to your family."

Hope nodded, barely aware. She inhaled, then exhaled slowly. *Always sound confident, even when you're not. Fake it 'til you make it.* The advice echoed down through the years, as relevant now as the day the words were first spoken.

Reaching up, she absently felt the mic at her collar, resisting the urge to rip it off and throw it away.

"Ms. Sanders?" The coordinator stood, waiting.

Hope started, only to find Alex had already disappeared to find her seat, so she followed the coordinator. She reached for the battery box on her belt and flicked the power on as she stepped out onto the stage amid thunderous applause. It had been a long time since Hope had seen so many people in one place. She took one more deep breath, and then stumbled to a halt, her rifle dangling from her nerveless fingers as she stared at the backdrop.

It was a grainy photo of a group of young people gathered in a meadow surrounded by trees. Hope knew every person in that photo. She knew what had happened to all of them. She drank in the sight, all of them smiling and laughing, their arms thrown around each other. Facing death every day, but knowing that right there, in that moment, they were *alive.*

Unable to stand any longer, Hope sank to one knee. Her quick, panting breaths echoed over the crowd from the speakers, the only thing letting them know she hadn't turned to stone.

"Hail the victorious dead." The words whispered throughout the stadium, silencing the audience as the woman rose and turned toward the crowd.

Chapter 1

My cousin Sonya stuck her head out of the window, pulling her shirt open at the collar. "Oh, man, I'm dying. Why is it so freaking humid? Hope, can we go back? There's a nice creek back there. I like that creek."

Sonya pulled her head back in, looking at me with midnight-blue eyes. Overweight, she had a comfortable belly and double chin, a stocky frame packed with muscle under the fat, and a missing tooth barely visible when she grinned. As a result of the extra weight, she got overheated easily, like now.

We even had a bet going, set up before we left. I said she'd lose seven pounds with the hiking. She bet five.

I glanced at her, laughing. "Yeah, but we all got bills to pay. One day off is about all we can manage. Dammit."

We'd just spent the last three days backpacking through the Opal Creek Wilderness. It'd been three days of hiking, plus camping when we were tired. Drinking from Opal Creek and swimming in the Little North Santiam. Walking the tracks and craning our heads back as far as the pack would allow, trying to see the tops of the trees. Spreading our arms and breathing in the loam- and crisp water-scented air. Feeling insignificant, dwarfed by the giant, regal trees.

Then I groaned, thinking about tomorrow. I had a crash repair, and the owner was a nightmare, calling every day to see if the damn car was ready. One of those new cars the government handed out to replace fossil fuel cars, they were so delicate that fixing parts couldn't be done. Instead, everything was replacement only, and I was still waiting for parts. Those cars spent more time with the techs getting the bugs worked out of their computer systems than on the road. Will, my cousin and Sonya's older brother, had more work than he could handle with those damn things and was also training his younger brother, Jake, in the computer work.

I patted the steering wheel of my '87 GMC. Ancient, yes, but it didn't fully run on petrol anymore. I'd converted it after I bought it from our neighbors four years ago. Sure, she took some gas, but the adjustments I made meant she went a lot farther on one tank than these cars were originally designed to do. I didn't have so much as a computer chip in this baby, and repairs were quick and easy. If the stupid government initiative had listened to mechanics, we could have made modifications to all vehicles. Instead, scrapped cars were piled in heaps in junk yards across America.

Morons.

"I need something pleasant to think about," I complained. "I'm not ready for real life again. Son, what's good and nice?"

She didn't have to think. "Dogs! And pizza. Speaking of which, wanna stop and get some on the way home?"

I did some quick calculations. "Will Toni be home? And you're stepping on a scale before you're allowed within *smelling* distance of that pizza. I want my Ben and Jerry's."

Sonya laughed, a great belly roll. I loved watching her laugh. Merriment seeped from every pore. Her shoulders shook as she leaned back in the seat. Store Santas at Christmas could learn a thing or two from her about how to laugh. But I digress. Our entire bet was based on Ben and Jerry's ice cream, and I stood to win an entire pint.

Then there was Toni, Sonya's sister and our roommate. I snorted softly. I spent more time with the Gatens—Son's family—than mine. I lived with Sonya and Toni in Silverton and worked with Will and Jake, just a five-minute walk from our place. Will was married and lived in the house with our work garage. Jake and Dana lived with their mom, my Aunt Rose.

My own family, the Wilkins, were based in Molalla—which is why I rarely saw them—though only Papa and Sean were there right now. Grace had just gotten married and was away on her honeymoon with her new husband, Charlie, and Peter, the baby of the family, had just gotten through boot camp three months earlier. I'm the oldest, followed by Sean, then Grace, then, like I said, little Peter.

I missed seeing Papa and Sean, but with the way things were, I didn't have time for the forty-minute drive twice a day that living in Molalla required. Couldn't find another job closer to home, either. Work was scarce. Everybody held on to what they had.

"Nah, she's planning to stay at Steve's this week." Son shook her head. "'Closer to work' is what she told me. I mean, she doesn't have to *lie*. She could just *say* she wanted to stay with him for a week."

Toni and her boyfriend, Steve, were spending more time at his house than ours lately. Me and Son thought that we'd either be looking for a new roommate soon or moving in with Auntie Rose. Couldn't afford our place with less than three paychecks.

"No worries," I said, smiling a little. My other cousin, Mercy, was from Australia, and she'd come into town for my sister's wedding. I'd picked up a few of her slang words while she'd been here. I glanced in the rearview mirror, checking out the clouds. "I reckon I've got enough for a pizza. Let's get a couple frozen ones from Safeway and take them to your mom's. Feed everybody. Pick up the dogs at the same time."

Sonya's dogs, an elderly Chow and Lab mix and a Border Collie puppy, stayed at my aunt's while we were gone. Usually we'd take dogs with us, but Cin was too old and Obelix too young. I missed having a dog on our hikes.

Lightning flashed behind us, illuminating the black clouds moving in from the south. For a moment, the evergreens were starkly outlined, standing in untidy rows on the foothills we'd just left.

"Nasty storm behind us," I commented, jerking a thumb over my shoulder.

Sonya twisted around in her seat as thunder rumbled across the sky. She began counting the separation between lightning and thunder. "I don't even know why I'm counting. Do you count between the thunder and lightning, or the lightning and thunder? The damn clouds are moving fast, anyway. Gonna be a bad one, too."

"Must be why we haven't seen any cars," I said, looking in the mirror again. "The hell if I'd want to be caught out in this shitstorm that's coming."

"Must've been building for a while, too. Remember that thunder the first night? Freaky shit."

Our first night out, we'd heard thunder and seen some flashes of lightning. Sounded like it came from the east, though. "Now we know summer's over. Two storms in three days."

"Should we check the weather report?" Sonya reached for the dial on my radio.

I snorted. "That thing hasn't worked in forever. Besides, we don't need a weather report. We can see it gaining on us."

Sonya stared in fascination out the window, watching the clouds loom closer and closer. "Maybe we should get a few other things from Safeway while we're there. Like candles."

I giggled. "I love a good storm."

Chapter 2

"Go faster!" Son yelled at me. She stared intently out the back window again, but this time she watched the drunken morons who'd tried to shoot us and were now attempting to run us off the road. "They can't handle corners for shit, but they keep gaining on the straight!"

I gripped the steering wheel tightly and tried not to shake. I hadn't seen a gun in *years*. No one had. They'd been reduced in the population during the previous president's first term. After all the gun violence, we'd been thrilled, but now we had a new guy in office who'd taken gun control and turned it into a ban. Get caught with a gun now, it's an automatic ten-year prison sentence and a ten thousand dollar fine that had to be paid before the perpetrator had a chance of seeing freedom again.

The people I'd heard of who got caught with a gun were usually in prison longer than ten years because of how long it took their families to pay the fine. My own parents had been slapped with a massive fine just for opposing the bill when it was being passed into law. Apparently, being the first ones to show up at the courthouse with signs meant you get to be the example. We were still paying the damn thing off, and probably would until my kids were adults.

If I lived long enough to have kids. Doubtful at this point.

The gun control had started mildly enough. Restrictions are what we asked for, and restrictions are what we got. It worked, too. Normal people had extra-strength stun guns—EM's. You could get one hell of a shock from one.

I spun the wheel, sliding around a corner, then whipped the steering wheel the other way, finishing out the S-bend.

"Will you go faster?" Son screamed.

"What about the cops? Call them!" I screeched, taking a sharp corner way too fast.

"Your phone's dead, remember?"

"Pieces of shit technology," I wailed. "They never work when you want them to! What the fuck is going on?"

No public holiday this weekend. No fireworks. So what the hell got into these guys? And where the *fuck* did they get guns? I took a corner, leaning into the curve. Sonya clutched the door with her other hand braced against the dash. The encroaching storm clouds cast a gloom over the valley despite it being mid-afternoon. The damn drunkards were in such bad shape they needed their headlights, and every time we hit a straight stretch of road their lights half blinded me.

We raced through the farm country of the Willamette Valley. That means rolling hills and blind corners. Have fun getting carsick. Straight bits were few and far between here, thank God. Every time we lost sight of them, I hoped they'd get bored and give up, but a few seconds later, there they were again.

Sonya screamed as bullets peppered my tailgate. "Do something!"

We snaked around another S-bend when I got a bad idea. Like, if it didn't work, we're dead. Then again, at the rate we were going, we'd be dead soon anyway.

There was a nice, long, straight stretch coming up in a couple miles. "Hold on!" I shrieked.

"I am!" Son screamed.

I gunned the engine, trying to get every bit of speed out of my poor truck as I could. A small hill was coming up, followed by more curves. A lot of curves, with a few side roads. If we made it past the hill, we had a tiny chance. The engine of my ancient GMC whined as it tried to keep up with my demands. I kept one eye on the lights in my rearview.

Sonya wasn't kidding. Those sons-of-bitches wallowed around the corners but really built the speed back up. We careened around the first corner, passed a side road, then went around the second corner. I flipped my headlights off, making Sonya screech, and stomped the brake, crawling around the corner onto the new road as quietly as a six-cylinder engine could. The road went uphill briefly, then abruptly down. At the bottom, I stopped and turned the engine off.

We waited, holding our breath.

The crazy drunk guys roared right past our side road. I slumped over the steering wheel as we both gasped. Thank God we'd been skipping in and out of their view. I hoped it might take them a few minutes to realize we weren't in front of them anymore.

"We lost them?" Son twisted around again. "Hope, you think we lost them?"

I trembled violently, fumbling the keys, then started the engine again, throwing my baby into gear. "Damned if I know."

"Why are we moving? I need a minute." Son had both hands braced on the dash, her head sagging between them as she hyperventilated.

"Ain't got a minute." I goosed the truck forward, keeping it slow so the engine stayed quiet. "Every book or movie out there, when the good guys are in a situation like this, they get caught 'cuz they stopped for a breather.

I am *not* getting caught by those drunk assholes. Do you know where we are?"

I wasn't familiar with the side roads between Stayton and Silverton. Never needed to be. I wished my phone worked. I really needed Google right now. Nevertheless, I took the first left I came to. Anything to get farther away. We worked our way down the roads, replaying every minute of the insanity just past.

"The way you took those corners was insane!" Sonya exclaimed.

"I know, right? Was it just me, or did they look like they nearly over-turned back there?"

"Wasn't your imagination. They were seriously tipping for a minute."

"What the hell was up with the shooting?"

"Right? I didn't know there were any guns left!"

"We need to go to the cop shop. As soon as we find Silverton."

"Amen, cousin."

I lifted a hand to tuck my hair behind my ear, but it was shaking so bad that I clamped it back onto the steering wheel. This was entirely too much excitement for me. Boring may be boring, but at least it's not near-death.

Thirty minutes and an eternity later, I breathed a sigh of relief. "I actually recognize this road."

Sonya peered around. "Me, too. Which one is it?"

"The hell if I know! I just know we turn right up ahead." That 'right' was Cascade Highway. We were nearly home.

Soon enough we approached Westfield Street and the Safeway. "Other than those drunk assholes, have you noticed any other cars?" I asked Son curiously.

"There've been tons of cars," Son replied absently, looking behind us again.

"Not parked," I said dryly.

"I can't remember, but—shit, it's those drunk assholes again!"

I looked in the rearview mirror. "Fuck! It *is* them!" I recognized their lights. Those Hummer-type trucks aren't common in Oregon. We're too poor here to afford those vehicles.

"Parking lot," Son said urgently. "Safeway's around the corner. Hide in the parking lot!"

"Do you think they got a good enough look at us to remember?" I asked, pulling into a parking space in the most crowded section. That wasn't saying much, with only a dozen or so cars in the lot.

"We're about to find out," Sonya muttered as we slid down in our seats. The drunks drove right past the car park and didn't even turn in. "Maybe they're too drunk to think straight."

"Well, hallelujah, brother," I groaned, straightening up. "Fuckers. I can't wait to tell the cops about them and get their asses thrown in jail."

We got out of the truck to stretch. I pulled my laces tighter and retied my boots. "I'm tired," I announced.

"Get cops. Get food. Then get sleep." Sonya flipped me off good naturedly.

I cracked a laugh, then stopped. "Hey, look!" I pointed near the first set of doors. "It's another Hummer-style truck! I wonder if it actually has all the bells and whistles?"

Sonya grunted, totally uninterested.

"Weird to see two of them around," I continued. "I wonder if the Resort's—" A scream from inside the store interrupted me.

"The fuck?" Sonya turned.

The woman—it had to be a woman, no man I'd ever heard managed to get to that pitch—screamed again, longer. My heart squeezed, then started again with a painful lurch.

"Call the cops." My voice trailed away as I remembered. "Dammit! C'mon!"

"What? Are you crazy?"

A muffled shriek sounded from the store. "Damned if I'm gonna stand by and listen! Your mama raised us better than this!" I started towards the doors.

Behind me, I heard "Fuck, fuckin' fuck shit, fucked, we're gonna fucking die!" Since the profanities followed me, I didn't care what she said. I just really didn't want to do something this stupid alone.

The doors didn't automatically open when we got there, which created new depths to the pit in my stomach. I pushed cautiously against them, and they opened slowly, catching a bit at first. Rough hands appeared next to mine, Sonya helping. We leaned into the doors, with her weight the deciding factor to get the damn things moving.

As we slipped in, we heard harsh male laughter. The woman had subsided into muffled sobs and moans. We followed the sounds towards the back of the store.

I leaned in close to Son so we wouldn't be overheard. "I hear three guys," I breathed.

She nodded.

"We should split, take them from two sides." I pointed to her, and indicated she stay put, and motioned that I'd take the long route. "If we're lucky they'll panic and run. If we're really lucky, some other person got the cops, and they'll show up soon."

"Our luck ain't been that great," Sonya grumbled. She winced when the woman got enough air to let out another scream.

"We're not dead yet. Wait for me to go first." *We are soo gonna die.* I clasped Son's shoulder briefly, then ran as quietly as I could down the aisle. These guys hadn't trashed the store much, I noticed, just a bit of random destruction. I shook my head. Why was I picking up on shit that wasn't any part of my immediate safety? Not just stupid, a friggin' moron, that's me.

I passed an aisle. Three dudes. The woman lay on the floor, naked, and there was blood everywhere. I almost changed my mind about all this. I thought we'd scare these guys *off*, but if they were spilling blood... Without realizing it, I slowed fractionally.

Then one of the guys hit the woman, and my auntie came to mind. Her sister had been abused by her husband and we'd never known about it until her murder. Aunt Rose said she'd wished someone had been able to help her sister, and if we ever met someone in trouble, we should give them any and all help we could.

My breath came faster, panic warring with adrenaline. With no idea which one was winning, I kept moving forward. I'd turned down an aisle and nearly reached the end.

Oh God, don't let us die here.

I didn't slow down at the end of the aisle, I didn't stop. If I did, I'd never start again. I just *knew* that I'd stand there and listen to a woman being raped and beaten and not do a damn thing to help her. I'd never be able to look at Aunt Rose again if I did that.

So I ran around the corner.

The young woman was securely held down by two of the men, Asians, I think. Her head thrashed as she tried to throw off the hand muffling her, her fingers bent in rigid claws of protest. The third man was atop her, bare hips pounding. There were half-empty liquor bottles scattered around, and one of the men had a bottle clenched in his fist, drinking as he pinned the woman's leg with his knee, free hand holding her arm.

The woman got in a lucky bite, and the owner of the hand gave her a heavy, open-handed slap that rocked her head. It centered me, seeing that. It left no doubt in my mind about what I should be doing. Suicidal or not, here I come.

It was too late for them by the time they saw me coming.

I stopped a stride away from the woman and snapped out a kick at the rapist's head. Something broke under my heavy boot, and his head bent at a weird angle. He flopped bonelessly over the woman, pinning her down. I kicked the man at her head in the chest, knocking him backwards towards the produce.

The third man, across the woman from me, scrabbled on the floor, trying to get fingers numbed by drink to function. He bumped an object, and I realized he was trying to grab a gun.

I screamed wordlessly and launched myself across the woman at the bastard before he could grab the gun. It was a mad scramble, both of us trying to stay on top, and I heard someone shouting. Took me a few seconds to figure out it was me.

"What the hell is wrong with you people? What is going on? Where the *fuck* are all these guns coming from?" I couldn't pay attention to what I screamed, it just poured out. At the back of my mind a little voice shouted *Shut up, you idiot! You're in a fight for your life and you're complaining?*

I struck out blindly and hit something soft. The man bucked suddenly, throwing me off and sending me sprawling. He slowly got to his feet, then pulled a knife from the sheath at his back.

"Fuck you!" I screamed.

He jerked suddenly, then again. The reports from the gun took a few seconds to register in my dazed brain, and I twisted, looking for the shooter. The woman stood mere feet from my head, holding the handgun, bloody and bruised, but up. Her teeth bared, mouth coated in blood, she turned to the last man, who scrambled away from Sonya, his eyes red and streaming from the pepper spray she held in her hand.

The woman's eyes were raw, merciless, as she emptied the magazine into the man, even as he held his hands up to show he was unarmed. All he said was "No, no!" over and over until the light left his eyes.

The woman looked at us, my cousin and myself, her face bruised, one eye closed, defiance radiating from her, daring us to judge her. I looked at Sonya, who didn't look as horrified as a person might, normally, then down at the man I'd kicked in the head.

He was definitely dead.

I looked back up at the woman and said, "Ain't gonna cast no stones. In your shoes, I'd have done the same." My throat hurt, and my voice was raspy but clear enough for her to understand.

She nodded once then sat down abruptly, crying. "They killed my baby. They swu-swung him by his-his feet and hit his head." She began sobbing uncontrollably.

I scooted towards her carefully. My legs were shaking too much to stand. She showed no resistance as I took the empty gun from her and hugged her gently. Tears started wobbling in my eyes, but I blinked them back. If I got to crying now there'd be no stopping me, and shit was seriously wrong here. I needed to think.

Over her shoulder I noticed Sonya suddenly blanch and turn away, falling to her knees, retching and crying. In amongst some fallen produce I finally spotted it: a small foot, blotched with drying blood. I stared numbly at it, and the shiny red apple next to it.

I almost missed it when the woman began talking, nearly incoherent, about running out of food, needing more, and if she'd just stayed home, her baby boy would still be alive, and why hadn't she just stayed home?

I crooned softly to her, the way I'd done for my cousin Dana when she was a baby and rocked her gently. "Ooookay, ooookay. No, no, don't go over there yet. We'll get him a blanket, get him wrapped, okay? Just wait here for a moment. No, don't worry, I'll stay in your sight."

I gently set her away from me and clambered shakily to my feet. I marveled at the woman's fortitude, that she'd managed to find her feet and shoot two men after all she'd been through.

I waved a hand to get Sonya's attention. *Get my pack,* I mouthed. She nodded, glassy eyed, and stumbled from the store. There had to be something around here that would work for a blanket. I scanned the shelves and found bath towels. Okay.

Grabbing a couple, I headed back to the woman and child. "My name's Hope. My cousin with the pepper spray is Sonya." I kept up a gentle sing-song as I spoke, as if she were a skittish horse or a frightened pup. "Can you tell me your name?"

"Alex," she finally whispered, gaze never leaving that one tiny foot.

"Okay, Alex. As soon as we can, we'll take you to the hospital. You need to get checked out."

"No," she shook her head. "No. No hospital. Closed. All closed." She stared, mesmerized, rocking gently back and forth. "Not home. No food. Not home. No."

"Is there anyone we can call?"

"No phone. No family. No one." Her voice broke and she shuddered, crying silently.

I looked around frantically. Where was Sonya? I really needed backup. Or a drink. I wanted my dad. My lips trembled and I tightened them, feeling the corners turning down. Nope, nope, nope, nope. I bit my lip.

No time for this, I told myself sternly. *We can break down later, when we have time. When we're finally home. Suck it up, buttercup.*

I continued on to the little boy, lying as if thrown carelessly to the floor. My breath hitched, but I unrolled the towel and gently wrapped the child in it, ignoring the tears that dripped off my chin, making tiny lighter patches in the blood drying there.

I ignored his cracked skull. I didn't see the gray matter peeking through. I definitely didn't notice his beautiful green eyes that should have been sparkling with life. I left the baby's face uncovered, closing his eyes one final time.

Right after that, Sonya came back with my pack, and I dug through it to find some bits of spare clothes Alex could wear. Wasn't much, but it would be enough to get her to the hospital, provided she was wrong and the place was open.

God, I hoped she was wrong.

We cleaned Alex up as best we could and got her into shorts and a t-shirt, with my sweatshirt over the top. She shivered constantly. Everything hung on her tiny frame, but at least it stayed up. At one point, Sonya looked ruefully down at her belly, silently acknowledging that she was too fat to offer clothes without safety pins to keep them up.

Then she shrugged. Who cared about size right now?

We placed the baby in Alex's arms and left her holding him, mourning the child lost and rocking gently. We went into a two-person huddle, just far enough away that Alex couldn't hear us.

"What do we do now?" Sonya hissed, looking frantically around.

"I don't know! I've never been in this situation before!"

"I can go get the cops." Son half-turned towards the door, but I saw it in her face.

"You don't think anybody'll be there," I stated flatly.

"I want there to be. Is that close enough?"

"Alex said everything is closed. They're not supposed to leave their homes. She ran out of food and that's why she came here. Then those guys. Who the hell *are* they? Son, shit is seriously wrong."

"What do you suggest?"

"Wellll..." I pursed my lips and looked speculatively at the stocked shelves.

CHAPTER 3

It might seem odd to go from "law-abiding citizen" to "let's rob the store," but I'd always felt there was a bit of the budding crook in me.

I'd bought spray paint once for a couple jobs, marking cutting points. The first thing I did with the rest of the paint was take it to Salem and try graffiti. It didn't last long. I discovered I had no talent for art. Then there was the time we rearranged traffic cones. Using the one-way streets in downtown Silverton, we created a loop. It worked, until the cops got caught in it. The fire at the sauna was a pure accident, though, and not the arson the media tried to make it out to be.

Apparently, it's only a small step from a misdemeanor to larceny, but it was almost fun.

Anyway, Son ran around with a shopping cart, literally sweeping entire sections of canned goods into it while I had a good look at Alex's assailants.

Their military-style clothing caught my attention first. All camouflage and tough fabrics, everything buttoned, zippered, or velcroed. Everything had the same style. Guns, belts, holsters, clothing. It made me think military.

The second thing I noticed was that they were all Asian. In big, metropolitan areas, that's nothing to talk about. But Oregon is a bit of a backwater. We have plenty of whites and Mexicans, with a sprinkling of Native Americans and, like, two black people. So Asian dudes stand out.

The damn guns freaked me out the most, however. People are severely punished for having weapons, and we run into two separate groups, both heavily armed, in the same day?

I had the sinking suspicion that Alex's words were far more accurate than we wanted. If there were more dudes with guns, no wonder this shit was going down. Best the cops had were electromagnetic shock weapons, called EMs (I know, we've got some real naming geniuses on our hands). They are very similar to the ones passed out to the general public. Also like our EMs, they were non-lethal. However, the cops' EMs had three rounds each. Even then, EMs are no match for actual projectiles.

We were happy when guns were made more difficult to acquire under President Cooper. We hoped it would reduce the number of shootings. And it did.

But then we had a new rash of gun violence when President Trembly took office and decided to fully disarm the populace. These laws were passed despite the rushed nature of the process, and we'll never know if it was a proper majority vote because if the senators and congress-people weren't in attendance *at that exact moment* they were never given a chance to vote.

Like most of America.

A few years later, my parents' fears were realized when the President decided to abolish the "two term only" limitation to the presidential position. After all, the only reason we have the Second Amendment in the first place is out of a general distrust for government and authority figures. It seems our mistrust was well-founded, in his case.

Now I've got three dead men with guns in a country where firearms are illegal.

I ignored the crashing as Son continued her looting and went through the dead guys' pockets hoping to find *anything*, but they were completely clean. All the guys had a country flag sewn onto the shoulders of their sleeves, confirming my "soldier/military" guess. The flag had a blue bar across the top and bottom with a thin white strip between the blue and the red center and star in the middle, outlined in white. I took one with me to show a cop or a doctor. Hell, a dentist would be good enough for me right now.

"Two groups in one day," I muttered, looking at the bodies. "What the hell is going on?"

"Can we go yet?" Sonya shouted from the front of the store. "I got two shopping carts full of tins!"

I took a deep, shuddering breath and looked at the woman rocking her dead baby. Whatever the hell was happening, that was real enough. She'd left her home to find food, and this was the result. "Let's get more. I don't want to have to come back here anytime soon."

I grabbed the guns and holsters and chucked them into the cart Son rolled down the aisle for me. She gave me a look as I put the guns in. "What? We've already killed people and now we're shoplifting on a major scale. Might as well add stealing from the dead *and* possession of firearms to the list."

"We are fucked, aren't we?"

"I really don't see how it could be any other way." I shoved my cart ahead of me and joined Sonya in looting the store.

***

After installing Alex in the passenger seat, we loaded the truck and covered everything with a tarp to hide it. The toolbox I'd installed kept everything from banging against the cab, at least. We checked the sky frequently, watching the black clouds roll over us. Lighting flashed periodically, and thunder rumbled often. I dreaded the rain finally breaking. This would be the storm of the year.

Occasionally, Alex would talk, but it didn't make any sense. Well, it made as much sense as anything else we'd seen since we left the mountains. She talked about an invasion, and people being forced to stay in their homes, and patrols.

When we asked, she couldn't, or wouldn't, tell us who'd done the invading. She also reiterated that hospitals and police stations were closed.

"Have you noticed regular drive-bys?" I asked Son.

She shrugged. "I did see a truck like the one that chased us, but I was just inside the front doors. Then I saw another one a while later..."

Sonya and I stared at each other, and she looked like I felt, like I'd just been sandbagged.

"So," Son drew the word out, "what do we do now?"

"Stop by the hospital?"

"And if it's closed?"

"Stop by the police station?"

"And if *that's* closed?"

"Hell if I know. You realize we've only been talking in questions?" I caught myself popping my knuckles and twisting my fingers, a nervous habit I'd had since my mom died.

"Whatever." Sonya waved me away. "We still need a plan."

"Right." I took a deep breath and let it out, thinking furiously. "Plan A, we go to the hospital, give them Alex and let them take care of her. Plan B, we go to the cops, tell them the story, give them Alex, let them take care of her, and never let on we stole from the store. Plan C, we go to your mom's house and hide. Sound good?"

"Close enough. I'm driving. You ride in the back."

"We hide in plain sight if any of those Hummers show," I continued, tying the last knot to fasten the tarp over the bed. "Move fast, move quiet. No talking."

"Commando?"

"Yeah. You realize we're screwed?"

"Yeah."

"Okay. Just checking."

***

We got the hell out of there before another patrol rolled by and noticed all the extra stuff in the truck. The quietest street took us past the hospital, and it frightened me to see it dark. Closed. Plan A was out.

As we got closer to Main Street, I slid off the tarp covering the truck bed and jogged down the sidewalk, slowing as I got to the corner. Peering around it trying to spot any movement, I silently blessed the fact that I'd finally patched my damn muffler three weeks ago. I'd had a hole in it the size of my fist and a rumble-roar to let even the hardest of hearing know I was driving by.

The block of apartments looked deserted, all the blinds drawn until I saw a curtain twitch and a pale face peering out of a window. As soon as they saw me the curtain jerked back into place, the resident determined to pretend we weren't there.

As I walked down the hill in the direction we needed to go, I heard the sound of a truck and saw the flash of headlights. My heart jumped when the lights turned up the hill towards us. I spun around and waved at Sonya, miming sleep, the signal to turn the truck off and pretend we weren't there.

I slid under the bushes and held my breath as the Hummer rumbled up the hill less than three yards from where I lay under a bush. I buried my face in my arms, hiding my skin as the lights flashed over me, and bit my thumb against the insane desire to laugh.

All this—hiding from cars, evading The Man—was the essence of Commando. We'd play a huge, elaborate game of hide and seek in my cousin Faith's neighborhood in California. The hiders would be on foot, running through the suburbs at night trying to get back to the safe zone, which was Faith's house. We'd hide under cars, in shadows, and behind bushes, dodging seekers and the cops. The seekers were in cars, a driver and a runner cruising the streets to find hiders.

It made life fun and scary and insane, and I wanted to smack myself for enjoying this moment. *Get a grip, woman! We're not here for fun and games.* I sniggered into my arms, my shoulders rustling the leaves.

As soon as the Hummer was out of hearing, I popped out and signaled Son to start my baby up again.

It took us nearly thirty minutes to go a distance we'd usually cross in ten. Mostly because we had to go my speed. We swung by the police station, but like the hospital, its windows were dark, the doors locked. We ended up hiding twice more, and once Sonya pulled into a driveway to get us off the road.

Once we crossed Oak and made it onto Mill, I hopped onto the back of the truck, and Sonya drove as quick as she could to her mom's house. Once there, she stashed my truck behind the fence, in a low dip next to the house.

The house was a brown two-story with five bedrooms and a large yard. Me, Sonya, and Toni had actually lived there for a while, but Aunt Rose now had it up on the market. She needed to downsize because even with all of us there, we couldn't afford the taxes and expenses on the place. The front door was up a short flight of stairs and opened onto a landing. Inside, one short flight led down to the lower floor, one led up. It was a weird setup, and one that made the house difficult to sell.

Well, that and the fact that the economy was dead and buried.

Son was out of the truck before the engine fully stopped and, ignoring the dogs who came running up to the side fence, rushed up the stairs before my boots hit the pavement. My heart dropped into my stomach when she just pushed the door open. I heard her thundering through the house, first upstairs, then down, calling for her mom, Dana, and Jake, but only silence met her.

I took the limp little bundle of Alex's baby from her and helped her carefully out of the truck. The dogs woofed softly at the smell of a stranger, but the elder dog didn't make too much fuss. Alex moved stiffly and had to use the truck for support. I cradled the boy in one arm as Sonya ran out of the house.

"I'm goin' to the neighbors, see if anybody knows where they are," she gasped. She jogged unsteadily down the driveway, her knees wobbling after the rigors of the last few hours.

I looked down on the small bundle in my arms, trying to decide what to do. Finally, I turned to the boy's mother. "What would you like us to do?" I asked her. "Do you want to wait until we find a mortician, or...?"

"We won't find one," she breathed, eyes vacant. "Can-can we protect him—bury him—ourselves?"

I hesitated, thinking furiously. "Uh, yeah, I guess. There's a nice tree in the back we can bury him near." Best case scenario, we could always move him to a proper cemetery when this was all cleared up.

I climbed carefully over the fence, shifting the body to do so. Once over, I lent a hand to Alex to get her over the fence, too. The dogs mobbed me when I turned around. The older one, Cinder, shuffled from paw to paw in a happy dance before leaning against me for a quick scratch and some reassurance. The pup, Obelix, made tiny growling noises in between shivers, unsure and insecure.

I glanced over to their food bowls and saw they were empty. Poor guys must've been starving.

I knelt down and scooped up Obelix with one hand and handed him to Alex. "Can you hold him?" I asked. "Don't know how long these guys have been alone." She took the puppy gently, eyes clearing briefly when he snuggled up to her, reassured by the human contact.

When I showed her the spot I had in mind, near the apple tree, she nodded silently. It was a peaceful place, with the tree and a flower bed. Aunt Rose had put a small bench against the little garden shed so she could sit and relax under the trees while reading. I helped Alex settle down on the bench, then placed her baby next to her. Alex carefully rested one hand on his chest, and when it remained still, she let out a tiny sob.

Cinder, ever mindful of the emotions of others, walked over and settled stiffly next to her, laying his head on her thigh. I filled the dogs' water and food bowls and brought them over so they'd stay near Alex. Obelix wriggled down and promptly buried his nose in the water dish. Thirst taken care of, he dug into his food.

Cinder was careful to never lose contact with Alex while he ate, his gently-waving tail brushing her hand repeatedly. When I exited the shed with a shovel, I found her with her head leaning back, her free hand stroking his head, her eyes closed. Obelix, finished with his food, crawled into her lap to cuddle.

"Cinder there, now he's a certified therapeutic dog," I said conversationally as I began shoveling. "Sonya regularly takes him to the hospital. Everybody really loves him. It's neat to watch him with people. He seems to know just what they need, which is to cuddle a fluffy dog." Right on cue, Cinder put his front paws on the bench. When he realized he couldn't get the rest of the way up, I stabbed the shovel into the ground and gave him a boost. He promptly lay down next to Alex, head on her thigh. She buried a hand in his thick ruff. "By the time he's done with folks, they're usually a bit more stable, a bit calmer." Cinder raised his eyes to look at me without lifting his chin and *humphed* softly. "See? He agrees with me."

Alex's expression lightened fractionally, and her fingers began exploring his ears. The dog groaned softly in delight, angling his head so she could scratch where it itched.

As I dug, the light took on an unreal quality, seeming to hang in the air. Clouds covered the sky almost to the horizon, where the smallest sliver of light shone through. It seemed to reflect from the clouds, bouncing between earth and sky. Instead of lighting the world, it colored it, lending everything a golden-red glow.

Lightning flashed for the first time in a couple hours, almost on top of us, followed quickly by thunder. My pragmatic side came out and shoved the romantic out of the way, rolling up its sleeves. I put my back into digging.

Nothing like a storm to give you incentive. I was grateful for the calluses on my hands. I shouldn't have to worry about...I paused and looked down at my thumb. Never mind. The blister hadn't even registered, it just went straight to broken skin. I sighed and changed my grip on the shovel.

The whole time I listened, dreading the sound of a vehicle, dreading even more that I'd hear shouting. But all that broke the thick silence was the rustling of leaves and the thunder that came ever more frequently. And me, grunting with every stroke of the shovel.

I'd made it nearly three feet, moving slower all the time, when Cinder's head came up and he woofed. I looked up without alarm. That was his "hi, friend" bark. Good boy that he was, he stayed with the human who needed him, though. Obelix raced over, his little puppy yip making me wince.

Sonya climbed over the fence, and she wasn't alone.

Son dealt with the pup first, shushing him quickly, picking him up for a cuddle for him and a face wash for her. The people with her, a family of four, two adults and two early-to-mid teen kids, a boy and a girl, looked at us with a mixture of apprehension and hope.

"These are the Blakes." Sonya indicated each of them in turn. "Walter and Kioni, and their kids Asilia and Jaali." Asilia looked to be the elder of the children, I figured maybe fifteen years old. Jaali was probably more like twelve and growing. Walter, balding, middle aged, and looking fit under a sweater that screamed "teacher," was about my height. His wife, Kioni, could've been a supermodel. Tall, statuesque, her skin was the closest to true black I'd ever seen in my sheltered life. "This is my cousin, Hope, and that's Alex." Sonya pointed to the bereft woman under the tree.

The Blakes looked at the small bundle next to Alex, and Kioni's eyes filled with tears. She headed directly to Alex, kneeling next to her and resting a hand on the other woman's knee. In the intermittent flashes of light, Kioni and Alex looked like statues carved from ebony and ivory by a master craftsperson. Each flash showed a new tableau, ending with Kioni holding Alex close as the younger woman cried anew.

Walter cleared his throat, then indicated the shovel in my hand. "Need a break?" he asked.

Wordlessly, I passed him the shovel and he took it, looking at the fresh bloodstains on the handle. Sonya gave me a hand out of the grave, and I winced when she grasped my proffered hand.

"You'll need to get those taken care of," Walter said quietly, pointing to my bloodied hands as he jumped in.

I grimaced and nodded jerkily, moving to stand with my cousin.

"The Blakes live just up the hill," Sonya said quietly, jerking a thumb behind us. "They know as much as anyone, and they're willing to talk. No one else would even open their doors." She took a deep breath, let it out slowly. "Went by Will's. No one was there either." Her voice trembled.

Walter had only gotten another foot down when the first, fat drops of rain came. "No more time," I told him. "It's deep enough if we use the border rocks to build a cairn."

My aunt had edged her flower beds with large rocks. I figured there'd be enough to make a decent mound. Enough to prevent any animals from digging down, anyway.

Walter passed the shovel to his son, Jaali, and Sonya gave him a hand out. We helped Alex to her feet, and Sonya lifted the little body. She held him while I jumped into the hole, then she passed him down to me. Alex knelt beside the grave, Kioni Blake next to her, holding her while she cried, keening sobs as I laid the boy down, covering his face with a fold of the towel.

Jaali and Asilia stood together with their father, looking shell-shocked. Poor kids. I heaved myself out of the grave as Sonya took up the shovel. She held a shovel full of dirt out first to Alex to take a handful and drop it into the hole, then to the rest of us. As she filled it in earnest, racing the rain, Kioni began singing *Amazing Grace,* her voice a beautiful alto. Her children joined in, harmonizing with their mother.

I closed my eyes and tilted my face up to the rain, feeling their cleansing drops mix with the tears.

***

After we placed the rocks carefully over the grave, Walter Blake brought a small cross he'd constructed from gardening stakes and twine and pressed it into the ground. We stood there uncertainly, not sure what to do next.

"Can someone please say something for him?" Alex choked out, looking up beseechingly at us.

We looked around the circle, and Walter held his hand out, *I don't know enough,* he seemed to say. Sonya gave me a little wave.

I gulped, pulled my baseball cap off and clutched it, searching for words. What had they said at mom's…? Oh, right.

"Lord, we lay to rest this young one," I paused, realizing I didn't even know the boy's name, then looked to his mother.

"Dylan Jameson," Alex whispered.

"Dylan Jameson," I continued, "who came to You too young. We pray he rests in Your arms, always and forever, and know that he is safe with You." I swallowed, listening to Alex's tears, and turned to her. "I wish there were words that could comfort you, but the best we can offer is our sincere condolences and what safety we can provide. May the Lord keep you and comfort you until you see your son again. Amen."

"Amen," the others echoed solemnly.

The rain came thicker, and we barely made it in the back door before the deluge began.

CHAPTER 4

"We got woken up two nights ago by what sounded like thunder," Walter Blake began quietly, holding his wife's hand tightly. "Soldiers burst into our homes and held us all under guard. It wasn't until yesterday we were told what was happening. Some Colonel informed us that they were the North Korean Liberation Army, and they had freed us from our corrupt government."

The North Koreans had bombed certain high-target areas, places with military or political significance. Portland had been decimated, he said, and people had been ordered to remain in their homes. Those who disobeyed were...disappeared.

"We heard a disturbance down here," he told Sonya apologetically. "Your mom?" Son nodded. "She was really laying into them, sarcastic as hell, pointing out every flaw in their so-called 'liberation'. Let's just say they didn't like it. The last we saw, your family was being loaded into a truck. I don't know where they were taken. I'm sorry."

Sonya nodded, clenching her fists and staring resolutely ahead.

"And this is everywhere?" I asked.

"The entire Valley, we believe. Don't know for sure about Eastern Oregon, or anything about the rest of the country, though. Maybe it's just hopeful thinking."

"So, you mean to tell me I don't have time to freak out?"

He shook his head.

"Rude." I sat back in my chair and scrubbed my hands over my face. On the one hand, I was terrified. My dad and brother lived in Molalla, roughly an hour's drive away. On the other, I'd been terrified for a few hours now, and it was beginning to lose its bite. I wondered when I'd be able to make it home to find Papa and Sean. Looking around the table, I realized that it wasn't "when." It was "if."

"The reason people didn't try to escape is that they've done something that's shut down all technology. Phones, cars, even lights, none of it is working."

"That's not possible," Sonya objected. "Hope's truck is working fine."

"My truck is ancient," I said dryly. "These new ones all primarily use computers to run. I'm one of like four people in the area who didn't turn in my truck when the government offered that deal."

Determined to prove Walter wrong, Sonya wandered around trying out everything. Lights, TV, the microwave. She had to say "Hey, Mia," three times before she gave in and tried things manually. I absently pulled my tiny, ancient flashlight out of my pocket and flicked it on.

Nothing. How disappointing

This sounded like some kind of an electromagnetic pulse. Shit. I vaguely remembered Will going on about EMP's and their effects on technology. I wondered if it was permanent.

"Why didn't you?" Jaali asked suddenly. "Turn your car in, I mean."

I smiled mirthlessly. "Because I'd just finished revamping the entire engine. I designed her to get two hundred miles to the gallon. I was hoping to patent my design. Then, when the initiative began, I wasn't just gonna throw away all my hard work."

Walter raised his eyebrows, impressed, but we didn't have time for my truck stories, so he continued with the tale. There'd been a brief attempt at a revolt that was ruthlessly put down in less than an hour. My aunt hadn't been the only one vocal about what happened, and every one of them was loaded into a truck. "All day today and last night, trucks have been rolling through, bringing in folks living in rural areas. Looks like they might be heading for Salem."

"They have been driving through town today," Kioni interjected, "on a loudspeaker, telling us the entire West Coast was 'freed' from tyranny, and that it was only a matter of time before the rest of the country followed suit."

"Well, fuck," I said. Not only my dad and brother, but I have an uncle and cousins down in the San Joaquin valley in California. "Beg pardon," I addressed Kioni and the kids.

Kioni waved it off. "Unfortunately, it's appropriate to the situation, and the kids have been exposed to worse in the last couple days. I think, with your family missing, we can give you a pass." She gave us a weak smile, teeth flashing white against her skin.

I looked around the table. The kids looked frightened and the parents both scared and determined all at once. Sonya looked like somebody had hit her with a shovel, and I thought a good breeze could knock me off my chair. Alex was focused on the story, pulled briefly out of her grief.

"So what are you gonna do next?" I asked.

"We-we don't know what we can do, really." Walter cleared his throat nervously. "Stay put?"

"Bugger that." I borrowed another phrase from Mercy, my Australian cousin. "Damned if I'll sit still and let them bastards push me around."

"How will you stop them?"

"Dunno if I can stop 'em," I replied. "But as of this moment, they don't know anything about me or Son. And I don't intend to stick around and let them find us." I wasn't really sure where the words were coming from. These ideas were all half-thought out, my brain pretty much running without a filter again, but I let it keep going. I wanted to see where I was going with all this. "I've been reading—"

"She does that a lot," Son mumbled.

I glared at her and continued. "Reading about military bunkers up in the hills. It's only a rumor, see, but Son's brothers like to go four-wheeling, and they've told us about areas that are fenced and gated, with armed guards. I think we should head there. They've told us basically how to find it." I sent Son a questioning look, and she nodded. The boys had spent a fair bit of time up there, trying to see if they could find another route into the claimed territory. They couldn't. They'd also spent a lot of time describing where they'd gone.

"Maybe we'll get lucky and find somebody up there. Find a safe place to stay until this," and here I indicated the world, "is fixed. We should be able to fit everyone in the back of my truck. It'll be wet, but preferable to staying here." I looked around the table.

"You'll gamble everything on a hunch and a hope?" Kioni protested half-heartedly.

I shrugged. "Best I've got right now," I admitted. "Unless somebody else has a genius idea?"

Silence.

Shit. I hated it when my half-assed ideas were the best we had. Like that time we went to Abiqua Falls because we were bored. That was stupid. Let's just say boogie boards and thirty foot drops don't mix.

Walter took a deep breath and reached over to take his wife's hand. "We want you to take the kids," he said tightly, "but Kioni and I aren't going." The kids immediately began protesting, but Walter raised his free hand, silencing them. "It's better for you two to get out of here. You know it is. But we can't." He looked at his wife and gripped her hand tighter as he continued. "Her parents are elderly and in no condition to go running around, and we can't just abandon them. They're right here in town, so we can easily keep an eye on them. There's no telling what will happen to the elderly with these animals."

"But Dad..." Asilia's lip trembled, and her eyes filled with tears.

"Oh, honey." Walter stood and pulled his daughter into a hug. Kioni and Jaali joined in, turning it into a family hug. Sonya and I looked away awkwardly. Walter looked over at us. "We've seen some young women being taken away. It's only been two days, but rumors are already flying, neighbors talking over fences, and it sounds like soldiers are having 'private parties.' Celebrations." His lips tightened with disgust. "I won't risk my daughter with something like that."

Quite frankly, I could see his worry. Asilia was...distinctive. Other types of beauty, such as I suspected Alex of having, could blend in to a crowd. Alex had blonde hair, green eyes and full lips. I don't know about the rest of her features as they were still bruised and swollen, but I could guess that when the swelling went down, she'd be beautiful. It's weird to think of beauty as being common, but perhaps "not unusual" for our region is the best way to describe it.

Asilia, on the other hand, was exotic. Her mother was incredibly dark skinned, African by her accent, with amazing bone structure. Asilia had inherited her mother's features, and her skin was a combination of both parents. Pair that with kinky dark hair, blonde streaks, and lovely, canted blue eyes, and the girl would be immediately visible in a crowd. All it would take is one glimpse for a man to notice her. Make that an unscrupulous man who thought he had rights to a woman's body, and that woman is in serious trouble.

"They ain't won yet," Sonya growled.

"Nope," I agreed, "but if we want to make sure they don't get comfortable—and don't catch us—we'd better get the hell out of here while it's raining and getting dark." I paused for a moment, thinking. They were all watching me intently, even the parents. I swallowed. "Son, get Dana's gear together, both packs."

Me, Son, Dana, and Toni were in Search and Rescue, and one thing every member was required to have were two packs, one for single day rescues, just the basics, and one for two days. Thing is, if you have enough gear for a couple days, you've got enough for a year. As long as you didn't run out of food.

Sonya nodded. "What about our house?"

"I'll go there and grab Toni's gear. We should have enough to keep us all dry. Dry-ish," I amended, listening to the downpour outside. "Maybe we'll get lucky and Toni will be there."

Alex stood up unexpectedly. "Do you have boots that would fit me?" she asked Son. She was puffy and bruised, and tears still filled her eyes, but she was resolute. "I don't know how well skaters will work in the hills."

Sonya blew out a breath as she stood up from the table. "We're bound to have something." She led the way downstairs. "What size are you?"

I moved to the window, checking that the coast was clear. "Right, I'll head to our place. I shouldn't be more than half an hour." I looked at the Blakes. "Pack a few basics and say your good-byes while I'm gone. If we're to have any chance, we'll need to leave as soon as possible. Don't be late!"

As I headed down the short flight of stairs to the front door, I could hear Sonya and Alex downstairs, packing and getting things together. Just before I shut the door, I heard Asilia saying, "Dad, I don't want to go with them. That Hope, she's scary."

"Good, I hope she scares them, too..." I closed the door before I heard the rest of what her father said.

Since no one was around, to see, I didn't bother hiding my grin. I never minded being thought of as scary. I pulled my beanie out of my pocket and tugged it on. I checked the truck as I passed it, making sure that the tarp was still in place, then headed down the drive.

As I jogged along the rain-slicked sidewalks, water formed small streams in the gutters and sluiced over the concrete. Droplets collected on my jacket, running off and soaking my pants. I thought about my family, wondering, scared. Well, I wasn't too worried about Grace. She'd just gotten married and was off on her honeymoon. They'd gone to Canada. Papa and Sean... I shied away from that. Too much thinking about them would just incapacitate me. Peter was in the Army, posted God-knows-where, so while he was likely in danger, at least he wasn't in *this* danger.

Uncle Dave, my dad's brother, lived just outside of Fresno, California. I wondered if they were okay. Especially Faith. She was closest to me in age, and me, her, and Mercy formed what our parents called "The Diabolical Trio" and we called "The Three Musketeers" whenever we were together. Faith and Mercy had been up for the wedding, then Mercy had gone back south with them.

I hoped that this hell was limited to just us, that's for sure. Mercy, my Australian cousin, should have flown out a few hours before the attacks started, from Los Angeles, so I chalked her up as safe. Good thing she left Oregon when she did.

While I'd been thinking, I'd puffed and panted my way up Robinson and onto Church Street. We were just around the corner from Robinson, in a tiny, single-story house. The once-bright paint was peeling, and the overall effect could be best described as rundown. It had three bedrooms and was listed as "cozy." This translated into "so damn small a mouse would have trouble turning around in it." Desperate times, desperate measures and all.

A twinge of nostalgia lanced through me as I walked up to the door. It may be cramped, dingy and the house equivalent of a rust bucket, but it was our home. Opening the door, I called for Toni, but I wasn't surprised when there was no answer. Hopefully, she and Steve were safe. Great. Another family member whose location was unknown.

I hustled through the house, careless of the water I tracked in, and dug through Toni's stuff. I thanked my lucky stars that her larger pack was mostly full. Trying to find anything in Toni's room is like finding a needle in a stack of needles. I waded through the clothes tossed carelessly around the room, covering every flat surface (including the floor) until I was sure I had everything.

I took a quick trip through Sonya's Spartan room to grab more socks and clothes (can't ever have too many socks) before running into my own room. As far as tidiness was concerned, I lived a happy mix between Sonya and Toni, with dirty clothes in a small pile in the corner, my smaller pack on top of the bookshelf, and a few random books and picture frames scattered around.

Yanking my smaller pack off the top shelf, I loaded it at high speed. Both Sonya and Toni were too fat for anybody else to borrow their clothes, and I had no idea if the kids had anything sturdy enough to survive rough living. Sure, Dana had plenty of clothes, but we could always use more.

I rifled through my shelves—*more socks, moccasins might come in handy, extra bottle of methylated spirits, big first aid kit*—and suddenly, I was nearly done. I wished I had time to change into dry clothes, but anything I put on would be wet in a couple minutes anyway. I shrugged. As long as my underwear stayed dry, I wasn't doing too badly.

Passing my bookshelf in the living room, I paused a moment. I had a smidge more space left in the pack, and I pored over the shelves, looking. I threw in three slim volumes about native herbs and their uses. I looked in the pack. I could fit one more...I vacillated between two before finally settling on one.

"Hope it's useful," I mumbled, stuffing it into the pack and buckling it shut.

Covering both packs in their rain tarps took barely a moment, though I did have a bad thought about the brightly colored fabric. I chewed my lip, then shrugged. Dry was important right now, and visibility outside was shit. It looked more like full dark than late afternoon in September. I grimaced, hoping for the best.

I stuck my head out the door to check but didn't see or hear anything. I scrunched my eyes up, hesitating. My heart thundered, I bit my lip, trying to nerve myself up.

"Fuck it," I mumbled, slinging the packs on, front and back, and waddling into the rain.

I huffed and groaned under the weight, grateful that the way back was all downhill. I'd never survive going up.

***

My legs were trembling by the time I made it back to Aunt Rose's and found that my little pickup had been reloaded. The tarp now covered a small mound. Sonya came up with a look of relief and helped me out of the packs. We shoved them behind the bucket seats in the cab on top of the packs we'd taken on our trip, three days and a million years ago.

Then she lifted the tarp, showing me what had changed under it. All the cans we'd stolen were blocked towards the rear of the bed by a board. The narrow space between box and board had blankets mounded in there, a couple bags, and Cinder, who *woofed* softly at his person.

"Wow! I never would have thought of this," I said, impressed by what they'd done and how quickly.

"Yeah," Son said wryly. "Just for fun I tried the other cars, but none of them worked. Not even a cough. Who'da thought you were the smart one, not taking advantage of the government? As for the back, the board was Walter, and the blankets Kioni, to keep the kids comfy in the back. Oh, and Walter gave us a Glock and ammo."

"What?" I choked, disbelieving. "Are you *shitting* me? He's got a *gun* and *ammunition*?" I exhaled, blowing water off my nose. Who would have thought a middle-aged guy who looked like your classic high school teacher had it in him? "That is one brave bastard. Government would crucify him if they'd ever found out."

I blew out a long breath. Enough time marveling at the size of Walter's balls. Time to think about how to get out of here.

We needed somebody to run interference like I did on the way here.

I looked at Son. Way too out of shape to make the three or so miles of suburban streets to get out of town. Alex could barely walk, the kids were...kids.

I groaned.

"Goddammit." I scrubbed my hands over my face for what felt like the millionth time, using the rain to wash off the last traces of blood and dirt.

"You just realized you're running again, didn't you?" Son grinned, her face still too pale.

"Fuck off," I said sourly. "You and your damn nearsightedness and glasses. I guess this is the moment I keep the New Year's resolution I never made to get healthy in a hurry. You do realize you're joining me on my health kick, y'know?"

"Hell no!" she leaned back from me as if I carried a deadly disease.

I smirked. "Dunno how you're gonna avoid it. You packed the truck. We don't have any junk food. We'll be hunting and gathering. All that fun shit."

It almost made me feel better, seeing the abject horror on her face at the thought of no more chips and soda. Almost.

Alex walked stiffly over, carrying Obelix, and eased herself into the passenger seat. I took two steps back to see the front door and the Blakes standing just inside, huddled together. I looked at Son, eyebrows raised, but she gave me a Death Stare, still pissed off at the thought of running, and I sighed. The walk to the door to get them moving stretched into a mile.

"I'm sorry, guys," I said when I got there, "but we have to go. Somebody'll find all the bodies we left at Safeway soon, if they haven't already, and they'll start looking around. If there's to be any chance for us, we have to go *now*."

Asilia let out a tiny wail and clung to her mother tighter. A tear tracked down Kioni's cheek as she and Walter urged the kids towards the truck. More tears fell, all washed away by the rain.

Once the kids were tucked in the back, cuddled around Cinder, Walter began fastening the tarp. They cried. It broke my heart. Walter's shoulders trembled, but his face didn't change until he fastened the last corner. Then he turned away and pressed his forehead against the house, shoulders shaking with sobs, uncaring who saw him now.

Kioni seized my hand, gripping it hard. "Promise me you'll keep them safe!"

"Uh." I flailed my free hand wildly around, indicating the situation and the world at large. I hated people asking for promises. Especially ones in situations that I can't control.

"I don't care! Promise me!"

"Best I can give you is an 'I'll do the best I can.'" Kioni scowled. I jumped in before she could get going. "I get that sending your kids away with complete strangers is insane in normal circumstances. And you've got to be having all kinds of doubts. But please," I was practically begging, "please don't make me give a promise I can't keep. I don't even know if we'll make it out of town!"

"Kioni." Walter roused himself from his grief and laid a gentle hand on his wife's shoulder. "Babe. If we send them away, they have a chance. If we keep them here…" He shrugged helplessly, eyes red from weeping but never wavering from her face. "We have to give them every chance, don't we?"

Defeated, she nodded and finally released my hand.

"Go get your parents," I said quietly to them. "Bring them to your house or go stay with them. Go now, while it's still raining."

I checked that all was clear on the road and circled a hand in the air. The truck started smoothly, the engine settling into a quiet rumble as Sonya eased her out onto the road. I did look back, but the rain poured, a solid wall so thick that I only imagined seeing the Blakes with their arms about each other, watching us leave.

***

Water gushed down the roads to the storm drains, and every footfall landed in an inch of water, splashing the hems of my pants as I peered around the corner. Not that a few extra drops made any difference now. As soon as I gave the all clear, Son pulled up next to me, and I hopped onto that greatest of inventions: the running board.

I'd never used them, since my truck is built so low that people sit down into it, and I have no idea why the previous owner had even put the damn things on. The only reason the running boards were still there is because I'd had no time to remove them, but they were proving worth their weight in gold.

When we were twenty feet down the road, lights flashed through the trees, and we got ready to stop. I nearly lost my grip with relief when the trucks never slowed, continuing straight. Near the end of Mill Street, I hopped off the boards and jogged to the end, checking the way.

I waved them across, then ran to join them. My right knee began to ache, and I had a vague memory of banging it into a refrigerated display unit at the grocery store. I tried to keep most of my weight on my left leg as we followed Third until it became a gravel track. We zig-zagged through the tiny streets with minute houses and postage stamp yards until we had no choice but to emerge briefly onto Water.

The first left we came to, Bodacious Drive, took us to a newer section of streets and the possibility of escape into the hills. We'd only gotten thirty feet down Bodacious when I saw lights shining ahead of us, and I quickly thumped the roof of the cab, signaling Sonya to pull over.

Sonya pulled into an empty space in a driveway, killing the engine. I dropped under a bush where I could watch the road. I sniggered at how quickly hiding from The Man had become routine. I watched the Hummer-style truck (these guys *seriously* had a hard-on for Hummers—compensating, maybe?) drive slowly down the lane, and then I frowned.

Why weren't they using spotlights? I could plainly see that the headlights worked just fine.

Instead, they used some antiquated method of flares in front of shiny backgrounds, similar to what lighthouses used back in the day. I guess it worked okay, but flares didn't offer a clear picture. Then again, I thought as I watched their red tail lights disappearing towards the town center, maybe that's why they missed our truck.

Meh. I shrugged, dismissing the mystery of the lights, and went to check on my people.

Son rolled down the window as I approached. "Everything okay?" she asked, worry tinging her voice.

"Fine. Just checkin'. You know, to see if you're still nice and dry." I couldn't keep the sourness out as I felt the warm air billowing from the crack in the window.

Sonya, that bitch, didn't even try to smother her laughter, letting it roll out. "We're fine. How about you? Washing your clothes while you wear them?"

I flipped her off. "Even my underwear." Son laughed again.

"Do-do you need a break?" Alex leaned forward, holding the sleeping puppy.

I shook my head. She was bruised, beaten and could barely walk, had buried her only child, and yet offered to take a turn on the running boards. What a champ. "I'll be fine. Eventually. No point someone else getting their nether regions chafed by wet pants."

I moved back slightly to talk to the tarp. "How're you kids doing?"

"We're fine." I could barely hear Asilia over the rain drumming on the tarp. "Are we out of town yet?"

"Not yet, kiddo, sorry." I felt a pang for these kids, being whisked away from their family by complete strangers. "We've still got a ways to go. Just keep your heads down. Try to take a nap. Keep the dog calm."

"He's sleeping." She sounded plaintive and a bit jealous about the old dog's ability to fall asleep at a moment's notice.

I moved back to Son and stepped onto the running board again. "Time to go."

Since we'd left Aunt Rose's, the final vestiges of light left the air, and an almost pitch dark settled over the suburb. Without lights or center lines, the only way to follow the road was to follow the lighter gray of the sidewalks. We knew we finally hit the road out of Silverton when the yellow center line appeared, and I breathed a sigh of relief.

The low growling of the truck was barely audible over the water as it burbled down the road. The truck lurched suddenly, flinging me from my precarious perch, and I hit the ground hard, then shrieked when the ground dropped away.

"Fuuuuck!" I groaned when I eventually stopped. I tried rolling over and pushing myself up. My left hand slipped in a patch of mud, sending me face first into a clump of grass. "Fukmmphrsibits!" I screamed into it.

Footsteps splashed across the road and squelched down to where I lay. "Oh, my God! Are you all right?" Sonya cried, panicking. She tried to help me up, stopped, started, and ended up sitting down abruptly.

If anything told me we were well and truly fucked, that would be it. Normally, Sonya is the most unflappable person I know. A spill like I'd just had would normally have sent her in fits of laughter, after which she'd take photos, before finally checking to see if I was okay. Then she'd laugh again. This panic was so much worse because it was completely foreign to her character.

Behind her, I could hear the kids crying in fear, asking what was happening.

"I'm fine!" I spat grass and mud out. "I'm fine. Just help me up, all right?"

I gripped her leg. Sonya grabbed my hand and hauled me to my feet. My right knee immediately informed me that it'd been whacked twice today, and I'd pay for it tomorrow. I flexed my leg back and forth, trying to work the joint, feeling a point just above the kneecap. I bent my leg again, musing. I guessed a rock, right into the top of my knee. *Oh, yeah. That's gonna feel good tomorrow.*

"How are you?" Sonya asked anxiously.

"Wet. Grumpy. Hit my knee on something. Again." I walked up the hill by stabbing my toes into the soil, gouging temporary stairs into it. Every time I pushed up on my right leg, the muscles all around the impact complained. "I'm okay!" I called to the truck.

Sonya, reassured by my irritability (it's easier to not panic when you're the one pissed off), took off past me, jogging to the truck to calm everyone there. Alex, I saw, had made it out of the cab and spoken to the kids, calming them. When Son got there, she filled them in on what had happened.

I could just make out a lighter patch in the asphalt a little ways behind the truck. When I tested it, I found it to be a nasty little pothole. I pinched the bridge of my nose, eyes closed and head tilted down to protect my face from the rain. Of course it's a friggin' pothole.

Welcome to Oregon.

I stumped back to the others, grumbling the whole way. "Pothole. Fucking cheapskate bastards can't even maintain the damn roads. Son of a bitchin' pothole."

Sonya grinned weakly when she heard me, then Alex hissed. I looked, barely able to see her head cocked, listening. "Something big's in front of us!" she whispered.

"Driveway twenty feet up, on the left!" I whisper-shouted to Sonya. "Go, go, go! I'll hide here."

Sonya actually obeyed, sliding into the driver's seat and going before Alex even got her door shut. I ran to the ditch I'd just climbed out of and went down it in a baseball slide, twisting at the bottom so I lay on my belly, ready to peek over the edge.

The earth trembled, then, when the lights came into view, my breath caught. This was more like a motor-cade, with two Hummers in the lead, both with mounted machine guns. I rubbed my face in mud to hide the paleness of my skin and went back to peering through the grass.

A short ways behind the Hummers loomed a large truck, a transport of some kind. I hardly dared to breathe as I waited for them to see an inconsistency to the grass and stop. As the transport passed, I could make out its cargo by the light of the next vehicle in the train. The truck was filled to bursting with people. Men, women, children, all of them huddled together, cold and miserable, pale with fear.

After that transport, another one rolled past, same cargo: people. Then another, and another. Four transports full of people. I lay there, shuddering with cold or anger, I don't know which. It was probably fear. After the last transport, another Hummer followed.

After it passed, I lay there, night-blind, my heart trying to pound through my chest.

A minute later, I felt it.

It started as a bone deep rattle that upgraded to the sensation of sitting on top of a washing machine when it's in the spin cycle. Cautiously, I poked my head up, ready to face-plant at a moment's notice. I saw a monstrosity grinding down the road, tearing up the asphalt.

A damned tank.

Turret facing forward, the thing rumbled blindly past, leaving ground-up bits of road in its wake. I wrinkled my nose. Didn't those things have shit-tons of computer systems in them? I found it difficult to get a clear look at the vehicle, but the sound of it...I cocked my head, listening.

"Rotate the turret, you bastards," I whispered into the rain. "Rotate it!"

They never did, and I scrambled up after it passed, standing in the middle of the road. Lightning flashed, illuminating the trees and blackberries crowding the road as I watched the tank's lights recede in the distance. They never saw me. Never even noticed. This was worse than I'd thought, and I'd thought it as bad as things could possibly get.

Note to self: Murphy's Law applies to All Things.

CHAPTER 5

Sonya didn't greet me with a hug or worry. Instead, she met me at the driveway entrance, spitting mad. "Where the hell have you been?" she hissed when I limped to the driveway.

"I took a nap!" I snapped, swiping a sopping sleeve over my sopping face. "That was a freaking convoy! Three guard trucks, four transports loaded with people and a fucking tank as rear guard."

"Wait, what? How do they have a tank working?"

"World War II era should work just fine, going by the looks of that thing," I said grimly. "We'll need to be extra careful. These roads weren't built for tank treads. Fuckers."

Sonya sighed, leaning against the truck, completely unmindful of the rain. *Easy to not care about a bit of wet when you know you're getting back into a nice, warm, dry truck,* I thought irritably.

She shook her head, tired. "You know what? Let's worry about this when we've found the Army and a safe place to stop. My eyes hurt." She rubbed them, then pinched the bridge of her nose to relieve pressure.

I looked down, ashamed She does just fine walking, but being near-sighted, Sonya needs glasses to drive. She'd been straining her eyes all evening in the dark, trying to keep us on the road, and then there's me, bitching about her being warm. At least I wasn't killing my eyes to see.

"You're right." I clapped her on the shoulder. "Let's get out of here before another truck comes through. We could all use a flat surface and a roof."

With the road a bit bumpier, hanging on got harder, the broken asphalt spinning away under our tires. Sonya rolled down her window so I could stick one hand in and get a grip on the handle mounted on the ceiling. I also got a wave of warmth from the heater, and I basked in the glow as she drove.

It must have taken half the night, but in time we began picking our way from blacktop to gravel and back again. Then we went to full gravel. The deluge slowed to a normal rain when we first hit gravel. I'd become so accustomed to the lightning that I don't even remember when it stopped. I was just grateful I wasn't breathing water anymore as I miserably clutched at the handle and the door, trying to stay on the board.

***

The truck lurched sometime near dawn, shaking me from my stupor as it passed from a narrow gravel track onto something that looked like two deer trails running side-by-side.

"Are you sure this is the right way?" I asked through the window.

"Fuck, no." Sonya's voice drifted out with the warm air. "But Will said it was in the middle of nowhere, and I'm pretty sure that's where we are."

I had to lean in close to the truck to keep from getting swept off by low-hanging branches. Sonya threw the truck into four-wheel drive, making it easier to navigate the mud. The truck listed sharply as she hit a pothole, and one of my feet slid off the running board. It's a testament to my exhaustion that nearly falling into a blackberry bush didn't even elicit a raised heartbeat. I just gripped my handholds as tightly as my numbed fingers would allow, and my left foot dragged and skipped over the ground until I could pull myself up enough to get both feet back on firmer footing.

Alex leaned over and whispered something to Sonya. Son nodded and said to me, "Alex needs to pee."

I flattened myself against the truck and tried to suck in my butt cheeks enough to not get scraped off. I stayed on, but the bark made a rasping sound as it dragged across my ass. "There's not enough space to get out yet," I grunted. "I'm really glad I got these pants, otherwise I'd be shredded by now."

Sonya snorted. She hugged the passenger side of the track to give me as much space as possible, and it wasn't enough. I really was glad for the pants, though. They were pricey, especially for this day and age, but also tough, made of ripstop nylon, and dried quickly, and were comfortable. The cargo pockets were an added bonus.

Ten minutes down the road, the blackberries stopped scratching over my legs, and I thumped on the roof. "I think we've got enough space here for a stretch."

Sonya eased the truck to a stop, but she left the engine running. I stepped down from the running board and nearly fell into a bush, barely catching myself on a low-hanging limb. I clung to the tree a moment before stumping awkwardly over the ground like a drunken sailor, my feet feeling like a pair of giant, squishy raisins on the ends of my legs. I shuddered. Taking off my boots wouldn't be a pretty sight.

While I re-learned how to walk, Sonya let the kids out of the back of the truck. Jaali immediately disappeared behind us, with Cinder trotting after. Alex wasted no time, squatting against the side of the truck to relieve herself. Asilia shifted, holding her legs stiffly and looked longingly at the top of Alex's head, all that we could see of her.

Then I realized we *could* see her. It wasn't light, by any means, but the trees had a faint silhouette instead of blending with the gloom. Sonya gave Asilia some of the wet wipes we always carried on hikes and a few tips on how to avoid peeing on her shoes. The girl seized both gratefully and disappeared in the opposite direction from her brother.

Alex groaned and used the truck to get herself upright. Leaning on it, she made her way around to me and Sonya, wincing when she extended her leg too far.

"How are you holding up?" I asked her.

"I'm here. I want—" She stopped, looking down at her empty hands, and cleared her throat. "I want to wake up and find out this was all just a bad dream. If not, then I want to be safe, and try...try to process." She choked, then began crying, dry little sobs.

Sonya and I froze, staring at each other. There's a reason I'm a mechanic. I'm not good at people-ing. Sonya, if anything, is even more awkward than I am. I remembered tons of hugs from a variety of people after my mom died, but...

Aw, fuck it.

I couldn't stand to listen to her weeping, so I reached out and tentatively laid a hand on her shoulder. When I wasn't rebuffed, I stepped closer, giving her every chance to say *no*. Instead she turned in and pressed her face to my shoulder. I patted her back and rocked her gently, like mothers do for their babies, and waited it out.

Jaali and Asilia came back while Alex grieved, and Asilia carefully wrapped her arms around Alex from behind. We held her sandwiched between us until she finished crying.

"Thanks," Alex whispered, sniffing and wiping her nose on her sleeve. Then she made her way slowly around the truck to clamber into the passenger seat, scooping up Obelix as she went.

"Time to go, guys," I said, walking stiffly back to the truck.

***

An eternity later I lightly thumped the cab. Sonya halted the truck, and in the pre-dawn light we could just make out a gate hidden amongst the bushes and trees. I stepped down from the boards to stagger slowly over to the gate. Sonya and Alex made their way over, closely followed by the kids. Cinder declined to exit the bed and join us in the drizzle, preferring the cozy nest he'd made there. Smart dog.

We perused the gate for a minute, looking it over carefully.

"Is it supposed to be like that?" Asilia asked. "All empty and abandoned?"

"We could be at the wrong one," Sonya allowed. "Jake showed me a photo, and this looks right. Finally. Except no one's trying to scare us away. Weird."

"We can just follow the road and see where it leads us," Jaali said. "Even if it's another wrong turn, at least we're far enough away that those people won't find us."

The conversation took a minute too long to seep in. "What do you mean, 'another wrong turn'? When did that happen?"

"There were a couple of dead ends," Son said, eyeing me. "I take it you don't remember?"

"No."

"Funny, since you were the one who pointed out that the road ended," Sonya remarked dryly. "Sleep talking again?"

Rubbing my face, I mumbled, "Talking, seeing, holding on, standing...the list of my accomplishments while sleeping never ends, apparently. I'm better looking and smarter while I'm asleep, too." I giggled blearily.

"Can we just go through the gate already and see where it leads? I'm cold. And tired."

Sonya and Jaali helped me muscle the gate open, then Alex drove the truck through and we closed the gate after us. At first, I wondered why we even bothered closing it, but put it down to me and Son growing up on farms, where shutting the gate is second nature. Then it occurred to me that closing it again makes it look like nobody's been through. Yeah. S-M-R-T, smart. That's me.

Alex stayed in the driver's seat, and I whimpered at the thought of riding on the running boards much longer. I could have curled up in the mud and fallen asleep. *Hang on. We can't be too much further. Think how stupid we'll feel if we fall off and it turns out we're just a few feet from the end.*

I need to work on my pep talks.

The track continued through thick trees for at least another four miles. Alex kept glancing at me out of the corner of her eye, looking worried. If the recently beaten lady looks at you worried, you know you look like shit.

Just when I thought I'd fall off, we rounded a corner to find the track's end in a small clearing. In the center of the clearing, a tiny bunker hunched like a glowering beast, with a low, grass-covered mound extending about ten feet behind it. Fir trees surrounded the small meadow, their scent rising in the early morning air.

My mom favored evergreen scents when she was alive. The smell brought up memories of home and safety.

I shoved the recollections back and tried to shake myself awake as we trooped over to the bunker to examine it.

"Is this it?" Asilia demanded, hands on her hips, a rising edge of hysteria in her voice. "This is ridiculous. We'll never fit!"

"Sure we will!" Jaali teased. "You just won't be able to spend an hour in the bathroom getting your hair perfect!" She swiped at him, and he dodged, laughing.

"Guys," I said, getting irritated. I cut off when I saw the slight smile on Alex's face at their antics, and that Asilia focused so much on getting her brother that she'd forgotten to be upset. *Jaali, you sly dog,* I thought, amazed at the boy's cleverness. "Whatever," I said when they looked at me. "Just don't wander off. We might have to leave again."

"So." Sonya drew the word out as she rocked on her feet. "What now, oh fearless leader? How should we go about this?"

"One, shaddup. I'm not any kind of leader, fearless or otherwise. Two, can't we just try the door?" I stumbled closer to the door and stared at it, trying to get my eyes to focus.

"Here." Alex stepped past me. "I've seen these kinds of doors on a submarine, once." She grasped a wheel and strained. Me and Sonya jumped in, and between the three of us, the handle slowly turned.

"We're in!" I shouted over my shoulder, then doubled over, a wracking cough shaking me.

"Don't die," Sonya said over her shoulder when she stepped into the gloom.

"Oh, yeah, sure. I'll get right on that, shall I?"

Stairs led downward just a few steps in, and blackness beyond. I fished a small flashlight out of my pocket, and to my disappointment, it didn't work.

"The Korean's lights were working on their cars," I complained, holding up the flashlight. "How come this isn't? Do we have any candles?"

"No—wait!" Son rushed outside. "I did grab some! The storm and all, I thought the power might go out, and Mom never has any..."

She ripped off the tarp covering the back half of the truck bed and rifled around briefly. "Hah!" Sonya turned, holding up some candles triumphantly.

"We got lighters in the backpacks," I pointed to the cab, then sneezed. "We'll have to try the lights on the truck, see if they work."

"Later." Sonya pushed past me to step back inside the bunker and lit two candles. She led the way down, the kids and Alex following while I came in last. The dogs, attracted by the commotion, picked their own way down.

"Son," I said, my voice cracking with exhaustion, "see if you can find a space for us all to fit. We'll bring in the packs and enough for dinner. We can deal with the rest after a good sleep."

The first door, on the right, looked like a storage closet. Some cleaning supplies and a vacuum occupied the tiny room.

The next door, on the left, proved much more interesting. A huge room full of all kinds of guns, rifles, even some bows and crossbows. It is a testament to the stamina of youth that Jaali immediately tried to explore. I collared the boy before he got too far and yanked him back into the group.

"Later," I said sternly. "We'll come back later."

Sonya turned in a circle, holding her candle as high as she could. "I think we found the right place. This looks like what I always imagined an armory would."

"Later," Asilia echoed me. "I'm hungry, and I want to sleep."

We continued down the hall. After passing a few rooms that looked like offices, and one big-ass computer room with an electronic map-type thing covering one wall, we finally found a common/dining room. The large room could fit a couple hundred people comfortably, with trestle tables and benches on the right and entertainment points to the left. Couches and a big screen TV in one corner formed a quiet area, with a pool table, foosball, and air hockey tables taking up the rest of that end. Past the tables was a big kitchen clearly visible through large, open, food service windows.

We looked around, and I nodded. "Good 'nuff. Let's get the gear."

I desperately wanted to sink to the floor and never move, but so did everybody. I stumbled wearily back to the truck. It only took two trips to get enough for the time being, but holy shit I hurt.

As soon as we brought the last thing in, I grabbed my pack and headed for a corner. Dumping the bag, I began stripping with my back to the room. "Right," I called over my shoulder, throat tearing with the effort, "this ain't a strip tease, so all you perv, I mean people, face the other direction. Especially the boy!"

That earned me a couple of giggles, and a yelp from Jaali. I huffed an exhausted laugh. Nothing seemed to stop him for long.

I had to sit down to pull the boots off, and I clenched my teeth, blowing hard to stay calm. I'd learned a long time ago that the best way to keep moving through pain was to stay relaxed. I unclenched my jaw, deliberately relaxing as I peeled the socks off. The soaked cotton had bloodstains where blisters had broken and bled freely.

Pulling on dry clothes took an effort of Herculean proportions, though once it was done, I felt almost like a new person. I slowly worked leggings on, whimpering as warmth crept up in the dry clothes' wake.

Sonya glanced over when she heard me shuffling back. She poured the first pot of heated water into a bowl and brought it over along with a first aid kit, letting Asilia refill the pot and set it to boil. Sonya then grabbed a candle and plonked herself down in front of me. I laid back and stared at the darkness, practicing my deep breathing as she did her best to tend the raw mess that I now called feet. I wondered how long it would take before they got back to normal.

I leaned on Sonya's arm to stand, and even to walk. Alex kept shifting, cocking up on one hip then the other, wincing with every move. Son snagged a cushion as we passed the couch, offering it to the injured woman, who took it with a smile that never reached her haunted eyes.

I smiled to see the young ones, hunched around the stoves, waiting eagerly for food. Courtesy of our home raids, we had four small spirit burners and accompanying pots, all of them beginning to steam. We passed around cups and bowls that Jaali had found in the kitchen and wiped clean.

Faces puffy from the terrifying days and sleepless night brightened as we gathered around a table. Packets of hot chocolate were produced from the Mary Poppins-like depths of the packs to the delight of all, bowls were filled, and we dug in.

There's something comforting about hot chocolate. It always seems to me that life wasn't over yet if you had a hot cup in your hands, and that proved true today. The world was upside down, our country invaded, our families missing or in danger, people prisoners in their own homes, we were exiles in an abandoned bunker, but with a cup of hot cocoa in my hands I could pretend that it was simply another camping trip, that in a couple of days I'd be home, watching a movie with my cousins or meeting Papa and Sean for Sunday lunch.

Looking around at the faces lit by candles, I could see some of the same comfort reflected there. That a beloved child still lived, that mom and dad were safe at home, that the family bustled around the house as they got ready for work.

Halfway through my cocoa another bout of shivers shook me, followed by a sneeze.

"It's bedtime for you, missy," Sonya said to me sternly.

"I don't wanna."

"Finish your cocoa and veg. Hup, hup, hup!" She clapped her hands briskly.

I took a deliberately slow sip from my cup, eyeing her defiantly.

"Oooh." Jaali looked between us, black eyes dancing above his own cup.

Five minutes ago the boy could barely keep his eyes open, now he's bright-eyed and bushy tailed. Lord give me strength. Why do I feel so old? Oh, right. I'd been hanging onto the outside of a truck all night.

I tilted my head back, waiting for the last drops of cocoa before setting the cup down and letting Jaali help me to my feet.

"The injured and elderly," Sonya looked at me as she said the second part, "get dibs on the couches. The rest of us can use the pads."

"There's another couch," Alex pointed out.

"I'll pass, thanks." Son smiled half-heartedly. "The sleeping pads are seriously comfortable and don't require extreme gymnastics to get out of."

Jaali and Asilia looked intrigued at the thought of sleeping on the floor. I didn't care anymore about *where* I slept, so long as I could lie down. Sonya grabbed sleeping bags and quilts from the packs and lobbed them to the couches while me and Alex made our slow way there. I flopped onto my couch and pulled my sleeping quilt out of the stuff sack. Alex eased her way down, wincing.

I tried to stay awake and make sure everything was good, but Sonya pressed a hand to my leg and murmured, "Go to sleep, I've got this."

I don't know if she said anything else. My brain shut off and I fell asleep before my eyes shut.

***

I turned over and moaned at the pain in my neck and shoulders. A stubborn line of fire reaching from my head to halfway down my back finally got too much to ignore and I tried to sit up, bumping my foot against something firm. I hissed in pain, pulling my knees up to my chest. Resting my forehead on my knees, I tried to open my eyes and briefly wondered why I was on the couch and not in my bed. It took a moment before the memories of the last twenty-four hours returned.

"You're awake. Good." Sonya's cheerful voice rattled through my brain.

"Huungh," I replied, clutching my head. I worked my tongue in my mouth to wet it. "Water," I croaked.

Sonya put a water bottle in my empty hand, and I chugged half of it before I felt remotely satisfied. "Yesterday really happened, didn't it?" I asked hoarsely.

"'Fraid so. Everybody else is up and walking."

"Alex okay?"

"Sort of. C'mon. We have canned fruit for breakfast. The kitchen is pretty well stocked with non-perishables, too, so we won't starve anytime soon."

The cold ground felt good on my sore feet until I had to put weight on them. Standing was an exercise and a half. Muscles I didn't even know existed protested my moving, but it had to be done. Son wouldn't leave me alone until I got up.

Bitch.

She filled me in on what they'd found so far as I slowly moved, whether to keep me distracted or to ease her own nervousness, I don't know. I listened with half an ear to her talk.

"We found these little plastic and wooden stick thingies. They were in a desk drawer, right next to some pads of paper." She laughed. "Paper! In a desk! This place is seriously weird."

"Huh. I wonder what they are?"

Later, we sat awkwardly around the table, realizing in the evening light that we were now saddled together. A bunch of strangers who'd shared more in the last day than most share in a year. The kids looked a bit nervous, though Asilia did her best to hide it.

"Do we have running water in here?" I asked after breakfast. Dinner. Whatever.

"No, but we found a creek not too far away," Jaali said. "The water's really nice. It's where we washed the dishes this morning." I resolved to pay that creek a visit at the first opportunity. He then held up a couple of thin sticks, one made from plastic, one yellow wood. "And I found these, too! Though I don't really know what they are."

I held out one hand. "Can I see them?"

He passed them over, and I ran a thumb over the points, looking at the marks they left on my skin. "I found them in a desk drawer. Well, Sonya found it, but she let me take a couple of these."

I licked the tip of the wooden stick, then grinned. "Son, didn't you have Thornton for history?"

She rolled her eyes. "Yes. I just about died of boredom."

"Too bad you didn't pay attention, otherwise you'd already know what these are." I leaned my elbows onto the table, continuing to inspect the sticks, enjoying Son's increasing irritation.

"Well?" she finally snapped. "Are you going to share with the class, or just keep all this useless knowledge to yourself?"

"This," I held up the yellow stick, "is a pencil. It has a soft lead core that people used to write with. The plastic ones are probably pens."

"Whoa!" Jaali took his pen and pencil back, eyes wide. "I heard about these, but I've never seen one before! Asilia, what do you think dad would do—"

The boy cut off abruptly and looked down at his cup, blinking rapidly. His sister wrapped an arm around his shoulders, giving him a squeeze.

"I think we found our destination," I commented, looking around the large room with fresh eyes. It really could fit a couple hundred in here. And then I drew a blank on what to say next. Yay, me.

"We need to get your feet re-bandaged," Sonya jumped in. "Let's head topside. I found moccasins in your pack. You should be able to wear those."

***

After a round of foot care I don't want to remember, we stopped at the gun room we'd dubbed the armory on the way back in. About the same size as the common room, it was filled with fully loaded gun racks and boxes of ammunition stacked neatly against one wall and under the tables.

The others joined us as we walked gingerly through the room. At the back, we found the explosives. Landmines, grenades, and shit I couldn't even identify.

I looked up from a gun inscribed with the words 'All my love, Lucy' and said, "Somehow, I don't think they destroyed the guns like they said they would. I am *so* not feeling reassured about the government's integrity right now."

"Maybe not," Alex said slowly, "but look at how much stuff we have here. Enough to start a war."

"Starting a war's easy," I said sourly. "It's finishing it that can be hard."

"Think about it." Alex spoke faster now. "These guys invade, imprison, and then kill us. This place was supposed to have the army here, but it's empty."

"Will was out this way five or six months ago, and they got chased off then," Sonya called out two tables down, where she checked out the bows.

"Right, so the official people have left. I think that means we're not gonna be saved." Alex turned a gun over and over, thinking. "Like, we have enough here to stay safe, but how can we do that when your families are down there somewhere? When these soldiers have done all the terrible things they did?"

There was an intensity about her that worried me. Her green eyes were burning and her smile was hard. "We can do whatever we want. Why not take the fight to them? Let them know this isn't the easy victory they thought?"

"Do you know how to use a gun?" I asked her. "'Because I sure as hell don't." The thought of finding my family was tempting, though. Damn...

Asilia looked up from the book she was flipping through. "We have instruction manuals for the guns." She held the book up.

We all rustled around, and sure enough, there were manuals for every type of gun in there. I skimmed through mine, about...I went back to the front page. Glocks. Okay. Use, care, maintenance, even diagrams for breaking them down and cleaning.

"Still," I said, "it'll be a while before we're ready to go anywhere. We have to think about all the things we'll need to know beforehand and actually train with them until we're competent. I ain't going on no suicide run."

As a method to dissuade the others, this failed miserably. Jaali immediately sat down with a manual and started reading. Asilia looked at the guns with distaste but kept reading her own.

"We'll need to know hand-to-hand," Alex announced. "I can't see us managing to always get away without getting close."

Sonya nodded. "Me and Hope spent a couple years learning jiu-jitsu until the dojo closed down. Though that was over a year ago. I think with a bit of practice, the skills'll come back." She looked at me for confirmation. "Let's take the fight to them."

The others nodded, watching me intently.

I closed my eyes briefly. Oh, fuck it. All or none.

"I've got some ideas about what we can do," I said, opening my eyes and wishing they didn't feel like sandpaper. "But it won't be easy."

CHAPTER 6

I guessed that it was mid-November and would be a cold winter. The wind cut through the scarf wrapped around my face like it was paper, but a scarf's better than nothing.

The last two months had been filled with training, a lot of reading, and more bruises. Sonya and me had spent hours trying to remember our jiu-jitsu moves in order to show the others what little we knew. Then there was all the time taking apart and putting guns back together and loading them. I found out the things you inserted into the gun to load it was a magazine, not a clip like they call it on TV.

Then there was the running. Oh, man, the running.

The paintballing was fun. We found paintball guns and gear with instructions and learned how to carry loaded weapons as teams. We split into two teams, different ones every time, and played. Definitely enjoyed that part, and we finally reached the point where no one was accidentally shot in the back and nobody shot themselves in the foot.

Less fun was that it'd taken nearly two weeks before my feet were healed enough for me to walk comfortably in shoes.

Which, strangely enough, we found. The bunker was fully equipped with clothes to outfit three or four hundred people. Well, men, anyway. We found an entire room dedicated to pants, shirts, socks, jackets, hats, and boots, without a bra in sight. It felt weird wearing army clothing, but for this trip and the weather, we'd really bundled up with extra clothing taken from the stores.

The time spent training had changed all of us, physically. Alex had healed, at least on the outside, and it turned out I was right. She was beautiful, lightly tanned, and her natural hair color of light brown was growing in, which gave her two-toned hair. She had always been slim, but now she added lean muscle. She was fast, and had the best aim for long shots, so she'd chosen a version of a sniper rifle to carry with her on this trip.

Jaali had grown. Not enough to pass his sister yet, but he was now taller than Sonya. He looked remarkably like Asilia, with the main difference being that he has his mother's black eyes and no blond highlights, though his hair is lighter than his mother's. I didn't see much of his father in his looks, but I noticed it in his personality. Jaali is practical, funny, and a thinker. And smart. He also drove me nuts.

Asilia, like Alex, toned down. She wasn't comfortable with weapons, and probably never would be, but she grew in confidence and maturity, once she got over the fact that there's no internet and no phones. The kids' complaining about that had nearly driven the rest of us insane.

I didn't see much change in myself until I realized I tightened my belt two extra holes and that my shirts were becoming tight in the shoulders. I'd wandered through the bunker until I could find a mirror, to see if the changes were actually *visible.*

I studied myself in it. I have dirty blonde hair, though a romantic might call it "honey blonde," with slightly slanted, pale, blue-gray eyes. No romantic terms for that. My features are blunt, my mouth too small, my nose too large. At best, I could be considered pretty, but only in ideal circumstances.

Nothing new there.

Physically, I toned up. All the soft bits had disappeared, and my shoulders were a bit bulkier with new muscle. I could run longer than I'd ever done in my life, and I didn't feel like I was about to die anymore, so that was a definite step up.

Out of all of us, however, the biggest change was Sonya. Her comfortable belly was gone. She was still stocky, but all the fat covering the muscle disappeared. She's not the fastest, but she could keep going long after the rest of us were dying of exhaustion. Interestingly enough, she's also the best at sneaking around.

Despite, or perhaps because of, her mediocre eyesight, she relied heavily on her other senses when running through the forest. When trees and bushes make it so you can't see farther than twenty feet, it doesn't matter if your maximum visual range is thirty. When we played hide-and-seek, she was the best at evasion and finding. It was really annoying how she did it. Natural scout, that one.

Now, after two months of running about playing soldiers, we finally left the bunker. Three days ago, there'd been smoke in the air down in the Valley, and I couldn't rein Alex back any longer. She was gunning for revenge, and she was right: we needed to get started. I could easily continue telling myself that we weren't ready, but the truth is, we'd never be ready. Best to get out there now, before I froze with fear and Alex went on a suicide run.

Which is how we found ourselves driving *out* of the mountains on a freezing morning. Everything looked so different in the winter daylight, the bare trees interspersed with evergreens forming patches of brown that were so different from that first night.

So far, we hadn't seen any signs of soldiers, but that didn't stop us looking. Asilia drove with Alex next to her, navigating. Jaali and Sonya rode in the bed with me, binoculars pressed to their eyes above the scarves wrapping their faces. Jaali still hadn't forgiven me for manning the machine gun we'd mounted in the bed instead of letting him do it.

I told him he was thirteen. If I wouldn't let him drive, I sure as hell wouldn't let him near that gun—his mom would kill me.

On the plus side, the truck's lights worked. Jaali had a theory about that after examining and comparing the bulbs from headlights and flashlights. It went something along the lines of "the filaments are sturdier in a car's lights." I chalked it up to magic. From my point of view, it came out to be the same damn thing.

Around us, the evergreens slowly gave way to leafless oaks and maples. The fallen leaves were piled into drifts by the merciless north wind. Years ago, we'd had another wind like this one. It resulted in the earth freezing solid, and three inches of ice across the water troughs. The sky was clear, now as then, and it looked like it should be a lovely spring day. If the temperature was the same, then we were looking at thirteen below zero wind chills.

Awesome.

As the truck bounced over another pothole, I marveled at how smoothly Son and Jaali moved with it, recovering their balance.

We were all leaner and stronger, but this would be our first test to see how disciplined we were. I sincerely hoped our haphazard training would be enough. Dying now would suck.

We had a plan—go for two weeks and check out the source of the burning. A quick jaunt around Salem, maybe. It really all depended on what we found as we went. If we did go into Salem, Jaali and Asilia would stay with the truck and the dogs would stay with them. I had every confidence that if the shit hit the fan, Asilia could out-drive anybody. The girl still squirmed when she held a gun but was more than happy to take sharp corners at the tops of cliffs at speeds that'd make professional drivers cringe and think twice.

Sonya and me were the idiots who got to make sure Alex didn't get herself killed and take us with her. I hoped that if we could pull off a simple reconnaissance, maybe disturb the soldiers a little and not die, she'd calm down a bit. Enough that I didn't feel like I had to watch her every second of the day.

We'd chosen our own weapons, though I didn't know how many more the others had stashed about their persons. The only thing I could see were the rifles Alex and I carried. Sonya had found out her eyesight was too poor without glasses to make using one a viable option.

I know they carried more because I had two handguns, both Glocks, one of them the gun Walter Blake had given us. I also had two grenades in the utility pouches on the belt, along with various knives. I even had a knife taped to my thigh under my pants. Maybe I couldn't get to it easily, but anybody trying to take off *my* pants would be in for a nasty surprise. I also carried four spare magazines for the guns in the cargo pockets of my pants.

I love pockets. So useful.

***

Jaali was the first one to spot the source of the smoke, and he banged the top of the cab, telling Asilia to stop. He passed his binoculars up to me and pointed. The worst of the smoke dissipated in the wind, but a few wisps of it still drifted, thin banners caught by the breeze.

"What the hell...?" I stared. It was a town. "Alex!" I called, my voice muffled. Impatient, I pulled down the scarf. "Which town is that?"

"Silverton," she said grimly.

"Fuck."

The few buildings we could see at this distance were mere piles of rubble, with maybe one or two walls half standing. I fancied I could see some with rooftops left, but I wasn't sure. I hung onto the gun while I got my breath back. Why would they destroy a perfectly good town? Where were the people? I didn't see any bodies, but we'd have to go closer to know for certain.

"We're going forward, right, Hope?" Alex's question had the ring of challenge.

"Yeah, we're going," I growled. "Depending on what we find, we might actually go into town. We came here for bloody recon, didn't we? Doesn't really work if we bail at the first sign of information. Still, eyes open, people! Let's try to see them before they see us, okay?"

I pulled my scarf back over my face as soon as I finished talking. Too damn cold to have exposed skin in this weather. I glared balefully at the clear, blue sky.

We took a slow route in, swinging wide around the town. Except that this is Oregon, and it's physically impossible to completely circle a town without going hours and miles out of the way, courtesy of hills, rivers, and infrequent roads. So we parked just outside of the town limits on Water Street. There were a few longer driveways that had sufficient cover to hide the truck. Couldn't leave it in the open anymore, not with a flipping mounted machine gun bolted to it. Why did I let them talk me into it?

Me and Alex went first, checking out the house and grounds, but the coast was clear, no one living or dead, so the others joined us. Cinder, that old dog, stayed with the truck, snuggled up in the cab with a blanket and the window cracked for him.

It surprised me how fast Alex and Asilia's scarves frosted over in the icy air. I pulled a glove off and felt my own scarf, wincing at the amount of ice coating it.

Sonya chuckled. "On the bright side, nobody will recognize us, bundled up like this."

Jaali thought about that for a moment. "Maybe we should get those masks like bikers wear. You know, the ones with skulls and stuff on them. That would be so wicked."

"Maybe, no," I said. Give that kid an inch, he'll take a mile. "Nobody goes anywhere alone. Check the buildings, see if we can find people. Street by street, slow and easy does it." I pointed at Alex and Jaali, "No running off!"

"Yes, Mother." Alex rolled her eyes. I glared and signaled *I'm watching you*. Her lips quirked upwards briefly before she turned away.

Our initial assessment was correct. Most of the buildings were reduced to piles of rubble. We walked in a loose group, checking streets as thoroughly as we knew how. Though I wasn't too worried. The place was a ghost town.

It nearly killed me, walking through this town. Silverton's so small, compared to most other places, and it's only gotten smaller over the years. Like, it's a great place to buy a gift, but if you need something sensible, like socks, you had to drive forty minutes to Salem. It is—it *was*—considered one of the most quaint and touristy towns to visit, and there'd been substantial renovations done to the town itself. Think "facelift." The new developments on the east side of town, the ones we'd escaped through, weren't new, not really. The original suburbs had gotten so old and worn that it'd been cheaper and more beneficial to the town to raze them and rebuild.

But seeing it like this...

Straight ahead of us, north on the 214, not a mile from where I now stood, was the garage I'd owned with Sonya's brothers, Will and Jake. Both of whom were missing, along with the rest of Son's family, and Will's wife. I'd been living and working out here for the last five years to save myself on gas bills and time. Just because I can get crazy miles per gallon doesn't mean that the price of gasoline hasn't skyrocketed. I even walked to work most days.

Not hard to do when you could walk across town in twenty minutes.

And now those sons-of-bitching soldiers from some random country had *killed* my home. My hands tightened on the rifle I carried until the metal bit through my gloves. I took deep breaths until my heart slowed down. No time for emotions. Push them aside, bury them deep, until we get back to the bunker and it's safe to feel again. For now, pay attention to the streets, to where I'm going.

"Having no people makes it all a bit...creepy," Sonya admitted.

"Yes, because walking through bombed buildings is perfectly normal," Alex jibed.

"Shut up in the peanut gallery! And keep your eyes open," I barked, turning away before they saw me smile. I turned to walk backwards a few steps and check out our rear. This was similar to sneaking through the bunker or the woods surrounding it with our paintball guns. Never knowing where my opponents were, afraid of getting shot with no warning—only no, a million times more intense.

I had to remind myself to keep breathing slowly to avoid hyperventilating. As I turned back to face the front, I caught a glimpse of one of the only roofs still standing on the east side of town: the library.

The bookworm in me, who'd had to keep its head down for survival's sake, was thrilled the library still stood. I really wanted to go in there and check out a book... An idea blossomed. Yeah, once we were reasonably sure no one was around to shoot us, we could go there. Maybe we could find some useful books at the library. Without the internet, finding good info was like stumbling around like the three blind mice.

I smiled. I liked the library.

***

Normally, for people like us, it'd take several days to go through the entire town, and I didn't really see how we could do it and still get to Salem and back before the weather really turned nasty. However, we had one advantage: Sonya's pup. Obelix was still young, only six months old, but smart. Smarter than me, at any rate. Add to that, Sonya's a regular Dog Whisperer, and she'd taught that little boy to keep his nose and ears sharp.

He trotted proudly next to his human at the front of the group, black and white fur ruffling in the wind, one ear flopping with each step. As much as we watched our surroundings, we also kept an eye on Obelix. We cleared streets so much faster with the pup's help.

As the sun settled farther into the western horizon and the shadows lengthened, we saw more of the same—empty streets, hollow, blackened buildings, and skeletal trees clawing at the sky. Time to head back and set up camp. After two nights on the trail we'd gotten the hang of it and had camp set up in less than twenty minutes.

I'd just spread my sleeping quilt out on my mat when Alex approached me. I'd wondered if she would.

"Will you take me to your aunt's house?" she asked, green eyes troubled. "I've been trying to remember, but I can't. Most of that day is just a blur."

I thought that might be a mercy but nodded. "We can head out now. It's not far." She gave a half-hearted, nervous smile.

I peered at her face through the shadows cast by the fir trees. She looked decidedly pale, and I couldn't blame her. I'd always found it difficult visiting Mom's grave, especially the first time.

I pulled Son aside to tell her where we were going.

"I searched that area myself," Son murmured. "You won't have to worry about her freaking out over a hole in the ground. Somebody took care of the place."

"Thanks." I exhaled, then beckoned for Alex to follow me.

We walked quietly through the desolate town, watching the shadows lengthen and rubbing our hands together to keep the blood flowing. We passed the game shop that'd also carried skateboards and snowboards. They had a small ramp and bar for kids to practice on. The owner's dad was the main driving force behind the skate park that popped up over twenty years ago. The shop usually had a group of kids outside it, practicing their moves.

Across the street from the skate shop was a chain link fence that always had wildflowers growing around it. The bachelor buttons were my favorite. The first left after that was a shop that specialized in restoring classic cars. We'd gotten some business from them over the years. Turn right at the intersection, next to the Norman Rockwell murals. The town was famous for murals. There was even a guided walking tour for them.

Down a straight stretch of destroyed suburbia, we walked past the house that had had a goldendoodle. I'd never known the dogs were so big. Alex walked silently by my side, eyes downcast, her thoughts turned inwards. We took another corner, and then we were at Aunt Rose's house.

I stood at the end of the driveway, looking up at it. The last time we'd seen it had been in the pouring rain. We were full of fear, panic, and trepidation. So, obviously, some things hadn't changed. I still carried the gun Walter Blake had given us, though I liked to think I had a slightly better idea of how to use it now.

I glanced over at Alex and saw the memories chasing across her face. Fear, fury, guilt, and a sorrow so deep you could drown in it.

I walked up the driveway, letting Alex follow as she wanted. I looked around, impressed so much of the house still stood. The eastern side had a bit of a hole in it, revealing both stories, but the west side, the street side, was in one piece. Alex caught up to me, staring with glassy eyes, looking like a sleepwalker. I let her take the lead as we came up to where the side fence used to be.

When we entered the backyard, I sucked in a breath, eyes wide in astonishment. Not only was the yard *not* destroyed, but someone had also obviously taken time and care in turning it into a small memorial. The little wooden cross we'd left had been replaced by a small stone, painstakingly carved with Dylan's name and the words *Beloved Son*.

Raised flower beds had been created around it, dormant now, but I thought that maybe, come spring, there would be life flourishing here. Auntie's small bench had been pulled forward, next to the tiny grave. Across from it a birdbath rested, though it was frozen right now. The apple tree was alive and unburned, so there would be blossoms gracing the tree next year, too.

I looked around, wondering how so much had escaped destruction, and saw the answer. Auntie had a twelve foot high hedge around the yard. 'Had' being the operative word. The destruction of the town reduced the hedge to mere sticks stabbing blindly at the sky. The giant maple tree that towered over the two story house and shaded the back yard was little more than jagged wooden shards thrusting towards the sky. I walked to it, resting a hand on the trunk and wondered if it was even still alive.

Alex stumbled to the foot of the small grave and dropped to her knees, uncaring of the frozen earth, as hard as concrete. I winced in sympathy for her knees. I could hear her speaking, her voice an indistinct murmur and stayed back, loathe to intrude on her time. Who knew when we'd make it back here again? Everything was just too...weird.

She stayed there, on her knees, crying and talking until the sun wasn't even a memory and the temperature had plummeted to well below freezing.

Returning from another walk around the house and down the driveway, I went over and rested a hand on her shoulder. I'd long since pulled my scarf more firmly around my face and my hat over my ears trying to keep warm.

"It's time to go," I said. "If we stay any longer, the others will worry." *And we'll freeze to death*, I didn't say.

Once Alex healed physically, we'd discovered that she was damned stubborn, even to her own detriment. I worried she'd fight me about leaving, maybe even try to spend the night, but to my surprise and relief she offered no protest. I ended up having to pull her to her feet and sling her arm over my shoulder and wrap my free arm around her waist to support her. She was close to half-frozen from staying in one place for over an hour.

As we walked slowly away from the memorial she didn't look back. "Thanks for letting me stay so long," she said quietly, after we'd been walking for nearly ten minutes. "I thought you'd have reeled me in a long time ago, especially since I've been such a bitch to you."

"Well," I kept my voice mild. "it's not like you haven't been dealing with shit." Was this almost an apology?

"Yeah, but everyone's had something to deal with. At least I *know* where my family is. You and the others don't. I mean, it kills me that my baby's gone, but I don't have to worry about what might be happening to him, if he's okay—" Her voice broke, and she stared forward.

I carefully blanked my face. I don't think she'd react well to my astonishment. Was Alex actually expressing concern for *others*? For the last two months, she'd been so mired in her misery and anger (I'm not blaming her—she's completely justified) that she'd talked of nothing but getting revenge and what she would do to all the bastards.

She'd been displaying so much aggression that me and Sonya had regularly walked away from training with bruises, black eyes, and split lips, and we never let Alex spar with the kids. Ever. She didn't walk into it with the plan to hurt anyone, but she worked herself hard, and the kids didn't have the stamina or the skill to keep up with her.

Plus, drawing blood is rather satisfying when you're hurting. Fighting Alex was good preparation for me and Sonya. Like Alex, any enemies we tangled with wouldn't let up or go easy on us.

The rest of the walk back to the camp, we were silent—Alex, hopefully contemplating a future, and me, worrying about my family for the millionth time and trying to figure out the next few days.

***

I woke with a start, listening intently. I heard Alex shift on watch at the far side of the camp and blew out a quiet breath. *Nothing, it was nothing. Just another nightmare.* I took a few more deep breaths, feeling my heartbeat settle. Everyone had been dealing with nightmares of one thing or another, though we rarely spoke about it. What was there to say? We were scared shitless, but scared shitless while doing something was better than scared shitless and hiding in a hole.

I honestly couldn't believe how much better I started feeling as soon as we actually left the bunker. The fear was still there but was buried under all the stuff I had to remember to do and look for. I snorted quietly and readjusted on my sleeping mat. I'd thought so much about all the things to be scared of that I'd created an emotional immunity. By thinking about being scared I'd actually bored myself out of it.

Either that, or the human body could only manage so much terror before it got used to the sensation and proceeded to ignore it.

Rolling onto my back, I caught a glimpse of the stars through the open tent door and sighed. No point in going back to sleep. Almost my turn on watch. Might as well start a bit early and give someone else the chance to catch up on this blessing called "sleep."

***

After breakfast, we packed everything up tightly and stowed it. Removing all the obvious signs of our campsite took a bit more time, but we were getting better at it. Best to be careful. No reason to let the soldiers know that there were free people running around.

We covered the ground on the other side of the creek, all the way to the Oregon Gardens and the hotel above them. The hotel looked in good condition, but too big for us to be comfortable or safe there. No way to see the enemy coming, either.

The burned wrecks of the houses didn't yield much by way of supplies. Made sense, if they transported all the people here elsewhere that they'd take the food, too. Even the grocery store had been haphazardly emptied.

Alex didn't enter the Safeway. She stayed outside and kept watch. I couldn't blame her. Walking into that store after what happened there made my skin crawl, and the slightest sound made me start and reach for a weapon. Even though the bodies were gone, I kept imagining the soldiers, lying there at the back, between the refrigerated section and the produce.

I did want to cry in the ice cream aisle. All that wasted deliciousness. "You still owe me a pint of Ben and Jerry's!" I bellowed to the empty air.

"How do you know you won?" Sonya shouted back.

"Have you seen yourself lately? You definitely lost more than seven pounds!"

"We never decided when I had to pay you."

"Bitch."

"Jerk."

I breathed a sigh of relief when we left the store behind, and Sonya visibly relaxed as we wandered down to the gas station. It was the only one left in town, used for buses and the few cars that locals didn't want to get rid of. Mostly classics. My favorite, the green '52 Ford pickup, could often be seen around town.

I picked up a nozzle and hopefully squeezed the lever. Nothing. I sighed. Damn no electricity. In the end, it took us over an hour to get the gas station to cough up the goods. It took a bit of experimenting, and a lot of damage to the pumps, before we realized we could break into the underground tank quicker and easier.

"At least we can hide barrels of gas," I stood, hands on my hips, examining the mess we'd made of the pumps before we'd figured out the tank. No way to hide that shit. "Anybody know a good place to stash the loot?" I waved at the barrels standing around us.

"A friend of mine lived up on Water Street," Jaali volunteered. "Their house is pretty well hidden by trees, and Fred and me had a small fort to one side. It's hard to spot. Plus, there's a lot of other properties along that road."

I shrugged. "Yeah, all right. Let's get this baby loaded."

It took a mere fifteen minutes to dismount the machine gun. Getting the barrels loaded took a lot more time. And panting, and groaning. Jaali came up with a rope system that allowed all of us to get the barrels up a short ramp and into the truck instead of only three of us breaking our backs. Quite ingenious of the little bugger. Sonya was our main brute force. Her forearms are the size of my upper arms, and they're *solid*. Rock hard muscle.

There were times, Before, when we'd be moving hay bales and Son would carry a sixty pound bale in each hand. Multiple times. She'd unload over half the hay *alone*. Without the fat to slow her down now and improved lung capacity, I actually had to force her, and the others, to take breaks. The aim was that we didn't break a sweat. In this weather, you sweat, you freeze; you freeze, you die. Simple as that.

We got Asilia to make tea purloined from the grocery store for us regularly, which we had with the few bits of edibles we'd found there. It wasn't much, but having stale crackers and twinkies beat the hell out of MREs.

And all day long, we hauled barrels of gas away to create caches for future needs.

On our fourth night out I *finally* started sleeping better. Probably because I dropped with exhaustion every evening. I woke up feeling...not cheerful, but content. We were moving forward. *Doing* something.

The others weren't so fresh in the morning, as they still hadn't adjusted to life without coffee. This morning, I at least, had tea. I was on last watch, and I took my steaming mug to the edge of camp and stood just inside the trees. Though I'd seen sunrises before, and many of them would have been as beautiful as this one, I'd always been too busy to appreciate them. Work, bills, family drama, the idiocy of the government, all of these things have a way of cluttering minds, but now everything was so much more basic.

Find supplies, shoot bad guys, don't die. Simple, right?

I leaned against my tree and sipped my tea, watching the sky lighten. I loved the color contrasts, the deep blue of the western sky, fading to a light, bluey-green. Slowly, so slowly, watching the blues become invaded by pinks, and reds, and oranges, before finally seeing the sun peek over the mountains.

Maybe my new appreciation is because we're dancing on the edge, I mused, breathing in the warm air over my mug. *Have to enjoy today what we may not be alive to see tomorrow.* I grinned.

As I watched the sun crest the horizon and finished the last swallow of tea, I turned my face into the wind. Something's different. I sniffed the air, trying to place it. Half a minute later, it dawned on me: I faced south. The wind had changed. So the cold snap was broken, but now the rains would move in. They always did with a southern wind. They usually did with a northern one, too.

Oh, let's face it. This is Oregon. A "ten percent chance of rain" literally means we'll be having rain. *Thinking* about rain means it'll rain, especially if you have plans. This is the Pacific Northwest.

I shrugged. Not much I could do about the weather, and I had to pee. I scraped away a few layers of loam from the base of a tree, dumped my tea bag in, and relieved myself. It was the work of a moment to scrape it all back over, hiding the evidence. Time to put introspection and philosophical thinking behind me. The day was calling.

"I hate you," Sonya mumbled blearily when I nudged her awake. The best part of having the last watch was waking everyone up. "You're unnatural. Nobody should be awake right now and happy about it."

I ignored her and continued around the camp, using my boot liberally, depending on how hard they were to waken. This morning, Alex was especially difficult to get moving.

"I changed my mind, Hope." I openly laughed at Alex, with her two-toned hair hanging in front of her face as she scowled at me, propped up on her elbows. "Last night I thought you were a nice person, but you're not. You're pure, undiluted evil. Go away." She flopped back into her sleeping bag, stubbornly burying her head in her arms.

I thought for a moment, then leaned down. "We're heading into Salem today," I whispered.

"I'm up! I'm up!" She straightened, groaning as she got to her feet. "I'm too young to feel this damn old."

"You and me, both," Sonya muttered into her steaming mug of morning tea.

I was a little disappointed that no one required more than a nudge to get going. I'm not squeamish about kicking a person when they're down. In fact, I figured that's the best time to do it. They're less able to kick back.

Breakfast, like always, was whatever we had in a tin. And tea and crackers. We still had some of those left.

CHAPTER 7

Sonya sniffed the air, turning to face the wind. "Rain's coming," I said. "South wind now."

She nodded. "Damn."

"How do you know?" Jaali asked.

"It's Oregon," I replied. "If it might rain, it will rain."

Jaali and his sister looked downcast by that, and us older ones had to laugh. "You haven't been here long, have you?" Alex asked. We usually avoided personal questions as it was so painful, but their ignorance of the weather was too cute.

"Six months," Asilia said. "We're from LA, but Mom," she choked a bit, "got a good job. She works in Wilsonville and Dad found one in Silverton. That's why we moved here."

I patted her shoulder. "You'll learn what Oregon's like." I grinned. She didn't look reassured. "Let's just say there's a reason we brought waterproof jackets.

"We should stop at the library while we're here, though," I said. "Just to see if there's anything we can use there."

"Like what?" Alex asked.

"I don't know! Useful shit. Herb books. Be nice to have something fresh once in a while. 'Sides, I heard you can get scurvy if you don't have enough fresh greens, and damned if I want to deal with that crap. Some local maps. Also," I continued thoughtfully, "it'd be nice to see if there's any information about Korea, as a country. Their geography and stuff."

"Who cares where they came from," Asilia said bitterly. "They're here. Isn't that enough?"

"I wanna know whether they're used to mountains or flats. What's their altitude? Rainfall? Highs and lows in temperatures? Maybe it'll help, maybe it won't, but those bastards'll be in the high country eventually, and we need to have an idea how they'll do."

"We're still going to Salem, though." Sonya managed to make it a command.

"Yeah. I just—I think we need to be better prepared for the way they think." *We're still looking for our families,* I thought at her. *I haven't given up on them.* Hers or mine. With Silverton empty, Salem was the logical place to look for them.

At the library, Sonya held me back and let the others go in first. "You've put some thought into all this."

"Only once we decided we weren't going to sit on our hands. We need to know more about the terrain *we're* in. I don't know about you, but if I haven't had to drive it, I don't know it, and that covers a shit-ton of roads." I scrubbed my hands over my face. "I just don't want this to be the one-and-only thing we do. Like I said, I ain't going on no suicide run."

"Well, lookit you." Son grinned, good humor restored "All 'let's save people' and shit! Feel like a rousing discussion about truth? Justice? The American Way?"

"Fuck off!"

The other three looked back, confused when Sonya fell over, laughing.

Eventually, when Sonya calmed down, all of us started rifling through the library. It made me sad all over again, seeing the wanton destruction of books. They were like dreams, as lifeless as the town around us. Most of the books were molded and mildewed. The only bits that survived were at the back of the building, closest to the river. Back there, you could still see some of the original paint, only faintly covered with soot.

We walked slowly through the rubble, picking up and discarding books as non-essential. Maybe fifteen minutes in, Alex hoisted a large book into the air.

"I got one! Called," she read the inside cover again, "*Mother Nature's Herbal*. Identifies plants and their uses."

"Bring it!" I shouted.

"Here, Jaali!" Asilia held up a book. "This one has small words. Perfect for you!"

I caught a glimpse of the title, *50 Shades of Gray*, before she threw it to her brother. "Don't give him that crap!" I chucked a book at it, hoping to intercept. Everybody froze when my book hit Sonya in the ass.

She straightened up slowly, her face like thunder. "Right, somebody's in deep shit!"

Three sets of fingers pointed right at me. I backed away slowly, hands held out towards her as I smiled weakly.

It degenerated into a free-for-all book fight. We raced through the building, leaping over piles of rubble and trash snatching up books and hurling them at one another, laughing and screeching. At one point I noticed the dogs sitting in the entryway, giving us puzzled looks. I turned to point their expressions out when I took a hardcover between the eyes, knocking me flat on my ass.

Asilia, who'd thrown the book, was the first one over, hovering and apologizing profusely. I looked blearily up at her, then shifted my hips until

I was able to reach the piece of wood poking me in the butt. I held it up, bemused, only to have it knocked from my hand.

"Hope! Hope!" Sonya was there, leaning over. "How many fingers am I holding up?"

I frowned groggily at her, scrunching my face in an effort to close one eye. "Three?"

"Close enough," She closed the fingers before I could see how many she'd actually been holding up. "She's fine," Sonya announced. "Just a little knock. She's had worse. Trust me."

Asilia looked ready to cry, standing behind Sonya's shoulder. "I'm so sorry, Hope. I didn't mean to hurt you, I swear!"

I waved it away. "No worries." There was Mercy's Aussie slang again. "Where's that damn book? Jaali, can I see the weapon of mass destruction?" The boy passed it over. "What is this? Oh. *War and Peace.* Of course it is. I'm lucky to be alive. Naturally. Whoever said 'words will never hurt me' never got hit by this thing." I carefully put my head down, hoping that it would stop throbbing soon.

Son took the book, thoughtfully turning over in her hands. "Here, Asilia. You should keep it. If you open it up and tie it to your chest you can use it as body armor. And when you're bored it'll double as reading material. Though you'd have to be pretty bored to read this sucker," she added under her breath.

She was right. I'd tried to read the book once, years ago. It was one of the few I quit.

One benefit to our book fight is we all went back into it with lighter hearts, and in my case, an aching head. I was especially pleased about Alex. She'd actually joined in the fun. Maybe this running around doing stuff was helping her get her head on right. Or distracting her from her thoughts. Either worked.

After an hour we gathered to pool the results of our efforts, which was little better than nothing. We had the herbal book, an Oregon map, a plant encyclopedia (courtesy of Jaali), and a mention about Korea that was briefer than the average bikini.

A bit of a mention about the highest peak (nine thousand and two feet) and that it had lots of plains. Also, lots of logging has left the country in environmental trouble, and it gets to between nine and twenty-seven degrees F in the winter, with an average of thirty-seven days of snow.

"Wow," I said dryly, looking at the paragraph. "I love how informative this thing is."

"Look on the bright side," Sonya put in, "it doesn't sound like they'd know what to do with mud."

"They don't need to. Those trucks are four wheel drive at least. They'll go through or over most anything we can throw at them."

A small gasping sob had us dropping the banter. Jaali stood there, arms hanging limply at his sides, staring at nothing as a tear tracked down his face and his thin shoulders shook with quiet crying. I was the first one to his side, and I wrapped an arm around his narrow shoulders.

"What is it?" I asked, hugging him tightly.

"Do you think we'll ever have a home again?" he asked, wrapping his arms around me and burying his face in my jacket.

I opened my mouth, closed it again, and gave it a bit of thought. Finally, I sighed. "It won't be easy, and it won't be the same, but I think we can. We'll get more help as we go, I know it."

"If that was true, the army would be here by now," Asilia interjected, an unusual note of bitterness in her voice. "Instead, people break their backs trying to pay taxes, and we get abandoned by those assholes."

I raised my eyebrows, and Jaali tensed in my arms. Asilia *never* swore, never used anything that could be construed as "rude language." Jaali teased her about it constantly, the little brat. So if she's using it now...

"As much as it may be fun to try to figure out where the government and all help is, it could be a blessing in disguise," I said. I got four astonished looks. "Think about it. Normally, we'd sit around, waiting for the government to bail us out. Then we'd be waiting...and waiting... and we'd just stay in a sucky situation. This way, we get off our asses and make shit happen. What the army does or doesn't do doesn't matter. Not to us. We'll save ourselves, dammit!"

While my little speech didn't lead to cheers or anything embarrassing like that, chins firmed up. I kissed Jaali on the top of his curly head, and we went to find a table to check out our map.

"So," I said, leaning in to find Silverton, "I've been thinking we should approach from either the north or south. Directly from here leaves us too much open farmland to cover, and we wouldn't be able to get very close by car. Personally, I like the north better. From there we can—Jaali, can you move your head, you're blocking the light—we can head towards Gervais, then take the 263...Oh, here, look, we can take the 260. That connects to the 263. That or head up Silver Falls way and take the 22."

"I vote we go in from the north," Sonya said slowly. "I'm more familiar with that, and I'd hate for shit to hit the fan and we're stuck at a dead end because we made a wrong turn."

"Seconded," Alex chimed in. "I'm all for not getting stuck at a dead end."

"North it is, then."

***

Later, everybody was back in their accustomed positions, Asilia at the wheel, Alex navigating, me on the gun, and Sonya and Jaali with binoculars. Asilia kept us to a slow, steady pace. The damn turnoff we needed was small and hard to spot, perfect for our needs. We drove through gentle hills and sharp bends, passing bare trees interspersed with evergreens. Along the way we saw a sign pointing to the Gallon House Bridge.

I wondered if it still stood. I wondered that a lot lately.

Clouds were moving in from the south now. Once the wind changes, Oregon wastes no time bringing back the rain.

"Hey, Hope?" Jaali patted my leg. "I hear something up ahead."

I rapped sharply on the roof. Asilia pulled to a stop and stuck her head out the window.

"'Sup? We're nearly there."

"Jaali's hearing things," I said. "We'd better check it out. Better safe than sorry."

"Oh, cool!" Jaali pumped his fist into the air, opened his mouth, and sucked in a breath like he was about to whoop. He lost all that air a moment later when Sonya whacked him in the stomach.

"Shut up," she told him sternly. "You want to bring the entire army down on us? Woohoo, let's die before we even started because Jaali couldn't keep his mouth shut?"

Jaali ducked his head, embarrassed, and mumbled something that sounded contrite.

I leaped about as gracefully as a drunken sailor from the back of the truck, staggering when I hit the ground. Ground that didn't bounce and sway was weird. Was this what sailors went through when they were on shore leave? Jaali followed me down, springing as lightly as a lamb.

Sonya just stopped Obelix from following him. The puppy was just so *excited* at the thought of going for a walk, his little rump wiggling as he wagged his tail. Kinda like Jaali.

Son took up a position at the machine gun and gave us a thumbs up. Yeah, that's right. Wish us luck, hope we don't die. Am I sure there isn't something stupider we could be doing? Sure, we could not be checking out a noise that the boy may or may not have heard.

"Are you always like this?" Jaali whispered.

I realized I'd been muttering under my breath, but fortunately too quietly for the kid to hear exactly what.

"Yes," I said shortly.

We moved cautiously off the road and through the dry shrubs and grasses lining it. I was about to shove sarcastic me into a box, out of the way, but then I decided sarcastic me was better company than morbid me, who was next in line. Panicking me went into the box, though. I didn't need all that extra mental jumping and screaming. I might physically be doing that soon enough.

As we crept through the tall grass, using every bit of our newly learned hide-and-seek skills, I waved a hand behind me. Jaali obediently slowed down and followed my footsteps. We took our time, and in fifteen feet I heard what Jaali had picked up on in the truck: the sounds of vehicles—lots of them.

We slowed even more, moving into a hands and feet crawl, the better to stay hidden. I pulled my scarf higher on my face to try to hide my pale skin and the white plumes of breath. Jaali bumped into me, eager for a glimpse. I pressed his shoulder *easy, easy, they're not moving too fast, neither should we.*

Crossing those couple hundred feet took forever, and the position of the sun reflected that. It sunk considerably towards the west as we crawled, gently parting the grasses to prevent an obvious trail being left. Once we made it to the cover of the trees and bushes lining this section of the highway, we bellied down and did our best elbows and toes wriggle.

I ended up lying full length next to a tree, with my head and shoulders under some bush. I didn't care what it was, as long as it had leaves. Jaali was behind a tree maybe eight feet away to my left, craning his head and trying to see as much as possible.

Trucks rolled down the highway towards Salem, so it looked like our guess about that was good. I wrinkled my nose when the stench from the trucks hit me. Only one thing smelled that bad. Silage, the fermented fodder reserved almost exclusively for dairy cows in this part of the world. Some trucks had livestock. Other trucks were loaded with vegetables. Corn, pumpkins, potatoes...It made me think of Thanksgiving. The last truck was full of people. Dirty, worn out, and depressed people.

The lightbulb finally went off. These guys were running around bringing in the last of the harvest. We may not have too many huge farms, but Oregon has shit-tons of small, family farms. Even we had one when I was growing up.

I shook my head, amazed at the scale of what they were doing, and even more appalled by the fact that we were out here planning to put a spanner in these kinds of works. We'd be lucky if we weren't squished like little bugs on a windscreen. Little panicking me started jumping up and down again in the back of my mind, screaming that we were all going to die, and what the hell am I doing?

My best. Now shut up! I closed my eyes, inhaling strongly through my nose until I'd stuffed the little panicked me securely back into its box and put my attention back where it needed to be.

The boy really did have exceptional hearing, picking up the sounds of all these vehicles from that distance, and over the sound of our own engine. He'd given us enough warning that we were able to see and count a good many of the trucks passing us, and to watch the tank that followed behind. I lay there, chilled, watching the huge, uncaring machine crunching down the road leaving bits of gravel in its wake. Reminded me of the first time I saw one, hiding in a ditch in the rain that terrible night.

A more practical consideration hit me. The countryside was cleared of people. They were also lugging animals towards the city. I really hoped they'd pen the animals outside of it, because how were they going to handle the sewage situation?

Even a top of the line sewer system wouldn't be able to handle the number of people I estimated were in the city. The rundown piece-of-shit system that was all Salem had would've been swamped within weeks, if not days. After all, they've been scooping people up since day one, so the soldiers must have been stuffing people into a small space for two months.

A freezing wind made its way up the back of my jacket, making the chill literal as well as metaphorical.

I slowly backed away from the road, keeping an eye out for stragglers while my brain worked in overdrive.

Hundreds of thousands of people, crammed into Salem, more added daily, for two months...Disease would soon be rampant. Who knows what the population was now?

***

"Jaali!" Asilia came running up to him as we emerged onto the road, just twenty feet from the truck, and threw her arms around him. "Why were you gone so long? I was so worried!"

"Yeah, mom, I'm fine," he muttered in her embrace, embarrassed but also pleased to be fussed over.

"Speaking of worried," Sonya interjected, "you guys were gone for nearly two hours. How far did you end up going?"

"Not far," I said dryly. "Do you know how hard it is to move fast when you're trying not to be noticed? I think this was pretty big." Understatement of the year—well, probably not the year. Understatement of the month, maybe.

I filled them in on what we saw, with frequent interruptions from Jaali. Boy was like a hyperactive puppy. Cute, happy, and couldn't shut up. I also filled them in on my thoughts about the sewer system, and the possibilities for disease in the city.

Sonya blew out a breath when I finished. "Now we really have to go there. We need to see if we can find—" She broke off abruptly.

Yeah. No need to finish that thought. We were all in the same boat there. It was a quiet group that plodded back to the truck to continue.

"Son, would you mind navigating for Asilia?" I asked. "I want Alex and her rifle in the back." Just in case.

"You think we'll run into trouble?" Asilia asked, worried.

"Hon, we're always in trouble," Alex told her wryly.

"You're only paranoid if you're wrong," Sonya chimed in.

"Try this: hope for the best, expect the worst, prepare for the ridiculous," I finished.

Everybody except Sonya gave me a blank look. "Something my dad likes to say," I explained. "It's as close as we'll ever get to a motto." They kept looking at me weird. "Just get in the truck, will you?"

I pulled Sonya aside quickly. "Can you refresh Asilia on what they should do if we don't come back?"

She nodded, blue eyes sad. "Gotcha."

Once we were moving again, I noticed Jaali was even more vigilant about keeping watch. I narrowed my eyes against the wind and gave that thought a bit of time. It seemed that because Jaali's contribution had value, he worked harder so as to not let the group down. I wondered if it worked for everyone.

If we didn't die in the next couple weeks, I'd have to try that. If I remembered.

Inside the cab, I could see Sonya having an intense conversation with Asilia. I saw the younger woman nodding periodically, her shoulders tensing. Yeah, that's about the right reaction. That girl has a level head on her shoulders, at odds with her kinky hair and pixie looks. Underestimate her at your peril.

CHAPTER 8

It was slow going. We were always expecting to run into the enemy around every bend. I wanted to scream in sheer frustration and terror at first. As the minutes dragged on, I was reminded of a lesson learned the night we ran away from Silverton: you can only be scared so long before it just becomes a normal part of your day. You start to ignore it.

I hadn't believed the books that I'd loved to read would be so accurate when they said that soldiering was nine parts boredom and waiting and one part danger and shit-your-pants. We were living the boredom stage now, and I decided to try enjoying it while it lasted.

It lasted maybe forty minutes before Jaali tapped my leg, signaling he'd heard something. I rapped on the cab, and Asilia quickly found a lot to pull into and a building to hide behind. Two months ago, this place had been a thriving plant nursery, judging by the sign.

"What is it?" I asked Jaali. Sonya and Asilia climbed out, leaning on their doors to listen.

"Don't know exactly. Sounds like machinery, trucks, heavy equipment? I'm not really sure, just that something's up ahead."

Awesome. "Son, you're usually out this way on your route, right?"

Sonya, the chartered bus driver, nodded. "We're maybe a mile from Salem now. The ground is," she hesitated, then burst out with, "I don't remember what it's like! I never had to know before, so I never paid attention!"

"Trees," Asilia said, looking up from the map she'd taken from the cab. "It's colored green, so it should be trees."

"Oh. Good." I stared at the ground, sky, trees, anything except the four pairs of eyes watching me so carefully. I wanted to snap at them to look at something else. Lose my temper. Maybe freak out. Actually, freaking out sounded better all the time. A bit of a favorite novel decided to cross my mind, reminding me that the best thing I could do right now is look and sound confident. Apparently, it inspires hope in the troops.

I sighed. Here goes nothing. "Asilia, you and Jaali take the dogs and hole up in that trailer park we passed not too long ago. Keep quiet, stay hidden. We may need a fast way out of here, and we're relying on you to not get caught. You know how long to wait."

Five days. We'd decided they should only wait five days. I hoped it gave us enough time.

Asilia's eyes were huge and terrified, but she nodded resolutely. Bless the child.

"The rest of us are checking Salem out," I continued. "We'll be back by the deadline," *I hope,* "unless shit hits the fan, in which case we won't. So don't worry, okay?"

"Right, so either you'll make it, or you won't, so don't worry about it?" Asilia snapped, eyes sparking. "How is that supposed to be reassuring?"

"Well, there's only two possible outcomes," Sonya said reasonably. "Oh, hell with it. There's not much you can do about it, is what she's trying to say. Badly."

Asilia's mouth opened and closed, and I could see a dozen arguments racing through her head, but in the end, she nodded, still glaring.

Alex was about to grab her pack out of the cab when Sonya reached out and stopped her. "We should leave our packs behind," she said quietly.

"What? Why? All our food is in there!" Alex protested.

"Because," I answered, "we don't want to stand out in there. Our only defense is blending in, and right now I doubt people are running around with nice bags full of useful stuff. If even half of what we suspect has happened in there, people will turn us in or kill us just to get a bit extra. I ain't taking that shit, thank you very much!"

"You really think Americans would turn on us?" Alex was aghast.

"I think that when people are starving, they're unpredictable. And while I'd like to feed them, we don't have enough. The only ways we could possible help is to either get them out or throw the North Koreans out. So fill your pockets. What we take will have to last us."

"Ugh, so much fucking work!" Alex threw her hands in the air. "Fine!"

Me and Sonya just grinned at each other and opened our jackets.

One thing I absolutely love about the gear left in the bunker: there are these utility belts, and they have pouches. Big enough to fit a few MREs, the pouches are out of the way and easy to cover with a loose jacket. There's also a holder with a flap and buckle for a water flask. We looked a bit bulky, but it was easy to explain away with the cold weather, if anybody got curious enough to ask.

Alex even went so far as to tape granola bars to her legs. Jaali, I love that kid, spun away the moment her hands went to her belt buckle, the boy's cheeks darkening with a blush. After she finished, the woman offered the tape to me and Sonya.

"Ah, thanks, but I'll pass," I said, waving the tape away. "I've got some things there already. The food will just get in the way."

The others gave me quizzical looks, but Alex just shrugged and held the tape out to Son, who also declined and didn't bother to give a reason why.

Jaali gave us a clownish, crestfallen look when I said I wouldn't be exposing my legs, completely forgetting his earlier blush. "No, Jaali," I said, sighing in exasperation, "I will not pull down my pants in front of you."

He shot me a quick sideways grin and I laughed, ruffling his hair affectionately. The little bugger never stopped making jokes, it seemed. He'd have women throwing their underwear at him in a few years, if he kept this up.

If he survives. Damn, damn, damn! Unless I constantly policed them, these cheerful little thoughts just kept popping up! I shook my head to banish them and motioned for Sonya to lead the way into Salem.

***

I leaned out from behind my tree, watching and counting under my breath. It wasn't as hard to see as I'd have liked, with a mostly full moon peeking between the clouds racing high overhead. Stupid moon looked like it'd be sticking around all night, so we'd voted and decided to go for it anyway.

It turned out our entry to Salem was blocked by a guarded gate at the road and a damn big fence everywhere else. Okay, so it wasn't the best built fence I'd ever seen, though it stretched to either side for more than a mile in this area, and was more than seven feet high, with coils of barbed wire guarding the top. We'd followed the fence to the south until we found our in. The builders left a small gap at the base of the fence and water runoff from the fall rains had worn a tiny gully, barely visible as a darker patch of ground against the fallen leaves drifted against the fence, but our best way in.

I smiled into the dark. Were we up against soldiers? Yes. Were they good at terrifying people? Also yes. But the fact that their fence building skills were so shit gave me hope.

No, the fence didn't worry me overly. What had me watching and counting were the regular patrols. At our best count, they showed up every five minutes. Almost on cue, two more soldiers came marching through, walking from north to south. This was the fourth patrol we'd seen, with no variation in timing, the size of the patrol, or the route taken.

This time, as soon as they passed out of sight I waved, signaling Alex and Sonya. They raced past me, running across the narrow piece of cleared ground and I lunged to my feet, following at a sprint. Alex aimed for the gap at a headlong dive, sliding and squirming on her belly while me and Son helped her get through, counting all the while. Then came Son's turn.

"Two more minutes!" I hissed, straining, holding the fence up. I didn't even wait for Sonya's boots to clear the fence before I ducked down, wriggling through after her.

Then I was inside the fence. Alex already headed for the cover of the trees when Son threw out a hand.

"We have to cover it back up," she whispered, panting with fear and adrenaline.

I dropped to my knees and started tossing blown leaves back at the fence, hoping to make it look natural while Sonya kicked drifts my way and carefully straightened the grass.

"No more time!" Alex hissed from behind us. "They're coming!"

I lay in the bushes lining the cleared zone, panting into my sleeve and trying to muffle the sound of my breathing as we listened to the two-man patrol walk past our entry point. As soon as they were out of hearing, I dropped my head back, chest heaving as I tried to catch my breath. I heard gasping from Sonya somewhere to my left where she'd entered the bushes in a diving roll just seconds before the patrol appeared.

"We all alive?" I whispered.

I got a grunt from Son and a barely audible 'yes' from Alex. Good. We're not dead yet. Did this mean we were winning?

I rolled over and pushed to my feet. "Let's get the hell outta here. This part of town sucks."

***

In the early hours of the morning I stumbled, barely catching myself before I fell. I giggled. Creeping through the forest in the middle of the night without causing a ruckus is exhilarating. And exhausting. Probably more fun than is good for me.

I giggled again. Considering our current circumstances, enjoying dangerous situations is a perk. If I was to do stupid and risky shit anyway, I might as well have fun at it.

A branch whipped across my cheek, chafed raw by the cold. A leaf brushed the corner of my eye and I winced, squinting and rubbing, wiping away involuntary tears. Aaand that's the other side of nighttime forest walks.

It wasn't even so much "walking" through the woods as "finding the way by braille." Everything was more visible from the corner of my eyes, a series of lighter and darker shadows. We managed a slow, steady pace interspersed with curses.

After a while, I heard Alex whisper, "Sonya, do you actually know where we're going?"

"Uh, no? Does it really matter at this point, so long as it's away from the fence?"

"I guess not."

Clouds had taken firm hold of the sky, blocking all light. I pushed past a bush and stumbled into a cleared area with a row of houses stretching away to my left and right.

Son leaned in and whispered, "Welcome to suburbia."

"What now?" Alex muttered into the cold morning.

The first thing I noticed, there behind the row of houses, was the stench. Seemed my earlier thoughts about the sewage system hadn't been far off the mark. I gagged and tried breathing through my mouth. When that didn't work, leaving me with a bad taste on my tongue, I went back to breathing through my nose slowly, trying to accustom myself to the smell.

We huddled together in the cold, looking at the nearest house. The back wall had a gate cut into it, allowing the inhabitants to enter the forest to use it as a toilet, judging by the smell.

"Haven't people ever heard of burying it?" Sonya whispered in disgust. Though it was still too dark to make out details, I knew her nose was wrinkled and her lip curled at people's lack of hygiene.

I mean, for goodness' sakes, we had an entire forest to use, since none of the bathrooms at the bunker worked, and we'd still gone and made some frigging composting toilets, which wasn't easy, let me tell you. We put them together from a bunch of half-remembered shit that Toni, Son's sister, had told us one evening years ago. These poor buggers didn't even have the sense to dig a hole and build an outhouse over it.

Still, smelly as it all was, we could dither over that only so long. "I don't know!" I said, exasperated in response to Alex's query. "Maybe we should knock on the damn door!"

"It's not the worst idea you've ever had," Alex told me.

"Are you crazy? It's a terrible idea!"

"We came here to find shit out, didn't we? Easiest way is to talk to people."

"I thought we were supposed to talk to your aunt?" Sonya inquired. "Unless you want to run the risk of being turned in..."

Either somebody was already awake inside the house or we were truly awful at being quiet, because our discussion came to an end when the back door of the nearest house opened. To say we were slightly spooked would be an understatement, with all our hands darting to various places on our persons, no doubt ready to shoot the poor bastard down at the first sign of trouble. The man (it was a man, his posture and the slight shine of his balding head revealed that) didn't see us, instead easing down onto the back stoop, elbows resting on his knees, and put his head in his hands.

Releasing the handgun I'd been prepared to whip out, I motioned for the others to stay and walked towards the man, hands held out at my sides, making no effort to conceal my approach. Something about his dejected posture made me think he probably wouldn't try to kill us. At the very least, Alex and Sonya had my back, and Alex wasn't wrong: talking to people would be the best way to get information.

When I stopped barely two yards away and he still hadn't noticed me, I cleared my throat, politely.

I think I startled him.

He reared up violently, slamming his back against the door frame, eyes bulging out wildly as he attempted to shout. I hurriedly took two giant steps back, holding my hands over my head, absurdly grateful he'd winded himself and could only croak, unable to shout down a guard, or police force, or whatever they had running this joint.

"Easy! Easy," I said, trying to calm him down, patting the air above my head uselessly. Belatedly, I remembered the scarf covering my face and used a couple fingers to pull it down, exposing my nose to the cold air. "We're just your friendly neighborhood... spidermen?" I looked over my shoulder at the women and back at him. "I really didn't think that through."

Behind me I clearly heard sniggers, but I kept my eyes on the frightened man in front. Being middle-aged, unshaven, balding, and gaunt didn't detract from the hardness in his expression as he looked at us in the pre-dawn light.

"You okay now?" I asked, lowering my hands and bending down to look him in the eye. He nodded, still staring. "My name's—"

"Don't tell me," he interrupted hoarsely. "I don't want to know. It's safer, not knowing."

"Uhh. Okay?"

"Can't tell what you don't know. Remember that," he whispered. "It might save your life one day."

I stood there, turning over the implications of that statement, the small hairs on the back of my neck standing up while the other two moseyed over in as non-threatening a fashion as they could manage. "Can we ask you a few questions?" I asked eventually.

"Not here. Closer to the trees. Don't want to wake anybody." He suited actions to words and led the way out of the yard to the trees we'd so recently vacated.

"What's actually happening here?" I asked.

"Why didn't anybody bother digging a hole?" Sonya interjected.

"Guess those two questions tie together," the man reflected. "Before I start, answer one question: Who sent you? The government? The army? Who?"

"Uh, us?" I shrugged helplessly. "We haven't seen anybody from the outside. Sorry."

The man sighed heavily, shoulders sagging a bit more. "Damn. Anyway," he continued with a fatalism that hurt to see, "we're from Three Sisters, brought here six, eight, weeks ago. Get fed just enough to keep us alive, not enough to fill us up. As you can smell, the sewer's shot to hell. Disease kicked up after we'd been here maybe two weeks. So many people fell sick, hardly had anyone healthy enough to dig a hole. Now the ground's froze. And people...people have been dying since day one." He paused to swallow, his Adam's apple bobbing violently. "I've lost one daughter. I'd just stepped outside for a break. My wife can't even walk, though we think she may recover. There's about half the people in that house as there was when it all started."

"Fuck," I whispered, staring at the man. It was worse than I'd thought. I heard Alex sniff. My own eyes stung with tears and cold.

"Carts go by every day, collecting the bodies," the man continued. He sounded as if he was talking to himself, needing to get everything off his chest. "And if the police aren't taking the dead, then the goddamn North Korean's pet Americans are taking the living in for questioning. Or punishment."

"What do you mean?"

"Girl living a couple houses down was taken from her family just four days ago. Excuse is that her dad isn't working as hard as he could—bastards have got us building the damn fence—but they'll take any girl they think is pretty."

Alex's head jerked up. "What happens to them?"

"Rumor mill has it a girl escaped, made it away. Briefly. We heard the girls are marked, then turned into prostitutes. Some bullshit propaganda about mixing the two cultures and races, making it easier for us to accept them since they're fathering the next generation. Sick way to describe rape, if you ask me."

I sagged against a tree, breathing heavily. Well, there goes burying my emotions. Fuck that, apparently.

Alex's face was suffused with rage, tears running down her cheeks, and Sonya leaned forward, hands braced on her knees, looking about to puke. On the one hand, I was sorry to know the truth. We'd felt a bit obligated to do something before, maybe bomb a building, burn some shit—lightweight terrorism—but this level of abuse... The other hand meant now we *had* to take action.

"We're doing something about that." Alex made it a statement.

"Yeah, but not here, not where he can hear," I said. I needed time to think. I needed more guns.

From the house came the sound of a thump, and the man's head cocked. "I need to go. Somebody's up." Without a backward glance he turned and disappeared into the house, shutting the door firmly behind him.

"That was weird." I stared after the man, nonplussed.

"Time we find your auntie," Sonya told Alex as we walked back into the trees.

"If she's still alive." Alex's expression was haunted.

CHAPTER 9

We walked parallel to the street, staying inside the trees. The lack of people walking around made me nervous. The last thing we needed was to stand out by being the only ones on the street. I looked up, watching the clouds coming in, herded by the building wind, and sighed. We'd likely have rain before the day finished. Lovely.

We kept a gap of a dozen or so paces between us, walking swiftly to keep warm. Despite the circumstances, or because they triggered the line of thought, my mind wandered to what could happen. Okay, I'll admit it, mostly I thought about the fact that one or all of us might not make it out.

Once the sun crested the horizon, we began to see more people out and about, and nervously we exited the last of the trees and made our way into suburbia. Unconsciously, we grouped together as we walked, eyeing the people around us. They were thin, dirty, wearing filthy clothes, but so were we. So why were they giving us odd looks?

I examined us and them as closely as those "find the differences" drawings and it finally dawned on me: we walked like we did in the forest, heads up and checking all directions, arms swinging freely, alert and looking for the next attack (Jaali's favorite thing, jumping out at us screaming, trying to get a reaction).

The survivors in Salem kept their heads down and tried to take up as little space as possible, scuttling around, shoulders hunched. If thinking could make a person invisible, the streets would've looked empty, I'm sure.

"Look at them," Alex muttered, "skulking around like frightened rabbits while their families are being torn apart. Why don't they *do* something?"

"They're sick, beaten down, and half starved," I said quietly. "They don't have the energy to do shit. I know I wouldn't if I'd been here two months."

"You wouldn't have stayed put for that long," Alex threw back.

"If my family was with me, and they couldn't leave, I'd park my ass and grow moss. Some things are worth dying for."

"Keep moving, morons," Sonya muttered, uncomfortable with the attention we were getting. "Last thing we need is questions. Where does your aunt live, again?" she asked Alex.

"Where are we...?" Alex peered at the nearest street sign. "Hayesville? Where the fuck is Hayesville?"

"There!" Sonya pointed to another sign. "Keizer. We're in Keizer."

"South then. Mary lives just off Silverton Road, behind Roth's." Alex turned and led the way, Sonya following with alacrity.

The farther south we went, closer to the city's main streets, the more soldiers we saw. Also kept seeing these white guys running around in red armbands. They were obviously better fed than the general population, swaggering like bullies in the schoolyard.

"Who the hell are those assholes?" Alex asked, watching them with narrowed eyes.

"Who gives a fuck? Get off the main road before they notice us!" I herded the other two onto the first side street we came across. "I'd rather try our luck with the damn maze back here than tangle with those guys right now. As for who they are, I'm betting they're collaborators."

"Coll-what?"

"They've sold out and are working with the soldiers. Basically, they're the enemy, too."

"At least they have the decency to make it easy to ID them," Sonya interjected before Alex could say anything.

Alex had been adamant that no American would ever cooperate with an invading force. She actually bought into all the crap they tried to teach us in schools about the US's moral superiority. Poor thing looked like she might vomit at the thought of anyone willingly helping with the subjugation of their own country. How to explain it's been going on since forever?

At the sight of these men and realizing what they were, she just looked sick. Then the paleness of her face slowly changed to red, and I recognized the look that showed up next. That bullish stubbornness that said, "Fight me." She'd been giving it to me for months.

Alex started angling towards the men with the red armbands, and I half-dragged, half-pushed her and Sonya onto a small lane barely half a mile from Roth's. Son caught Alex's expression and grabbed her arm to help pull her away from the main road.

"What the hell?" Alex sputtered.

"Get your shit together, woman!" I snapped. "We are not starting a damn fight in broad fucking daylight with unarmed people everywhere!"

"One problem," Sonya stated. "We have to find our way through the soldiers, in the suburbs."

An observer might think it odd, the way we kept referring to the suburbs, but honestly, as far as me and Sonya were concerned, those streets are worse than the corn-maze we did every October. Dead ends, lanes that turn out to be crescents, and windy little shit roads that go nowhere. Only the people who live in them can navigate them, especially now that Google Maps was just a memory.

"We'll climb a tree," I growled, still pissed off, even though I was expecting this kind of behavior from Alex.

"I'd need binoculars to see farther than thirty feet." Sonya quickly voted herself out of tree-climbing.

"I-I haven't climbed a tree since I was, like, five." Alex followed Son's lead. "I might fall out."

"At least it'd be funny." I glowered at both of them, but neither budged on their convictions. "Bitches." I set about trying to find a tree tall enough. Courtesy of this being an older neighborhood, there were a few options to choose from.

I picked a nice fir tree, on the assumption that an evergreen would provide a bit more cover to my semi-disreputable endeavor. My progress up the tree was...hampered. It went something along the lines of: "Son of a bitching—who put that—ow! What the hell...? Urg. Branch. Gonna cut every fucking branch off this piece of shit—motherfucker!"

By the time I reached a branch high enough to have a view, my hat was half-off, my hair was sticking out everywhere, and I needed to empty my bra of all the little bits and pieces that'd fallen inside. A twig that'd gotten into my underwear poked my butt, and I couldn't get it out yet because I needed both hands to not fall out of the damn torture device masquerading as a tree.

I spent a few breaths up there, carefully looking and counting, then began my descent. Well, maybe "descent" is too kind. "Fell out" isn't quite accurate either, with so many branches between me and the ground. Suffice it to say that gravity had more to do with my exit from the tree than any arboreal climbing prowess on my part.

Thank God most people don't look up.

Alex and Sonya were both red-faced by the time my boots (and a shower of dead twigs) hit the ground, and their shoulders shook. "Fuck you," I told them rudely, and they burst into laughter.

Sonya ended up sitting on the ground, squealing around the hands she'd clamped over her mouth, while Alex leaned against the tree I'd just left, gasping and snorting through the scarf she stuffed into her mouth.

"When we get back to the bunker, I'm making everyone climb trees," I said, glaring at them. They just sniggered more. I sighed. "I hate you both. We're also not far away from Silverton Road, and Roth's is swarming with soldiers and workers. Yay! Will you two get up already? We have business—oh, for fuck's sake!"

I walked away to give them some space to get their shit together. While I waited, I fished around in my pants and pulled out the offending twig and emptied an amazing amount of bark, needles, and a couple of insects out of my sports bra by the simple expedient of pulling up my shirts and lifting the bra out. Every girl has done this at some point in her life. More than once, usually. I stared at the sky. How much time do women spend emptying out their bras?

"So—so," Sonya's breath hitched with residual laughter as she clambered unsteadily to her feet, "where to next, oh fearless leader?"

Alex took one look at my face and dissolved back into giggles when I growled, "We'll need to head east, towards Silverton to get around all the guys working around Roth's." I talked over their chortles because if I waited for them to calm down, we'd be here until next week. "We've got a few normal looking people wandering around, and there's a guarded gate to the outside world in view right across the road, but as long as we keep our heads down, we should be fine. Note, I said *should*."

"Another gate? With guards?" Sonya moaned theatrically. "Why is it that just when I think it can't get much worse, it does? What's wrong with these assholes? Don't they trust people to stay put and follow orders?"

"Learn to love trouble," I said sardonically. "It ain't going away anytime soon."

"And here's the world's tiniest violin playing a sad song just for you," Alex put in, rubbing two fingers together. "Can we go before you guys get too far into your favorite sport? I want to get to Aunt Mary's before dark, thank you very much."

"Oh, *now* she wants to move," I muttered to Son as we got going. "Yes, when *I* want to move it doesn't happen, but when *Alex* says go, everybody runs."

Sonya rubbed her mouth to hide her smile. The smile disappeared when the street dead-ended and a fence blocked the only way forward. It turned out that everything we'd done over the last two months had actually prepared us for hopping through strangers' backyards, and we progressed quickly enough. It was also a lot more fun than walking on the sidewalks like normal people. Even Alex enjoyed it.

I suddenly realized Alex had laughed and engaged more with us in the past week than she had in the last months. Well, my mama always said busy hands lightened the heart.

We lost track of our location until I stuck my head over the next fence and saw the chain-link barrier barely forty feet away. I turned back. "Uh, people? We went a bit too far. We need to go that way now." I pointed south-and-west-ish.

The last stretch involved crawling under some bushes before we abruptly emerged onto the sidewalk. We gained our feet quickly enough, but as we brushed the twigs and dirt off each other a cop cycled past. The presence of the police made me acutely aware of all the things I had hidden under my clothes. The guns felt like they were burning holes in the fabric. The cop gave us a look, long enough to make me sweat, though he thankfully didn't stop.

"Wonder if he's one of them?" Sonya muttered after he was out of hearing.

"No red armband," Alex replied.

"Maybe cops don't need them."

"More moving, less talking," I interrupted. "I don't like being on main streets like this. People can see us."

"Maybe the cops aren't on the payroll like those armband guys," Alex continued as if I'd never spoken.

We crossed the street without incident. Once on the other side, Alex took the lead. In this area we saw more people hanging out in yards and wandering down the streets. It was a dichotomy, their clothing and their bearing. Most folks we saw looked much as they would have the year before. Perhaps their clothing was a little more worn, a little more tattered around the edges, but that's fairly common in Oregon anyway.

Their expressions and their posture, however...all tense features and nervous glances. Walking too fast and looking over their shoulders. If they weren't twitchy and trying to see everywhere at once, then their heads were hanging, attempting to avoid the gazes of others. They barely spoke, and the few I heard talked in low mutters or with a forced air of geniality.

We didn't have to stand the odd vibes of the street for long. Mary's house lay less than half a mile away, easy enough after everything we'd done the last weeks. A small house with a tiny yard on a dead end street. Neat enough, but even a small yard in winter shows signs of neglect.

Alex walked quickly to the porch, knocking before she'd even stopped. Inside we could hear feet approaching, overlaid with a crotchety voice yelling, "What do you want? It's not like we have any food here, either!"

The voice's owner turned out to be a grouchy woman slightly shorter than Alex, in her fifties, with the coolest hair I'd ever seen. She'd left the upper layer a natural white while the underside was dyed a brilliant red.

My first thought was *I hope I look that good when I'm that age.* My second thought was, *I probably won't make it to that age.*

The woman's eyes filled with tears and she lunged at Alex, pulling her into a tight hug. She looked at me and Son over Alex's shoulder with gratitude and mouthed *thank you* as she held her niece, both of them shaking. The moment ended quickly as it began, with Mary pulling back and dragging her niece into the house, calling for us to follow her.

As I stepped inside, the smell hit me like a brick wall. My eyes watered and I pressed a hand to my nose, trying to suppress the stench. It smelled like fear, despair and desperation, like too many people in too small a space. The second thing I noticed after I got myself under control was the sparse furnishings. Anything burnable, other than blankets and one comfy chair, was gone.

The older woman coughed as she walked, a nasty, chesty cough, and my lungs hurt to hear it.

"You're sick?" Alex asked, concerned. "What do you need?"

"Just to see you again, dear." Mary led the way to the tiny living room, sinking down into the single chair in exhaustion. "As for what I have? Who knows? Everybody has something. I'm just grateful mine doesn't seem to be a killer." She shivered in the room's chill air.

We were so used to being in the elements that we'd acclimated to the freezing temperatures. I found being out of the wind practically balmy. Plus, from the looks of things, we were the healthiest people around. Maybe we'd trimmed down, but we still had more body fat than these poor buggers.

"Do you have enough food? Any heating?" Alex bustled around the little room, pulling another blanket out and tucking it around Mary, fussing over the older woman like a mother hen.

Me and Sonya hung back, trying not to stare at the side of Alex we'd thought died with her boy.

"We have food," Mary told her. "Your cousin and her family are here, as well as two other families, and while you have to work to be fed, they do and we are. I keep an eye on the children most days. Today they're out with their parents. Everyone does their 'part,'" she said sardonically, making air quotations around that last word. "Stupid propaganda."

"Now," Mary turned her attention to us, "who are your friends?"

"Uh," I said intelligently as we shifted uncomfortably, "we've been told it's a good idea to keep that to ourselves, particularly as we're not exactly 'regulars.'"

Mary smiled. "Very well. I dub you 'Tweedle-dee' and 'Tweedle-dum.'"

"I'm Tweedle-dee," I said, before Sonya could get a word in. "This is Tweedle-dum."

Sonya stuck her tongue out at me. "How come I'm Tweedle-dum?"

"Because you were too slow."

"Whatever." Sonya wandered off to check out the pictures Mary had on her walls. None of them were framed, not anymore, judging by the marks on the walls. Mary had apparently lived an adventurous life. There were photos of her in exotic locations, with even more exotic people. I sighed, envious. I'd always wanted to travel, but bills and fines made that impossible.

Behind us, Mary asked, "Where's Dylan? Is he here?"

My interest in the photos became acute as Sonya and me gave them some privacy. Mary let out a short cry, and in the reflection of a photo I saw her and Alex embracing as they wept.

Long minutes later they parted, Mary keeping a tight grip on Alex's hand as she invited me and my cousin to take a seat next to Alex on the mattresses piled on the floor. "Now, where have you been keeping yourselves? I've had people looking all over for you, my girl."

"Not in the city, Auntie," Alex said. "Probably better if I don't say more. We're safe, and we can provide food for ourselves."

"What brings you here? Surely more than just reassuring a worried aunt."

Sonya and Alex turned to me where I sat sandwiched in the middle and waited for me to speak. Put on the spot like that, I was rather uncomfortable. "Um, we were hoping for some help, erm, finding some people we know. Also, we're trying to get a grip on what the hell is going on, and we were hoping you'd know. Alex says you've got friends everywhere."

"Can you get that book and pen, dear?" Mary pointed to a plastic tv tray doing double duty as a side table and Sonya leaned over to grab them. "Write down the names of the people in there. I'll put the word out. When did they disappear?"

"You have a pen, auntie?" Alex reached out to touch it. "I didn't know that."

Mary snorted. "You have no idea how hard it was to get people to understand what I wanted. Or how hard it was to find."

"We haven't seen them since the Invasion," I said, taking the book from Sonya to write down my family's and Asilia's parents' names. No matter how hard I tried, I couldn't keep from sticking my tongue out with the effort of writing on paper instead of a tablet with predictive text. "No idea what exactly happened, although some of them did protest the soldiers."

"As for the 'what's happening' question, well!" Mary leaned forward, still holding Alex's hand. "We've got people in here from all over! Wilsonville, McMinneville, Grant's Pass and places in between. They just crammed thousands more people in here than it was ever built to hold, and disease was rampant. I suggest you spend as little time indoors as possible. From my sources, upwards of a million people have died here."

Mary gave us a moment to try to take that in, looking at our white faces with genuine sympathy. "Don't worry, dear," she told Alex, "Olivia and the children are all fine. They all got sick, and it was dicey for a while, but they're making a full recovery."

"We heard people disappear," I made it a statement.

Mary sighed. "Yes. Mostly girls. The women face taunts, catcalls, groping. That's pretty much business as usual. The girls, however…You hear a bunch of different things. One says they're being made into wives for Steve, another one that—"

"I'm sorry." I held a hand up. "Who's Steve?"

"Oh, yes," Mary said, smiling. "We needed a way to talk about them without *talking* about them, if you know what I mean. So we picked a name. Anyway, there's only rumors about what Steve wants with the girls, but prostitution and victory parties are some of them."

"How many are there?" I asked. "How widespread is this? Is it just the North—I mean, Steve? Is anybody else involved? What about weapons? Vehicles? Placement of troops?"

Mary stopped me before I could go on. "I don't know most of these, but let me try: How many? Nobody knows. Ten? Twenty thousand? More? And that's just Oregon. How widespread? The entire west coast. The police chief is a friend. She told me herself. It's how Steve convinced her to work with them. They feel that it's the only way to minimize deaths. Weapons? No idea. They've completely blocked us from passing west of Lancaster. If there's an armory, or anything important to Steve, it's over there. Cars? I've seen all kinds, but they look weird. They remind me of when I was little."

"They're not very high tech," I said. "They can't be, if they're working now. Which reminds me, how did they do that to the tech? It practically destroyed computer bits."

Mary shrugged. "No idea. I'm sorry, I don't have a lot of good information. The last thing you asked about was troops, correct?" I nodded. "I've heard they still patrol the countryside. Sometimes they bring in more people. Steve also takes people outside sometimes to work. Spring time should see more people leaving the city to work. We're supposed to be a farming region again. Or so I hear. They must have some use for us, otherwise why pack us into Salem like sardines? I'm afraid I have no idea how many troops are driving around, where they go or, well, anything."

"Who else is working with the, uh, Steve?" Alex asked.

"That idiot of a mayor practically handed them the keys to the city, for one." Contempt dripped from every word. "The police are too, like I said. They're convinced it's the best way to reduce the damage." Mary snorted. "Anybody with any money has been trying to curry favor. Some of the poorer have found an in with the Corps."

"Who are they? Are they the red armband dudes?" Sonya leaned forward, hands tight on the armrests.

"You've seen them, then?" Mary raised her eyebrows. "Yes, the North American Liberation Corps, or some such nonsense. There's too much of this 'the end justifies the means' shit happening right now."

My lip curled. Sonya's dad is an asshole like that, too. We'd all gotten fed up with his bullshit to the point that we'd mess with anybody who used that as an excuse. Just because. Now, as if we needed another reason to protest...Steve...stupid justification reared its head once more.

"So the armband dudes..." I spoke slowly, ordering my thoughts. "They have a fair amount of power and freedom? Like, they go through the gates and everything? Don't get stopped too often?"

Mary shrugged. "I suppose. Too soon to tell. They were only formed recently."

"Are there women in the Corps?"

"None that I've seen. Steve seems to prefer people with more muscles than brains for the Corps."

I looked at Alex and Sonya speculatively. "I can work with that."

I sat there, running through various scenarios to see what might work better, eyes flickering around the room without actually registering anything until I saw Mary smile. "Slow down, girl, before you overload that brain of yours. Are you—do you play chess, by any chance?"

I smiled innocently. "Maybe once or twice."

Next to me, Sonya guffawed. "She never learned formally, but she's handed a few chess people their asses over the years."

I sighed. "Woman! The whole point is you play it close! You don't just *tell* people about shit like this."

Mary laughed gently, degenerating into another coughing fit. "We should talk again at a later time, once I have a chance to find some answers for you," she said when she'd caught her breath. "Now that I know there's some resistance happening, I'd like to be a part of it."

"You want to spy?" Alex was horrified. "My *aunt* wants to be a *spy*?"

"A resistance!" I exclaimed at the same time. "Who said anything about a resistance?"

"You did," she replied tartly. "I'm too old—and sick—to fight or run, but I know people, and they like to talk to me. Why not let them?"

I stared at her, mouth hanging, then shrugged. "Why not?" I said sarcastically. "Though maybe we should call you by another name. Or by anything not resembling a name. Like Steve."

"Kitten," Mary said, smiling, ignoring my tone. Her eyes became unfocused as she remembered yesteryear. "My husband, God rest his soul, sometimes called me that. When he wanted to annoy me."

"You want us to call our spy 'Kitten?'" Alex couldn't get more dramatically dismayed.

I closed my eyes and pinched the bridge of my nose. I'd had no intention of being more than a minor irritant, but this was quickly turning into a runaway train wreck. Fuck it.

"On the bright side," I said to the air, "nobody would ever think a spy would be called Kitten."

Mary pulled the blanket higher around her shoulders, a look of contentment settling over her features. I struggled against a desire to laugh. Is this what we'd come to? Four women and two kids deciding to try to bring down an entire army? We were going to die, horribly, in ways I wasn't capable of imagining. What was I thinking? I should end this now, before we did—

The front door opening had my head whipping around, hand diving for the small of my back. I noticed Sonya and Alex also reaching under their clothes as my gun leveled on the door when it swung back to reveal a man, woman, and three kids.

"Wait!" Alex flung her hand out just as I'd relaxed marginally. "That's my family!"

The small group froze at the sight of armed strangers in their home, and the man stood between us and his family, arms spread to shield them. The woman caught his arm, leaning around him.

"Alex?" she asked incredulously.

Alex made her gun disappear as quickly as it had appeared a few seconds ago, and jerked her head, eyeing me and Son, commanding. I slid the gun back into my waistband, feeling a bit sheepish. I don't know exactly why. Overreacting, maybe?

Alex leapt off the couch to hug her cousin, crying and laughing simultaneously. "Olivia! I'm so glad you're okay!" She pulled back to look at the kids. "And you're all here," she breathed.

Olivia's husband continued to watch me and Son with a suspicious eye, Mary's tranquility notwithstanding.

I stepped towards the man, a few years older than myself with a pleasant face and work roughened hands, and held out my hand, once more empty of weapons. "Hi! I'm Tweedle-dee, and this is my cousin, Tweedle-dum!"

"Huh?" Under the circumstances, I had to admit that was a fairly intelligent and eloquent answer. Manners (or reflex) made him reach out to return my grip. "Sam. Ashton. What?"

Maybe not as intelligent as I'd thought. "I'm Tweedle-dee," I repeated. "Your mother-in-law named us, if you want to blame somebody." I finally took pity on him. "In the current conditions, we decided it was best that not every name was known."

"Down, child," Mary chided gently. "Don't mess with the poor man. He already lives with me—and two other families," she added under her breath. "'Livia, dear, would you take everybody into the kitchen? I need a private word with Tweedle-dee."

Olivia gave me a stern look, not budging. A stern look from her was something else. She had a stubborn jaw that I bet could break granite. "What are your intentions?" she asked. "Walking in here like this. Not that we're not grateful to have Alex back, but..."

Sonya snickered. "Yes, what *are* our intentions? Are they strictly honorable?"

"Shut up," I told Son, folding my hand into a fist so I didn't flip her off in front of the kids, "and you can follow that up with a 'piss off.'"

Sam and Olivia looked horrified, Alex rolled her eyes, and Mary laughed until she coughed. Waving away her daughter and niece, she concentrated on breathing once the episode stopped. "Olivia. I'd like a few minutes with her. She won't hurt me," Mary told her daughter, in response to the glare I received.

"How do you know?" Olivia folded her arms.

"Because Alex vouched for her," Mary said simply.

"Because if she wanted to, you'd already be in trouble," Alex said at the same time.

"Your idea of reassurance sucks," I muttered to Alex out of the corner of my mouth, watching Olivia's reaction to that little tidbit.

Olivia took some deep breaths, but it wasn't until Sam spoke quietly to her, gesturing to the children, that she relented. If looks could maim, I'd be whimpering as she took her family past, gathering Alex and Son into her wake by virtue of personality alone.

As they shut the door behind them, I turned to Mary, eyebrows raised inquiringly. Inside, I braced myself, expecting a lecture on the idiocy of our little crusade. Mary surprised me, though perhaps it shouldn't've.

"You seem to have taken the leadership role." Her hair should have given it away. Any woman her age with fire-engine red in her hair wouldn't take the typical route. "How are you finding it?"

"I just sort of...fell into it," I said wisely. "Nobody wanted to be the front guy, but somebody had to break the ties in votes. Soo...yeah."

"Alex was a little...sketchy on the details of how you met," Mary finally said. "What exactly happened?"

I grimaced, but the woman was Alex's aunt, and maybe she'd have some insight into Alex's future behavior? Probably too much to hope for, but what the hell. I gave her the outline—our current home, Asilia and Jaali, and exactly how we got out of town remained vague.

Her face went through a gamut of emotions, from sorrow, to anger, relief, and maybe a hint of appreciation?

"Alex has been on a freaking suicide mission ever since, wanting to make somebody pay. If she dies in the attempt, I get the feeling she wouldn't object too much." I sighed. "The nightmares are...yeah. I can understand dying for a cause, but dammit! There's no point if your death ends the damn cause!"

Mary took a deep breath, held it for a moment and let it out slowly. "Thank you. For taking care of her, I mean. Taking care of both of them." I nodded silently. She continued after a moment. "You've taken a lot on yourself, here. Deciding to fight when it's literally you and two others. Are you sure you're up for it?"

"Hell, no!" I exclaimed without hesitation. "Not a snowball's chance in hell I'm ready for it! Not much choice, though, is there?"

Mary snorted. "You get to my age, you realize there's always a choice. You could've run. You could turn yourselves in. You could just hide in the hills and never come out again." *I may still do that*, I thought. "But if you said you were up for the challenge, you'd be a filthy liar. I won't sugarcoat it. What you're starting will be dangerous beyond your wildest nightmares. If you make it out alive, it'll be a miracle, though it probably won't feel like it."

"Thank you so much for your words of encouragement," I said dryly. "You're a font of good wishes. Are you sure you want to work with us?"

Mary cracked a laugh. "Wouldn't miss it for the world, girl! You keep that attitude, too. You'll need it, where you're going."

I cringed.

"How old are you, anyway?" she asked.

I looked at her, puzzled. What did that matter? "Twenty-six."

She grinned. "Young enough to get up to trouble, old enough to get out of it. One thing," she cautioned, "always sound confident, even when you're not. Fake it 'til you make it. It gives people confidence in you as a leader."

"I ain't a leader," I said automatically. Sonya has me trained *good*. I could probably deny it in my sleep.

"What do you think being a leader involves?" Mary sounded exasperated.

"I don't know!" I pulled off my beanie and ran a hand over my hair, agitated. "I'm making this shit up as I go along! I've read a bunch of books, and lemme tell you, none of 'em's a how-to guide, so I'm putting it together as best I can!"

Mary gave me an appraising look. "So everything you just told me is bull? You didn't make decisions that helped people? Hate to break it to you, but that looked like leading to me. Just so you know, Steve's been reeling in people from all over the state, and you lot are the only ones I've heard of who have evaded them.

"Then you made the choice to do something about it. I think it's about time you faced the facts and *named* it. You're leading those two. They're following you. You're not just doing *something*. You're rebelling. You're fighting back. Name it. Own it. Once you do that, well, it doesn't get easier, but it does get clearer."

Chapter 10

S on and Alex had decided discretion was the better part of valor and kept everyone in the dark about us. They'd put out that we were making our way along trying to find our families, which was partially true. When I came into the kitchen, the kids were sent back into the living room to get some sleep, malnutrition and hard labor having exhausted the poor tykes. Even strangers and the return of "Auntie Alex" weren't enough to keep them up.

The other families who were living in Mary's house had come back shortly after Mary and I had finished our conversation. Sonya, in a massive effort of socializing (and one question) had managed to get the adults to start talking about their days, and their efforts in the "Great Endeavor," as the enemy occupation was being called by the mayor.

The whole scene had a surreal look to it, lit by a single candle set in the center of the kitchen table. We were perched on a motley collection of chairs that were here only by dint of the fact that they couldn't be burned. Even the table was one of those horrible aluminum and Formica creations that belonged in the 1970s.

Alex, Mary, Sam, and Olivia sat close together. Then there was Mona—whose husband Dan had died in the plague—followed by Evelyn and Steven. I idly speculated that the name for the soldiers hadn't actually come from the old kid's movie but rather him, despite what Mary said. I got the feeling, listening to him, that he was one of those pompous assholes who loved to hear his own voice.

Under the circumstances, talkative people are good. Sometimes.

"The women are set to cleaning," Olivia said as I sat down. "Everything west of Lancaster is held by Steve and those guys in the Corps. Red armbands everywhere. I'm starting to hate the color red. Just cleaning. Every. Single. Day. We work different areas, take turns in the hospital. You know that's still running? Just not for us."

"We're also on the west side," Steven interrupted. "We end up having to clean out the rubble. I know, I know, cleaning is hard, but have you ever had to gather and cart concrete and wood day after day? And with the slop they feed us…"

"Do you get trouble from the soldiers?" Alex asked Olivia, pointedly ignoring Steven.

Steven looked irritated at having his pearls of wisdom ignored, but Alex didn't even register. I snorted softly. One man's irritation was less than a speck of dust in her eye.

"Comments. Leering." Olivia's eyes were haunted. "I haven't heard about anything worse, but," she hesitated, "we've seen women who are indentured to the Corps. As in, slaves. And there's the rumors about brothels for soldiers. I don't know anything for sure, though." Sam stood abruptly and went to his wife, pulling her out of her chair and taking the seat, tugging her onto his lap. Secure in her husband's embrace, Olivia continued.

"Occasionally women don't show up for work again. They could be reassigned to a different group, but…there's just…so much we don't know."

She shrugged helplessly. "That's the worst of it, not knowing." Olivia wiped tears from her cheeks and leaned her head against Sam's, fingers twisted in his shirt.

Steven filled the silence. "Men are also split into gangs. I've only worked on clearing rubble, but there's other groups building fences and repairing what they can. They're very generous with their favorites." Going by the sullen tone, I didn't think he'd become one of the chosen few.

"Beatings are pretty common," Sam offered. "And if you have pretty daughters, well, they'll use them to frighten their fathers and keep them in line." Lines deepened around his eyes and mouth. A man with a wife and kids had extra reason to worry. Olivia kissed his forehead gently.

"How much longer until the fence is done?" I asked. Yeah, subtle, right?

"Nearly finished circling the city. After that, we'll be topping it with barbed wire. Then," Sam shrugged. "Who knows?"

"I overheard a rumor," Mona, the woman who'd just lost her husband, put in. "I heard they'll be sectioning off the city and limiting travel between places."

"Great," I muttered.

"You'll need to be careful," she warned us, concerned. "With the curfew, you don't want to be caught outside while it's dark."

Of course the city had a curfew! We thought we'd do most of our travelling at night, but...I snorted. I'm rather bad at this whole planning thing. Like, sure, time and experience would help, but a wrong decision could end in immediate death, or worse.

"Still," Sam tried to lighten the mood, "we're still here, aren't we? Somebody's bound to do something, come up with a plan that will actually work."

I stared at the ceiling, studiously avoiding the gazes of my three co-conspirators. *Is this guy for real?* Sure, somebody *is* coming up with a plan, but the people doing the planning would get a vote of no confidence from any sane, rational human being. I sighed, glancing at the others. Sonya bit her lip and stared at the floor, and I got the uncomfortable idea that she was trying not to laugh. Alex just looked guilty.

Then, to top it all off, Sam finished with, "We just need to be prepared when the moment comes."

I cleared my throat to quell the hysterical laughter attempting to escape. "I think Ben Franklin said it best 'God helps those who help themselves.' Or we could go with: 'All it takes for evil men to succeed is for good men to do nothing.'" I shut my mouth after that, afraid if I didn't stop now, I never would and one of these relatively normal folks would turn us in for being insane.

Later that night, I leaned against the post on the tiny porch in Mary's backyard, secure in the knowledge that even if patrols could see through houses, it was too damn dark to make out more than the barest silhouette of a house. I was grateful for a few minutes' respite, unused to the sounds of so many people sleeping in such a small space.

As bad as the sniffles and coughs were, it was the small whimpering noises from the children that made sleep impossible. They sounded so frightened. I didn't want to know what they dreamt.

The door opened with a slight whining from the hinges, but I didn't turn around. Alex probably couldn't sleep either. I almost started when the voice coming from the dark wasn't female.

"Couldn't sleep, either?" Sam asked.

"No." I shifted against the porch rail. "What's got you up so late?"

He remained silent, blending into the night. Finally, he sighed. "Worry. I worry about my wife, my kids. Even my mother-in-law, though she's the toughest person I ever met. I pray about my worries, but unfortunately, that doesn't make them go away."

"You and me, both."

In companionable silence, we went back to staring out into the night.

***

As soon as the sun lit the sky the next morning, we were ready to move out. We'd discovered that fencing work crews did leave their houses before dawn, but only with an armed escort. As Sam pulled on his jacket, Olivia gave him a kiss, as if he headed to a normal day at work. Only the tension around her eyes and mouth gave away her fears.

"I wish we could leave this place," she murmured after the men had left. "I wish…" Her voice broke, eyes reddened by unshed tears.

Screwing up my courage (why was breaking into a guarded area less scary than talking to a person?) I asked her if I could have a word. She led the way to the back yard where I'd just had a conversation with her husband a few hours before.

"What do you think about Alex?" I asked once we were alone. "Does she seem stable to you? Or is she likely to, uh, explode?"

Olivia looked troubled. "I have no idea. She's barely speaking. She did say you and your cousin saved her life, but she didn't sound particularly happy about it. She also said you were doing your best, and you're her best chance for revenge."

"Wonderful," I mumbled. "We're gonna die."

"Mom told me about Dylan and everything, but how are you supposed to help her get revenge? I thought you were looking for your families."

I gave her my best innocent look. Going by her disconcerted expression, I was failing miserably. "What do you mean? We're just…erm…looking around, you know, trying to find our families. Not, uh, sure where she got the revenge idea?" I shrugged, acknowledging that I'd failed that one miserably. "Listen, she was going crazy sitting in one place. Moving around, feeling like she's doing something has really improved her mood."

"'Improved her mood'?" Olivia's brown eyes, so like her mother's, blazed. "You're telling me you think she's doing better? She not! She's an angry mess who's talking suicide!"

"Yep. Believe it or not, that's actually a step up." I left Olivia staring after me with her mouth open.

Before we left, we took a look at a city map Mary produced where she had marked out the boundaries that she knew about.

"Right," I said once we were on the porch, "we try to stick together. If anybody gets lost, we all go to the Capitol. Most importantly, don't get dead."

"Yes, Mother!" Alex and Sonya chorused.

"I hate you. Let's go."

***

It was surprisingly easy going at first. There were enough people wandering around that we didn't stand out as long as we kept our heads down and tried to look depressed. That wasn't difficult. My stomach gurgled and reminded me that the portion sizes in this town weren't big enough to feed a mouse, much less an active girl. First chance we got, we ducked between buildings and had a snack. It wasn't Aunt Rose's strawberry and rhubarb pie, but it temporarily shut my gut up.

Walking through the streets had an objective fascination. All our media was about America and American soldiers occupying other countries. We'd never seen it before from the other side. It was interesting, being the occupied rather than the occupier. The only difference was that the faces and skin colors were different.

Alex's fingers twitched constantly, eyes darting around trying to keep every soldier and asshole in a red armband in sight. "Listen," I muttered through clenched teeth, "either you keep your hands a hell of a lot stiller, or you're walking in the middle and we're all holding hands."

Sonya looked untroubled by thoughts of revenge or useless philosophy, but her eyes never stopped moving, cataloging the soldiers and their weapons. If I knew her, she had her eye on something.

We pushed closer together to get past a group of Corps guys loitering in the middle of the road, swaggering and shoving those who got too close. Think high school bullies with fewer brains and less muscle, but larger numbers.

"It might fit?" Son mumbled to herself, so low I'd thought I'd imagined it. Then I saw her look down, assessing the length of her jacket, back up to a rifle, down again, her hands opening, fingers spread wide as she touched thumbs and did some mental math. A sad shake of her head gave me her answer, but the acquisitive gleam in her eyes stayed put.

As we bunched, I slid a step to the outside, putting myself between Alex and the assholes—H*ey!* my moronic brain jumped in, *what a great name to call them!* I lowered my head and scratched my cheek to hide a snigger. Running the gauntlet past the Corps wasn't too bad. Some catcalls, a shove, and me clutching Alex to make sure our headstones didn't have today's date.

All in all, not a whole lot different from walking down the street in LA when I visited it with my cousin Faith a couple years ago.

A turn and a short walk down another street whose name I didn't even bother to look at and suddenly Alex lunged forward. Only sheer reflex allowed me to snag her collar and stop her. She snarled in frustrated rage and tried to break free.

I looked up from the hell-cat I'd grabbed, down a cul-de-sac, trying to see what set her off. I saw a group of soldiers. One of them was pushing around a middle-aged couple, laughing at the man's futile attempt to protect his wife. The soldier—Steve, right, Steve—knocked the man's legs out from under him.

Alex tried charging again, nearly wrenched my arm out the damn socket before I could haul her back. It took me and Son to muscle her out of sight, into a mercifully unoccupied building that had been stripped of anything burnable. We charged right through to the back with our cursing, struggling bundle, not even giving her time to yell.

We slammed her into a wall, leaning heavily on her back to keep her still. "Will you—" I clamped a hand over her mouth to muffle her shouts and twisted awkwardly to look outside. "Shut up! Steve's leaving—son of a bitch!" I snatched my hand away before Alex could bite me again.

"You bitch!" Alex rasped, still pinned to the wall. "You fucking left them there! How could you? We're supposed to *do* something! In this entire fucking city, *we're* supposed to do something! Let me go. I'll do it myself if you're too chickenshit to help them!"

I leaned in close. "Idiot, Steve's already leaving. If we'd charged straight in, us and that couple would all be dead. Congratulations. We would've accomplished nothing."

"There were only like two soldiers!" Alex hissed. "You're just a coward!"

"Alex," Sonya warned softly, "don't say something you'll regret later. And there were five."

"Five what?" Finally, Alex's struggles eased, and she sagged against the wall, exhausted.

"Steve," Son said. "Five soldiers. That we could see."

"Eh, actually, there've been a few posted here and there on taller buildings. Snipers or lookouts," I said. "There was one, maybe two, who would've had eyes on that little show."

"Oh."

"Yeah, oh. And next time, let's take a second to figure out where the bad guys are *before* we go running in, yeah?"

After a quick check of the couple, we were off again. Once we were well away from the area, having seen both people walking slowly and a few brave souls offering assistance, Alex turned to me. "How'd you notice all that is such a short time?"

Sonya rolled her eyes. "Have you not listened to her at all over the last two months? Let me tell you this: whatever team she's on usually wins." She turned to me abruptly. "You can play chess against Alex next time. I'm tired of losing to you."

"You don't lose *every* time," I protested.

"Yeah, I win just enough to keep me going. Thanks. Bitch."

"Jerk."

"My original question?" Alex prompted me.

"What? Uh, yeah." Then I stopped. Remembered Mary's advice from just last night. Pretend to be confident. *Fake it 'til you make it.* I took a deep breath and let it out slowly while keeping a constant eye on our surroundings. "I paid attention. It's really that simple. Oh, yeah, and keep emotion out of it as much as possible. We've really covered all this back...home. Remember?"

"I just got so mad." And scared, though she'd never admit to that. Not yet. Not while she was trying to prove to us that she could do this.

I sighed and let it go for now. Best to let her think about it a bit.

***

It took forever to walk through the city that we usually drove into once every couple of months. Alex was quiet, pensive, biting her lip and looking down frequently, but that didn't stop her from keeping pace. Son stayed half a dozen steps behind, watching the rear. Every once in a while, we'd duck into a narrow alley for a few minutes of respite from the wind and to see if anybody had followed us.

It was almost a relief when we began turning west and hit a roadblock. Heavily-armed soldiers screened people crossing both ways. Papers were passed and examined before pedestrians were allowed through. The few vehicles were scanned, and sniffer dogs were brought out.

I nudged the girls and jerked my head farther up the street, and we quickly left the roadblock behind us. Down a side street, then another turn into a cul-de-sac, and we approached the end. Just some houses with blocked and locked side fences and gates. I accelerated down the walkway and had a moment of sheer panic.

I'm not gonna make it, my hindbrain screamed. *You moron, the roof is too low!*

I didn't even register grabbing the top of the fence. It was all a blur until suddenly I stood a few feet inside the yard. My cheek throbbed, and I touched in tentatively. No swelling, not yet, but I was pretty sure I scraped it as I landed. A big bush sat awfully close to the fence. I must have half stabbed my face on it.

"Watch out for the bush on this side!" I warned when the next set of hands grasped the top.

Alex grunted as she pulled herself over, and nearly took out her eye on the corner of the gutter. "Fuck me!" she swore, rebounding from the sharp blow to her forehead.

I hurried forward and helped her the rest of the way, then Sonya came over a little slower. Her foot slipped on the up part, so I knelt down and Alex stood on my back so she could pull Son the rest of the way over.

We stood in a small circle once we were safely inside the protection of the fence and just stared at each other. "Well," Sonya broke the silence, "there's no way we'll blend in if we keep this up. What happened to your face?" She asked me.

"I decided it'd be fun to try to shish kebab it on that stupid bush over there." I pointed to the offending plant.

"Heh."

"What, are we planning on standing here all day?" Alex demanded. "Let's keep going!"

"Yes, ma'am." I threw out a lazy salute then ran to the back fence and the next yard.

I couldn't believe it. A month ago we'd never have been able to do this. So what if the fences only got harder as our muscles got tired? I was still amazed at how well we were doing. And it was *fun*. Until I half jumped/half fell over a timber fence and found myself face-to-face with a little boy.

He was tiny, maybe four or five years old, with adorable round cheeks ruddy with cold and a knitted cap pulled snugly over his ears. I barely managed to snatch him up and clamp a hand over his mouth before he could scream.

He struggled in my arms, squirming and wriggling. In his bulky winter jacket it was like trying to hang onto a greased eel. Alex thumped to the ground next to me, sending the kid into a fresh round of panic.

Alex froze at the sight of the boy, not moving a muscle until I plopped the kid in her arms. "Can you calm him down? I usually just make strange kids cry. More."

Alex slowly unlocked and sat down, her grip changing until she cuddled the boy and started up a low croon. "It's aaalllright. Everything's aalllright. We're not here to hurt you. It's oookay."

When Sonya came over the fence, he barely moved, instead staring at Alex as if hypnotized. Once he was calmed, she removed her hand and asked him in the gentle, high-pitched sing-song reserved for children, "How come you're outside, sweetie? Where's your mommy?"

"Mommy's talking to the man," he whispered, so quietly I leaned in to hear him.

The boy became alarmed at being the center of attention from a bunch of strangers, so I wandered away, keeping an ear out.

"What man?" Alex asked.

"He comes here lots. He started coming in the fall." The boy looked around, proud of his knowledge. "They talk. Mommy lets me play outside when he comes." He stuck a thumb in his mouth, sucking quietly.

Through the window I could make out a coat hanging over a chair.

It had a red armband on it.

"Do you like the man? Is he nice?" The gentle interrogation continued. A noncommittal shrug was the only answer. "What's your name?"

The thumb was removed. "Corey."

I motioned urgently to them, and we gathered in close. "There's a red armband guy in there," I whispered. I could see the blood rising in Alex's face, but we didn't have time for it.

I was willing to bet everything I owned that banging an asshole was the only way Corey's mom knew to keep them fed and in decent housing. I ran across it in a lot of books, and what are books but studies of human nature set in fantastic surroundings?

"Do you want to come with us, Corey?" Alex asked the little boy.

I exchanged an alarmed look with Sonya, and she began shaking her head vigorously, but the boy beat us to it. "Why?" he asked. "Mommy's here. And I'm not s'posed to talk to strangers," he finally remembered.

"Alex," I hissed. "The kid's obviously well taken care of. Here, at least he has a chance. We take him with us, who knows what'll happen?"

Alex muttered something, and I pretended not to hear "..beat the crap outta..." as she stood and set Corey on his feet, straightening his hat.

"Think we can trust the kid to not say anything?" Son asked, worriedly looking at the boy.

"He's five, at most," I said, rubbing my dripping nose. "Who's gonna believe a kid that little?"

"Good point," she conceded.

The boy glared at us fiercely. "I'm not little. I'm big. Mommy said so."

I held my hands up in surrender, grinning. "I stand corrected. And now," I inclined my head towards the side gate, "I believe it's time we were on our way. You first, Alex."

I felt bad, leaving the kid alone in the backyard. Sure, his mom was in the house, but still…In a way, this was worse than the couple getting terrorized in the street. At least they were old enough to process what was happening around them. This kid only got a tiny portion of the picture.

Though it seemed like we'd gone miles, the truth is we'd cleared barely two miles in an hour and a half. Walking on sidewalks, you could get about four miles an hour, if you were very fast. Hiking over dirt trails dropped that number to two or three miles. Apparently, going over fences and through backyards lowered that number to where it took forty-five minutes to go a mile.

What a depressing thought.

Alex kept glancing back, probably thinking of the kid. We'd talked about him briefly when we paused for a break, but even Alex had to agree. In the same circumstances, all of us would most likely have made the same decision as his mother.

***

As evening closed in, we had to find a hiding place.

We ended up spending an uncomfortable, frozen night huddled together in a rundown backyard somewhere along Sixteenth Street. Half-buried under fallen leaves, only Alex, who was in the middle, could say she was warm. Exhausted, I fell into a light sleep, waking occasionally to pull my scarf back around my nose and rub sensation back into my hands before dozing again.

Old memories and new thoughts surfaced, masquerading as dreams, marching through the uncomfortable night. Aunt Rose used to work in this area, back when I was a kid. So had Papa. Rose had been closer to the Willamette River, and she'd told us stories about the riots that started when people were forced to sell out so the government could rebuild the 99 as a "proper" highway. Thousands of people lost their homes and had to move from small houses to tiny apartments at exorbitant rates.

If they were lucky.

Auntie lost her job in the city. Her employers tried to hire more locally in an effort to support the poor already in Salem. She told us she couldn't fault them for it. After all, she had a lovely, roomy house to go back to. So she rented her extra rooms out and went back to commercial sewing.

Back and forth, memories, old stories, and new experiences jumbled together in an endless nightmare until a careless elbow in the back pulled me out of it. I settled my back more firmly against the warm body behind me, clamping clammy hands between my thighs.

In my hazy mind, I couldn't be sure exactly where Sixteenth put us. Part of the maze of residential areas that appeared randomly in Salem, occasionally entire streets were bought up and redeveloped. Between the constantly changing landscape and the exclusivity of housing within the city, my one to two visits in my lifetime didn't give me enough to draw on.

CHAPTER 11

I n the morning, sore and stiff, we decided to chance the sidewalks again and try to head farther west. My arms and shoulders screamed if I lifted them higher than my chest and my neck could barely turn. I wasn't sure how much of it was due to our efforts the day before and how much to sleeping on the cold, hard ground. I swung my arms in widening circles, slowly warming stiff muscles.

Yesterday, we'd had to boost Alex over the last three or four fences, and I'd been one fence away from needing help myself. Sonya was fine, though. What else would we expect from the woman who could carry two bales of hay at a time for half a day?

Walking down the street, the normal people we saw on this side of the barrier seemed...different. I looked around, puzzled.

"What is it?" Alex muttered.

"Dunno. Something." I scratched my head. Beanies were not meant to be worn twenty-four hours a day, five days in a row. "Anything look weird to you guys?"

"Other than you?" Sonya looked around. I elbowed her sharply. "Is it just me or are people here cleaner?"

The lightbulb finally went off. I almost raised a finger and said "Aha!" because that wouldn't have been noticeable *at all*. The soldiers over here were also different. It was little things. Guns weren't held at the ready, the men spoke quietly to each other, and there was a general air of relaxation.

"This is their Green Zone," I said as understanding dawned.

"What?"

"This is the area they control most tightly. Betcha once the outer fence is done, they do a proper one around this entire section. Security will go through the roof then." I nodded to myself. It's what I would do, and they were actually trained to be soldiers. I wondered if there was anything else they'd add to it. More guard stations? Towers? Were towers even effective anymore? Then again, in many respects we had less technology now than was present in World War II, and guard towers worked pretty well then.

I nodded decisively. We were definitely screwed.

"I'll take that bet," Sonya said calmly. "Hundred bucks?"

"Pfft." I waved a hand. "What do I want that for? Make it a candy bar. Those things shouldn't go bad anytime soon. If we ever find some."

"If I win, I want a Mars Bar." Sonya grinned as we ambled down a side street angling south. Best to get out of sight before Steve talked to us out of boredom.

A quarter of a mile later, it dawned on me that the side street may not have been our best idea. Bear in mind, this was in a series of brain farts that involved trying to overthrow our occupiers. It occurred to me that we really made a lot of stupid choices, because once we got to the cross street, we saw the Capitol building rising up to our right.

"So that's why Twelfth Street sounded familiar," I said, staring inanely at the gray dome rising above the park. "Also, the gold dude on the top of the Capitol building is missing."

Alex stuck her head out for a better look, then pulled back quickly. "On the plus side, if we want to watch Steve, we have plenty to look at."

She wasn't joking. The grounds around the building were a hive of activity, and we finally saw the bureaucratic arm of Steve. Instead of the standard rifle, handgun, and baton, now we saw files and briefcases.

Son pursed her lips in a soundless whistle. "Is it just me, or does it look like they're setting up their own government here?"

"I do believe you're right, cousin mine," I concurred, trying hard to rubberneck without looking like gawking. "The bastards are getting all kinds of comfortable, aren't they? Kinda makes me want to mess it all up. Just for shits and giggles."

"There's more women here," Sonya observed. "I've seen maybe two this entire time, but here...they're even wearing sensible heels."

"Aides? Dress uniforms? Do we care?"

"Can we throw a grenade?" Alex pleaded. "Just a little one?"

I shook my head. "We'd need a grenade launcher to hit the Capitol from concealment. I don't know about you, but I really don't feel like walking up to the front steps and lobbing one in the double doors. We wouldn't have a snowball's chance in hell of getting out."

I took a deep breath, smelling the coming rain and watching the clouds rolling in from the south. It'd been two days since the north wind broke, and the temperature now was practically warm.

"I feel like writing some poetry," I announced.

"Poetry?" they chorused. I loved it when shit like that happened.

"Well," I said reasonably, "we need an excuse to sit around and observe, right? I can't draw to save my life, and the best I have on me is a pen."

"Why do you have a pen?" Alex asked.

"Because they're there."

"You're insane."

"Yeah, but at least I'm not talking back to myself. Yet. Give me time." I grinned at Alex. "Get ready to start counting."

We moved slowly, never staying in one place too long. I kept a tiny notebook tucked in one pocket, the first half of which had notes to myself since we'd gotten to the bunker. Now I filled page after page with tiny diagrams and notes with observations on how many rifles we saw, any sentries and checkpoints and which areas saw the most traffic.

The only heart attack came when a soldier demanded to know what we were doing. I showed him a couple pages with the plagiarized bits of poetry we could think of. It was bad. The soldier ordered us to move on, and we were more than happy to, skittering off under his suspicious glare.

We went as far at the next group of bushes we could lurk in.

By the time we'd worked our way to the south side, between the Capitol and the university, we had one glaring flaw in our half-assed plan. Don't get me wrong, there were a multitude of minor flaws as well.

"This would be easier if we knew exactly what kind of rifle they had." Sonya pointed out the elephant in the room. "I mean, we're still no closer to knowing what kind of firepower they actually have. Are they automatic? Semi? Do they have magazines? What's their capacity?"

"I've seen you eyeballing them," I told her. "I have every faith you'll get your hands on one soon."

Sonya grinned so widely that the gap at the corner of her smile showed and the laugh lines at the corners of her eyes deepened.

"I think we need to know more about all kinds of different weapons," Alex said. "If we did, we might be able to tell by looking at them. Sentries on top of the university, north and south."

"Weapons training when we get back, then," I said, dutifully noting the sentries. "We'll read through all the booklets and train with every type of gun in there."

"D'you know," Son said casually, "I think the university might be in use as a barracks?"

"Huh? What makes you say that?" I kept scribbling, sketching a rough outline of the back of the Capitol and the position of a gun nest on the roof.

"Well, the number of Steves walking around is a hint. Lots of dudes going in and out. Quite a few of the assholes visible through the windows. That sort of thing."

"Ooh, lookit Sherlock over here," I teased, nervous sweat breaking out across my skin, an itch crawling up my spine to my neck. "We're done here. Let's take the scenic route out."

I got no argument from them. Not even Alex, which I considered a victory. Our level of casual as we walked away was a step below "whistling while rocking on your heels and looking around unconcerned." We took the direction with the fewest people, which was—I glanced up at the sun showing through patchy clouds—west-ish. The first side street was too close to the university still, so we took the second one, a left.

Church Street, and there was an old church on the corner. *Yes, nice to see how much thought went into street names,* I thought with a grimace. The church still had a sign up advertising it as a nightclub. I doubted it was used for that anymore, either.

I risked a quick look behind as we passed a tall, pale building—once a theatre—to spot a lone soldier behind us. Easy enough to spot by simple dint of being the only other person besides us on this street.

"Don't look now, but we have a friend," I said in a low voice.

Ahead of us, the new 99E rose up in all its concrete glory. Once upon a time, that highway had narrowed to a two-lane road through the city. When I was a kid, the city bought up land around it in order to build it up more like a freeway. That was when Aunt Rose lost her job here. The houses that were left were in shit condition and took twice as many people as there were bedrooms to be able to afford it. So, a two-bedroom house needed to have four people in it. As a result, gangs and the homeless had ruled. The only law-abiding folks here had been the truly desperate.

Now, the buildings rose around us, empty. I wondered if the place was as abandoned as it looked, or if the people were just out working. The street was creepy, like walking through a ghost town or a horror movie, compared to yesterday, when we saw massive overcrowding.

Sonya watched the windows intently as we passed them, then gave us reports on our tail. "It's been ten freaking minutes and he's still there!" Frustration welled in her voice.

There was nowhere for us to go without looking more suspicious. I hoped that when we made it to the highway there'd be a chance for us to lose the soldier. Maybe disappear before he decided he was bored with—

"You!" The male voice echoed off the empty buildings in heavily accented English. "What you doing? I see you wit' book! What you doing?"

Reluctantly, we turned to face him. I held up my hands to show him they were empty, and clearly irritated, he pointed to my side pocket where I'd stashed the notebook and pen.

"P-poetry," I said, hoping he didn't catch the stutter. "I was practicing my poetry. My friends came with me because...our parents won't let us out alone."

"What is po-et-ly?" he demanded. "I hea' dis now."

My mind raced frantically as I tried to think of something, anything. His eyes narrowed, irritation turning to anger, so I opened my mouth and what came out didn't even bother checking in with my brain before it exited.

I walked one day and saw a thyme

I thought it'd make an awesome rhyme

Until I saw those distant shores

I realized I really suck at this

Awesome. I clenched my hands, grinning insanely.

He glared at us and dropped a hand onto his sidearm. I blinked. I hadn't even realized he wasn't carrying a rifle. "You come wit' me, now. We go back. Talk more there." He leered at us and licked his lips.

Okay. Maybe it wasn't anger I'd been picking up on. Why did I have to be so fucking clueless?

"Ah." I frantically wiggled my fingers behind my back and prayed the girls could read my mind. Or my fingers. Whatever. "I can't do that...We have to go home...Our parents will be getting worried about us..."

I could just about feel Sonya's groan. I'm a terrible liar unless I have about an hour to prepare. Apparently, the soldier didn't buy it either, because he simply stepped to the side and waved for us to precede him.

As I walked towards him, he said, "You tell me 'bout you fam'ly. What is they name? Why they let you wander. Nice girls no wander." He leered again.

I was beginning to think this creep only had the one expression, but I tried to placate him anyway. "We're, uh, the Smiths?" I swallowed a whimper. This just kept getting better and better. When I tried to pass him, he reached out and squeezed my hip familiarly. "Oh, fuck this!" I grabbed the hand on my hip and turned towards him, my right hand coming around in an open palm strike to the chin, snapping his head back.

Sonya, poised right behind the bastard, had an arm raised with a chunk of concrete in her hand when he fell. We stared at each other in shock, or amazement (I'm not sure which), only broken when Alex cackled and darted away to check our back trail.

"What do we do now?" Son wondered.

"Fuck if I know!" I hissed. "I don't exactly make it a practice to beat guys up. Let's at least get out of the damn road."

"Sure you do," Sonya grunted as we dragged his skinny ass between a house and an empty apartment block.

"I do what?" I shook my head, trying to dislodge two hairs poking the corner of my eye.

"Beat guys up."

"I do not!"

"What do you call Andy?"

"Self-inflicted via sheer stupidity."

We sat on the guy to make sure he wouldn't unexpectedly wake up while we weren't looking, Son on his legs, me on his chest.

"Theo. No way a guy kicks himself in the nuts AND gives himself a broken nose."

"Don't forget the sprained wrist. He really wanted me to. I think he was a masochist."

"How's that?"

"Said he'd like to stretch Peter's ass."

Son winced. "What about that other guy, Aaron?"

"Grabbed my crotch."

"I do have other examples, you know."

Alex saved us from continuing by arriving back and reporting that the coast was clear. "Have you decided what to do with him yet?"

"No."

Alex had the simplest solution. "Kill him. One less to deal with later."

The soldier shifted beneath us, slowly waking up. I thought frantically, trying to come up with an idea that wasn't likely to have him hunting us down. Death. I grimaced. I'd already killed in the heat of the moment, but this...this was premeditated. It also made a lot of sense.

My stomach heaved, and I swallowed heavily, trying to keep it in place.

"Fuck...you...beetches," the soldier gasped under my weight. "Rape...you...cunts..."

I clamped a gloved hand over his mouth and stared down at him, my nausea dissipating. "His grasp of swear words is excellent. And unfortunate. For him."

Alex started forward eagerly, knife already in hand. The soldier's eyes rolled wildly.

"Wait!" I stopped her.

"Hope, you know we have to do this," she snapped.

I glared. "I know! Especially since you threw out my name. Thank you! But you won't be doing this." I took a deep breath and held a hand out. "I will."

Under us, the soldier thrashed, trying to get free. Sonya adjusted her grip on his legs and rode it out. I didn't even have that much trouble. I'm a tall girl, taller than either of the others, and well-built with plenty of muscle. Taller than the soldier, come to think of it.

Alex started, surprised by my assertion. "I'm more than happy to kill the misogynistic fucker. You don't have to do it."

"Yeah, well, it's about time I decide exactly what I'm willing to do, right? Until now we've been pretty vague. Gonna do 'something'. Your aunt told me I need to get clear. This is me getting clear. I'm putting down a rapist, or soon-to-be rapist, like the rabid dog he is."

Privately, I acknowledged another reason: Alex was too eager for it. I honestly think she'd kill the guy and never give it a moment's notice. What would it do to her, though, if she looked back on these days? How would she feel later, knowing that she'd happily cut a man's throat and left, eager to kill again? I worried that it might send her into a downward spiral of blood and retribution. One she'd find it difficult to get out of.

The soldier's eyes flared with panic as he listened to us, and he began shaking his head, whimpering. I flicked my fingers, wanting Alex to give me the knife so we could get this over with. He began crying, sobbing into my hand, tears running down his temples, snot bubbling and popping against my glove, biting and wriggling frantically.

I positioned the knife above his solar plexus, angled to drive it under the breastbone and into his heart. Hesitated. Tried to nerve myself up for it. I had a flash of memory. Papa with a needle poised over the cow's rump, trying to give her a muscle shot. It always took him five to ten minutes to steel himself to do it. I'd managed to pick up on that reluctance.

Now, I knelt astride a human being and tried to brace myself to drive a knife in and snuff a life out. I gritted my teeth and pressed. The man squealed and thrashed. I thought of the animals we'd butchered on the farm, but that was different again.

Behind me, Sonya rested a hand on my back. I stiffened. Sonya doesn't touch people casually, so for her to do it now meant I'd better pay attention. "If we let him go now, he'll just go back to hurting girls."

"How do you know?" I gritted, readjusting my grip on the knife.

"Remember who my dad is? I know the signs of an abuser." She patted my back. "Do it for the girls we both know he's hurt. Let's keep him from ever hurting more."

I nodded jerkily. Then, before I had a chance to think any more about it, I threw my weight behind the knife, driving it straight in. It caught on his uniform briefly, but once it was through the cloth the razor sharp steel entered his body easily, needing just a single upward wrench to drive it home. I felt the skin, muscles and organs parting in front of the blade like, well, like every other time I'd ever gutted an animal.

He thrashed some more, shivered, shit himself, and finally fell still.

I left the knife embedded and crawled a few feet away to vomit into a pile of drifted garbage. I heaved until there was nothing left to come up. I stayed there, on my hands and knees, head hanging for I don't know how long, before Alex came over and helped me up.

"Why didn't you let me do it?" she asked me curiously. "It wouldn't have bothered me anywhere near as much."

"That's why," I said, fishing my depleted canteen out and rinsing the taste from my mouth. She gave me a confused look. "Someday, you'll reach a point where you're not so angry anymore. I don't want you to look back at some of the things you did and hate yourself." *Or think you're a monster.* "What happens when you realize you killed a man and *enjoyed* it?"

Unsure how to respond, Alex ignored that and showed me what they'd found while I'd been puking my guts up. There was little enough to see: identification papers that we couldn't read but did contain a photograph, the handgun, no spare magazine, and interestingly, a small notebook and several pens tucked into his breast pocket.

"Looks like, I don't know, lists, maybe?" Sonya flipped through the notebook. "How the hell am I supposed to tell? I can barely read English. No way I'm gonna be able to figure out Korean."

"He doesn't have much by way of calluses." I put down his right hand. "I'm pretty sure if he was a normal soldier, he'd at least have a callus on his trigger finger." We'd all developed blisters that turned into calluses on our index fingers. I absentmindedly rubbed a thumb over mine through the glove, suddenly drained.

"Shit. Shit, shit, shit, shit." I rubbed my fingertips over my eyebrows, hoping to relieve the tension there. This...was exactly what I'd expected, I just didn't want to be right. I pressed my palms to my eyes, struggling to hold back tears. "We have to hide the body, and the scene," I said thickly.

I'd always figured that under the right circumstances I could kill. I wasn't dumb enough to be one of those 'Oh, no, I could *never* hurt someone!' types. Of course I could hurt someone! I have done it. Sometimes, I even think I enjoy it. But still, to think a thing and to have it proved are two very different things. It hurt. I hurt. I sighed and turned back to the work that still needed doing.

Sonya was busy burying the body under the torn trash bags piled against the bridge...thingies...girders? Girders sounded right. Or maybe it was pilings. Hell, I'd never learned much about bridges.

I walked over with a handful of trash to scatter over the stains left on the concrete when Sonya stopped me. "What?" I asked irritably.

"Do you see any of that type of garbage floating around this area? No? It'll stick out like a sore thumb! Use that stuff over there." She waved a hand to indicate the greasy rags a few feet from me. "Rub that over the ground to hide the blood and shit. Then we'll find some dirt...here! And we'll add some of that to the top..." Putting action to words, we worked quickly.

Seeing the bloodstains, I lost the rest of my lunch ("Under the trash!" Sonya yelled) against the girders, then went back to work.

"How do you know all this?" Alex watched us, handing over whatever items Sonya asked for.

Son smirked. "I've seen every episode of *Bones, NCIS,* and *Hunting Amelie* ever made. I could make it look like Winnie the fucking Pooh did it."

"What are those? E-books? I've never heard of them."

"How do you not know what...?" Sonya was aghast. "I can't believe—Hope, did you *hear* her? She's never—aaarrrgghh!"

"Can it, guys," I said, leaning against a girder. It took everything I had to keep my eyes open at this point. "We need to get the hell out of here before someone comes looking for this asshole. Last thing we want is to get caught before we've even done anything."

Sonya grumbled but scattered a few leaves over the area to hide the work. "Wouldn't say that was the *last* thing I'd want to happen," she muttered. "Last thing *I'd* want to happen is dying. *Dying* before we've done anything would suck."

"I want to put some distance between us and them." I jerked a thumb over my shoulder. The university stood only a mile or two behind us, *way* too close for comfort.

CHAPTER 12

We set a fast pace for the next hour to put some distance between us and the scene of our crime. Some jogging and a few turns, and we started to feel better. Well, they did. I still wanted to collapse in tears and sleep.

We didn't find a good place to hole up until well after dark. A large building loomed out of the gloom. Plenty of places to hide, plenty of ways out for an enterprising mind. I nodded. Good.

What might it once have been? A conference center? An office building? Both, likely, and more. Papa had worked in Salem for a time, before the reconstruction of the 99 had so drastically changed the city, and he did tell us that places close to the Willamette River (as we currently were) often doubled and tripled as locations for family outings, weddings and the like.

I had a brief flash of memory, a sunny day in a park. The broad Willamette sparkled just a stone's throw away. I rode on Papa's shoulders and he raced through the grass. I screamed and clutched his thinning hair as Mama laughed in the distance and called for him to be careful with me.

Then they redid the highway, the current president got into office, and everything went from bad to worse.

I pulled away from that and remembered Papa as I'd last seen him. I'd gone home for dinner a few days after Grace's wedding, a few days before leaving on that last, fateful camping trip with Sonya. It'd been just him, Sean, and me. It was odd not having Grace and Charlie in the house, but she'd be back in a week, and we were happy, knowing she'd found a good man.

We'd laughed and teased, and Papa showed me Grace's room, and how they were moving the furniture and getting it ready for when the newlyweds got home. I'd hugged him before I left, basking in the smell of the machine oil and grease that never left him. Despite the fact that this memory was only a couple of months old, it had the same warmth as ones from my childhood.

Emerging from the glowing memories of youth to return the dark reality we now faced hit as hard as ice water.

"Where have you been?" Sonya asked, fully breaking my reverie. We were inside the building, and Sonya had gathered some old cardboard boxes to protect us from the cold ground.

"Right here," I replied, looking around. When had we gotten inside? Regardless, I struggled upright and pitched in to help. It'd be nice not to freeze tonight.

"Hah. I know when someone's a million miles away."

My mouth quirked sadly. "Only a million years."

Our quiet conversation was broken by Alex, cursing as she tripped again. "How are the two of you walking so easy?" she demanded. "Why am I the only one who keeps falling?"

"Well, for a start, stop squinting. It doesn't help you to see at night." I shook my head, dispelling the last of the golden memories.

Alex was startled. "How'd you know I was?"

I huffed a brief laugh. "Because you're tripping over junk every other step. You need to soften your eyes. Unfocus them a bit. It helps your pupils dilate and lets in more light."

It took her a few minutes and a few more stumbles, but eventually her gait evened, just in time to keep her from walking into a door frame. "It actually works!" she said, pleased, as she pressed a hand to the frame.

"Don't sound so surprised," I replied dryly. "I occasionally know something useful."

Finished, we stood back to survey our work. Cardboard boxes were piled on the floor, enough to keep us off the ground, more nearby to cover ourselves with.

"I never thought I'd see the day when I'd miss the bunker." Alex looked sourly at our rude accommodations.

"Guess what? This is what striking back at the bastards who own everything looks like." Sonya's teeth gleamed in the dark as she grinned. "And you're the one who was pressing so hard for that."

I couldn't help smiling a little. Alex glared at me. "What?" I said. "Living rough is always a little fun."

Alex rolled her eyes but sat down equitably enough as we huddled together and pulled out bars for dinner. As I ate, my nose twitched. Something in this place smelled bad. I raised my nose, coursing for the scent and followed it, pulling out the collar of my shirt and sniffing.

I curled my lip but didn't stop eating. "I hate cold water, but right now I'm almost tempted to jump in if it meant finally being clean."

"Mmmm," Sonya agreed. "You do smell. We'd fit right in on the other side of town."

"Not so much this side," Alex spoke around her food. "Everybody, even the Americans, seem a lot cleaner on this side. Not as beaten down."

"Classic example of class distinction." I washed down the dry bar with a mouthful of water. "History's full of shit like this. Soap wasn't readily available to lower classes in Regency England or thereabouts, and the cleanliness of the person as well as their accent dictated how they were treated. Hell, it's been happening here. We just don't realize it 'cuz we're too poor to ever see rich people. I mean, how often did you take showers, Alex? Our place, you can't shower more than twice a week. We couldn't afford the water. And then, to make life really fun, the chip that regulates water temp was broken so the best we could get was lukewarm water. *Real* fun in winter. Couldn't get it replaced either, right?" Sonya nodded, chewing steadily. I continued. "I mean, for fuck's sake, I'm a mechanic that rarely drives!"

"Why didn't you drive?"

I grinned mirthlessly. "Too afraid the government would realize I didn't need to fill up very often and start asking questions. People have been disappeared for doing what I did."

"You know what?" Son looked up. I couldn't make out her features, but the somber tone of her voice told me all I needed to know. "After we're done here, we should have a little talk with our own government. Because you're right, this is stupid."

"The way rapists get—" We froze when a thump sounded from the floor above. Abandoning the relative comfort of our boxes, we were on our feet and moving in formation before the sound faded. *We're not jumpy at all, are we?* I grinned as I led the way. It was either that or scream and run. Right this moment, I only had the two settings.

We moved quickly and quietly, and I honestly gained new respect for cops and soldiers. Being the first person around the corner is fucking terrifying. On the second floor we checked the rooms. All the paintball practice we'd done was...less than satisfactory. It couldn't come close to the adrenaline rush of a live scenario. Trying to breathe quietly while my heart raced a hundred miles an hour was difficult at best.

In a small room halfway down the hall we found them. Dim moonlight filtered through the small window illuminating a huddled mass.

"Hands up!" I barked. "We are armed! Come out slowly!"

A child began crying in fear as the shape separated into three. One large, two small. Tiny, in fact. "Please, don't hurt us," a female voice quavered. "I'm just a mother. I have my girls with me. Please, woman to woman, don't hurt us!"

Not for the first time, and definitely not the last, I wished we had flashlights. Or even lights.

"Shiiit," Alex breathed behind me. "Lower the guns, you idiots." Turning back to the woman, she spoke in a soft, soothing tone I'd never heard from her before. "It's okay, we're not going to hurt you. We thought there might be dangerous types here and didn't want to get jumped in the middle of the night."

The woman took a deep, trembling breath. "Are you with the Corps?"

I paused a moment, trying to remember. "Assholes with red armbands," Alex reminded me.

"Right! No, not them. We're just normal people, wandering...around...at night." I tried again. "We're not with the soldiers. You're safe with us." Yeah, that seemed like a good way to go.

"You can put your hands down, now," Alex added.

The woman immediately pulled her kids close, cuddling them until they calmed. We took them downstairs to the crude nest we'd built. The inconstant moonlight disappeared behind clouds, and a light rain started up. Finally.

Like a magician, Sonya produced a thin sheet of flexible plastic from under her shirt, rolled it into a rough cone shape, clipped the top to hold it together, and took it outside to collect rainwater into her canteen.

"Where the fuck—uh, heck—were you hiding that?" I asked Son, glancing quickly at the kids. She just chuckled.

Unasked, we dipped back into our supplies, pulling out generous portions of food for the newcomers. They tucked in, eating quickly. Going by the hurried, watchful way they ate, I thought maybe they were used to food being taken from them. As they ate, we told a little of our own story, enough to set the mother's mind at ease.

Afterward, she told us her story. The first part, the bit about the Invasion, was old hat by now. It was after they were gathered into Salem that things got interesting. And sad.

"My husband was sick off and on for years, but then the work gang they put him on..." Her voice thickened. "It killed him." She paused to get herself under control. "After that, I came to the attention of the Corps. They drafted me and a few other women for cooking, cleaning, and—other things."

Sonya growled softly, and the woman shrank back. Alex slid a hand behind her back, to where she kept her knife, probably contemplating murder. Again. I rested my chin on my fists and thought.

"The...Corpsmen. Are they marked? We heard they have the same tattoo," I said, pulling the woman out of her personal hell.

"Oh, yes, they're marked. With a brand. Those of us who work for them were also branded." She pulled back her sleeve, but we couldn't make it out in the dark.

"Those mother—" That was as far as I got before Alex punched me, hard.

"Language!" she scolded me. "Kids pick up bad words so quickly. And you're probably scaring them!"

The woman sighed in the darkness. "Thank you. Kindness is a rare commodity these days."

"How did you get here?" Sonya asked. "If you work for them, where are you housed?"

"With them." The young mother gathered her girls to her, holding them tightly. "We ran away, just this morning. I caught...I caught a man trying to corner my girl here." She indicated the elder of the two, who looked no more than five. "He was talking about what he wanted to do to her.

She swallowed, then continued. "I'm not going back," she said, desperation and hysteria rising. "I'd rather be dead. I'd rather my girls were dead than live like that! I won't—" She broke down. The girls began crying quietly, frightened by their mother's outburst.

Alex turned to me. "We're taking these ones with us," she declared.

"No problem," I told her. Then back to the woman, "You can come with us. If we get out of the city in one piece, we can guarantee more safety than you've known here. And if we don't get out, I'll personally make sure they never touch you or your kids."

Weeping softly, she reached out blindly, trying to find me. I took her hand, and the strength of hers surprised me. Maybe it shouldn't have, though. "Thank you," she whispered through her tears. "Thank you."

"We should call you something," Sonya broke the quiet. "We've been told using names is a bad idea. Apparently, it can lead back to people you know. So you need new names."

"Leo," I said, smiling. "We can call her Leo."

The woman jerked as if she'd been slapped. "You don't have to make fun of me. I know I'm not brave. I've been scared for years."

"Ah, but you are," I replied. "Lack of fear is a sign of stupidity or psychopathy. But doing something *despite* fear...that's a sign of bravery."

"Pleased to meet you, Leo." Alex held out her hand. Leo reflexively let go of mine and shook hers.

The littlest girl, tears forgotten, giggled sleepily, stood up, took a few steps to me and plopped herself in my lap. I froze, unsure what to do with a strange small person. The kid apparently had her own ideas of what should happen, as she promptly curled into me, stuck a thumb in her mouth, and closed her eyes.

"Uh, is this...?" I waved at the kid, arms raised, looking helplessly at her mother, "...okay?"

Leo shook her head ruefully. "She likes you. You don't have to do much. Just wrap her up and keep her warm."

"The lion's cub has guts," I murmured, opening my jacket and tucking the girl inside.

"What about you, little one?" Alex asked the older girl. "What should we call you?"

The little girl thought long and hard. "Moana," she said eventually.

"It's her favorite old movie," Leo explained. "She knows every song by heart." Leo looked fondly at the little girl. "You'll know she's feeling better when she starts singing it again."

We gathered up a few more scraps of cardboard to act as mats and blankets and bracketed the mother and daughters between us. Dawn was a long time coming, with the three of us taking turns keeping an ear out, shaking the next person awake when the time came.

I rolled over to warm my back and give my hip a break. Three nights of really rough sleep started to wear on me. On all of us. Alex, triggered by Leo's story, tossed and turned in her sleep and now both of them had nightmares throughout.

I don't know if I slept, but I woke for my final shift feeling like I'd rested a bit. It's an odd thing. Sleep badly in a bed and you feel as if you hadn't slept at all. Sleep badly while camping, with lots of fresh air, and you're surprisingly functional.

I turned over the problem of Alex as I waited for dawn. She'd settled a bit, and I no longer worried that she'd up and attack me, but at the same time, she was far from stable. I could see her itching for a fight, and if she didn't get one soon, I feared she'd make one.

Having one's mind going in circles on problems that can't be fixed is a marvelous way to stay awake, I had to give it that.

CHAPTER 13

I can't really say that dawn broke the next morning. More like it slouched sullenly over the mountains like a teenaged vampire wannabe forced to get up before sunrise, accompanied by its older, heavier brother—last night's drizzle.

The plus side of the rain is that we managed to refill all our canteens. Alex looked fretfully up at the sky. "I hope Corey won't be sent out into the rain today."

"His mom's sensible," I said from where I knelt, laying out more bars of food. "She bundled him up well enough yesterday. Besides, her benefactor visited yesterday. Dudes like that rarely see their women two days in a row."

She fidgeted, picking at her fingernails as she paced. Wonderful. Back on edge again.

We ate, though nobody was by any means satisfied. I surveyed my empty pouch dismally. "We'd better wrap things up and get the hell out of here." I sighed. "I'm out of food."

"I'm sorry," Leo said miserably. "We've ruined this, haven't we?"

I waved her off. "We had no idea how long we'd be here, and honestly, getting you out and away from the Corpsmen will be more good done than we'd thought."

"You know," Sonya said, staring out at the watery sky thoughtfully, "I don't think I've ever seen a kor before. Like, what is it?"

"You've seen it." I rolled my eyes. "It's spelled C O R P S."

"OH, you mean *corpse!*" She grinned with delight. "Suits them. They're dead meat walking."

"No." I sighed heavily, staring at the sky and begging it for mercy. "Just...no."

Alex shook her head at us, and Leo looked bemused. Probably wondering how we were still alive. I asked myself that every day.

***

By noon, I was ready to shoot someone out of sheer frustration. Every time we tried to angle back towards the east and freedom, we ran across roadblocks with security checkpoints.

"What's all that?" Sonya asked, waving behind us. Done with being cold, wet, and tired, we huddled under a lone evergreen growing between two commercial buildings on a side road running south from State Street. It gave us a chance for a rest out of both sight and hearing of Steve. I was surprised that the kids hadn't uttered a whimper all morning. The assholes in the Corps must've done a real number on them.

"All right! That's it." I looked up at the startled faces around me. "I need something to call them besides 'those assholes in the Corps.'"

"I *said* Corpses." Sonya gave me an aggrieved look. "But *nooo*, you didn't like that. It was too simple for *you*."

"I'm willing to...recons:der." I grimaced. "It's just...we have Steve, and we know what that is."

"We do?" Leo asked, bewildered.

"It's the soldiers," Alex murmured, watching us like we were her new favorite soap opera.

"So why can't we think of something more like that?" I finished.

"What about Dorothy?" Sonya offered.

"How'd you get that?" I shook my head. "No, don't answer that. It works. I'll take it."

Alex rolled her eyes but didn't look at us. Something well down the street caught her eye, and now she barely paid attention to the conversation.

Leo shrugged. "Back to the *original* question." She gave us pointed looks. "On the far side of that gate is the prison. Steve?" We nodded happily. She continued. "Steve uses it as an armory. Tanks are parked and serviced there. Men talk freely when they view cleaners as furniture."

Alex ignored us now. I got worried. Alex should've been salivating for a chance at that kind of target.

Sonya poked her head around the corner of the building, looking north for a moment. "I think the parking lot for the district's school buses isn't too far from here. That building is hard to forget." She pointed across the street to a sea-green monstrosity towering over the rest of the drab, gray concrete blocks passing as architecture.

"Could be useful," Alex murmured. "Guys, check out that building there." She pointed through two windows to a two-story block south of us. "I saw three Steves walk in a while ago, and two Dorothys walked out. The Dorothys looked...messy. I don't know. That place is giving me the creeps."

"Fine. Let's go have a little look. Just to see what has them so interested. I know you want to." I held my hand out, indicating that Alex should take the lead. We headed behind the buildings and were rewarded with a short alley that dead-ended on another building. That one relied on a keypad to lock its doors, so Alex pushed straight through. We found a traditionally-locked door next to a broken window, then took the window through and out the other side. The little girls thought it was fun, being passed from person to person through a window. Their faces lit up and Cub raised tiny fists over her head, grinning.

Thank goodness for the window. I don't think anybody knew how to pick a lock. A guy I knew growing up had taught himself that for fun, but he'd died in a motor accident three years ago. Best I could do was hot-wire a car. Fat lot of good that did, with most cars being out of commission...Well, a bus might be susceptible to hotwiring. Most of those were *old.*

The fourth building down from our starting point put us directly across the street from the creepy place. I never saw any other people enter or leave in that time, though let's face it: there were periods (I'm looking at hanging upside-down over a window frame here) where nobody watched the place. Still, if Alex thought something was hinky, I'd follow her gut.

The building we squatted in had a strong draft, and most of the windows looked like they'd been boarded up for more than a year. We lit a tiny fire at the back, behind a broken wall, watching the flames dance in the breeze. The children and Leo were pressed to sit closest, to warm them quickly. I looked away to let my eyes adjust back. Wouldn't do, becoming night blind while we were running around in occupied territory.

Being out of the rain was great; it highlighted the fact that we were cold, wet, and sore. It also helped me notice every ache. Getting up this morning had been painful all around. Finding out that the muscles in my ribs could scream in protest just by breathing was something I'd have been happy to never know.

I stretched before trying to sit, for all the good it did. *I'm too young to feel this damn old,* I thought, rubbing my shoulder. Alex insisted on being the one to keep watch, and I gladly let her. The window was chest high to her, and I guessed her to be in her mid-twenties, well past the age where crawling over an object three-quarters of her height was easy.

I'd just closed my eyes and saw that skinny Steve's face again when, from the front, I heard "Fucking hell! It *is* a brothel!" My eyes popped open in time to see Alex heave herself through the window.

I lurched to my feet, leaning heavily on Son to wake her as I did. By the time I made it to the window, Alex leapt onto the sidewalk, crossing the street without slowing down.

"Shit, shit, shitshitshit*shit!*" I spun towards Sonya. "Do you still remember how to hot-wire cars?" I'd shown her a few times, for shits and giggles. Son nodded. "Find those buses and *get me one!* You're our exit." She spun, running for the back without question. "A small one!" I shouted at her retreating back. She waved without turning.

I whirled towards Leo, who stared at me with wide, frightened eyes, clutching her kids. "Gimme five minutes head start, then follow me in. Shit's about to get bad."

"How will I know?"

"Count!" I bellowed as I flung myself in a rolling dive through the window. It was a rare occasion that I made a perfect landing, and thank God this was one of them. If I hit wrong, there's a good chance I'd've busted a shoulder, or broken my neck or back. But when you get it right, it's one of the sweetest things in the world. The concrete felt like a hard mat instead of a bunch of, well, concrete, and I rolled straight to my feet in a run.

Halfway across, the shooting started.

I burst through the door into a large, open room. To my left was a door labeled "stairs" and to the right a hallway opened with enough space to have rooms on both sides. I had a gun in one hand and saw a man down on the ground, writhing feebly in a growing pool of blood. A teenaged girl huddled against the wall, hands up, trying to shield herself. I gave both no more than a cursory glance that took in a horribly-scarred spot on her right flank and continued down the hall.

More shots sounded, and I could tell they came from the rear of the building, but which floor I didn't know. In a burst of false bravery, I flung open the first door I came to. A naked Steve frantically threw clothes around, searching for a weapon. Movement on a bed tucked in the far corner showed a girl, not more than eighteen, sitting up groggily. She was naked, making it easier to see the bruises and welts marring her skin. She too had scarring on her flank, and I had time enough to register a K branded on her.

The soldier looked up, holding his belt and holster. I shot him, point-blank without warning. I missed. Two more quick shots followed. There would be no mercy for rapists. No prisoners, and no enemies at our backs.

"Get dressed, now!" I told the girl over my shoulder. I checked out the hall to see if anybody would stick their head out. "We're here to help."

The girl stared at me, uncomprehending. From everything we'd been told, these girls were taken to punish their families. They're marked, so they can't go home, and if we left them here they'd probably be killed. She still didn't move, too shell-shocked or stunned from the beating. I repeated the order in my best bellow. It startled her out of her funk, and she began fishing around for clothes.

I continued down the corridor before she finished. The next two rooms were empty, and the only thing left was to clear the other side of the hall. Gathering up my stupidity, I opened another door. Empty.

One left.

As I reached for the last doorknob, I heard a crash in the room. I flung the door open with my right hand, left ready to shoot somebody, only to find Steve on the ground, wrestling with a woman. She looked a bit older than me, her face twisted in the grimace of a life or death struggle. I danced around the edges of their fight, looking for an opportunity. When the opening came, I stomped on his shoulder, making him howl and pinning him down long enough to shoot him.

A part of me was mesmerized at the sight of the small hole that occupied the spot where his eye used to be.

The woman jerked her chin upwards from where she lay, unable to stop trembling. "There's more upstairs," she gasped.

"There's two girls out there who can use your help. We have a bus coming and a woman with kids. Get ready." She nodded as I raced back down the hall to the stairs. The girl in the front room was moving, though slowly.

I took the stairs quickly, my gun held in front, pointing up. These stairs were the kind you saw in commercial buildings: five or six shallow steps then a small landing with a right-hand turn and repeat. They were the kind that could make you dizzy if you ran up enough flights. The door on the top (and only) floor swung loosely on its hinges.

I cautiously poked my head around the frame, but only saw a derelict hallway, ceiling panels loose or missing, with doors opening off it, just like the lower floor. In the back of my mind, I'd been aware of more shots being fired, though I was more concerned with keeping my own head in one piece. The deep barking of Alex's Ruger was offset by another sound, more of a staccato, that made me think Alex had run into some trouble.

More trouble, I amended.

I moved to the closest door, to my right, and checked the room. I had to make sure we wouldn't have anybody shooting us in the back. Inside the room was yet another girl in her mid-teens, red hair in a floating mess around her head, staring in deep shock at the body sprawled across the bed in front of her.

"Get dressed!" I barked, then moved on without waiting to see if she had heard. Across the hall, through an open door, crouched another teen, this one wearing lingerie, the soldier lying in front of her still dressed, still alive—and moving. He crawled slowly toward the girl, who moved back, casting around desperately for...something.

I stepped briskly in and pulled the trigger. *Bang. Splat.* The slide locked back, and I triggered the magazine release, dropping the empty magazine into a pocket and pulling a full one out of a cargo pocket and sliding it in. Racking the slide was automatic at this point. We'd drilled for hours to be able to do this without any input from the brain.

Which was a good thing.

My brain, hung up on the horrors of the last few minutes, had quit all higher functions. If it was left in control, we'd all be dead in another five. The girl moving snapped me out of it, and I motioned for her to follow me out.

The third and fourth rooms were empty, and the fifth had two women in it, looking about my age. There was another man down, this one definitely dead.

The hallway took a turn to the right, and just around the corner I saw Alex crouching in a doorway, bullets peppering the hall around her. She'd pop out like a jack-in-the-box and fire off a round or two then duck back in. From the way she moved, there was definitely one Steve on my side of the hall and maybe another one on hers.

Shit.

I wasn't fond of heights if I had nothing solid to hold onto. So, after climbing up a tree, trying to prepare to jump onto the rope swing from fifteen or twenty feet above the ground, I'd often stand up there for ages, trying to nerve myself up. Eventually, I'd realize I'd never be ready, and there was nothing for it but to let go.

This felt like that, only this time, the possibility of dying wasn't just in my imagination.

I never stopped, moving in a diagonal down the hallway with a gun in each hand, firing the whole time. The Steve on Alex's side of the hall fell first, caught by Alex when he tried to shoot me. I crashed into the wall and used it to rebound, pinballing back. The remaining soldier had stood up, the better to hit me since I was making such a wonderful target of myself. Alex got him, too. I didn't even bother firing by that point.

I'd swear I felt the wind of the bullets tearing past my face. I'm still convinced that the only reason I didn't die right then and there is because I never stopped moving.

I managed to make it through a doorway the second time and finally had a degree of cover as I caught my breath.

"Don't shoot!" A woman's voice called. "We're all unarmed. There are no more soldiers down here!"

"Come out. Slowly," I called back. "Hands where we can see them."

Three women stepped carefully into the hall, hands held above their heads. A middle-aged woman took point, doing her best to shield the younger women behind her. She was unusual in that her dress actually covered her body. The other two were teens, again, a blonde and brunette, and the black-haired girl had tears streaking her face.

I mentally reviewed the women I'd seen since entering the building. Considering these girls were supposedly taken to punish their families, Steve had managed to only steal the beautiful girls.

Naturally.

When they were halfway down the hall, the eldest of them asked, "Who are you people?"

Name it, Mary had said. *Own it.*

"We're the rebellion."

"What rebellion?"

"Honey, we're the only one in town."

CHAPTER 14

The older woman, the spokeswoman, had an elegance about her. It was in the way she moved, the way she held herself. The younger women gravitated to her like moths to a flame. Or like frightened children to their mother. I felt like a filthy vagabond next to her. Then I remembered that I *was* a filthy vagabond.

Still.

"What's next?" the woman asked.

I was about to hem and haw when I remembered Mary's advice. *Always sound confident...Fake it 'til you make it.* Unwillingly, my shoulders scrunched closer to my ears. "Next, get everyone together, we're heading downstairs. Hopefully our ride will be here soon."

The woman stared at me, thinking, before nodding to herself as if she'd come to a decision. She turned to chivvy the girls along, speaking gently but firmly. The dazed looks slowly cleared, and the girls disappeared into various rooms.

Alex grinned triumphantly at me, nodding and inviting me to take part in the win.

"You," I growled around the sudden flash of rage, "can get your ass downstairs and make sure Leo and the kids got here okay. Then you can keep watch. Pray you see a bus before you see soldiers."

"I just—" she began.

"Shut up!" I snarled. "I don't have time for excuses, courtesy of you! You had something like this in your head ever since you heard about the fucking brothels, didn't you?" Alex nodded, but wisely didn't try to say anything. I think I might've decked her if she tried again. "Because of you, I had to send Sonya out alone to find us transport out of here. You better hope she's fucking good, or else you've just handed all of us to the North Koreans on a damn platter," I hissed, not two inches from her face.

Alex paled, leaning back and licking her lips. It took her three tries before she managed to croak out a week "You keep not helping people. We could have insisted that guy leave with us. And my aunt. And cousin. The kid. That couple. I thought you'd see another reason not to help. You-you don't want to take any chances," she finished sullenly.

"I could answer that. Again," I whispered. "But I could swear you were there, that you saw their situations. Now go watch the fucking road!"

After the women headed downstairs, I took a quick trip around, just to make sure there weren't any living bodies and to pick up any weapons I could find.

Downstairs, I saw the soldier I'd first encountered had his throat slit. By the blood, it looked like the tough chick had finished him. I was marginally gratified to see Alex actually keeping watch. The oldest woman had the others, including Leo and her girls, gathered in one corner, near the lower hallway. They wore a mixture of lingerie and uniforms, anything to cover up.

I did a quick head count. Fifteen of us, far more than I'd expected. I sincerely hoped Sonya got here soon.

"Yo!" Alex called. My hopes rose. "We got company! Soldiers headed this way."

My hopes plummeted. *Fuck.* "Anybody here have shooting experience?" I asked the room at large. "At this point, I'll even take video game experience."

Only one person stepped forward, the tough one. "I'm ex-Army," she said, straightening her shoulders.

"Cool!" I spread out the weapons I'd brought down with me. "Take your pick. Take a couple."

Ex-Army took two handguns and a knife. I took an extra gun, taking my working total up to...two. Yeah, maybe I needed another one. Moving over to Alex, at the window to the right of the door, I checked where she pointed and cursed under my breath. We were heard, all right. Two patrols of six men each were heading our way from the south.

"We'll have to wait until they get into range, dammit! Assholes got rifles," I ground out. I looked to the north, where Son had gone. "Come on," I muttered.

The soldiers kept to the edges of the street, six to a side. There was caution, sure, but a lot of arrogance, too. They just looked...like the popular kid at high school, the one who rocked up fashionably late to everything, who had perfect hair and wardrobe. They knew they were the top dog, and they walked like it.

I always had the urge to mess with their hair. It annoyed them so much.

"I can hit them," Alex whispered. "I know it."

I waited, calculating the distance. "All right, mess up Steve's hair," I finally said.

She sighted down the barrel, choosing her target, waiting. I cracked the door open while the soldier set up in the northern window. I was sweating, my base layer growing clammy as I waited for Alex to start shit.

I waved for the woman to get all the others down and spared a moment to feel grateful for the building. A solid structure, it had an added benefit: after they'd built the walls and run the cables, concrete was poured between, sealing everything. My brother Sean worked for a construction company, and he'd told me about it, walked me through a job site. Said there was no artistry to it, though. I rapped on the wall, just to reassure myself we wouldn't die in the next five seconds.

"Gotcha," Alex murmured, exhaling as she fired.

Once she opened up, Ex-Army and I joined in, picking at the edges and keeping them bunched up for Alex. I pulled the door closed and jumped back from it, away from a spray of splinters. So, yeah, that thing wasn't bulletproof.

"I can't see the other team!" Alex cried, frustrated. Two Steves were down, not moving, and the four we could see were hiding as best they could. She'd picked a moment when they were walking past a glass-fronted building, minimizing the amount of cover that they could find. I enjoyed watching them squirm and try to squeeze behind bits of furniture and walls.

"I might get a view of the other team from upstairs," the soldier called. She detoured past the remaining weapons, grabbing another gun on the way, leaving one more. The older woman took that last and positioned herself in front of the girls.

"Is there a back door?" I asked the air. We didn't have to worry about windows. Everything on the ground floor had bars, which twenty minutes ago was a bad thing, but now I was eternally grateful for.

"There is," the woman replied, "and it only opens from the inside."

The soldier upstairs began firing, and judging by the spacing, she picked her shots carefully.

"I can see flashes of the other team," Alex said fretfully, "but not enough for a good shot. You wanna give them something extra to aim for?" she asked me hopefully.

"I hate you," I informed her as I moved to the door. Two quick breaths and I stepped outside, firing wildly. I fell backwards into the room, tucking into a roll as bullets peppered the space I'd just occupied, and I heard a whoop from upstairs while Alex punched the air. "Got some?" I inquired.

"Do it again," she commanded. "There's some who made it into the building directly across the street. I want a shot at them."

I flung the door back, stuck my head out then shrieked with joy as I ducked back in. "Our ride's here!" Screeching around the corner from the north came a short, bright yellow bus, my cousin's stocky frame visible through the window.

The soldiers saw her, too.

Shit.

"Here goes nothin'!" I fished one of my grenades out, pulled the pin and hurled it at the window across the street I'd climbed through a short time ago. By some miracle I actually made the throw just as the bus screeched to a halt in front of the door.

It was impressive, seeing the bus open its doors against a backdrop of smoke, flying bits of building and the occasional *plop* of organic matter. Too bad we were too busy to appreciate it.

Son leaned over. "Get in," she bellowed.

"Move!" I bawled, taking up a covering position with Alex between the bus and the building. The smoke and dust from the grenade combined with the coming dusk created a murky half-light that was difficult to see in. It's a good thing we were leaving now. Maybe we could use the dark to lose them...

Someone slapped my shoulder. "Time to go!" the soldier cried.

As soon as I got a good hold and a foot in the bus Sonya gunned it and we shot off, taking the first right, then right again so we were heading back north.

"What took you so long?" I asked Son, panting.

She grinned and pointed to something laying on the floor next to her. "There might've been some folks who objected to my liberation of a bus." I laughed when I saw two rifles, the same kind Steve carried.

I caught a glimpse of a street sign as it whizzed past. "We're on Twenty-fifth Street," I said, hanging onto a seat for dear life. I scrunched up my nose, thinking. Didn't Twenty-fifth connect with—

"Down!" screamed Alex.

I hit the floor with everybody else and heard glass shattering interspersed with women screaming. "Where are they?" I gasped.

"They came out of a side street just ahead of us." Alex was pale, blood running from a shallow cut made by the flying glass. "I think it's that other team."

"Here." One of the younger women wriggled up to Alex with some torn cloth formed into a pad. I recognized her as the bruised woman from downstairs, the Latina. With quick, efficient movements interrupted by the jarring of the bus, she pressed the pad to Alex's head and wrapped a strip of cloth around, tying it roughly.

"Catch!" Son yelled, sliding one of the rifles to me.

The rifle *thunked* into my leg and I grabbed it, giggling madly, and slid down the aisle to the back door. I took a moment to familiarize myself with the rifle (mostly making sure it was on something other than "safety") and popped up, squeezing off short bursts at the soldiers through the broken back window. Just enough to keep them occupied while we put them in our rearview.

The bus braked suddenly, and I flew backwards, sliding a few feet. The training kicked in enough that I managed to not bite my tongue in half or slam my head onto the floor. I twisted onto my belly and scrambled the rest of the way to the front, still clutching the rifle.

"What *the fuck* is happening?" I screamed. "Why are we stopping?"

Sonya pointed silently in front of us. A roadblock hunched across the two-lane road, fifty feet away. The bulk of it had been hidden by the buildings, which is why we'd made it so close before Son noticed it. The block part was nothing more than sawhorses with a wooden pole across the single lane. It was the sandbagged machine gun nest on the left and the soldiers with rifles behind a barricade on the right that freaked me out. The curly barbed wire topping it all was really just overkill.

A quick glance showed we'd passed the last intersection, and the enemy team behind us had managed to find a truck.

"Fuck it!" I snarled.

No sooner had the words left my mouth than Son stomped the gas and we lurched forward. Cue shrieking, though it sounded more angry and shocked than afraid to me.

"What are you *doing?*"

"Are you crazy?"

"Estas loca!"

I think we surprised everybody, because it took Steve long, precious seconds to comprehend what was happening. Long enough for Alex to lob a grenade with a classic sidearm dodgeball throw through the window into the machine gun nest. I fired out the door at the soldiers on the right while Sonya made herself as small as possible, screeching at everyone else to hit the floor. The remaining glass on the left side of the bus blew inwards at the grenade concussion.

A line of fire high on my right arm and the *whap* of a bullet's passing told me Steve had finally pulled their collective thumbs out of their asses, just in time to watch us barrel through the flimsy barricade.

"Shit, I've been shot!" I couldn't believe how much it burned. "Those assholes put a hole in my jacket!"

Alex and the Latina arrived next to me at the same time. "It's not too...*malo.*" The Latina had more bandages in her hand. Bedsheets? I looked further back and saw three rescuees frantically tearing a sheet into strips. And there were blankets everywhere.

When did blankets happen?

Reading my expression, the young woman jerked her head, indicating the spokeswoman. "*Mi madre,* her, she took blankets from *el armario. Comprendes?*"

"Uh, maybe? Your...mom grabbed blankets and stuff from...*armario*...wardrobe? Closet?" Utilizing my distraction, the younger woman wrapped the strip snugly around my arm, ignoring my sharply indrawn breath.

"*Si,*" the woman replied, tightening the knot as we screeched around a corner.

"Ow!" I snapped.

"Suck it up," Alex said carelessly from where she watched our rear.

"Do you need me to pull over so we can take care of your owie?" Son called, never taking her eyes from the road. She took a left, then a sharp right a few minutes later.

"You can both jump off a friggin' cliff," I informed them primly. "If you can't find one, I'll be happy to give you directions!"

Those assholes just laughed, a little hysterically, reassured that I wouldn't die from the graze. Our ex-soldier had a tiny grin on her face as she listened to us. She also kept her eyes on the sides, joining everybody else in watching Steve running to catch us. The others looked frightened, though here and there, little glimmers of excitement showed.

"Head for 99E," I called to Sonya. "We gotta pick up the kids."

"Can I have the other rifle?" Alex shouted from the back. "Steve's gaining on us!"

"Pass her the rifle," Son announced to anyone who was close, then louder, for Alex, "I want that back! I worked hard to get it! Won't it be safer if the kids stay hidden?"

"Dunno how these dudes roll." I nodded my thanks to the young woman for bandaging me. "Personally, after watching us bust out of this place, I'd be all over the countryside, making sure there weren't more lil' shits like us floating around. Besides, we need the gun."

"You don't like to make things easy, do you?" she asked sarcastically as Alex began taking shots at the truck still pursuing us. "Just, y'know, *drive* across the entire damn city while being chased and shot at and make it out the other side in one piece. No problem."

I patted her shoulder with my left hand. "I knew you'd see it my way."

"Bitch." Sonya's voice was high pitched as we approached another roadblock, this time from the rear.

The women all hit the floor again, two of them helping Leo with her girls, curling around them.

"Brat." I readied the rifle, wrapping the strap around my arm to make sure I didn't lose it and leaning over the barrier and out the door. Waiting.

There were no buildings to hide this roadblock, and immediately on the other side of it was a T-junction. We needed to go right. If we missed this, we were fucked. Steve held their fire, waiting for us to get close enough for them to be sure of a hit. Thing is, Murphy's Law: if you're close enough to shoot me, you're also close enough for me to shoot you.

Our windshield became more hole than glass, cracks spiderwebbing over the rest of it while Sonya drove with barely more than her forehead showing over the dashboard. The manufacturer's boasts held true; the windshield cracked, but it didn't shatter. It should also be mentioned that not all of those holes were caused by incoming bullets.

Some of them may have been mine, exiting.

We roared through their little roadblock, sending sawhorses and men flying. I braced myself as we screeched around the corner onto Center Street, the bus barely righting itself. I chanced a quick glance back. The girls were mostly all right, just shaken and scared, though the redhead had one hand pressed to her head, her other hand tightly gripping the seat in front of her.

"Sloppy," I muttered, shaking my head and watching Steve scurrying around like ants whose nest had been kicked.

"What?" A blonde girl, I think she was one of the two girls with the spokeswoman earlier, asked me, puzzled.

I shook my head, "They're fuckin' sloppy. Look at 'em." I pointed behind us. "No coordination. They're totally surprised. Like, sure, they've got roadblocks, but they weren't expecting to have to *use* 'em."

"Hawthorne!" the soldier shouted. "Left on Hawthorne if you want the 99!"

Son took the corner so sharply I found myself with my cheek plastered to a window. It did give me a great view of the Hummer that'd just turned onto Center from Lancaster.

Fuck.

"We have another stalker!" I bellowed.

"I see it!" Alex shouted back. "A little help here!"

"No good!" Sonya called. "I got one coming up on the right."

I peeled my cheek off the glass and awkwardly stepped into the bus's stairwell, bracing my back and knees against anything that would hold. I raised the rifle, grimacing as the motion pulled the damaged muscles and fired at the windows. I scowled when the bullets didn't even ding the glass.

"Fuckin' bulletproof glass," I muttered. "Stupid bastards, can't even take a little..." I aimed low this time, hoping to get a tire. I missed the one I aimed at but got lucky and hit the other side. I giggled as the Humvee listed, and I riddled the front grill with bullets. I whooped when steam gushed from under the hood.

"Didn't bulletproof your engine block, did you?" I crowed. "Who's the idiot now, Steve?"

Some of the girls gave a ragged cheer as that truck had to break off, and we watched the soldiers pouring out of it. One of them popped up into a—my eyes widened. "Gun!" I roared. "Everybody DOWN!"

That soldier manned a machine gun from a small turret in the middle of the Hummer and peppered our beleaguered little bus. I heard a short cry about half-way down the aisle.

I turned to see a girl slump into the aisle, blood pouring from a gaping hole in her chest. The oldest woman flung herself down by the girl, stuffing a wad of sheets against the girl's chest, trying to stem the flood. She whispered softly to the young woman, stroking her hair tenderly. Leo, closest to the two of them, scooted over and helped raise the girl up, and between the two women, they cradled the dying girl.

I heard Leo crooning a lullaby and quickly, so quickly I almost missed it, the young woman was gone.

Around us, the bus's engine still strained, roaring away, glass fell tinkling to the floor, metal shrieked as it was rent by bullets, and over all this, the harsh, staccato report of gunfire marked the passing of a girl who'd been thrown into the fire by an uncaring army.

Gasps and cries sounded from the others who'd shared this poor girl's captivity. I watched frozen. It wasn't until our soldier hushed them and reminded them that this time was for helping the living, that we would mourn her later, that I snapped out of my daze.

Looking up to check our progress, I saw Son repeatedly twisting, trying to look over her shoulder at us and watch the road at the same time. "How is she?"

"She's gone," I said, throat tight.

Sonya's shoulders slumped, but her foot stayed glued to the pedal, maintaining that fine line between maximum speed and wasted gas. God only knew when we'd see a gas station and have time to fiddle with refilling. Damn automation made it tricky. In this one instance, I had to be content that Oregon is a poor state: we couldn't afford the fancy new gimmicks that richer states could, even on our few remaining gas pumps.

That Hummer, whose radiator I'd ruined, had decided to stay in the chase. I laughed, but there was no humor to it. They'd thrash their engine, melting all the little bits of it, driving like that.

Good.

So a truck and two Hummers. We've had better days. I made my way to the back to help Alex deal with our pursuit while the soldier watched the front with Sonya.

"How're you doing for ammo?" I asked Alex when I reached her.

"Hell if I know." So while I watched, she checked her magazine, and found it only a quarter full, maybe ten rounds left. Then I checked mine and found it maybe two-thirds full.

"Got any spare mags?" Alex shouted at Son.

Without looking around, my cousin reached into her jacket and fished a couple spare mags out and sent them back to us. "I love her," Alex breathed, scooping them up when they reached us. "She really thinks of everything."

"Got any more grenades?" I asked. I swiped my face against my shoulder, wiping away tears. When had I started crying? "I've only got one."

We still had the gates at the 99 to get through, and I preferred fast and dirty to slow and caught. That gate had been blatantly designed to keep people in, prisoners. Alex silently unzipped her jacket and pulled it open, displaying the lining. I pursed my lips in a silent whistle, eyes wide. She'd sewn pockets in there, and she was carrying *six* grenades, all right next to her. It was a miracle she hadn't spontaneously combusted just breathing.

I slumped in shock, propping my butt on the back of a seat, staring. "How are we not dead yet when you've got all that?"

She shrugged. That lunatic just *shrugged*. I decided I'd kill her later, provided we survived this. "You know what?" I asked. "Why don't you take your arsenal to the front? That gate should be coming up soon." We swayed as the bus took another corner too fast. "Real soon. Have fun!"

As she stepped carefully to the front, I fired a few rounds behind us, just to let Steve know we hadn't forgotten them, as I pondered our suicidal friend. With a shiver, it occurred to me that we'd been closer to dying than I'd even *dreamed* of over the last few days. I paused with my cheek resting against the barrel of the rifle: *How did she manage to sleep in all that?* And another thought: *I'd slept next to her!* Chalk it down to one more thing to not think about.

I looked through the window again, and found the truck weaving across the road, making it harder to hit. *Smart*. Dumb, because it took them so long to do it, though. The injured Hummer had dropped back significantly, blocking the last Hummer and slowing that one down. *Good*. A soldier stood up in the truck behind us, hefting a large caliber rifle.

"Evasive action!" I yelled.

"Aye aye, captain!" Sonya shouted back and I flopped to the floor, that being the quickest way to get out of the line of fire.

"Fuck you!" I screamed at her. A bullet tore through the door, a massive hole appearing where my chest had just been. I giggled madly, sliding side to side in the aisle as Son swerved to try to make a fucking *bus* a more difficult target.

As the bus swayed clumsily, I wished we had Asilia. Her skills, or recklessness, would come in pretty handy about now. So would the mounted machine gun on the GMC, come to think of it.

A bullet *pinged* through the door, destroying the latch and making the rear door swing wildly, loudly banging each time it shut. Everybody was screaming, including me, as I wriggled around to sit with my feet braced on either side of the door, firing short bursts in those moments when the door swung open.

"You need help?" Alex yelled, preparing to come to the back.

"Stay put!" I shouted back. "We'll need you there!"

A bullet plowed through the top hinge, making the door hang awkwardly as it flopped on its remaining support. It gave me a longer window to shoot through, but now Steve could see me, too. I was doing okay, with my feet still braced, when a sudden turn had me crashing sideways, into my right arm. I shrieked, hand spasming, and lost my grip on the rifle.

It slid under a seat, out towards the back. It bounced part way over my leg and I lunged for it, swearing. I missed and I *knew,* with every fiber of my being, that it was gone. A hand shot out from the last seat in the bus and snagged the strap just before the rifle slid out the door. A young (they were all young), frightened (we were all frightened) face peered at me, and the blonde girl passed the rifle to me, giving me a small smile. I grimaced back and should have kept that to myself as she just gave me a strange look and pulled away, pressing herself into as small a bundle as she could manage again.

I re-looped the strap around my arm and aimed for the grille as the truck rounded the corner after us. The harsh sound of large caliber bullets tearing through the side of the bus got my attention next, and I struggled to see out the side window. The bastards behind us took advantage of my distraction, obliging me to flop to the floor, sucking in my stomach, thinking *flat,* and hoping to avoid getting shot.

Well, until a shrieked "Mommy!" filled the bus.

"No!" I howled, sitting back up, firing wilding out the door, forcing Steve to slow slightly.

All the wild gyrations became too much for the beleaguered door and it gave way, bouncing merrily down the road. The truck had to swerve abruptly to avoid it, and for a split second I had a chance to shoot without fear of being hit. I put four bullets directly into their grille. Within seconds, the truck slewed to the side, nearly throwing the gunman on the back from his perch as the engine, already under extreme pressure and heat, gave up, all the little moving bits fusing together.

Now that my immediate problems were solved, I had the attention to notice the shots being fired at the front of the bus and to realize I still heard children sobbing. I chanced a quick look over my shoulder and saw Alex and our soldier at either side of the front, firing steadily. Alex passed over a grenade and fished out another for herself. It finally dawned on me that the last turn we'd taken had brought us onto the 99. Between us, I could see a cluster of people, and from the center of that, two little girls, crying.

Two booms, the concussive forces rocking the bus, let me know the women had thrown. I just hoped they'd been accurate. I peered out the back door, but the only vehicle currently on our tail was far enough back that I could take a minute. I twisted around and began a slow crawl up the aisle to check on Leo. My right arm didn't want to support my weight and I limped heavily, my knees taking a bruising as we bounced over the road.

The spokeswoman was in the center of the small cluster, and when she saw me, she shook her head silently. Leo was gone.

I slumped back closing my eyes and slamming my left hand onto the floor. Trying to pound out my guilt and rage. Trying not to scream. Two dead already. Someone shifted in the seat I leaned against, bringing me back to my senses.

Breathe.

Just breathe.

After a few moments I opened my eyes. A quick swipe of my sleeve over my face and I was ready to pretend again. We didn't have time for anyone to fall apart now. As I looked up, I made eye contact with the spokeswoman. The woman who obviously acted as a mother to all the girls under her care.

She cradled Moana, and another girl, the Latina, had Cub. Those two were right in the middle of everything.

The spokeswoman nodded firmly, never breaking eye contact. Giving me silent encouragement. I'd known her less than an hour, and I already knew, to my bones, that she's a rock to everyone around her. A calm, quiet, utter badass.

Screaming from the front got me moving, and everything was soon drowned out by a crash and screeching metal as we barreled through the gate and tore it from its hinges. Seconds. If we'd evaded them for a few seconds more, Leo would still be alive.

We shot down the road, leaving the gates as nothing more than wreckage in our wake. I hoped it took Steve time to replace them, and that people heard about the broken gates in the city—a breath of hope, of freedom, wafting through the fetid air.

Yeah, that didn't last long.

"Behind us!" cried a girl in the back. I turned towards the door and saw the blonde chick who'd caught the rifle before I lost it. She pointed frantically toward the city, rapidly falling away behind us.

What wasn't falling away were three Hummers and two of those massive road tanks. Not only were they not receding, they were *gaining*.

My heart sank back into my boots. "We got company!" I bellowed.

"Fuckfuckfuckfuckfuckfuck!" Alex turned the air blue with one simple word.

The soldier paled but grit her teeth and ejected the magazine to check how many shots she had left. Not enough, naturally.

"Got it out of your system?" I asked Alex cheerfully. "Take this." I shoved my rifle at her. "Get back there and slow them down. Maybe use a grenade, too, if you think. You've got the last of them."

"Not quite." Son, who'd been eavesdropping, interjected. "Here." She passed me a handgun, a spare magazine for the handgun, then, like a magician, she withdrew a landmine from under her shirt with a little flourish.

"How the hell did we not explode?" I asked the air as I took the landmine from her gingerly and passed it to Alex.

Alex grinned, the light of a pyromaniac shining in her eyes as she carefully scooched to the back of the bus on her ass and took up a position with a foot on either side of the open door, like I'd done.

"Aim for the grille," I shouted at her. Without bothering to reply, she began carefully picking her shots, aiming low down at the engine and tires.

I turned back to find the soldier watching me attentively. "Orders, sir?"

"I ain't army, you know. Keep an eye on the front, make sure Steve isn't surrounding us. I just gotta borrow this," I held up the handgun, "for a sec, then you can have it. Need to call the kids."

"Is that code for 'help'?" the soldier asked hopefully.

"No? Kinda? You'll see." I stepped to the front door and fired three carefully spaced shots, waited a moment, then fired three more. That's the backcountry signal for "help," which we'd decided to use for "shit's happening." Hopefully the kids were ready.

There's something to be said for boredom, because no sooner did the nursery's sign come into view than my old GMC came roaring out. The kids saw me hanging out the door and pulled level with us. Jaali bounced happily and waved from the passenger seat. Asilia had a look of grim concentration on her face, though she spared a moment to smile at me.

The smile turned quickly to shock when she saw the condition of the bus, and the extra people in it. Her eyes widened and she visibly drooped when she followed the finger I pointed behind us. Asilia punched Jaali, probably telling him to settle down, though it took a few moments longer for him to get Obelix calm.

Asilia rolled down her window, and before she could say anything, I jumped in. "No names! Don't use any names! I'll explain later!"

"What do you need?" the girl asked without hesitation. I felt a surge of pride. Most people would've asked a million questions and completely ignored the fact that we were in danger of death in favor of having an explanation. Not this kid. She had her priorities straight.

"Pull up a bit more." I leaned out farther so she could hear me. "I'm gonna jump in the back." *Like an idiot.* "We need the machine gun and our rifles and spare mags."

Asilia pulled forward, edging closer to the bus. There was some canvass-y looking stuff back there. I hoped it'd cushion me "Where's Cin?" I screamed to be heard over the wind as I belatedly remembered the old dog.

"Sleeping in the back!" Asilia shouted, jerking a thumb over her shoulder.

I stretched up and could barely make him out, hidden under a pile of canvas stuff, tucked into the corner closest to me. No worries, then, I shouldn't land on him. I licked my dry lips and tried to pretend I wasn't staring at the asphalt as it whizzed by barely a foot away from my feet. I crouched, preparing to jump. Sweat dripped between my breasts, my worn underwear chafed the creases of my inner thighs, and my right arm screamed as the muscles bunched, readying myself for the leap.

I told myself I was a second away from jumping, but that's almost certainly a lie. Before I could get to the point of realizing I wasn't going anywhere, the bus jerked to the side, nearly flinging me from the steps.

"What the *hell?*" I shrieked.

Sonya was sweating freely in the cold air. "The tank nearly had us in their sights! We don't have time for you to nerve yourself up! JUST DO IT!" The last was a roar that carried over everything. The crying from the middle of the bus, the rifle reports from the rear, the straining engines, all died in the force of her shout.

"I hate you," I shouted, and jumped on the last word, tucking my knees to my chest.

My feet clipped the side of the truck bed, spilling me across the stuff in the back in an undignified heap. I blessedly landed on my left side, the ribbed bottom dragging across my shoulder and hip as I skidded across, slamming my head and shoulders against the opposite wheel well. Before I had a chance to recover, something warm landed heavily on top of me.

A strangled scream escaped as my right arm took the brunt of it. *Thank God we're not a hemophiliac*, I thought dimly, *I think we're still bleeding.* I shoved back hard and was rewarded with a pained grunt. The thing that'd landed on me was a person. Our soldier, in fact.

"What the hell you doin' here?" I struggled to my knees, using the machine gun's stand as a crutch. "I told you to watch the front."

The soldier looked at me, unrepentant brown eyes mere inches away. "Your trigger-happy friend can do that. There should be at least two people guarding our rear." She nodded to the gun as she found her feet. "One for that, one to act as a sniper."

I sighed and rolled my eyes. "Make yourself useful then, and get the boy to pass us some ammo."

Asilia was already dropping back, cutting to the left so we were behind the bus. Alex waved at us then moved to the front of the bus.

"What do I call you?" the soldier shouted. "It would really help if you had a name!"

"Tweedle-dee," I yelled back, getting the machine gun unhooked and loaded.

"What?"

"Tweedle-dee," I repeated.

"I can't call the person who broke us out of a North Korean brothel 'Tweedle-dee!'"

"This name was given to me by a very nice lady," I said huffily, lining up the sights on the first vehicle in line, a Hummer. "And while she was not my mother, what does that currently matter? What should I call you?" I pulled the trigger, absorbing the recoil as I swayed with the little truck.

The lead Hummer slewed sideways to avoid me, opening up an opportunity to shoot at the guy behind.

"Call me Seahorse," the soldier said, after much consideration, as she knelt, braced and began picking shots.

"Seahorse?" I turned my head to see if she was serious.

"I like 'em," she said simply. I pursed my lips and shrugged. Okay then. "That's how you pick a name," Seahorse threw me a quick grin, dark eyes dancing merrily.

Tweedle-dee and Seahorse. Seahorse and Tweedle-dee. There should be a punchline in there somewhere. I went back to firing at the enemy.

CHAPTER 15

Sonya continued north for as short a time as she was able, taking the first road to the right, trying to give us some space and freedom from Steve's return fire. The tanks fell behind, but not as far as I'd hoped. Those metal monstrosities could move.

Son took another right, the northern turn taking us away barely before we were cut to ribbons. Each time, Asilia followed as close and precise as if we were being towed by the yellow school bus, even down to sliding off the asphalt and onto the verge, causing me to jostle the machine gun. The first few times it happened I sprayed bullets into the air, trees, even the ground, kicking up mud and gravel. Once I got the hang of it, I managed to get my finger off the trigger in time to stop wasting precious ammunition.

Steve disappeared behind a corner and I tried to swallow, my tongue sticking to my teeth. Those few mouthfuls of water at breakfast now seemed like they'd happened in another century. My mouth got a whole lot dryer when we hit a straight stretch and I found myself looking into the barrels of Steve's guns.

I kept pulling my own trigger gently, taking deep, deliberate breaths, exhaling hard enough to move the scarf over my mouth, trying to keep from fainting and doing as much as I could to hide behind a skinny stand and an entirely-too-small gun. Seahorse pounded on the cab, screaming at Asilia to dodge *right now*.

We swayed heavily as Asilia swung the wheel frantically trying to keep us alive when a high-pitched voice caught our attention. "Here!"

I twisted my head to see what was going on and barely retained the presence of mind to turn *only* my head and not everything else, too. Jaali held a rifle out the window to Seahorse. It looked like...my rifle?

Seahorse took it, delighted. "Where on earth did you guys get this? For that matter, where did you get any of this? I thought all the guns were turned into paper clips."

"Ah, you know our government. Never throw away anything that might someday be used to kill someone or rob them." I took advantage of the narrowing road to concentrate my fire. Bastards couldn't avoid me now.

I whooped when the lead Hummer began steaming, then smoking, and slewed to a stop. Steve got out and ran around, frantically trying to open the hood and check their engine. I took advantage of the lull by grabbing more boxes of ammunition and stacking them at my feet, then shook my head at Cin.

The old dog still snoozed against the cab. He'd looked up briefly when the shooting started, put his head back down and decided it was nothing to do with him.

I turned back to the gun, my elation dying abruptly as the next Hummer in line simply cut around the broken Hummer and the tanks muscled it out of the way, pushing it to the side of the road. The soldiers from the downed vehicle leaped onto the tanks as they passed. Seahorse fired, and the soldier manning their machine gun toppled, giving us a moment to breathe. I could barely make out the other Steves as they dragged the fallen man out of the way and put another in his place.

Seahorse turned her attention to the next man in line and grunted in satisfaction when he fell. "Just like shooting ducks at the county fair."

"We still have the truck and tanks to deal with," I said dryly.

"Ah, you're no fun."

We were forced to slow our fire when we hit a winding stretch of road. Steve had to slow even more. It seemed Oregon's windy roads were a natural defense for us, because Sonya and Asilia, well used to our roads, took the corners in the dark like they were competing in a cross country race.

Come to think of it, we were.

I took the time to take stock of my truck and the holes peppering her. It was worse, and better, than I expected. There were plenty of holes in my tailgate, a few low down on the cab, and more through the windows, but since nobody was screaming in the truck the kids must've been okay. Despite all the damage, she was still running. I cocked my head and listened, frowning. The engine was noisier than it had been. Bastards must've put a hole or three into my nearly-new muffler.

There was only so long we could keep running. We needed to slow them more. The lightbulb went off. "The landmine!" I turned to the soldier. "We need to tell the bus to drop the landmine. *Some* asshole should hit it."

After all, this is a narrow, winding road at night. Everybody's swerving all over the place. Yeah. My logic was working okay.

I hoped.

I continued to shoot anything that showed while Seahorse spoke to Asilia through the open window. Asilia stomped on the gas, and we slowly gained on the bus. Seahorse screamed for Alex to drop the landmine *carefully*. As we passed over the landmine, I saw the tail end of the torn fabric Alex used to lower the landmine to the road without setting it off. Stroke of genius, that. I probably would have dropped it and hoped for the best.

I could only hope the thing still worked. After all, Sonya's been carrying it for days, Alex dropped it out the back of a speeding bus, and it still hasn't exploded. I just hoped that if something *really* heavy, like, say, a *tank*, ran over it, something should go boom. And if it was a dud, well, our lives really couldn't get worse.

"Hold on!" Asilia screamed.

I crouched, spreading my feet and bending my knees while holding onto the gun's stand for dear life. I wasn't sure what to expect, but that girl screaming was never a good sign. I'd barely finished bracing when we screeched around a sharp right corner. I lurched and Seahorse slid, banging her shin awkwardly against the wheel well.

Barely a quarter mile down the new road, a huge ball of fire lit up the dark sky, silhouetting the trees that hid us from Steve's view. A moment after that, the *whumpf* of air reached us, a gust of hot wind rocking the trees and making them dance.

I whooped, punching the sky in triumph. Behind me, screams of victory erupted from the bus. I twisted around. The girls who'd been sullen, dazed, and afraid so recently were hugging each other, flipping off the fireball and generally showing so much more life. A couple of the girls were crying, hands covering their mouths as they stared at the fire dancing above the trees.

Seahorse reached up and slapped my leg enthusiastically. A short scream tore from me as a line of fire shot up my leg and through my hip.

"What the *fuck?*" I swore, jerking involuntarily as the leg gave way. Only my death grip on the gun stand kept me from falling and hurting it worse.

Seahorse scooted closer, gripping my ankle to hold me still while she examined my leg by the light of our boom. "Congratulations. You're missing a little bit of meat just above your knee. Not as much as your arm, at least. We'll need to go over everyone when we stop and make sure there's no other hidden injuries." She indicated her own side, and I saw the slowly spreading black stain.

I clumsily knelt next to her. I had no idea when that bullet nicked me, but now that I knew it, my leg and my arm were all I could feel. Dammit. As I dropped down, it also dawned on me that she only wore a pair of stolen pants and a flimsy negligee style top. Outside. At night. In winter.

"Well," I said, checking out her side, "you're so cold you're not bleeding as much as you could be. So that's probably a good thing. Lemme just..." I pounded on the roof of the cab. "Hey, kiddo! Can you pass us a blanket? Seahorse is freezing!" I turned back to the injured woman. "Anyway, this looks more like a deep graze. Or a hole that's not too far into your side. I hope there's nothing important behind there."

The soldier huffed a pained laugh. "Your bedside manner is terrible. And no, I don't think there's much important stuff back there. I think it's mostly fat right now. Can you—"

"Hey!" Jaali interrupted her. "Here's your blanket!"

I took it from him with thanks and wrapped the freezing woman up in it. "If we're lucky, soon you'll start to bleed like a normal person," I commented.

Seahorse needed liquids, rest, warmth, and soon. The biggest problem, we'd learned, was infection. No more readily available antibiotics. Well, no antibiotics at all, but... "Kiddo?" Jaali stuck his head out the window, the wind whipping through his curly hair. "Got a first-aid kit somewhere in there?"

While the boy rummaged through the packs, I locked the machine gun down. From here on out I'd be using my rifle. No sense wasting bullets we can't replace. I peered through the scope, checking out the glowing fire growing smaller with every spin of the tires.

"Hey! Help!" I turned to see Jaali hanging half out the window, waving a little red first-aid kit.

"Pass it here," I stretched back.

The boy shook his head, stubbornly refusing to hand it over. "You're watching the back. Besides, you need bandaging too, and someone should keep an eye on her." I could barely make the kid out in this light, but I knew the look on his face too well: big, pleading eyes begging to help. Something, anything to contribute. "Please?"

"Your mother will kill me." I shook my head. "Fine," I added, resigned. She'd have to catch me alive before she could kill me. At the rate we were going, I'd be lucky to last another month. I braced my knees and stomach against the corners and top of the truck bed and stretched forward, feeling the dampness in the wind numbing my face as I reached for the boy.

He pushed off from the seat and I grunted, feeling the weight of him as I pulled, straining to get him over the edge. One last heave...I groaned, the muscles in my stomach tightening as Jaali slithered over the side and into the safety of the bed.

"Weak," his teeth flashed white as he grinned. "Getting tired, are we? Nearly lost me there."

I sagged down, feeling like I'd just run a mile. "Piss off. I barely slept for three days. *Some* people need their sleep."

Jaali was already cleaning Seahorse's injury, clean pad and bandage laid out, waiting to be opened and used. "Or you're getting old," he suggested.

Jaali jumped a little when I fired two shots at a Hummer, forcing them to slow a little more. "Old?" I muttered under my breath. "I'll show you old."

Seahorse walked him through the steps for properly bandaging the wound, her voice tight with pain. She was the perfect assistant to her own case, passing him what he needed as he needed it. I cast my mind back, walking through the last few hours, trying to remember if anybody else had been hurt, and my heart stuttered over the thought.

We should probably see a doctor for our hinky heart, it's obviously not working right. I snorted softly. As if near-death on multiple occasions on one day wasn't enough reason to have weird heart rhythms. I caught a glimpse of something way back on our trail, but my eyes felt like they were full of sand, and I couldn't be sure what I'd seen was accurate.

"Ja—" I barely caught myself. "Kiddo, can you take a look at this?"

Jaali turned away from Seahorse, looking pleased with himself at the neat job he'd done. I made to pass the rifle so he could look through the scope, but he waved me away and pulled a small collapsible telescope, like the ones you see in pirate movies, out of his inner pocket. I couldn't see it, but I *knew* he had a shit-eating grin on his face.

That lil' shit.

Seahorse readjusted behind us, completely covering herself in the blanket with just her face peeking out. I shivered inside my layers, envious that her part in all this was done and she could rest.

"There's at least two more trucks back there," Jaali announced, pulling me back to the rather important present. "They've just passed the remaining tank."

"Remaining tank? You mean you think we blew up the other tank?" I grinned. That left one tank and two trucks. The next second I wanted to collapse where I sat and just sleep. All these changing emotions were exhausting.

"I only see one tank," the boy confirmed. He continued in a small voice, "They're chasing us a lot longer than I thought they would."

"They gotta make an example of us. Them soldiers been getting fat, thinking they're the only fish left. Now we come along and throw a rock into the works, messing up their roadblocks and shit." I grimaced. Those roadblocks were damn scary in hindsight. "Anyway, we made them look bad. Since there's more of us than them, they can't let us get ideas in our heads, like maybe we can beat them, if we work together."

I stopped and went over what I'd just said. My mouth had been on autopilot, throwing shit out without running it by any brain cells first, but even so, had I really just said we could beat a freaking army? I came to the reluctant conclusion that I had indeed. Fuck.

"Maybe," the boy sighed, an entirely too world-weary sound from him. "Did you manage to find our parents?"

"No. Sorry," I said gently. He looked down, stray curls blowing across his face before raising the telescope again and watching our back trail. I rubbed his back, hugging him to me.

"Too bad we don't have night-vision goggles," he said eventually. "We'd be able to turn the lights off and lose them."

"We'll turn 'em off when we hit gravel again." The asphalt proved too difficult to follow at any speed at night, but the gravel was a different matter. I looked up at the patchy clouds, assessing them. If the moon came out, maybe we could shut the lights off sooner.

The truck slowed, and I turned to see Son braking to make a turn. Her lights flashed over a sign: Scotts Mills. Asilia pulled up next to the bus, and I leaned on the cab to talk to my cousin.

"I need gas," Son said without preliminaries. "We're too low to get back. You guys?"

"The soldier's been hit in the side, but she's still alive. The kid bandaged her up. How are we on gas?" I asked Asilia.

"We just filled up a few days ago, so we're fine. But if we're hitting a gas station we may as well put in that half-gallon we just used." I could hear the excitement in the girl's voice. We'd outrun an enemy that'd been the stuff of our nightmares for two months, bloodied Goliath's nose.

I think she liked it.

"Right, then." I waved a tired hand at Son to lead the way. "Let's get on with it. Steve's still back there, and I'd like to sleep sometime tonight."

Five minutes later we were at the only gas station in town. When Son got out of the bus, she was immediately mobbed by Obelix, with Cin finally finding the interest to stand up and get her attention, too. She crooned to them, calming the puppy who'd been whining with anxiety.

Jaali and me got started on the pumps, and I was grateful that the little town was ancient. No automation here, so it only took us a few minutes to get the gas flowing. Asilia opened packs and passed out additional clothing and sleeping bags to the freezing girls. While Jaali filled the tanks, I helped Alex get Seahorse into the bus so she could lie down without having something digging into her.

"What's up with this?" I asked Asilia, fingering the tough fabric in the back of the truck.

"Oh, it's this shade cloth stuff we found in the nursery," Asilia replied. "Jaali got the idea to use it as camouflage for the truck. Worked, too. We had two patrols exit by that road, though only one has gone back, so far."

Dammit. There's another patrol floating around? I leaned against the truck and closed my eyes just for a moment. The ground rolled under my feet. My eyes snapped open, and I clutched the side of the truck only to realize that the ground hadn't moved. I shook my head, trying to rid myself of the sensation, but it refused to leave.

"Blood loss." I looked up, my head weighing heavily on my neck to see the spokeswoman standing next to me, holding a first aid kit.

"What?"

"That swaying sensation?" The woman checked my arm. "That's blood loss. Drink some water. You need to stay hydrated. I'm Eleanor Rey—"

"Don't tell me that!" I exclaimed, flinging up a hand in a lame attempt to shield myself. A few short days and I already felt allergic to knowing anybody's name.

"Reynolds," she repeated deliberately, with a hint of bitterness. "The only reason we say don't use names is if you have people to protect. All the people I need to protect are right there." She tipped her head indicating two girls. One was the Latina who'd done the first bandage job on my arm. The other was the blonde who'd caught my rifle. The blonde carefully eased the battered Latina into some warmer clothes, helping the other girl pull them on over dark bruises.

"How *did* you end up being a brothel madam?" I asked, too tired for tact. "And is everybody branded? What is it?"

Eleanor's lips compressed as she knelt down to check out my leg. Jaali passed me the nozzle for the gas pump, and I shifted to fill the tank while Eleanor worked on me.

Eventually the woman looked up at me with scraped-together dignity. "Yes, we've all been branded. And it wasn't by choice, I can assure you of that. I tried to protect the girls, and when I couldn't do that, I could at least tend to them. Bind their hurts."

Eleanor stood wearily, brushing dust from the knees of her skirts and faced me squarely. "My daughter saw fit to join the enemy, and her entry into those ranks involved putting myself and her two best friends into that hell-hole." Tears shone in her eyes as she made the admission, the patchy moonlight reflecting there.

The girls, seeing Eleanor's distress, came to stand beside her, the blonde helping the other. The Latina's head wobbled with weariness, but they stood there, daring me to say something about Eleanor.

"Good enough," I sighed, unhooking the nozzle. "Welcome. You've just stepped from the frying pan into the fire."

"That's it?" Eleanor leaned in, trying to see me clearly. "Maybe you're feeling worse than I thought. How many fingers am I holding up?" She held up three fingers.

"All I need to know about you, they showed me," I nodded to the teens. "Whatever. Welcome to the rebellion."

Name it. Own it. The words Mary had spoken just a few days ago echoed in my head. I closed my eyes for a moment, enjoying the sweet relief of pretending I could find oblivion. When I opened them again, Eleanor and the teenagers had gone.

Chapter 16

Son started shuffling everyone back into the vehicles, and I clambered back into the bed of my pickup truck. Alex elected to join me, first collecting her own rifle from the stash in the cab. I snorted, watching Son's dogs follow her into the bus. Over the rumble of the truck's engine, the sound of the girls exclaiming and cooing over them came clearly, and I knew those dogs would be the most comfortable out of the lot of us.

"You okay?" I asked Alex once we got going.

"Not even a graze," she boasted.

"Good." I kept my eyes on the road, staring into darkness with my rifle cradled in my arms. We rocked as Asilia swerved around a pothole. "That means you got two good arms, because you're on added duties until I say when. And," I turned on her, and she shrank back, startled by my sudden rage, "if you pull any of that shit again, running in without a damn clue, I will fucking shoot you myself, got it?"

I faced the road again, breathing deeply, clenching my jaw until my teeth hurt and trying to get myself under control. Alex stared fixedly into the night. I hoped she was thinking, damn it. I had neither the time nor the energy to watch her constantly.

A tiny sob escaped her. As if that was the feather, her shoulders began shaking as she cried silently. "Leo and-and that other girl...That was my fault, wasn't it?"

I sighed and awkwardly reached out with my injured arm to hug her. "No. If Steve had never shown up, they'd've been fine. All I do know for certain is that if we hadn't been along, none of them would ever have made it out. So let's look at the ones who now have a chance to go through some PTSD. We can't change the past."

"I'm sorry," Alex mumbled through her tears. "I was an idiot." She took a deep, shuddering breath. "I'm—I'm—I don't know!"

"I know," I whispered. *I know.*

***

"So," I said conversationally about ten minutes later. Alex startled beside me, surreptitiously wiping her eyes. "You think you can do anything about those lights following us?"

She sighted down her scope, checking out the distance. "Moving targets, from a moving platform, at night? You're cracked, but what the hell." Alex rapped on the window.

Jaali, riding shotgun, rolled his window down and stuck his curly head out. "What? I was about to take a nap!"

"Tell Asilia to keep her steady. I'm gonna try to slow down our friends back there."

"Gotcha!"

"Hey," I interrupted. "Any chance we can go dark yet?"

"Waiting for the moon," Jaali reported. "We've got snaking roads ahead."

"Better get shooting, then." Alex sighed. She moved to her knees, bracing herself and trying to keep the muzzle steady. "Shit!" she cussed as we turned a corner. "Can you—?" She gestured in front of her. She wanted to use my body as a brace to keep the gun steady.

I exhaled heavily. "Yep." I didn't bother keeping the resignation out and settled myself in front of her. I gripped the tailgate to keep myself steady and braced.

"Here." Alex thrust something into my view. "Use this." It was a pair of earplugs.

"Yippee," I grumbled, stuffing them into my ears. I might actually be able to hear once this was done. Maybe.

It took an effort of will to keep my shoulders loose and prevent them from scrunching up and bringing the muzzle closer to my ear. I closed my eyes and took deep breaths through my nose, clenching my stomach and hands, trying to ready myself for the boom. I could imagine Alex's face, set in concentration, waiting for the right opportunity.

The rifle exploded, and I jerked involuntarily, my head ringing from the sound. I looked, but the lights were still following.

"You missed," I said. I think I said. I could barely hear anything.

Alex's face appeared as a pale blob in my view as she pulled me around, and she yanked an earplug out. I heard *human*, *ice*, and *person* for sure, though I think there was more to the sentence than that. I gave her a thumbs up for lack of a better idea. It must've been the right thing because she turned me around again and put that damn rifle back on my shoulder.

I kept my eyes open this time, watching the lights carefully. This shot didn't hurt so much. Perks of being half-deaf before you start.

"You still missed." I *felt* my mouth moving, I just couldn't tell if it came out at any volume. Alex merely patted my head and re-positioned the rifle.

This time, she fired twice in quick succession, adjusting her aim slightly in between. The lights of the tank vanished in a small shower of sparks. I grinned. That woman was a royal pain in my ass, but she could shoot.

A Hummer now pulled in front to lead the way. *Nice, narrow, windy roads...* I twisted so she could hear me. "Betcha a can of peaches you can't do it again."

She stuck a hand in front of my face, thumb up. A silent "I'll take your bet." Alex pressed firmly on my shoulder, telling me to stay still. This time she targeted the rear Hummer, taking the opportunity to liberally pepper the space between the lights as well. I snatched up my scope and whooped at the sight that met my eyes. The front grille had a pretty little hole punched in it, and I didn't have to imagine the steam whitening the air from the damaged radiator.

"If you can take out the front one too, I'll even consider shortening your cooking and cleaning punishment." My lips moved, I felt the vibrations in my throat, but not a hint of sound made it through the dead silence weighing my ears. I pushed down a breath of fear.

Either I was deaf, or I wasn't. Worrying wouldn't change anything.

Her teeth flashed whitely, and she nodded vigorously. Looking past her, I could make out some faces visible through the back door of the bus, and judging by their wildly gesticulating arms and open mouths, they were either encouraging Alex or trashing Steve. Or both.

Stay still, Alex mouthed to me. *Don't move until I say.* She rapped on the roof of the truck, and a moment later we came to a full halt. I braced myself, tensing. The muzzle appeared over my shoulder, and Alex waited.

The convoy passed a tiny break in the trees before disappearing again. Then another. Still, she waited. Finally, I spotted what she waited for. The lead truck rounded a sharp bend, leaving it unobstructed. Alex fired rapidly, the short time between shots telling me she must be holding the bullets in an easy to grab place, like her mouth.

The truck slowed abruptly, unable to maintain its uphill momentum any longer, causing a traffic jam behind it. Alex pounded my back in jubilation, and I took that to mean I could move now. Rolling to my left to avoid the hot muzzle, I turned and gained my feet.

The bus had stopped a few yards ahead, waiting for us. Girls crowded the windows and door, waving, mouths open. Screaming, presumably.

"Quiet!" I said, feeling a strain on my throat. "Lights off, and quiet! Now's the time to lose them. We need to move out!"

Alex stepped up next to me, and I could see her mouth moving, steam gusting from her mouth as she yelled. Guess I wasn't very loud, then. She got people settled down, and within a minute we were driving away using nothing more than moonlight and the contrast of road and bushes to guide us.

***

I was huddling and half frozen in the truck bed in the early hours of the morning when the truck lurched suddenly. The clouds had come back, blocking the moon, but not before we'd managed to get ourselves thoroughly lost. I'd breathed a sigh of relief when Son announced she didn't know where we were anymore.

Jaali, who'd been helping by being Son's night vision, directed her to a side track that ended in a small clearing. As the vehicles were shut down, we could hear a stream burbling close by (yeah, my hearing returned) and smell the pine trees that surrounded us, deep as we were in the Cascades.

Alex had to help me out of the truck. The hours spent in the cold, hard bed had stiffened everything, and I could barely move. I was dying for the chance to lie down on a surface that didn't move, preferably with a blanket, though that wasn't a requirement.

"What'll we do if it starts raining?" Alex asked, giving the sky worried looks.

"Doubt it'll be a problem," I mumbled. "Too cold to rain. More likely we'll get snow."

"As if that's better!" The woman looked at me, alarmed.

"Not wet. Snow can act as insulation, keep us warmer. Worst comes to it, we'll load everyone into the bus." I could barely form sentences, and as soon as I got both feet on the ground, I forgot what we were talking about and stumped off to gather firewood.

We couldn't have a big fire, but maybe enough to heat some water. I shrugged, trying to loosen muscles, and the bandage on my arm pulled against the scab that'd formed and I winced. Straightening to take my load back to camp, I groaned.

"Will you quit creaking and groaning in the dark, oh fearless leader?" Son said sharply, taking my burden from me.

"Piss off."

"Well, at least now I know you're not dying on me."

"I wish I was. Might not hurt so damn much."

She pointed sternly back towards the cars. "You can get your ass back there and sit down before you fall down and I have to drag your sorry carcass back."

"Fine," I grumped, limping in the direction she pointed, still carrying my load. "See if any of the others have got the energy left to lend a hand gathering more sticks. We need enough for—"

"Yeah, yeah, I know the drill." She put a hand between my shoulder blades to keep me going.

Back in the clearing, she directed a girl to drop my pack wherever and for me to "siddown" while she kept going to the bus. She returned shortly, carrying an exhausted Cub and leading Moana. "Here." She set Cub down in my lap and helped Moana curl up next to me. "This is a job you can do sitting down. Keep 'em company."

Gingerly, I settled Cub on my good leg. She buried her face against my shoulder, and a fatigued mewling issuing unabated, one icy little hand clutching my collar. My right arm made it awkward, but I unzipped my jacket and did my best to tuck both kids inside.

Eleanor saw me trying to help the kids and left starting the fire to Alex to collect a blanket, bringing it over. "Here." She shook it out, spreading it over us. "We took some blankets out of that place."

"Thanks." We readjusted Moana, tucking some of the blanket under her and me so we weren't in direct contact with the bare ground. The little girl burrowed underneath it, pressing her head against my side. There, in the safety of darkness, she finally let her tears flow. Her narrow shoulders shook as she sobbed, tears wetting my sweatshirt.

Alex soon had a small fire going, using bits of dried moss, pinecones, and slivers of wood we'd picked up every time we went out, gathered against such a time as this. A small pot of water soon steamed nicely, and Sonya and Jaali were working with the able-bodied girls to string up the large pieces of heavy cloth the kids had found at the nursery.

Seahorse had been carefully placed on blankets near the fire, the Latina tending her as the young woman was also unable to move easily. She had more bruises than the rest of the girls we'd rescued, poor kid.

A lovely aroma drifted through the air as Alex skewered the rabbits the kids had caught and got them roasting over the flames next to the pot. Slowly, as jobs were finished, women trailed in, dressed as warmly as we were able to provide, and settled in. Food was passed around, and people ate like they'd never seen food before.

I sighed and settled against my pack, cold quickly seeping into my butt, two warm spots on my chest and side from where the girls now slept the deep, immovable sleep of the grief stricken.

"So." Eleanor was the first to speak after many long minutes, talking as she carefully cleaned Seahorse's side. "We need to call everyone something. All of my girls," she indicated the women we'd rescued, "had names given to them by the soldiers, and I think I can speak for them when I say we'd rather not keep them."

There were nods and murmurs of assent from around the fire.

"I was wondering." I stretched my neck carefully. "How important is the name thing?"

Eleanor gave me a bleak look. "There was a situation, about a month ago, where a young man was pressing his attentions on a girl. She refused him, and he went to the soldiers and told them that her father was trying to undermine their rule. It was a lie, but they took him in for questioning. Let's just say that torture makes people say whatever they can to stop the pain. He told them whatever they wanted to hear. His daughter and several girls from named families were sent to brothels. That's how I heard about it." She paused a moment, staring off into space before shaking out of it. "The moral of the story is that everyone breaks under torture, and you will give them every name you know. But if you don't know any names..."

I pursed my lips, trying not to show how badly that scared me. "So, it's important, then," I said with false levity.

"Maybe." Eleanor leaned her forearms on her knees to keep her hands steady. "After we've got names for everyone, then we can talk a bit more about who we all are, and you can tell us what's going on, how you managed to get all this equipment, and where on earth you found guns!" Seahorse gasped as Eleanor got too rough in her agitation, and Eleanor halted immediately, pressing the back of her hand to her mouth in horror.

"It's all right," Seahorse reassured her quietly. "Everything's just swollen. I'm fine. You didn't hurt me, okay?"

"So, names?" Jaali, as always, talking with his mouth full.

"Heh. Yeah." I tried wriggling a hand free, couldn't, and settled for indicating my cousin with my chin. "I got something to call you."

"Can't call me something bad," Sonya said promptly. "There's little ones around, so nyeh!" She stuck her tongue out at me.

"Gonna call you Sirius," I told her.

"Serious?" echoed several people, puzzled and incredulous.

"No," I explained. "Sirius, as in the Dog Star." I spelled the name for them. "Think *Harry Potter.*"

Son thought about it for a moment. "I can live with that." She shrugged, passing on the canteen.

"I'm Seahorse," Seahorse informed the group. "I like them," she added defensively.

"That one," I indicated Jaali, "you're smart, wily, and a lil' shit. That, in my books, makes you Anansi. He's an African trickster god. Or he is in a fictional novel."

"I'm a god!" the boy said, delighted.

"You're a pain in the ass," I told him, and he just laughed.

"We should call her something to do with driving," Alex said of Asilia. "She's good, and damn scary at it."

"Dereva," Jaali said, rolling the *r.*

"Say what?"

"Dereva," Jaali repeated. "It literally means 'driver' in Swahili. Mom taught us how to speak it," he explained, a slight quaver to his voice.

"How about 'crazy driver'?" Sonya, I mean *Sirius,* asked.

The boy thought about it. "Too many words. You'll have a hard enough time with this."

"Dereva," I repeated it to myself, but no matter how hard I tried, I couldn't say it like Jaal—*Anansi*—did.

"What about me?" Alex asked, a hint of trepidation audible to those who knew her.

"Phoenix." I sighed. "The firebird reborn from the ashes."

"I—Oh." Alex sat back, surprised.

"That's—that's really cool," the blonde from earlier said, staring moodily into the flames, dinner forgotten. "I want to be called Storm," she said abruptly. The fire displayed her fine, delicate features, slightly tilted eyes, and full lips. In short, I couldn't imagine anyone looking less like a storm.

"Storm?" asked Eleanor, looking up from the contusions she was examining on the Latina.

"Yes!" she cried. "They're free! They can't be caught, locked up, or caged. You can admire them, but you can't hurt them."

"Fuuuck," Son—dammit, Sirius!—murmured to me.

"She's beautiful," I whispered back. "I always figured we were lucky for being plain."

"Amen," she breathed, watching the girl.

Eleanor looked down at her hands, bloodied and clenched into fists, a look of pain and understanding on her face. She nodded, shoulders slumping in defeat. "You always did have to deal with that," she said quietly. "How about you?" she asked her other foster daughter.

"Amanacer," she said. "It means 'dawn.'"

I said it a few times. "I guess I can get used to it. Is there a nickname we can give you?"

She gave it serious thought. "Aman, or Amana."

"We can do that." Alex nodded. "I want to ask why," she added, smiling, "but if we did that, we'd never actually name anybody, would we?"

"Also," Amana added, "I will no' fight. I 'ave 'ad *suficiente violencia para mi*." She paused, looking at our confusion, and sighed. "I will no' contribute to *violencia*. I will 'elp 'ow I can, but no' fighting."

Several of the girls looked outraged, protesting and calling her a coward. Storm surged to her friend's defense, denying them hotly. Sirius and Alex began struggling to their feet, but we'd been going full-bore for nearly twenty-four hours on minimal sleep and food for days before that, and I was afraid they'd be too slow.

This was the typical catfight that most people expected when they imagined a group of women trying to work together. I'd always thought we'd do better, but here we were, less than a day of freedom, and it looked like we'd be torn apart before long. I didn't know whether I should laugh or cry, so I found a third option.

"ENOUGH!" I bellowed, startling the children, who began a thin, wailing cry. Alex—*fuckin' Phoenix,* I corrected myself—came over and took Moana, cuddling and whispering to her. This left me with two hands to hold Cub. As soon as the girls realized no one was angry with them, and that they were safe, they fell back into an exhausted sleep.

I glared around the circle, making a point to look at each and every one of them, staring them into silence. "If she don't want to fight, she don't have to," I said firmly. "She's already proved she's a badass, bandaging people up in the middle of a damn car chase. There's a ton of jobs to be done and picking up a gun is only a tiny part of it. I'll not force anyone to fight." *They'd be unreliable, anyway,* I added privately.

"But—" a lovely brunette protested weakly.

"Can it," I snapped. "How would you feel if I forced you to do work you didn't want? Oh, wait, you already know! I could go on, but you'll figure it out in time."

I readjusted the sleeping baby in my arms, hoping no one could hear my heart pounding. I hated speaking in front of people, and having to yell at a group of strangers felt weird.

Amana nodded thanks, with calm serenity, seemingly unperturbed by the vitriol aimed her way. Then again, from the looks of her, she'd been dealt harder blows than opinions.

The other's names came together quickly after that, Eleanor providing suggestions where needed: Fox, for the young redhead; River, for a quiet woman a couple years older than me who had the look of an old soul; Kestrel, of a similar age to River, who had hair the same brown-gold as her namesake, and expressed a desire to fly; Jewel (I rolled my eyes at the presumptuousness of it, but whatever), the girl with black hair who'd tried arguing with me; and Hightide, a girl in her late teens with a smidge of Native blood who'd grown up with her uncle's tribe near the coast.

Choosing names was rather more emotional than I'd have thought it would be and took longer than anybody cared for. By the time we were done, I slumped, limp as a wrung-out dishrag, and I could see the others weren't any better off. Except our Anansi. That boy could get hyper on air.

Seahorse had long since passed out, and Eleanor and Amana had taken care of most of the injuries. Eleanor just started on my leg, though, so sleep for us would have to wait a bit longer.

"Wait!" the newly-named Dereva said abruptly to me. "You don't have a name yet!"

"Sure I do," I mumbled, breathing deeply against the pain of Eleanor's work, "I'm Tweedle-dee. Those were good sweatshirts, you know," I said to Amana as she began cutting away my clothes to get to my arm.

"Now dey are good rags," she said serenely. "'old still."

I couldn't stop myself from twitching as the two of them bathed my cuts, getting out the bits of debris that'd been rubbed in after hours of ignoring it. Before too long I was biting my lip and scrunching my eyes shut, vaguely aware of the conversation around me.

"Nuh-uh." Storm shook her head. "No way do we have someone named 'Tweedle-dee' in the group."

"Our leader, no less," Sirius said helpfully.

"Who said I'm leading?" I grunted. I indicated Seahorse, who'd come out of her doze. "We got an honest to goodness soldier right there."

"Seems to me like you already are." Seahorse smiled wanly. "I can't believe you dislike me so much so soon that you want to saddle me with this lot. Besides," she added, "you'd probably go nuts watching somebody else botch a job you've been doing well enough on."

"'Well enough?'" I laughed shortly, tipping my head back. *Two people died today,* the words hovered on the tip of my tongue. Looking at the building hope, I swallowed them back. I sighed, shoulders slumping, resignation and exhaustion bowing my head.

"Most of us made it out, and you've been free since the beginning," Eleanor said gently. "If not you, then who?"

Who, indeed? I sighed again. "This can't be one hundred percent a democracy, you know."

"We'll work that out as we go." Eleanor smiled, tying the bandage at last, and I relaxed at the lessening of pain. "Now, we need to find you a name."

Suggestions were thrown out wildly, mostly from my ever-loving cousin and Phoenix, ranging from Rock to Eagle to Chicken-Wings (that one was all my cousin).

"All right, all right." Eleanor patted the air with one hand, settling them down. *About damn time.* "We all need our sleep, and we'll learn more about each other over time, but I really think everybody should have a name before we turn in for the night. Serious options only, ladies."

Seahorse, who'd been silent during the earlier hilarity looked thoughtful. "I was thinking we could call her Captain."

"I told you, we're not an army," I protested.

"No," she replied calmly, "but we're planning on fighting, right? Which means military, or at least militia. Which means a command structure. That means you. And it might help confuse the enemy."

I yawned, wanting it to just be over so I could go to sleep. "Anything that confuses Steve is a bonus."

"Who's Steve?" three voices asked at once.

Sirius giggled sleepily. "The North Koreans. We heard it and thought it was funny."

"Any objections to her name or her being the leader?" Eleanor asked.

There were none, probably because everyone just wanted to sleep. Sirius' pup, Obelix, would be the main watch this night, and thank God for the little guy's ears and nose. Before sleeping, I struggled upright, pulling off my boots and socks to check my feet.

Ever since our escape and the mess my feet had become, we'd made it a thing to regularly check our feet. Being in Salem, we'd ignored that, but sweat and the cold had gotten me worried. Son, at some point, had had the presence of mind to ransack her mom's medicine cabinet, which, fortunately for me, included antibiotics. I probably would've gotten an infection that first week if not for that one small act. It wasn't a performance I cared to repeat.

After pulling on another pair of socks, I finally fell into oblivion.

Chapter 17

"Ssssst! Hey, wake up!"

I lifted my head, blearily aware of someone talking near me, then a hand grabbed my injured arm and I roared awake as they squeezed my bullet graze wound. I lurched upright, snarling.

"What? Oh, sorry!" It was Sirius, snatching her hand back like she'd touched a hot pot.

I wondered irritably how long it would take me to get used to this whole "new names" thing. "Whaddaya want?" I mumbled, remembering to check next to me. I breathed out, relieved to see Cub still sleeping. "It can't be morning yet, can it?" I didn't feel like I'd been asleep more than a couple hours.

"It's not morning. It's snowing." She sounded like she couldn't decide between childish glee and concern, so instead she channeled both.

"Snowing? Cool." I flopped back down, already half asleep. "Oh, shit!" I shot back up. "Bad. Damn! You reckon it's gonna stop anytime soon?"

"Nope." Sirius sat back on her haunches. "We're about a thousand feet higher than normal, so we're screwed. It's wet snow at the moment, if that's any better."

Wet snow. Not dry. Slippery and treacherous. We might still have a chance to hide our tracks if we got moving. "Get everyone up and loaded. We're getting going while the getting's good."

Sirius moved quickly, shaking shoulders and nudging people awake. Not surprisingly, Eleanor woke immediately and quietly. Next to her, Seahorse was groggy, lethargic and running a fever, but conscious. Eleanor followed behind Sirius, helping calm the girls frightened by the sudden awakening. Sirius had to pull the sleeping bag off Jaali, earning herself dirty looks from Jewel and Kestrel. They probably thought Sirius was cruel.

"Why are we getting up?" Jewel asked.

"It's snowing," I said shortly, wrapping Cub in the blanket we'd shared and slowly climbing to my feet.

Sirius crisscrossed the camp hiding the decomposable remains of dinner, flinging bones into the bushes and tossing the cut ferns as far as she could. Phoenix chivvied the newly awakened, bundled in blankets, into the bus.

"So what?" Jewel complained. "What difference does it make?"

It took me longer to answer than normal, trying to shake life into my limbs, so Seahorse answered her before I could. "Get going!" she rasped. "You agreed last night that Captain was leading, which means doing as she says. So move!"

I adjusted Cub in my arms. "Reckon none of you know me well enough to take everything I say on face value—"

"Except, you know, the part where you *broke us out of Salem,*" Seahorse muttered sarcastically.

"—so we got enough time for me to explain," I finished quietly.

Jewel folded her arms and stared at me belligerently. I sighed. Why was it always the pretty ones who caused the most trouble? Even at the shop, I'd always get sneers and superior looks, and they didn't like dealing with me because I wouldn't give them discounts for having their tits hanging out. Come to think of it, only Jake gave discounts for that. I shifted the toddler uncomfortably. "We're leaving now in the hopes of making it back to our base before the snow gets too deep, so it'll cover our tracks. This way, we can disappear into thin air as far as Steve is concerned."

"It's a pretty good idea," Jewel said grudgingly.

"I'm glad you think so." If my tone got any drier, we'd be in a desert. "You haven't spent much time in forests, have you?"

"No."

"It shows." I turned and walked to the bus before I dropped the kid, leaving the girl staring after me.

***

I scratched idly at my cheek as we bumped cautiously down the track, following the bus's bright yellow behind. "Is there something on my face?" I asked Phoenix and Anansi, who rode in the back of the truck with me.

The boy peered at my face closely. "Ugh!" he said, halfway between curiosity and disgust. "You've got something on your shoulder. It's big. And ugly," he added.

"What?" I swiped frantically at my cheek, scratching, but I couldn't find anything.

"Oh." Anansi suddenly lost interest. "Never mind. It's just your head."

I tried. I really tried, but I burst out laughing. "You little shit!"

I ended up sitting on the floor, holding my sides, getting strange looks from Phoenix while Anansi grinned proudly. Twerp was living up to his name already.

"Seriously," I gasped a quarter of a mile later. "My cheek really does itch."

"Well," Phoenix said after a short evaluation, "you do have a rash. How'd you get that?"

I rolled to my side, slowly calming. "Must've been that blanket. I thought it felt like wool. Damned sensitive skin," I mumbled, more to myself than them. "Guess I was too tired to care." Wool always annoyed me so much I never kept it on for long.

Fan-fucking-tastic.

The truck bumped over the road, Dereva driving, Hightide riding shotgun. The two girls were of a similar age, and I could see Hightide's hands waving as she talked. River hung out the door of the bus as Sirius drove again, the girls huddled inside whilst freezing air blew around them.

The snow came down ever more thickly, and we were forced to slow to a crawl. Two days ago, I could've walked faster than this. The truck lurched as Dereva shifted it into four-wheel drive, causing those of us in the back to rock. We huddled together, with Jaali in between, but eventually the boy's shivering became too much. It wasn't so much the cold as the damp when the snow melted on our clothes.

"All right, Anansi," Phoenix muttered through clenched teeth, "you're making me feel cold. Time for you to get inside."

It was the space of a couple heartbeats to lower the boy over the side of the truck, and a quick jog took him to the bus. I could barely see their silhouettes as River gave him a hand into the bus. Me and Phoenix stayed in the back, beanies pulled firmly over our ears, hoods up, scarves wrapped around our faces, gloved hands firmly holding our rifles. The only good thing about it all was that the cold finally numbed my cheek enough that it no longer itched.

"Call me crazy," I said, muffled by my scarf, "but I'd swear that if it wasn't for being wet, it's warmer than last week."

"You are crazy," Phoenix answered, "because we *are* wet. And it's *damn* cold!"

The bus slowed even more, the tires unable to cope with the slushy ground, and it was taking everything Sirius had to stay on the track. In

Oregon it didn't rain but it poured, and it snowed the same way up here. Finally, Sirius stopped. We watched for a moment as she hopped out, searching around the sides of the bus.

"Whatcha lookin' for?" I asked, curiosity beating out the cold.

"Chains," she answered shortly, crawling under the bus. "Ow! Shit!" She wriggled out, sucking her thumb. "Bent the nail back," Sirius mumbled around the digit. "Stupid tires are nearly bald. Fucking budget cuts. Didn't have time to check everything."

"Anything useful down there?"

"No, dammit!" Frustrated, she pulled off her beanie, beating it against her leg. "Found a jack, but no spare tires and no chains. How are you guys doing? You need chains?"

"Nope," I said laconically and pointed down. "Got me some nearly new mud tires here. Don't need no chains. Though," I added, smiling and slightly abashed, "now that we're talking about it, I may have something buried in the box."

Sirius threw up her hands in exasperation, stomping over to throw open my tool box. She dug around in the back, muttering a stream of less than complimentary things about me.

I grinned and shrugged helplessly. "What can I say, getting shot, a new name, and freezing my ass off has made me a little forgetful."

Phoenix sniggered.

"How can you be laughing at a time like this?" Jewel angrily stuck her head out the back door of the bus. "People have died, we're stuck in the middle of nowhere, we're hoping we don't get caught and you three are making jokes?"

Phoenix, irritated by the shrillness, snapped. "What? Are we supposed to sit around crying all the time?"

I winced. Not the best way to handle that, maybe. "Look, kid…"

"I'm not a kid!" Jewel reached a higher pitch, if that were possible.

"No, guess not." I rubbed a hand down my face, pulling the scarf with it. "Jewel, if there's one thing we've managed to learn, it's that at times like this, when shit just keeps happening, you've only really got three ways of looking at this. You can either laugh, cry, or get angry. Ain't nothing to get angry at, crying's no good, so we might as well laugh. Later, when it's safe, we'll cry. Make any sense?"

"Well," she began snappily, and my heart sank. No good ever came from a sentence started like that. "We've got two little girls in here who've just lost their mother. The least you could do is show some sympathy!"

Save me from the self-righteous know-it-alls. I rolled my eyes. "I've got some understanding how those girls feel—"

"How could you be so insensitive as to say that!"

"Oh, for fuck's sake!" I snapped, holding onto my temper by a thread. "Shut up and listen to people for once! Everybody here has lost family and friends. I hate telling people to not be stupid, but dammit, stop being an idiot and use your brain for something other than being offended all the damn time! Now sit your ass down and contemplate the fact that there are people in this world beyond you."

Jewel retreated sullenly, lower lip poking out. Seahorse gave me a thumbs up through a broken window before sinking back down.

"How old do you think she is?" Alex muttered as we got the chains laid out.

I moved slowly but having my feet on solid ground let me finally stretch properly. My leg wasn't having to make constant adjustments.

"Three," Sirius volunteered.

"Three year olds got more brains," I replied. "I say seven."

"She's eighteen," Eleanor told us quietly. I hadn't even noticed her stepping out of the bus.

Phoenix rolled her eyes. "God, I hate it when people run around policing everybody's language and still behave like that."

"From what I've gathered, her parents were involved in everything from pro-life to animal cruelty," Eleanor said carefully. "I understand they were particularly against farmers."

"Oh, my God," I moaned as we stepped back to let Sirius drive onto the chains. "As if we didn't have enough problems with that type Before, we're saddled with one now."

"She hadn't yet been...used," Eleanor said delicately as we started buckling the chains on. I grunted as I tugged my side. The chains were barely large enough for the bus's tires, and it took two of us to put one on. "Tonight was supposed to have been her introduction, and, well, she has blinders on. I don't think it's sunk in yet, what the others went through."

"Will go through," I said quietly. "Phoenix is barely holding it together, even if she's been doing better since we got out of our...house. Acting against Steve has really helped, though we haven't had enough sleep to tell if it's done anything about the nightmares."

"Then we'll just have to make sure that they have a safe place, and we'll get some therapy sessions going." Eleanor stepped back, wiping her hands clean with snow. "Having others around who've experienced the same thing helps."

***

We were dead on our feet by the time we rolled into the bunker, but it was worth it. Snow filled in our tracks within an hour, and the knot of anxiety in my chest slowly unraveled. The women piling out of the bus looked so disheartened at the sight of our bunker that I couldn't help laughing a little.

Except Seahorse. She looked happy enough. Maybe she felt like she was coming home. Anansi raced to be the first to the door, throwing it open with a flourish and handing a lit candle to the first girl to reach it, Fox, bowing her in.

"Welcome to our super-cool hideout!" he announced.

Dereva hurried in, returning quickly with her arms full of sheets. While Anansi got the others inside and situated, Eleanor, Sirius, Dereva, Phoenix, and I got the two bodies wrapped, and we carefully carried them inside, laying them in the utility closet near the entrance.

Tomorrow, we'd dig the graves.

As the newbies saw how spacious the place was, they slowly brightened. Jaali, that little wonder worker, showed them to empty rooms that they could take and began collecting mattresses from the barracks.

"Clothes, kiddo!" I yelled down the hall towards the racket. "They need clothes!"

"Right!" his voice bounced back.

I rubbed my face, trying to get circulation going. "We'll need more toilets, too."

"Why don't you get the stove going?" Sirius suggested. "It's something you could actually handle." I flipped her off, and she continued. "We can't risk you getting an infection too, since we don't have enough antibiotics for you and her." She waved to where Seahorse was laid out on a couch in the common area.

"What do you mean, more toilets?" Eleanor asked, interest piqued.

The two of them walked down the hall, Sirius' hands moving as she told Eleanor what they were about. "We'll need to take apart some bed frames," she said, just before they disappeared around a corner.

"You and me for food." Phoenix faced me squarely.

"Yup. We need snow for water. Lots of water."

***

In surprisingly short order, people began filing back into the common room, looking for warmth, food, and companionship. Phoenix began dishing up the rough stew we'd made from canned and dried goods, along with some dried rabbit meat.

"While they eat," I told Phoenix, "I want to see about a place for a cemetery. I'm thinking that meadow to the south of us."

"Gonna check the map?"

"Yeah. About time that useless room did some work."

"What useless room?" Eleanor said from right behind me.

I had to be thankful for my brother Sean in that moment. He liked to sneak up on me and try to scare me. It would be so undignified if I jumped and squeaked right now. My heart racing, I turned slowly to face the other woman.

"We've got some kind of command room, with all the latest tech and gadgets," I replied to Eleanor's query, keeping my face bland. "As you know, ninety percent of that shit is useless. We can't even burn it. But there are a few maps on the walls, and one of them is geological. We've got types of soil, and at what depth rock is, plus altitudes. Anansi likes looking at it."

"Yup!" the boy said as he passed us with his bowl of stew.

"May I come see it?" Eleanor asked. "I'd like to know more."

I nodded and waved for her to follow me. We threaded through the girls finding seats at the tables, conversation filling the air. I hadn't realized how quiet we'd been until this moment. Soft laughter, chatter, and occasional tears all filled the room. Kestrel and Amana were taking care of Leo's kids, making sure they had comfort, support, food, anything. Those little girls had lost their mother, but from the looks of it, they'd at least have the love and support of a whole bunch of aunts and one uncle.

"Can I ask you something?" I asked as we walked down the hall.

"You just did." Eleanor smiled.

"A personal one."

"Oh." Eleanor bit her lip, the first sign of nervousness I'd seen from her. "Yes, of course."

"Aren't you worried Steve will target your friends, since you're going by your real name?"

"Ah. Yes." We walked in silence while she thought. "I can't say I have friends anymore. They turned their backs on me shortly after the Invasion..."

I kept my mouth shut, waiting for her to continue.

"I-I'd rather this didn't go beyond us," Eleanor said eventually.

"As long as it doesn't impact others' well-being, no problem." I kept my voice non-committal. Seemed to me that Eleanor needed to talk but was afraid to.

"Anything that can point to me will lead to my daughter, Anna."

*The fuck...*I bit my tongue, questions bottling up in my throat.

She took a deep breath, steeling herself. "Storm and Amanacer used to be good friends with my daughter. They practically lived at our house. Amanacer's parents didn't have the resources to care for her, and Storm's were neglectful, bordering on abusive, so I nearly raised them side-by-side with Anna. I hadn't realized how much Anna resented that until the Invasion. Or at least, that's what I think. Anna...Anna decided the best way to look out for herself was with the North Koreans. She deliberately seduced one, and the next thing I know, soldiers were at my door, marching us away.

"I only saw her once, when she told me she would 'let me keep watching over them' and had me appointed as a whorehouse madam." Tears clogged Eleanor's throat, and I opened the door to the command center silently, ushering her in. "I don't know what happened. Where I went wrong. But Anna used the soldiers to make it very clear to our neighbors that I was collaborating with the enemy. I tried to see my oldest friend once. She spit in my face, and I had to run. I think they would have killed me if I stayed."

"What about Amana and Storm? When Anna realizes you're alive, won't she target their families?"

"No." Eleanor shook her head, wiping away the tears. "I implied that they died. It wasn't difficult. So many girls didn't survive the abuses."

"What do you think they'll do to her?"

"I try not to think about it. Keeping my own name isn't so much about that. I-I guess it's about redemption, as silly as that sounds. I used to be a woman with a good reputation, and now..." She covered her eyes, shoulders shaking gently. "I watched two wonderful young women that I helped raise, that I love as daughters, be degraded, hurt, and broken. Essentially at my daughter's hands. And I couldn't do anything to help them! What kind of person does that make me?"

"Sometimes," I said slowly, thinking it through for once, "it's harder to watch others be hurt than to bear the abuse ourselves. We feel helpless, but Eleanor, you did help them! They're still alive, and now that they're here, they have a chance to heal. We'll do our damndest to give them the skills to protect themselves, I promise." The vehemence in my voice surprised even me. I'd never believed in a cause before, but it seems I finally found one.

***

"That place gonna work?" Sirius called when Eleanor and I walked back into the common room.

"The meadow's a bit shallow," I said, "but better than anything else around. We'll just have to go old school and gather rocks to top them with."

"What will that do?" Fox, the redhead, wanted to know.

"Keep animals from digging up the bodies," I answered. "They used this method back in the day, when they couldn't bury their dead very deep."

"Have you been somewhere like that?" Hightide asked.

I nearly panicked at being the center of so much attention, pinching my arm to stay grounded. "I just read a lot."

I breathed a sigh of relief when Eleanor called order and invited us to tell them more about what we'd done for fun the last couple months. We gathered near Seahorse so she could participate, maybe offer an opinion or two as our resident person-who-knows-something-about-shit.

"Do you know the rank of the soldier?" Seahorse asked at one point.

"No?" I glanced at Phoenix and Sirius. "You guys get a look? I was too busy."

Phoenix bit her lip, forehead wrinkling in thought. "There was a gold thing on his sleeve. With a red stripe and some stars in a triangle.

"How many stars?" Seahorse couldn't sit up, but she managed to radiate intensity pretty well.

"Four? And the red line went through the triangle, not around it."

Seahorse relaxed with a grunt. "That's like a captain. Wonder why he was following you?"

I pursed my lips, looking up.

"I think he wanted a private harem, instead of one he had to share," Sirius said dryly.

"Oh."

"How did you find this place?" Eleanor looked around the room. "You didn't tell us that."

"Eh, rumors, a general distrust of the government, and a dash of good luck." I waved a hand airily, brushing away the hours of discomfort and fear, the two weeks of my feet healing, and the traumas of losing family. The newly rescued gave me puzzled looks. "What? Hasn't anyone ever heard the rumors of the 'natural disaster bunkers' the government was building?" I made air quotes as I talked.

"I heard something," Seahorse admitted, "but I thought it was just the usual end-of-the-world crap going around again."

"My brothers spent time driving up here," Sirius volunteered, "and they saw a few things. Like soldiers where there shouldn't be any."

"And you also tend to notice when they disappear," I finished.

"What do you mean, 'disappear'?" Seahorse struggled to sit up, alarmed.

Eleanor kept the injured woman down with one hand and no effort, shaking her head in warning.

"About six months before the Invasion," Sirius continued the story, "the boys saw soldiers. We get here, nada. After two years, they just packed up and left."

"Did-did they..." Seahorse was so agitated she could barely catch her breath "...were there any...devices left here?"

I shook my head, a sinking feeling in my gut. The others did likewise, except Anansi.

"Oh, yeah!" the kid bounced up. "I found something! It kept blocking the front door, so I moved it. I found more scattered around. I've been collecting them." He ran off to get one, unable to keep still in his excitement.

He returned quickly with a little yellow block that looked like modelling clay, with a small plastic box attached to it. He handed it to me, and I passed it to Seahorse, who took it gingerly.

"How many of these have you got?" she asked the boy.

"I don't know," he shrugged. "Twenty? Twenty-five? Something like that."

Seahorse went pale and giggled, the edge of hysteria plain to hear. My heart sank. This was bad. This woman had been kidnapped, raped, tortured, then rescued by the seat of her pants, in an extended firefight and shot, all without raising an eyebrow. I was very worried.

"Oh, God," she wheezed between breaths. "Twenty to twenty-five?" Anansi nodded. "This is enough Semtex to level this entire area plus some. They were probably rigged to go off in case someone unauthorized tried to open the front door. Everything would have exploded and taken you all with it," she said bluntly for the tired and confused.

"Oh." Yep. It was exactly as bad as I'd thought. "So we should all be very grateful the electronics were fried?"

Seahorse nodded.

"Guess the detonators were broken, too."

"Your lack of concern never ceases to amaze," Eleanor said dryly. "Are you sure you have blood?"

"You tied my arm up," I pointed out. "Besides, we busted in here two months ago. I've had time to get used to the fact we haven't blown up."

"I wish," Seahorse, said, lying back down, breathing heavily, "you weren't so sarcastic about the military. It was my home for eight years."

"Hard not to be, when they build a barracks in the middle of nowhere with a massive-ass armory of confiscated weapons," Phoenix said wryly.

"No!" Seahorse hitched forward in a panic. "No, there can't be any weapons here! They were destroyed..."

Kestrel, sitting near her head on the next couch, leaned over to restrain her while Eleanor bent close, murmuring.

"Get Lucy," I instructed Jaali.

The boy took off like a shot, then quickly returned carrying the rifle we'd found on our first day here. The effect on Seahorse was devastating. Her face crumpled as she stared at the inscription—*All my love, Lucy*—tears starting in her eyes.

"They told us these were being made into paperclips, things like that. They told us we'd made people safer. Why did they keep them? What were the guns being kept here for?"

"We had active service members on US soil, not a base," I said sardonically, "in a secret underground bunker that can comfortably house two hundred, with a ginormous armory full of illegal weapons. I wouldn't care to speculate."

Seahorse closed her eyes. The girls around us were deathly silent, watching the play intently. I wondered how any of them were awake enough to pay attention. I was dead on my feet.

"They were preparing for an invasion," Storm breathed.

"Considering they buggered off before one hit?" My voice was so dry it would have been right at home in Death Valley. "They also weren't figuring on invading another country, not based near tracks that can't take large vehicles ten months of the year."

"Fuck 'em," Phoenix interrupted our doomsday talk. "They ditched us and haven't bothered to come back. Who cares about them? They've left us, fuck 'em. We'll save ourselves."

I grinned at her. Phoenix may be a pain in the ass, but she had a way of hitting the nail on the head. "That is the point, ain't it?"

Unbelievably, after we left to let Seahorse rest, the girls decided to explore, with Anansi and Dereva playing tour guides. I heard voices echoing through the tidy mass of tunnels, feet scraping the ground as they left the smooth concrete nearest the entrance for the rougher stone of the deeper passageways. I don't know what they thought. Most of the rooms were relatively boring, uniformly sized spaces that could have been used as officer's quarters, meeting rooms, or storage. It was impossible to tell.

They gathered for a while in the useless room full of dead computers. There was a large table in the center with a 3D map across it. The map was a closeup of Oregon, northern California, and southern Washington. I totally understood their fascination with the map. I'd spent hours in there, myself, looking over that map from every angle.

They were all banned from the armory. Eleanor and Seahorse agreed that all the girls needed time to heal emotionally and receive training before they'd be allowed anywhere near guns and shit with pointy ends. They thoroughly explored the gym, shooting range, and barracks, but finally stopped at the garage. They didn't have a choice. The large bay doors were operated electrically and frozen shut. Sometimes, in the evening, Anansi and me would sit down and try to figure out how they could be opened.

The boy said he got ideas from these Tinker Toys his grandpa had gotten him a few years ago. Well, he'd build structures with the toys, scan them into his computer, and run simulations to see how they would perform. I'd asked him once if he'd wanted to be an architect, and he went silent.

"I'm sorry," I'd said awkwardly. Bad idea to ask a kid about a future that didn't exist.

The garage walls were unfinished rock, and the tunnels around them were rough, barely high enough for a tall woman (i.e., me) to walk through. Except for that one spot where the ceiling dips down. I'd hit my head on it several times. We couldn't break the rock, and we were unable to make padding stick to it, so I just walked the entire thing with my head pulled in like a turtle, praying it made me short enough to avoid another headache.

"Why don't you look at the doors from the outside?" Jewel asked when Anansi mentioned the sealed garage doors, nose in the air as if the answer should be obvious to a blind man.

"Because," I heard Anansi respond, "the tunnels are twisty, compasses don't work down here, and we can't find the stupid things."

"Maybe you're not looking hard enough."

I pursed my lips to hide a grin.

"You know what?" he replied brightly. "You're *right*! Why didn't we think of that? We should just look harder. How could we be so dumb? Tell you what? Why don't you show us how tomorrow?"

A quiet snort just ahead let me know I wasn't the only one keeping an eye on the kids. Sirius walked silently back, shoulders shaking from suppressed laughter. "The sarcasm is strong in this one," I murmured as she passed me. Her shoulders jumped with a fresh round of laughter as she clamped a hand over her mouth to keep it in.

Between the mountain-scape, the layout of the tunnels, and a few other factors, unless we knew exactly where to look and what we were looking for, finding those doors from the outside was virtually impossible. Maybe if we had a couple years and plenty of free time, we could do it. The decorators of the map room had left out one critical piece of information: the blueprint of the bunker, and how it corresponded to the outside.

Damn useless room.

Even the air vents were carefully hidden. Going by the fact that there were levels, and even the lower levels had vents, we figured it filled the mountain. The two vents we found gave us some useful information. A fine steel mesh covered the vents at ground level, where it was sunk into concrete carefully disguised. Inside, the vents were open, so that even if an enemy dropped a grenade, it would explode in the corridor, preventing it from causing too much damage to the bunker's structure.

CHAPTER 18

I sat up abruptly, breathing hard as I stared wildly into the blackness, sweat coating my skin. The sudden wash of cold wiped the remaining sleep from my eyes. I was in my room, in the bunker. Pain radiated steadily from...everywhere. I stretched gently.

Flashbacks from the latest nightmare, this time about that creeper soldier, scrolled behind my eyes. Instead of killing him, though, he was killing me. He laughed the whole time. I laid back and tried to go back to sleep, until the unsettling thought that maybe this was a premonition made my eyes stay open.

"Fuck this shit," I muttered, climbing out of my warm bed. I pulled on a new-ish sweatshirt and stepped into my moccasins to take a little walk. Checking in on Seahorse was as good an excuse as any.

I'd taken the empty room closest to the entrance, so I cracked open the front door first, just to make sure a stray gust hadn't blown the tarps off that bright yellow bus. I relaxed on seeing it covered in a healthy, stealthy layer of snow. Back inside the bunker, I walked down the corridor, trailing my left hand over the wall, counting doors.

There were candles and matches stashed around, but I did okay in the dark, all our games of hide-and-seek coming into play. All I had to do was look for the door with light around it. I took the first right, heading towards the barracks, and halfway down I saw light shining through an open door. I peeked in to see Eleanor resting in an office chair next to a sleeping Seahorse.

Eleanor opened her eyes when I poked my head in. "How's she doing?"

"She'll be fine." Eleanor smiled, mostly with her eyes, crinkles showing at the corners. "She's strong, and the fever's broken. What brings you here?"

"Oh, y'know," I shrugged. "It's the only time of day I'm free of Sirius and Phoenix. I like to imagine what it's like not living with them."

After a few minutes' idle chat, Eleanor refused my offer to sit with Seahorse. "You'll have your hands full in the morning. You should go back to sleep. I'll call if anything changes."

She wouldn't be budged. As I exited, I could've sworn I heard a quiet "Thank you," but when I turned to look, Eleanor's back was to the door as she carefully dripped water into Seahorse's mouth. I shook my head as I headed back to my room and sleep. *Must be more tired than we thought if I'm hearing things.*

***

I groaned as I woke the next morning, rolling onto my left side and getting out of bed by the simple expedient of falling onto the floor. I had no bed frame, as the mattress was left over after we'd used the frame to build our first composting toilet. I groaned my way to my hands and toes, not bothering with pushups today. It hurt enough just holding a plank. After that, I moved through the rest of my morning sequence slowly, giving everything time to warm up, skipping a couple exercises for the sake of my injuries.

In the common room, I wasn't surprised to see both Sirius and Phoenix there, grumpy as usual. On the trail, Sirius could live without coffee, but the moment she had a roof over her head, she needed two cups just to wake up in the morning. I grinned as I gave them a cheerful "good morning!" just to piss them off.

Sirius grunted, unimpressed. "You've been volunteered to wake the new campers."

"Hah! You just don't want to deal with them."

"Yes." She went back into the kitchen to help Phoenix with breakfast.

I stuck my tongue out at her retreating back but did as I was told.

All the girls had chosen rooms in the same corridor as Jaali and Asilia. Probably because those same two helped them find and pick rooms. I knocked on doors, making sure to give Anansi a full drumroll on his. While I waited to see who would wake and who wouldn't, I stuck my head in Seahorse's room again. Today I saw what I'd missed last night: Moana and Cub sleeping on a pallet in the corner. Eleanor, sound asleep in her chair, had kept watch over them all. I tugged the blanket higher over her shoulders and left the room quietly, leaving the door cracked open behind me.

River, Dereva, and Hightide were the only ones who'd made it into the hallway. I sighed, greeted them, then proceeded to knock on doors again, louder this time.

"Good morning, my darlings!" I called through doors. "Wakey, wakey!"

One door flew open behind me as I turned away from it, and an imperious hand clamped down on my bad arm. "What the fuck do you think you're doing?" Jewel demanded. "I'm still tired!"

I spun towards her, right arm going up and over hers to break the grip, then around, finishing with me holding her arm, her hand pinned against my side with my own hand locked under her elbow, keeping it straight. I held her like that, watching the other faces peeking out of their doors. The corridor was better lit in daytime than the rooms were. The air vents let in a fair bit of light, all things considered. Not for the first time, I wondered how the builders had kept the trees growing over the bunker alive while building the entire thing so close to the surface.

"There are a few rules," I said evenly. "Number one, don't grab people. We work very hard to react in ways that hurt the people who grab us." I squeezed for emphasis. "Number two, work and training need to be done, which requires us to be early risers. Number three, you will work. Number four, you haven't earned the right to be constantly questioning. As far as we know, you have mud for brains, and we'll waste precious seconds telling you the why of it, by which time we'll all be dead. So until we know you can ask intelligent, pertinent questions, we'd like you to shut the hell up." I looked around, trying to think if there was anything I'd missed. If I did, I could just add to the list later. "Understand?"

I still held her arm, even though she'd been subtly struggling for the last minute. I squeezed again, waiting for an answer.

"Yes." Jewel glared at me resentfully.

"Yes...?" I cupped my free hand around my ear.

"...Captain."

I released her arm abruptly. "Excellent! Remember this, and it'll all go a lot smoother."

By now we had a full audience, including Eleanor, who watched from the doorway of Seahorse's room. She gave me a brief nod when I saw her, and I stuck my hands in my pockets to hide their shaking. I hate being the center of attention. I didn't make it five feet before River stopped me, and I braced, waiting.

"Will you show me how you did that?"

My eyebrows shot up. Not what I was expecting. "Uh, sure. Later. We have things first. Like breakfast."

I led the way down the corridor, listening to the women's excited chatter as they rehashed my bad manners. I felt Jewel's glare boring a hole in my back the whole way, too.

***

After breakfast we walked to the snow-covered meadow to bury our dead. Maybe it was stupid, to try in winter, but nobody felt right leaving them in the cupboard for the season. We had some tools we'd found in a closet in the garage. Everyone except the injured and those too small took a turn with the pickaxe and shovel, which meant everyone except me, Seahorse, and the little girls.

As the map said, we only made it three or so feet down before we hit rock, so all of us collected loose rocks, enough to make cairns like we'd raised over little Dylan's grave at Aunt Rose's house.

Asilia sang *Amazing Grace*, accompanied by her brother, and for a moment I stood in my aunt's back yard, rain clouds building overhead and a small hole in the grass below. I could see from Alex's face that she barely held on.

"Their deaths were so pointless," Hightide said as we laid the last stone. "They died for nothing."

"They died trying to escape," Eleanor told the girl gently. "They died full of hope for a better life."

"But they didn't get it," Hightide protested. "That makes it pointless."

"Leo's daughters are safe now," Eleanor pointed out. "As a mother, I can tell you that that makes it all worth it. Knowing your children are safe."

"Hail the victorious dead," I murmured to myself, listening to their talk.

"What's that?" Anansi, who had sharp ears, asked. "How are they victorious if they're dead?"

"It's just an old quote," I replied. "It means that when you die for a good cause, for others, you can't ever really lose."

***

At Eleanor's suggestion, we kept the girls busy for the rest of the day. We started in the gym, teaching them the move I'd done on Jewel earlier. This set the routine for the next few weeks, with hand-to-hand training in the mornings, followed by weapons in the afternoon.

During that time, I learned these girls would bet on anything, swapping chores instead of cash. The most popular was the weapons drill, where we'd take apart a handgun and put it back together, racing to see who could finish first. I competed with Sirius and Phoenix in the common room, the others gathered around, shouting. There's something about hearing fifteen- to twenty-four-year-olds making bets, and having a thirteen-year-old offering the odds...

The girls who were betting on me swore and threw their hands up when I fumbled the barrel alignment, their jeers mixing with the cheers of those who bet on Alex while Anansi moved through the group, redistributing the wealth.

The evenings were saved for busy work and repairs. For cleaning weapons or mending tears in clothing and gear, people would gather in the common room. I glanced up once to see Eleanor looking around, contentment relaxing her features as she listened to the girls talking.

After a week, we decided we needed to try hunting. With so many more mouths to feed, and so long until spring when we could begin gathering, a decision was made to send out a small group.

"If we're not careful," Sirius pointed out, "we'll eat through the stores in like two or three years."

"Is it safe?" Eleanor asked, worried.

"No," I said bluntly, "but if we use bows and arrows, at least we can be quiet."

"Are you any good with them?" Seahorse asked.

"I plead the fifth," I said, laughing. Sure, we'd practiced, but hitting stationary targets in a shooting gallery is vastly different from tiptoeing through the woods trying to not alert everything within a twenty-mile radius of our presence.

We won in the end, and Sirius, Phoenix, and me were released into the wild. We left under low, heavy clouds, trapping the cold in with us, giving us a good chance of snow. I walked through the halls, an extra bounce to my step, a small pack on my back next to a quiver of arrows and a bow in my hand.

"Come *on*, guys!" I shouted. "Let's go!" Any excuse to get outside.

A clatter announced Sirius' arrival. "Fuck." She glared at the quiver in her hand as if it were somehow to blame.

"Don't break 'em," Phoenix admonished as she followed Sirius down the hall. "We don't have *that* many extra." Sirius stuck out her tongue at the other woman.

Phoenix had a compound bow, Sirius a recurve, and I carried a longbow. The aim was to try them all and see which one was easiest to use in the forest.

"Are you sure we can't just shoot the deer?" Sirius asked for the umpteenth time.

"Yes," I rolled my eyes. "We have no idea how far the sound of a shot carries, and whether Steve is still in the hills, and..."

I trailed off as Sirius' eyes glazed over and she let out a snore. I twisted the door handle and threw my shoulder behind it to push back the snow drift. A wash of cold air blew in, and Sirius grinned. She'd never admit that she enjoyed this high-activity lifestyle, and that she was the best sneak in the place.

"Be careful," Eleanor said, walking over with Cub on her hip as the little girl carried a handmade dolly.

"We'll be fine, mom" Phoenix said, patting her shoulder, bouncing on her toes, anxious to get going.

Eleanor looked stricken for a moment, then forced herself to relax. "Just come back in one piece."

"No promises!" Phoenix sang as we stepped outside.

"We'll be careful," I promised Eleanor just before we muscled the door shut.

Eleanor, beginning to get used to our humor, just sighed.

"I changed my mind," Sirius announced as the door thudded shut and we got a face full of icy wind. "I want to stay in the bunker."

***

I leaned out slowly from behind a tree, extending my left arm to bring the bow up, drawing the arrow back at the same time. It was noon on the third day since we'd left the bunker, and we finally felt we were far enough away to begin hunting. A buck stood roughly seventy feet away, nibbling on a tiny piece of greenery at the base of a downed tree.

I inhaled, drawing the arrow back another inch, sighting on a point just behind the foreleg. I exhaled, releasing the arrow which flew straight...into the tree as the buck stepped back, looking for more food. Damn him. The impact of the arrow startled the buck, and he raced away, leaping over the downed tree.

"Son of a doe!" I shook the bow at his retreating white ass.

A snigger drifted through the still air as Phoenix walked to collect the arrow. "Don't worry," she called softly, "you would've missed anyway."

Sirius wasn't so contained, clamping both hands over her mouth to muffle her laughter.

"Oh shut up," I told her. "It's not like you even saw the deer at that distance."

Sirius' face turned bright red with the effort of restraining herself.

Phoenix froze. "Car!" she hissed, the word carrying clearly through the winter air.

Immediately we crouched, taking advantage of any cover. I held my breath, bow held low and horizontal to hide it. The sound of the engine grew louder until I swore I could reach out and touch the car, then it slowly faded away.

"I didn't know we were that close to the road." Sirius looked up, breath frosting her scarf white.

"I'm more worried about how often we're hearing them." Phoenix said, appearing from behind a snow covered bush.

"Meh," I said, brushing it away. "It's only been a month—or is it two weeks?—since we broke out. It's too soon to stop looking yet."

"Amana's keeping track of time," Phoenix volunteered. "I think it's been three weeks."

"Either way, they'll keep searching," I said. "I think they're daring us to mess with them." I finally put into words what had begun running through my mind the first time we heard only one engine.

"Whatever." Sirius had her mind on the task in front of us. "We need to get going. Since you missed that last shot."

Phoenix sniggered.

"Go jump off a cliff," I told them genially while giving them the finger. "If you can't find one, I'd be happy to give you directions."

***

We set up camp that night a mile away from where Phoenix had killed the second buck. We had both of them gutted and hanging in the tree we had our tent set up under. Last thing we wanted was to forget which tree we'd hung our deer in.

"Once upon a time, I'd never be able to sleep if I was cold," I yawned. "Now...I just hope I don't wake up with frostbite."

"Dunno what you're talking about," Phoenix murmured. "I'm nice and warm." She burrowed down, sandwiched between me and Sirius. We took it in turns to be the warm one in the middle, and tonight was Phoenix's turn.

I pulled my sleeping quilt higher around my ears, shifting my head to get the placement just right on my pack and sighed in contentment when I hit it. The tent grew quiet, the silence only broken by Sirius' gentle snoring and the occasional rustling of sleeping bags and mats as somebody shifted for more comfort. I relaxed and let sleep take me.

A horrific scream shattered the night, followed by a scrabbling sound, and something heavy crashed onto the tent. The poles snapped, and that terrifying scream sounded again, supported by our own shrieks. I thrashed awake, floundering in my quilt and the tent's ripped rain fly. Something punched my back, and I heard Phoenix scream.

I got an arm free and lunged forward, only to fall back again from a blow and momentary pain across my forehead. I blindly put a hand out and felt the rough bark of the tree and twisted around to sit up. Next to me, the shrieking continued, interspersed with snarls and coughs. The heavy thing had disappeared, and I didn't know where.

I heard scraping over our heads, and I tilted my head back, blindly looking just in time to see a shadow come crashing down with another scream. It crashed onto my legs, and I found myself face-to-face with a fucking *cougar*.

I forgot how to breathe.

It stared at me, just a few inches away, golden eyes fierce in the moonlight, fangs bared and furious. Time slowed, spun, lasted forever as it glared its rage at me, and a distant corner of my gibbering mind mentioned our deer meat. The moment broke when the cougar scraped its back paws, one at a time, over the tent.

Another scream sounded from under the shredded tent, and I smelled the metallic tang of blood. The big cat snarled, probably because its next meal was closer than it thought. It swiped with a heavy front paw and I gasped, feeling lines raking across my thigh. I lashed out, surprised to see a knife in my hand. I didn't remember drawing it.

I caught it across one shoulder, and it whirled back to me, snarling. I did the only thing I could think of; I flung myself forward. I had one thought in my mind, and it went along the lines of *ohfuckshitGallifrey!*

Time turned into a rollercoaster as I got a foot against the tree and *pushed*. I had one arm under its foreleg, and it fell backwards. I screeched as I landed on top of the thing, my arm jerking the knife over its ribs. A warm gush of blood washed over my hand. The cat screamed, arched, and this time it fell on me while I landed on a tree root.

Agony shot through me, radiating from my back. I gasped, trying to catch a breath around my galloping heart. The cougar yowled, its claws raked my side, and I shrieked, wrenching the knife around. Its back legs scrabbled frantically. I had my free arm up, forearm braced under its jaw trying to keep it away. Suddenly, the entire cat just collapsed on me, fangs scraping my raw forehead.

I lay there, trying to process what the hell had happened, unable to move under the dead weight of the cat, unable to care. I wheezed, lungs suddenly working since we weren't dying after all. I nearly choked on the musky scent of the cat when I noticed the sobbing breaths weren't mine.

"Are-are you alive?" Sirius' shaking voice finally penetrated through the haze.

"I think I peed myself." I heard my voice from a long way away.

"Oh, my God! You're alive!"

Footsteps crashed closer, and I grunted as the cat shifted on top of me. A fresh wave of panic hit until I realized the others were trying to move it off. I pushed with them, and between the three of us, we rolled the cat off.

"Well," Sirius said, surveying me, dropping her bow, and swiping away the tears before they could freeze on her cheeks, "no one will notice the pee with all this blood." She swallowed, bending over me with her hands fluttering from my head to my side to my leg, trying to decide where to start. "Are you okay?"

"'Okay' is a relative term," I groaned, flopping onto the freezing ground. Turning my head mostly by letting it fall sideways, I saw the cat had two arrows buried in its side. It had already shrunk from a hulking nightmarish monster to the smaller proportions of a good-sized dog. "I'm breathing, right? How are you guys?" I rolled limply onto my left side, pressing the bleeding portion into the ground to slow it.

"Terrified, scratches from branches," Sirius reported.

"He got me good on the shin," Phoenix wheezed. "And I think I broke a rib when it fell on me."

"Her first." I jerked my head at Phoenix. "We need to strap her ribs before anything moves. You're the one who shot the damn cat?"

"It seemed like a better idea than trying to play with it!" Sirius snapped.

"You're bleeding worse than I am," Phoenix protested at the same time. She held onto the tree to lever herself up.

"Yes, because bleeding on freezing ground is so much more dangerous than a hole in your lungs," I glared weakly at her. I shivered.

"Fine!" Phoenix made the word sound like "fuck you." She helped Sirius lift her sweatshirts and shirts, holding them up as Sirius thriftily used the shreds of the tent to bind her ribs.

After that, general campsite cleanup happened. I was moved onto the sleeping mats. They'd all been punctured, but by piling them up, they provided a small barrier between me and the ground. Phoenix got the cook stove going while Sirius cleaned and bandaged me as well as she could.

Sirius was *very* thorough in cleaning my wounds, informing me that animal scratches and bites are the most likely to get infected. I bit into a wad of cloth to muffle my grunts and screams, breathing hard through my nose, trying to relax. When Sirius finally finished, she flopped back onto the ground, sweating more than me.

"Guys, guys." Phoenix poked Sirius with an arrow. Sirius snarled and flopped a hand, trying to brush it away. "I figured out why it went after our meat!"

"Why?" I grunted, shivering and trying to pull my shredded sleeping quilt around myself.

"One of its back legs looks like it got broken and healed wrong."

"Cool." Sirius rolled onto her back. "Since you have so much energy, why don't you butcher it before it freezes, then."

"We can eat it?" Phoenix sounded like she didn't know whether to be happy or scandalized.

"Why not?" I groaned, wiping away half-frozen tears and snot. "Bastard tried to eat us. Fair's fair."

Shrugging, Phoenix got to work.

***

A week passed by the time we made it back to the bunker, but courtesy of the weather all the meat was still good. We were halfway to frozen, having spent every night on piles of fern fronds topped with our tent's footprint. Sirius had the only whole sleeping bag, but with some creative stitching we were able to salvage the other two. We had to cuddle, and we draped the rain fly over ourselves each night, but we made it home. I was conscious of the fact that if any one of us had been out solo, we would've died—alone.

At the bunker there were actually guards set out, just inside the tree line. We met River maybe a quarter mile away, and she raced ahead of us to let the others know we'd returned.

Eleanor was first out of the bunker, marshalling the others like a general at war. In short order we found ourselves relieved of our burden, fed, bathed, bandaged, and tucked into bed. I had the joy of getting everything cleaned *again*. Eleanor said that with my fever and the way the cuts looked, it was that or die slowly.

I also discovered that Sirius and Phoenix had been more than willing to impart an embellished story of the cougar to a rapt audience.

"What the hell would they know?" I grumbled when Eleanor chided me for my stupidity. "They spent most of the time buried under tenting."

"You're still not denying it," Eleanor pointed out as she and Amana scrubbed my cuts and I bit down on a wadded towel, squealing into it.

It took me and Phoenix nearly a month to get back into working shape again, starting slowly with light chores. During that time, Anansi supplemented us with meat from snares. He taught everyone how to set them, and the girls would go out in pairs to set snares in likely spots.

For the first two weeks, I could barely hobble, and spent most of my time in the kitchen, helping get meals together. Okay, fine. I can open a can as well as the next woman. And all around me, people talked.

The only truly interesting kitchen gossip I heard is that Kestrel used to be kept in an outpost at the edge of the mountains. Apparently, Steve had set up bases for the patrols instead of having them constantly go back to the city. She'd been removed from her home with her friends, and the soldiers had taken her off the truck before it went to Salem. They had her for nearly six weeks before they traded her in for a different woman.

Kestrel even knew the name of the town: Cascadia. A careful search of the maps showed it lay an hour or two south of us.

Chapter 19

"Okay, are we missing anything?" I rubbed my hands down my pants to dry them, scrunching the heavy fabric in my fists. In a couple hours, once it got full dark, a small group of us would set out for Cascadia to see if we could mess with Steve.

We finally had a thaw and could get out without drawing a map for Steve to find us. It'd also been a little over a month since what was now being referred to as "The Cougar Incident," and Eleanor deemed us well enough to go, though Phoenix and me still got tired easily.

A group of us stood in the Useless Room. Gathered around the table were Sirius, Kestrel, Phoenix, Dereva, Storm, Seahorse, Eleanor, and myself. Since Storm was the most advanced of the girls, and the most level-headed, she was going. We needed Kestrel as a guide, so she was in, while Seahorse and Eleanor stayed put to make sure the others didn't implode.

"I wish you weren't going," Eleanor said to Storm, again.

"We talked about this," Storm replied, gaze and voice even. "I won't stand on the sidelines anymore."

"We'll keep an eye on her," Phoenix assured Eleanor.

"Yes, I've seen how well you do without supervision." Eleanor took in Phoenix's leg and all of me with that simple statement.

"Look on the bright side," I said wryly, "she won't be the first one in. That's supposed to be me."

"Back to the topic," Sirius interrupted. "I think we have everything, and we know where everyone's supposed to be. I want a nap before we go." Shaking her head at the rest of us, my cousin left, waving as she left the room without turning back.

"Will she actually sleep?" Storm asked, still staring at the door.

"Oh, yeah." I leaned on the table to check out a small detail near the town. "She'll sleep."

***

We left a solemn crowd behind us that night. Little Cub clutched my hand as she walked me to the door. "I'll miss you while you're gone," the child said seriously, hair floating around her head like dandelion fluff. "You have to come back to the Lair, okay?"

That term had been floating around the bunker the last couple weeks. The Lair. I had no idea who started it, but I really wish they wouldn't. Life was weird enough, with all these different names for shit.

But still...

My heart twinged, hearing that small voice say I'd be missed. "You betcha, darlin'." I smiled down at her. "I'll miss you, too. Be good for Amana, all right?"

She nodded, then pulled my hand. When I crouched, she kissed me on the cheek and hugged me tightly around the neck. I blinked back tears and patted her back gently. "I'll see you again," I whispered into her wispy hair.

Eleanor took the girl from me as I followed Kestrel out the door, the last of the good-byes done.

We piled into the truck, Dereva and Kestrel in the cab and the rest of us bundled into the back. I noticed Sirius smile.

"What's got you so happy?" I began preliminary checks on the machine gun. "Good dream?"

"No," she said, stowing packs and making herself comfortable. "I'm just happy that 'the Lair' is taking off."

"You're the one who came up with that?" Phoenix got into the conversation. "Why?"

"We have a seahorse, a bird, a dog star, a phoenix, and a whole freaking menagerie living here," Sirius said reasonably. "A lair is the perfect place for all of them to live. And I like the sound of it."

I rolled my eyes and made sure the machine gun was loaded, leaving them to debate the pros and cons of calling the bunker "the Lair." I hoped it didn't catch on. Sounded a bit lame to me, but I'd never tell Sirius that, not when it made her so happy.

That, and the fact that she was carrying one of her spoils of war. I'd never seen a person so pleased to have a rifle.

The drive took longer than we'd thought. On paved roads, we could have been there in two hours max. But by back roads, it took at least twice that. It's easy to take paved roads for granted, and in a state the size of Oregon I gained a new appreciation for the luxury of paved streets.

And then it started raining about two hours into the drive, so the others wrapped up in the old shade cloth Anansi found, and we took turns on the machine gun. I huddled under it when my turn came to rest, pressing up against Sirius and Storm to share their body heat.

Dereva didn't stop the car until the early hours of the morning, and the rain had dropped to a steady drizzle. I was rousted out of my doze by the stillness.

"I think we're a mile or two away," Dereva called, trying to stay inside the cab as much as possible.

"Mmmm. How long we been driving?" I blinked and yawned, shaking off the sleep. My neck twinged, protesting the awkward position I'd slept in. Next to me, Storm pressed her face against my shoulder, determined not to wake up.

"Five hours."

"Guys, catch an hour's sleep." I twisted my neck and rotated my shoulders. "I'll keep watch."

It was maybe three hours until dawn when we moved out single file. I mean, maybe not the best idea, sneaking into the town where Kestrel had first been held captive, but by this point we were running on plain food and bad decisions.

Dereva and Storm stayed with the truck, ready to act as the cavalry if it all went to hell while four of us crept to the town on foot. By the time we got to Cascadia, it was light enough to see the outlines of the buildings, and I got a good look at the town.

The houses were tiny and in poor condition, with peeling paint, warped boards and missing shingles. There were a few shops—sad attempts at being a tourist attraction—a café, and a gas station. On the far side of town stood a newer, two-story colonial style house, halfway down a cul-de-sac, and Kestrel froze when she saw it.

"That one," she whispered, clawed fingers digging into the frozen earth. "That's the house."

"Where do they keep the truck?" I examined the building through my rifle scope. It looked different from how Kestrel described it. Less haunted house, more on the verge of ruin.

"That driveway." Kestrel pointed and I saw it, one of those big-ass Hummers, to the right of the house.

"How boring," Sirius mumbled. "Couldn't they have hidden it with a secret stash, made it more fun?"

"Why the hell would Steve have stashed their car if they think they control everything?" Phoenix demanded. She also had her rifle unslung, but her finger wasn't on the trigger. Yet.

"Not now, children," I admonished, feeling like a school teacher. "Let's try to stay on topic." I scanned the Hummer, looking for any marks or damage. "Pretty car," I sang under my breath. "Preeetty little car."

"Oh, no." Sirius groaned, dropping her head onto her arms. "You want one, don't you?"

"I always wanted one," I said primly. My heart began to pound heavily. It would continue like this until we were done. *Helloo, adrenaline!* "Besides, *you* wanted one of their rifles, and you got two. I see no reason I shouldn't get one little truck. It's nearly Christmas, after all."

Kestrel stared at us, mouth hanging open. "What happened to the grim stoicism? Speaking in grunts and being all regimented?"

I grinned. "A necessary evil, until people learn to listen."

When we were sure the coast was clear, we made our way to the house slowly, pausing often to listen. I was pleased, and surprised, at how well we moved together. Only halfway there, we saw the lights of the truck as it left.

"Right on time," I murmured.

"We'll have all day, at the least." Kestrel panted, eyes wide as panic threatened. "One...one always stays behind."

To have a day all to himself. Though the words remained unspoken, the thought lurked behind everyone's eyes.

Because there was nothing we could say to that, we didn't. We did cluster around her, offering silent support until Kestrel could move again. Keeping to the trees, we didn't stop until we were within a hundred yards, where the trees ended at a lawn. Once, that lawn was kept trimmed and manicured. Now the grass grew wild, beaten down by rain and snow. It would provide little cover, but that didn't matter. We wouldn't move until we knew where Steve was located.

"No repeats of Salem," I warned Phoenix, who shrugged uncomfortably. She still had dish duty when we were at the bunker.

I kept my hands tucked under my armpits, body scrunched up in the cold and damp, watching the house. Lights came on inside the two-story building, dim candles lighting a room upstairs. We watched a second light make its way up, disappearing as it passed between floors.

"Those're women upstairs," Phoenix reported. She rested in the tree above us, cheek nestled against her rifle stock, protected from the cold wood by a scarf. "Two. Looks like a bedroom."

"Steve in the front yard," Sirius said a few minutes later. "Bringing wood inside."

Add that to the man going up the stairs, and that gave us two bad guys and two civilians. My hands trembled slightly.

"Door's opening in the women's room." Phoenix's voice was tight, agitated.

Kestrel began to stand. "We have to—"

I grabbed her jacket and yanked her flat. "Oh, no. We are *not* going through this again."

"Steve's got a hand on his crotch."

"Right." If we were to keep these two from exploding, we had to go soon, and since this was the only movement we'd seen for nearly two hours…"Phoenix and Sirius, take the verandah upstairs, you got the guy in the bedroom. Me and Kestrel will take the back door. Move!"

Sirius and Phoenix took off to the left, sticking to the trees until they got to the shrubs lining the old property boundary. Kestrel and I cut to the right, crouching and crawling down the depression running towards the street. Halfway there, the light moved into a rear-facing room, and Kestrel froze, breath coming in short, panicked gasps.

"It's him! It's him it's him it's him," she moaned, swaying.

Fuckin' fuckity fuck, fuck! I turned to her, taking her hands carefully so as not to startle her. "It's okay," I whispered, sweat pricking between my shoulder blades. I expected to hear an alarm at any moment. "Ssshhh, you're safe, you're safe. Take deep breaths." I breathed with her, like Kestrel had taught us. "Name five…" I glanced around wildly, "things that are green."

Long minutes ticked away while we crouched in the dew-laden grass as she named four things before the glazed look of a trapped animal passed and I saw her features relax as she came back to herself. "Did-did I mess everything up?" Kestrel was still tense, but that could also be put down to our purpose here.

"Nah." I tugged her gently forward once more. "Sirius and Phoenix are waiting on the verandah roof for us. It's all good." Kestrel moved with me, her motions smoothing out as she fell into the familiar rhythm of walking in the dark. "Remember to stay behind me. I'm the tank, you just mop up the edges, okay?"

Kestrel nodded.

I grinned, anticipation bubbling up inside me as I slung my rifle over my shoulder and pulled out a handgun. This time I'd come prepared with the handguns in holsters strapped to my thighs, within easy reach rather than stashed under several layers.

I stepped lightly onto the porch, sticking to the edges. On the roof, somebody tossed a bark chip over the edge, the signal to go. In a silent burst, I made it to the door, testing the knob. Unlocked.

My teeth were bared. Steve's such a cocky bastard, I almost couldn't stand it. We entered in a rush, Kestrel sticking close. I checked the kitchen. Empty. Left was the hallway heading to the front room, right went towards the bathroom and another bedroom. A light shone under a door.

From upstairs came the faint sound of a struggle as I ran to the door and kicked, right under the knob to break it. Apparently interior doors aren't built very well, because I nearly put my foot through the door. This left me caught in the awkward position of standing on one foot, with the other one stuck in a door and slightly extended, the door partially open.

Not as awkward as Steve, though, who sat on the toilet, pants around his ankles. I saw half of him and shot through the door to try to hit the side of him that had his heart in it. The toilet's tank shattered as the bullet passed through the soldier, and he slumped, blood coloring the water cascading over the floor.

Footsteps came thundering down the stairs, and I jerked, trying to turn and face the new threat. "Aaaaaahhhh!" I overbalanced and fell, my foot still stuck as I landed. I thrashed, then arched up, balancing on my head and hips to point the gun down the hall, one foot still stuck in the door…only to see Sirius snorting with laughter and using the wall to hold herself up.

"Fuck off," I snarled, twisting and wriggling on the floor.

Phoenix sat down, then flopped backwards, wheezing.

"H-he-here," Sirius gasped, staggering over to yank on my leg. "Shrnsfusup!"

When I made it, upright I was greeted by the sight of two hysterically laughing women and three very confused ones. "Here." I collared Phoenix and Sirius and hauled them to the door, shoving them out of it. "You can come back in when you've calmed down!"

More laughter sounded through the closed door. "Assholes," I muttered.

"Jerk!" Sirius screeched. A dull thud sounded through the door, followed by another screech of laughter.

"At least you guys are calm." I eyed the new women. They were in their late teens, I reckoned, definitely no older than twenty and alike enough to be sisters, with light brown hair showing above their hair dye and hazel-ish eyes.

"They're calm," Kestrel said, "but not *calm*, if you get my drift."

Oh. "Uh, have they eaten?"

Shaking heads. "Okay, let's find some breakfast then." I got more confused looks. "What? No reason we need to do this shit on an empty stomach. I'm hungry." Now that the first part of the mission was over and the nerves had passed, my stomach let me know it didn't appreciate its empty status.

Letting Kestrel sit the new girls down and talk her counsellor stuff, I washed my hands and got busy, opening every cupboard and drawer in the place to find food. They had a lot of dried and canned stuff. The only fresh food was eggs, potatoes, and pumpkins. I could work with that. The wood stove gave off waves of heat, explaining what downstairs Steve had been doing.

I clattered away at the stove, putting water on to boil and cutting potatoes and a pumpkin. What we didn't use, we'd take with us. "Hey!" I shouted out the window. "Make yourselves useful and go get the others! We're gonna have breakfast!"

Sirius flipped me off as she and Phoenix obeyed, still giggling, their eyes wet with tears.

"What about the bodies?" Kestrel asked.

"What about them?" I scooped potatoes into a bowl.

"You're a bit of a psychopath, aren't you?"

"...no?"

"That's not something you're supposed to answer with a question," Kestrel replied dryly.

"I don't want to bother lugging them around. Besides, we won't stay here long. Just enough to eat. Then we can burn the place—"

"Whaat?" Kestrel interrupted.

"*I* don't want to wait two or three days for them to come back! A fire should get 'em back quicker, right?" I dumped the potatoes into the frypan. "Plus, Steve might not realize those two," I pointed the knife at the new girls, "are still alive. Win, win."

"You never said anything about burning the place down!"

"It was a recent revelation that I'm a bit of a pyromaniac."

"Who are you people?" the oldest of the two girls interrupted.

Kestrel waved at me with a "go ahead" look on her face.

"We, uh." I shut my mouth a moment. *Always sound confident, even when you're not.* I took a deep breath and tried again. "We...are the rebellion. We don't do names, it's proven a bit dangerous. I'm Captain. She's Kestrel."

I nodded. *Yep. That's that job done.* I turned back to the stove and the potatoes frying there.

Kestrel poked me. "Is that it?" she hissed.

"Yeah."

"You should be trying to reassure them!"

I looked at her, puzzled. "Since when have I been the reassuring one? Even Before, I wasn't the reassuring one. I'm the bitch one. You're the counsellor. Besides, you're better able to connect with them. You've been in their shoes, and you know better than I do what they need. I can feed them."

"You're impossible!"

"Yes."

Kestrel threw her hands up in frustration, but she did sit the girls down and start explaining the situation in detail. I gave Kestrel and the girls plates of food and got more on the stove for the others. I'd nearly finished when my truck rolled past and pulled behind the neighbor's house. The sun poked over the horizon, allowing us to keep an eye on the road without having to be outside, and I enjoyed the warmth of the kitchen.

"'Sup?" Sirius greeted us when they walked in the door.

"Yo." I nodded. "Breakfast is almost ready. Plates there." I jerked my chin, concentrating more on the scrambled eggs than the conversation. They were cooking fast, and I hate burned food. "See anybody?"

Dereva sighed, eyes closing in pleasure as she soaked in the warmth of the kitchen. Her nose twitched. The food smelled pretty damn good, if I did say so myself. Storm didn't wait and came straight over to the oven, grabbing a plate as she passed the stack.

"Nope." Dark blue eyes gleamed as Sirius stared hungrily at the eggs. "Can we take the chickens that laid those eggs? Passed a café in town. Might be supplies there we can take, too."

"Sure thing. We'll get that sorted, then we'll torch this joint." I ladled food onto the plates, being generous. Sirius took burning a building in stride, never batting an eye.

There wasn't a lot of conversation while we ate, just some quick introductions. We'd gotten into the habit of eating as much as we could, when we could. We never knew when our next meal might be. The new girls stared, their mouths agape as they watched us putting it away.

"I've never seen anybody eat that much," the older one admitted, watching Sirius. "Even the soldiers didn't eat that much."

"Going by the ones we've seen," Sirius said between bites, "they're a damn sight smaller than us. If that means anything."

As soon as we finished eating, we got the girls outfitted with warm clothing instead of the lightweight leggings and shirts they had on, most of which we stole from the soldiers' quarters. After that it was a quick jaunt down to the café.

We rifled through it like professionals, leaving mayhem and destruction in our wake, searching every nook and cranny. In less than fifteen minutes we had everything edible loaded into the truck and ready to go.

"We could actually have bread," Sirius breathed reverently as we loaded the last bag of flour. "How long has it been since we've had fresh bread?"

"Fresh? About four months." I grinned, though it quickly died at the next thought. "I don't know how to make bread. Do you?"

"Meh." She brushed it aside as irrelevant. "Somebody's bound to know something. Maybe we can find a cookbook?"

A quick search didn't turn up anything that looked like a recipe book, so we ditched that thought and headed out again. Back at the house, we stashed the pickup across the street and planned an ambush. We'd never done one before, so it was a learning curve for all of us. Around the circle there were bright eyes and quick, nervous movements, hiding the shaking of our hands. My heart started thundering the moment we began planning and I had to fight to keep my voice steady.

We ended up placing Phoenix up high across the street and four houses down from our target, and Storm on top of a house at the end of the cul-de-sac. Kestrel and Sirius were posted to either side of the house itself. The rescued girls were with Kestrel, and I heard her telling them about the Lair and our training. No mention of the Lair's location. Even I had a hard time finding it on a map.

I knelt in the back of the truck, surrounded by bags of canned goods. The cab pointed into the yard, ready and waiting. When Steve showed up, we'd reverse far enough that I could shoot, and we'd hopefully catch them in a complete crossfire.

Soon, there was nothing left but to light the house and wait.

CHAPTER 20

The ambush left me with a bad taste in my mouth.

Steve came roaring up after the house burned enough to leave a huge, black, smoke mark in the light gray sky. We waited while they debated. Waited until three soldiers had exited the truck looking for their buddies. Waited until they were in point blank range of Sirius' hiding place.

My breath came in quick gasps, waiting for Phoenix to start the show.

Then we cut them down.

Phoenix took out their own gunner, a neat shot just above his left eyebrow. The driver tried to back out, but I banged on the roof of the cab, shouting for Dereva to move. We boxed the bastard in and left him nowhere else to go.

I hesitated once he was cornered, unsure what to do with him from there, but not so Kestrel. She knew him, and when she stepped forward, I saw the recognition in his eyes. The moment of bewilderment left, and he gave her a contemptuous look, dismissing her. I saw the moment she snapped, but I was too late. Too slow.

Kestrel snapped her rifle up, firing quickly. She missed but recovered quickly, firing twice more. It wasn't a clean shot. She hit him in the stomach, and we all stood frozen as the man sank to the ground, stunned. Within moments the shock wore off and he began to scream, holding his belling and crying. Me, Dereva, and Sirius rushed to him, checking the wounds, both front and back.

"I don't think he's gonna make it," I said, swallowing convulsively and talking loudly to be heard over the crying man.

"You don't know what he's done." Kestrel watched him with a flat expression. I'd never seen that look on anyone's face before, and it scared me. It was cold, hard, full of memories she didn't want.

"We shouldn't leave him like this," Sirius said quietly. "It's cruel."

"So was he!" the older girl exclaimed, voice trembling. "The others mostly just wanted sex. He-he liked to hurt us. Kestrel's right. You don't know what he's done."

I stared down at the man moaning on the ground in front of us, blood oozing and a bad smell wafting from him. I think Kestrel had punctured his intestines with that shot. "Either way, I wouldn't leave a dog like this, and I won't leave him."

I clenched my teeth so tightly it would've taken a crowbar to pry them apart and stood over the man, breathing deeply through my nose. He stared blindly up, crying, completely unaware, even when I drew a gun and cocked it.

Kestrel and the rescued girls never looked away, even when I shot him.

***

Dark began settling over the land when we left town. We weren't willing to stay in that place, particularly with the plume of smoke still rising above it. Thing is, I had to do one thing before we left—open the hood of that Hummer.

I did not expect what I found. The engine had a lot of modifications and parts that weren't machined by the brand. The body was probably chosen because it's a great, bottom-heavy, all-terrain vehicle, but the innards...

"This shit ain't right," I said, shaking my head slowly. "It's gorgeous, but it's a chimera. Bits and pieces taken from different muscle cars and remade to fit. It's expensive and would've taken a shit-ton of money and connections."

"How the hell would a po-dunk country like North Korea get their hands on this?" asked Sirius, the only person who could follow me. Comes from living together the last few years.

"Couldn't they have just bought the parts online?" Phoenix looked from me to the truck and back again.

"Not a snowball's chance in hell," I pushed my hair back. "*I'd* have a hard time getting the crap for this, and I'm capable of machining some of this stuff."

"So what's it all mean?"

"I think they must've had help." I closed the hood.

"Here's a question." Phoenix looked around. "Anybody ever see somebody who wasn't Asian in that lot of soldiers?"

After a round of *no*'s, we figured additional debate was pointless and decided to bugger off. We left the house burning and headed into the hills.

Once we found a safe, hidden spot, we heard the girls' story. It was all too familiar, but instead of being locked in one building, they'd been taken from post to post, all over the valley. Cascadia was their fourth prison, and they'd been here two weeks. The girl before had died. Malnutrition, beatings, they didn't know for sure.

I looked around the tiny fire at the exhausted faces.

"You know they still need names," Dereva said.

The two women conferred quietly while we finished getting the camp set up. After the water boiled and we got food heating they told us their choices. Lightning for the younger, who'd barely said two words, and the elder chose Thunder. For a brief moment, curiosity almost had me tight enough to ask their reasons, but food and a goldfish memory won. By the time I remembered again, I also remembered our basic creed to not ask for explanations. It could take all our time.

I slept poorly that night, the gut shot man and the man I'd stabbed in Salem blending in my dreams. I got up several times, walking around the camp, checking on the others.

Once, I found Lightning curled on her side, whimpering softly as she twitched and jerked in her sleep. I feared touching her would make it worse, but I didn't want to leave her like that. I sat next to her, roughly singing a lullaby my mom used to sing to me. I'm not good, and Dereva, who stood watch, grimaced and came over to help. I faded out and left the last verse to her pure, sweet voice. Lightning slowly calmed, and I touched Dereva's shoulder gently.

"Go to bed," I whispered. "Let Phoenix keep sleeping. I'll stand her watch."

***

"Okay, good, but remember, don't yank the trigger. You gotta squeeze it on an exhale."

I lay in my patch of less muddy ground, watching Phoenix coach Kestrel through her first hunt. Hunting hadn't been on the agenda, but when you see four large bucks grazing and there's a ton of mouths to feed, you make time. I'd gone out with Phoenix, Kestrel, and Storm, leaving Sirius and Dereva at the trucks with the new girls, who needed time to heal before they'd be ready for serious physical activity.

I exhaled deeply myself to keep from twitching at the report as Kestrel followed instructions and fired. A buck jerked, making him a second slower than the others to turn and flee, and my heart sank. We could spend all day and then some, if we had to track this guy down. Turned out Phoenix was ready for this situation, and her shot brought him down before he made it to the cover of the trees. The only thing we saw of the rest of the bucks were their white tails disappearing into the forest.

Kestrel grimaced, dejected. "I can't believe I missed that badly."

"Don't worry about it," Phoenix reassured her. "You're still learning the rifle, and actually having to shoot something is hard. My first one, I missed completely."

"You really can't do worse than our last hunting trip," I said dryly. We walked slowly towards the downed buck, lifting our knees high to step over the hummocks hidden in the tall grass. We were only halfway there when a whistle pierced the air.

I turned to see Dereva waving frantically. "-omp-ny!" She pointed towards Cascadia. "—got coooompaaaanyy!"

"We got company!" I shouted, bolting for the deer, Phoenix hot on my heels. Kestrel and Storm hesitated a moment before following. "Everybody, grab a leg and MOVE!"

Running with a deer carcass bouncing next to your legs makes life awkward. What made it worse was the antlers, and I nearly impaled my leg on one before I grabbed a tine, holding the head on an angle while we ran. It's amazing, the kind of incentive not wanting to be shot can give you. We unceremoniously threw the deer into the back of the running GMC and dived in, piling on top of each other in our haste.

I found myself spitting deer hairs, glad we'd moved all the foodstuffs into Steve's truck. Dereva punched the gas as soon as the last pair of boots left the pavement, the tires screeching on the chimera truck as Sirius followed behind.

We disentangled ourselves, sitting up and trying to figure out where the danger lay. "What the fuck?" Phoenix exclaimed.

I looked and saw Thunder, the older sister, standing at the machine gun on Steve's truck. It wasn't a protected position, though it was more than we had in the pickup. "I wonder if she'll be able to figure out how to work—"

A new chimera-style truck appeared like magic from around the corner in front of us, and we had nowhere to go. Bullets raked the top of the cab and spun off into the air as we ducked. Dereva yanked the wheel to the left, stomping on the gas. I lunged to my knees, barely able to reach the trigger on our machine gun and hoping to keep them from killing us for a few more moments.

Phoenix squirmed, bringing her rifle up, firing from where she'd been thrown into a corner. Storm and Kestrel joined in, but they were erratic, slow. We passed so close to Steve it was only the windiness of the road and Dereva's driving that saved us. It took all the quivering scraps of courage I could find to stand up and use our damn machine gun properly.

Forewarned by us, Sirius and Thunder were more prepared. The girl kept her finger on the trigger, screaming the whole time, catching Steve by surprise. Dereva threw the pickup into reverse and chased after Steve while they were distracted by Thunder, knocking all of us except Phoenix over.

She pulled a grenade out from under her jacket and lobbed it at the enemy. It missed, exploding on the far side of the vehicle. Phoenix immediately followed that with another grenade. My breath caught as it bounced on the roof, then fell through the gunner's position into the truck.

"Yes!!" she shrieked, punching the air. I listened to the others cheering, lurching as Dereva put us back into drive and got the hell out of Dodge, but paid more attention to how the truck reacted. Hinges and doors came loose before that glass did.

Our celebration was short-lived. Thunder fired at the truck until Sirius passed it, then, still screaming, she turned the gun onto a new target: us.

"Oh, FUCK!" was the common theme as we hit the deck, barely managing to fall down before the bullets whizzed through the space I'd just occupied. Dereva weaved around, though that action was hardly necessary, considering the twists in the road. We bounced over the rough road, knocking into the gun's stand, the deer carcass, and each other, all over the ribbed fiberglass of the truck bed.

"What are you DOING, you crazy bitch!" screamed Phoenix over the tailgate, ducking down as a fresh hail blew past. We screeched around a corner and had a few seconds of bliss. A flock of black birds shot into the air when the bullets peppered their trees, the racket of their cawing lost in the sounds of straining engines and squealing tires.

Above our heads the machine gun spun, proving that not all the bullets missed, and even the untrained get lucky sometimes. The barrel swung down as the locking mechanism broke, catching Kestrel above the ear and tearing a patch of skin. She collapsed boneless to the floor.

"Stop shooting my truck!" I bellowed uselessly, pressing my sleeve to Kestrel's head. "Sirius, why are you still driving?" I peeked up over the edge of the tailgate. "Well, shit."

"What?" asked Phoenix, from where she and Storm were frantically digging out bandages, pushing my hand away from Kestrel's head, the first-aid kit from my pack open and scattered next to them.

"There's another truck back there," I explained. We left Storm to finish the nursing job and scrambled through the mud, blood, and limbs, trying to find the rifles we'd had to abandon and were now bouncing and sliding through the muck around us. I popped up, holding my Marlin rifle, and took another look behind us.

"Fuck. Get a couple grenades ready," I barked at Phoenix. "Storm, leave her for now, and get ready to make Thunder keep her head down. Dereva!" I bellowed. The girl waved. "Veer left and brake. NOW!"

We screeched to the side and all of us in the back slid towards the cab. Storm, fortunately, never had to deal with Thunder. Sirius kept her foot pressed down and they blew past us, leaving those enemy soldiers to our untender mercy.

Phoenix began firing three-round bursts at Steve, and I blessed the versatility of the M21s. Behind me, Thunder's machine gun finally fell silent, empty or jammed, I didn't care which as long as she wasn't shooting at me anymore. I fired at the enemy's engine block, hoping to hit the radiator while Storm prepped and flung a grenade. She missed so badly the truck was driving over it when it exploded.

I revised my opinion of "missed" when the resulting explosion sparked the gas tank. Two of the truck's tires left the ground, lifted by a glorious, orange ball of flame. The heat from the explosion kissed my face, closely followed by a light hail of shrapnel

"Go, go, go!" I yelled, ducking down. Dereva obliged, racing to catch up to Sirius.

Phoenix switched her rifle back to single-shot and aimed at the survivors of the truck explosion as two men stumbled away from the flaming hulk. I pushed the barrel up before she could fire. "Let 'em go," I said hoarsely.

"What? Why?"

"Fear." I settled back, shattered now, as the adrenaline faded. "Steve should get just enough information to piss them off. Make them look in the wrong area."

Phoenix grumbled under her breath, but she listened. I'd take the win.

***

"What the hell were you thinking, letting a traumatized girl near a damned machine gun?"

As soon as we found a good, out of the way clearing, we pulled over and made camp. Phoenix showed Kestrel and Storm how to properly skin and gut a deer while I dragged Sirius into the trees for a little privacy.

"I didn't 'let' her do anything!" she protested. "They were just supposed to sit in the back while I drove. Kid figured out the rest on her own. Maybe, instead, we shouldn't have stopped!" Sirius glared at me.

It was like being threatened by a wombat. Small, compact, could probably kill you, and would definitely fuck up your car.

I swung away from her, angry at how close we'd come to losing everything. I clenched my teeth repeatedly, trying to calm down. In truth, Sirius was right. We shouldn't have stopped to hunt. It was my decision, not hers. My fault, not hers.

"I'm sorry." I breathed deeply through my nose, hands on my hips and stowing the angry, pointless words that wanted to spew out. "We're still trying to figure this crap out." I took another deep breath, then let it out slowly. "Who'd have thought, last year, that we'd be doing crazy shit like this?"

Sirius grinned at me, wide enough that I could see the gap from her missing tooth, all forgiven. "I know, right? Guess we're not 'useless women' anymore." Our medieval grandfather thought single women were second-class citizens, and he hadn't been afraid to tell us.

"Nah, he'd still think we're useless. 'Specially after the way Toni schooled him last time!"

We laughed, remembering the dumbfounded expression on the old bastard's face when Toni, Sirius' sister, had lambasted the old man and gave him a piece of her mind.

"Mmm." Sirius made the sound deep in her throat. "Good thing for you we had this talk in private. If you'd done this in front of the others, I'd've had to kick your ass. Got a reputation, y'know."

"Hah!" I tossed my head back, reminding her who was taller. "As if you could. I'd have to be dying before you had a chance."

Sirius stuck her tongue out. "You wish! Remember when we were kids and you- mmphmhm!"

I clamped an arm around her neck, muffling her, and noogied her beanie-clad head. She pinched my ribs, and we scuffled, neither trying very hard as we tumbled, laughing, into the firelight.

Phoenix and Dereva ignored us, used to our idiocies, but the others stared, mouths hanging open. Kestrel gave us a sideways look, the fresh bandage showing brightly against her golden-brown hair, open disapproval on her face.

"There is just something wrong with you two. You both could use some therapy to respond like normal people. Feel free to come talk to me any time."

We only laughed harder. I cropped to the ground on top of my new sleeping bag (which was really my old one, before I got the quilt) between Phoenix and Storm, crossing my legs in front of me. A pan of mixed green beans and corn warmed to one side of the fire, while thinly sliced meat from the earlier kill roasted on wooden skewers over the other.

"You people are kind of weird," Storm commented as Sirius sat next to her.

"Only 'kind of'?" Sirius said with mock horror. "We're doing something wrong if we're only kind of weird."

I shrugged, smirking at the teenager. "Guess we need to try harder." I eyed the sisters and tried to decide what, if anything, I could say to them, when the decision was taken out of my hands.

"Captain," Thunder began timidly, "I wanted to say I'm sorry for-for what I did, earlier."

"Good," Phoenix muttered.

I shook my head at her, warning her to stay quiet. "I won't say 'no problem,' because that's definitely an issue, but I'd like to know what was going on in your head."

"I was scared. Afraid that if we didn't stop them, we'd be taken back, and I can't go back...I can't," she whispered.

I pinched the bridge of my nose, thinking. "Right. We get that—"

"Then," Thunder continued, "then I felt...powerful. Like I had control over my life for the first time."

Oh, boy. "Either way, you'll go through a fuck-ton of training, discipline, and hand-to-hand combat, plus group counselling sessions with Kestrel, before we let you near a gun again." It's as close as we'd come to a standard procedure, with all the traumatized women running around. Even Phoenix attended.

Lightning, that quiet little mouse, finally spoke up. "We're not in trouble?"

"No, kid." I smiled, feeling the sad turn of my mouth. "It's as much my fault for stopping. All I can say is we're learning, too."

By this time dinner was hot, and we tucked in using tin mugs, knives, and fingers to eat. Everybody ate silently, hungry after the day's insanity.

Kestrel shifted, arching her back and trying to stretch without spilling her food. "All this running around without a bra is killing me. How do you guys stand it?"

"Sports bra," I mumbled around a mouthful of food. "Didn't you guys get something?"

Kestrel and Storm shook their heads. "There aren't any," Storm offered. "We've been using the smallest t-shirts, but a lot of us are small enough that they're still too big."

"Oh."

"We could try tanning hides," Sirius offered.

"You know how to do that?" Kestrel raised her eyebrows, surprised.

Sirius laughed. "No."

I chuckled. "Not like ignorance has stopped us yet. Slowed, yeah. Stopped, no. After all, necessity is the mother of invention, or some shit like that." I finished another mouthful and gestured with my knife. "We'll mention it to Eleanor, and she'll see who wants the job."

Chapter 21

"Oh, you're back!" Eleanor was the first to greet us after the perimeter guards. She'd been walking outside when we returned, driving carefully down the road. Me and Phoenix had followed behind, brushing out our tracks as much as we could and hoping for more snow or a melt to hide them.

Eleanor went straight to Storm, hugging the girl until she squeaked, then ushered us inside. Despite the cold, she had on an ankle-length skirt that swirled around her legs when she walked, sweeping the snow.

"Who are our new friends?" Eleanor smiled warmly at the girls, causing them to visibly brighten. At that moment, a little whirlwind blew past us as Anansi ran to his sister, hugging her tightly.

"The girls are Thunder and Lightning," I pointed to them. "Any way they could have a warm wash? Life's been hard."

Amanacer and Seahorse pulled us into the common room, and Amana immediately went into the kitchen to get some pre-melted water on to heat. "We need *mas agua*," she told us. "Thees was *para la cena.*"

"No worries, we can—"

"You can sit down," Eleanor said firmly. "There are plenty of others who can bring in more snow for melting. Now."

We sat. Moana and Cub came racing in, shrieking, and I smiled to see them so exuberant. Cub threw herself on my lap and yelled, "You came back like you promised! I was scared you wouldn't."

Cub chattered away, no doubt telling us about the exciting things that happened while we were gone, but she talked so fast I couldn't follow her. Still, we nodded, made the appropriate comments, and looked to Moana for a translation when things got too confusing.

"Seahorse." I turned to the ex-soldier when Cub settled down. "How were things while we were gone? How was Anansi...?"

She laughed a little, then stopped, surprised at the sound. "It was good. He was a help, most of the time. Except for when he tried to figure out how to get the faucets running again."

I winced. "Was there a big mess?"

"Just a fire. It was more smoke than anything," she hastily added.

"Mostly smoke." Eleanor smiled fondly at the boy, where he huddled with his sister, sharing their experiences over the last few days. "The air vents work just fine, if you're wondering."

The rest of the girls slowly wandered in and listened as we told them about our excursion. Fox and Hightide then bundled the new girls off to find rooms and clothes while we waited for the water to heat.

No one here had seen bad guys other than North Korean soldiers and American collaborators from the North American Liberation Corps, either, which was a disappointment. I had a feeling that there was more than just Steve involved, but if the women who were at the center of things hadn't seen any other people, how could we find them?

"One thing at a time," Sirius said in my ear. "Let's deal with the problem in front of us, okay?"

"Okay, okay." First things first then. "How was Anansi planning to get the faucets running?"

"Oh," Seahorse said, looking up from playing patty-cake with Moana, "he found the well, and said something about bypassing the need for a computer chip? I lost him after 'I found the well.'"

"He found it? Where?" I sat forward, holding Cub snugly. "We've been looking for that damn thing since the beginning. Like the freaking garage doors, the builder decided to lose the blueprints and maps."

"You know that service corridor on the far side of the gym?" I nodded. "In a dingy corner of it, under some ancient gym shorts, there's a trap door leading under the gym, to a whole bunch of pipes and plumbing. I think it runs under most of the corridors on this level. He disappeared for nearly twelve hours the day after you left."

I winced. We were lucky the boy just made a bunch of smoke. Despite his intellect, he still didn't know that much about mechanics, though he was rapidly filling the gaps in his knowledge. And what he didn't know, half the time he could make up.

"I'll go down there with him later, after I've had a chance to clean up a bit." I surveyed myself and thought I didn't look in too bad of shape. "Between us, we should be able to figure something out."

"You know electronics?"

"No, but we don't want electrical stuff. We want gears and levers." I remembered something we'd left out of our little debrief. "Do you guys know if anyone here can work with leather? Kestrel says we need bras, and I don't think I noticed any last time we were in town."

"That's because we were in Silverton," Phoenix said dryly. "You can only buy gifts or groceries there. If you want anything useful, you have to go to Salem."

"Hightide has already been trying to tan leather," Eleanor informed me.

"Since when?"

"Since she saw her first deer hide." The older woman straightened her shoulders a little more. "Haven't you noticed that terrible smell in Section Eight?"

Built in sections, the bunker had painted signs telling you where you were. Section Eight, an area next door to the garage and out of the way of everything else, stayed largely empty. So, yes, I had noticed a funky smell, but I'd put it down to poor air circulation and spent two days trying to find a blockage in the vents in that section.

"Those are her attempts at tanning leather. She's trying to go from stories she's heard from her uncle's tribe, though they weren't exact in their amounts or methods."

Later, after I ate, I spent a surprisingly pleasant afternoon with Anansi down in the bowels of our bunker. I pursed my lips in a soundless whistle, impressed the kid had managed to find the damn pump. Sure, once we knew where it was it seemed obvious, squatting at the center of the water pipes like a spider in the middle of her web.

Anansi's jimmy-rig was a mess after the fire, but I could follow what he'd been attempting. He wanted an automated system that could draw water from the well into the cistern, but that just wouldn't work. Not in this situation. The best I could see would be to create a draw using a hand pump. Once the water had a steady flow drawing it should get easier. I'd prefer siphoning it, but considering the depth of the well, that was impossible.

We made detailed drawings and went back up top to see how we could implement the whole thing. By the time we made it to the common room, we found that dinner was ready to be served, so we rushed to clean up. Amana didn't tolerate unnecessarily filthy people at the dinner table and had proved willing to dump a bucket of cold water on anyone who didn't listen.

Me and Anansi took up an entire table so we could spread our drawings out, deciding what parts we had on hand and what we needed to scavenge. I absently placed my bowl over one corner to hold it down and Anansi set his cup on another. I glanced up once to see Sirius watching us, a little smile on her lips as she shook her head.

I needed this, though. After all the blood in the last two days, I needed to make something again, to build.

Phoenix called me back to reality after dinner. We needed to talk about heading back into Salem. Mary—Kitten—had asked for a month to dig up any information, and it'd been longer than that. We'd made arrangements to leave notes in the hollow of a specific tree, one that Phoenix and Olivia had used at various times in their lives to store the treasures children everywhere collect. Now, it was a dead drop, a place to leave notes and information. Kitten would be getting worried if she'd left a note and we hadn't collected it yet.

Eleanor, Seahorse, Sirius, Phoenix, and I gathered in the Useless Room around the map table. Phoenix urged a full attack, preferably bombing the city center. Seahorse and me automatically vetoed that.

"Four people," I said sternly. "Two to stay with the truck, maybe do some looting, two to go into Salem."

"We need more intel before we can attack the city." Seahorse sat straight in her chair, every inch the soldier. "We're too inexperienced. The girls aren't ready for the unpredictability of combat."

"I was thinking we could start them on something smaller," I informed the group. "Deliberately hitting a patrol truck, instead of accidentally running into one. You know, an ambush."

The others considered. "I think that would work," Seahorse said cautiously. "If we chose the spot. We'll need everyone here, though."

I let the others debate while I waited for my cousin to speak. Sirius liked to take her time with things. It wasn't good in the field, but in the planning room, it was perfect. "We can set up watches, keeping an eye on the roads," Sirius began slowly. "Find routes they frequently use. Scope out the area, hit them when they least expect it."

Shrugs and nods around the table. Close enough. "Seahorse and Sirius, you guys want to collaborate on that?" I asked.

They looked at each other. Sirius shrugged.

"Yes, sir!" Seahorse nearly saluted.

I winced. "Don't call me 'sir.' You know that. Now, back to Salem."

We decided to have a single person dedicated to talking to Kitten. Her job would be to infiltrate Salem on a regular basis, checking the tree and carrying messages. "She'll need to be good at working alone," Eleanor mused.

Sirius volunteered, but we vetoed her. She was too good with the dogs, and her distance vision was shit now that her last pair of glasses broke.

"River," Seahorse eventually said. "She prefers to spend her time alone."

"She's good at hide-and-seek," Sirius offered.

"Decent shot," Phoenix added. "Not great, but decent. A loner."

"Like Sirius, then?" I grinned at my cousin.

"Less grumpy in the morning." Phoenix ducked away from Sirius' swipe, laughing softly.

River, it turned out, didn't have a lick of sense, because she was more than willing to be the go-between. I'd go with her the first time to show her the way, while Dereva and Phoenix stayed with the car and went looting.

Over the next few days, while we got supplies together, Anansi and me went through everything, cataloguing what parts we had and seeing what we needed to make the pump. We were cannibalizing the bus the day after River agreed to take the messenger job when Hightide tracked me down.

"Captain, I need more information," she announced from near my feet. I lay on my back under the bus, a muffin pan and baking sheet stolen from the kitchen next to me, each filling up with parts or connectors.

"About what?" I could hear her hands planted on her hips as I wriggled out from under the bus.

"Tanning. I don't know enough. There's something I'm missing. Can you look for books while you're out?"

"You're kidding, right?"

"You've been to a library!" Her hair was sticking up from where she'd been running her hands through it. "All you have to do is find me the information. I can take care of the rest."

How hard could it be to tan leather?

Seeing the skepticism on my face, she threw her hands up in frustration. "I've tried everything I can think of! Scrambled brains alone don't work. I've tried mushing them up and straining them to get the oils out but—"

"Gross!" I held a hand up to stop her. "I believe you. I don't want to know more. Tell the shoppers."

"Thanks, Cap." Hightide grinned happily at me, now that this problem was passed on, and practically skipped away.

I'd just gotten back under the bus, with my arm in shoulder deep, trying to reach a stubborn bolt, when there was another interruption.

"*Capitan*?" The accent placed her as Amanacer.

"Yes?" I growled. What did it take to get some work done around here?

"We need pads and tampons," she said bluntly.

"Oh. Shit. Do we still have some?" I extracted my arm and wriggled out again.

"Enough for," she tapped her fingers on her leg, "two more periods."

"Shit." Another thought occurred. "Has everyone had their period?"

"*Si.* Eberyone except T'under and Lightning, but they have no' been here long. River and Storm say theirs were...bery heaby."

Very heavy. Could that have meant...pregnant? A very real possibility, and I had to admit, if no one was pregnant we'd definitely dodged a bullet.

At some point, however, we'd have to deal with a woman pregnant by rape. It was a bridge I was happy to put off until I got to it.

"Right. Tell Phoenix and Dereva." I brightened. "Better yet, write it down. Write down a list of things you'd like them to keep an eye out for. Also, can you brainstorm with everyone and come up with some suitable alternatives to pads and tampons? They won't last forever, no matter how many we find."

"*Si, Capitan. Me pondre en eso.*"

I sighed and wished for the millionth time that I'd taken Spanish in high school. "I'll take that as a 'yes.'"

***

"Did you find any grease?" I asked Anansi.

We were under the gym the day after I talked periods with Amana, messing with the pump. We'd managed to mickey-mouse a system, but I needed some grease to smooth things out.

He shook his curly head. "Nothing. We'll have to go looting for it."

"Dammit." Animal fat was all we had, and it would have to be enough. I hoped. I continued tightening the bolts, surveying our work as I did so. We'd set up two large wheels on either side of the new system. They were connected to the crank shaft and acted as our handles, at least until we had supplies to get a better system up and running. We should, in theory and by all calculations, be able to draw enough water to fill the cistern, giving us enough water for a day or two. We'd left the pipe unhooked just so we could tell when the water finally made it up. I had no idea how many more adjustments we'd have to make before we were through.

Anansi applied a little more grease, and then it was time to put it to the test. We hauled on our wheels, and I went so far as to brace one foot on the bottom of the pump, the other on a pipe brace halfway to the roof in order to get a better grip.

"Is this even working?" Anansi cried breathlessly, his young frame straining.

"Gotta...get the grease...worked in," I grunted. "First time's...the bitch."

After five revolutions it moved a bit easier, so we stopped and applied more grease. Anansi's stomach growled. I laughed.

"What?" he said defensively. "I'm growing!"

"As long as you don't faint..." I exhaled, pulling once more. My stomach growled. Anansi cackled. "Can it, kid."

"What?" He blinked innocent black eyes at me. "At least I'm growing taller. At your age, there's only one direction left...!"

"AAAAAHHH!!!" I bellowed, pulling the wheel through the last sticky bit. "That's it! You're my example now!" I finally got my feet under me. The wheel picked up speed. "By the time I'm done with you, nobody'll ever give me grief again." I laughed a little, arms moving faster.

"You'll have," he panted, "to catch me first. Sure you can do that? You're what? Twenty-five? Getting pretty old."

"Older than you'll get, at this rate. You can't outrun a bullet, boy." Every turn got easier, but still no water. I wondered if there was any left.

"Will the toilets work again?"

"Probably. Damned if I know what shape the septic tank is in." My arms ached all the way through to my back. "Actually, I don't wanna know how that's doing. We can keep the composting toilets for all I care."

"Are we there ye-AAAHHH-mmlblergh!!!" Water shot up out of the open pipe, blinding Anansi.

I stepped back, shaking my head and pawing the water out of my eyes. "Shit! It wasn't supposed to do that!"

Anansi made use of the mouthful of water he'd been given and swallowed it. "It's good! Sweet, like the creek."

I tasted a handful. He was right. It was cool, refreshing, and better than the creek because it was right in front of us. "Quick, let's get this hooked!"

We hurriedly fitted the pipe back on and tightened the O-bolt. I didn't want to lose the flow and have to start from the beginning. As we hauled with renewed vigor, I could hear the boy singing softly. "I'm taking a baaath tonight! I'll be taking a baaath!"

Our rigged system held, though barely. I kept a close eye on it, gauging the shaking as the water gushed through. It would hold for now. I screamed with joy, Anansi giving war whoops, all fatigue gone as we rushed to fill the cistern.

"What the hell's all this noise?" Seahorse appeared through the tangle of pipes, her glare set on 'kill' mode. "I'm trying to—"

"We have water!" Anansi screamed.

"What?" Seahorse impatiently shoved short brown hair out of her eyes.

"We got water!" I repeated. "Tell them to turn on the faucets! Turn on everything."

Seahorse wriggled through the pipes like a snake through vines, and when she exited, I could hear her yelling at everyone to *go*.

***

Dinner that night was the cleanest I'd ever seen us. Not a smudge of dirt anywhere. The girls were more animated, chatting and laughing, stroking and smelling their hair, pleased to be entirely clean. Me and Anansi had been the last ones out, and we'd had to refill the tank again, but seeing these shining faces made the effort worth it.

My hair still dripped when I finally sat down with my bowl of stew between Eleanor and Sirius, my bare feet stretched out in front of me. Amanacer set her bowl down opposite me, giving me a shy smile as she did.

"What do you t'ink of de soup?" she asked us.

"The soup is delicious, dear," Eleanor replied, smiling at her daughter.

I nodded, mouth too full to speak.

"What's the green stuff?" Sirius asked. "It's nice."

"Stinging nettle, *y diente de leon.*" At our blank looks, she tried again. "Yellow flower? Leaf look like, uh, saw? Teeth?"

"Dandelion?" I asked, remember Mom's obsession with herbs.

"*Si!*" Amana said happily. "Dan-de-leon."

"I didn't know you could put them in soup," Eleanor said.

"I don' know," the girl shrugged. "De book say is good for you. So I put where I can. In soup."

"*Bien,*" I took another bite. "I like it."

"Oh, *madre,*" Amana said to Eleanor. "Tell *Capitan* about de pads, *por favor.*"

I transferred my attention to Eleanor, who said, "My mother told me about how her mother used to deal with periods. They used to use strips of fabric, fastened to a belt tied under their clothes."

I leaned back, horrified. "You mean like a *diaper*?"

"Erm. Yes. Exactly like that."

Sirius wrinkled her nose. "Won't we be going through a lot of cloth?"

"Nooo." Eleanor gave us an apologetic smile. "They're reusable. We'll just have a lot more washing."

"Fu-" I caught Eleanor's look. "-udge. That'll add a lot to the list."

"Well, that's why it's so important that you've gotten the indoor plumbing fixed," Eleanor said, smiling Madonna-like.

"What do we need," I sighed, already resigned to mountains of laundry.

"Not much! Safety pins, soft cloths and tough ones, for both the belts and the outer layer of the pads."

"Soo, sheets, jeans, and safety pins?" I summed it up.

"Yes, exactly, thank you."

"Yay." Thick, chunky pads, and no chocolate on top of the cramps. Yeah, that'll really make our months. *Fuck.* "More for the shopping list, then."

CHAPTER 22

We took Steve's chimera truck this time. More storage space and we'd have the opportunity to actually blend in. Dereva refused to let anyone else behind the wheel. We'd taught the girl to drive, and it seemed we'd created a monster. I smothered a smile, watching her competently handling the big truck.

Seahorse and Sirius would get started on stalking Steve while we were gone, and hopefully we'd have an ambush option or two within the next couple weeks. Everybody was getting antsy to fight, and we knew we couldn't wait too long. Didn't want Steve getting complacent. Or someone to go off half-cocked.

Just as we were pulling out, Amana came racing out of the Lair, shouting and waving a scrap of paper. "Wait!" she cried. "Wait, *por favor! La lista!*"

Dereva brought us to a crashing halt and Phoenix hopped out from the back. "What? Oh, thanks." She perused it for a moment, then looked at the other woman. "We probably won't find everything, you know."

"*Si*, I know. As much as you can." Amana smiled broadly at her. "So you don' forget, eh?"

"Can we go now?" I complained through the open door. "You're letting all the warm air out."

Phoenix cheerfully gave me the finger as she hopped back in the truck, calling out a last *thank you* to Amana. As quickly as that, we were underway. "Man, she doesn't ask for much," Phoenix commented a few minutes later, after she'd thoroughly read the list. "Antibiotics, aspirin, the usual foods, more clothes, *sewing needles*? And what are the safety pins for?"

"Our new pads," Dereva informed her.

"Fuck."

***

Taking advantage of dirt roads, they dropped me and River off in the orchards just south and east of Salem, shortly after dark, right next to an area I discovered was actually called Pratum. "I always thought this was called Salem," I said, examining the road map.

"Live and learn," Phoenix said, grinning.

The drop lay only fifteen minutes' drive from Salem, which should take us two to three hours of walking. We'd spotted Steve twice, from a distance, but they never even looked at us, and I was more than happy to take advantage of them while it lasted. *Bless their unimaginative little hearts,* I thought fondly. That's what happens when all creativity is killed. Nobody ever *thinks.*

Dereva and Phoenix dropped us off behind a ragged, dirty-white farmhouse in the middle of an orchard, and in the spirit of superstition, we avoided saying goodbye. I hated that word normally, and in these perilous times, it was too ominous to use. So we mocked ourselves and each other, promised to meet in three days, and they left, with Phoenix's parting comment: "Don't get shot in the ass!"

I jauntily flipped her the finger as they pulled away, and River and I waited until their tail lights disappeared. I turned to the other woman and bowed with a flourish. "Shall we?"

River just shook her head and started walking.

***

As we ran, it occurred to me how much I'd improved over the last few months. In September, I'd've been puffed out and dying after a minute or two. Now, I had to slow down for River. While I was breathing hard, I wasn't working like a bellows or feeling like I'd bust a lung.

I estimated we still had four hours before dawn when we reached the fence. I held River back when she would have made straight for the barrier, motioning her to wait. I took the time to re-tighten the straps holding all my holsters down. This time, we went in fully armed minus rifles, and I had four handguns, two in shoulder holsters, two in thighs, plus spare mags in my pockets. I was *not* risking running out of ammunition again.

"Hey," River hissed, poking my arm. "What's that?"

I peered in the direction she pointed, my heart sinking. "I ain't positive, but I think that's a half-built watch tower." I'd only seen them in movies, but it was a logical step, and fit with what Sam told us a month ago. "How many others can you see?"

We spotted two more, all of them maybe two hundred yards apart. I sighed, feeling a weight in my chest at the sight. Wonderful.

***

I reached inside the hollow of the tree, feeling for the bottle Kitten said she'd leave for us. Nothing. I breathed slowly, trying to get my heartbeat under control as my anxiety skyrocketed.

"Is everything okay?" River shifted slightly behind me, nervous.

"There's nothing in here." I couldn't keep the tightness out of my voice and fought to think. "I'm gonna swing by her house. Maybe she's just sick again."

It took a bit of preparation, fixing my holsters so they wouldn't show. I ended up stuffing the thigh holsters and guns into my waistband and zipping my jacket up just a bit higher. Bulky, but a quick bounce test had things shifting without falling out. Kinda like my boobs, so it worked.

In order to keep Kitten safe, I left River two streets away with the promise to return by midday. I waited tensely in the shrubs outside her house, waited while men were collected by Steve before dawn, waited while women and kids left in streams that turned into trickles. Then I waited a little longer.

Once I was as sure as I could be that there was no one else left in the house, I gathered up my courage and knocked on the front door. "Come on," I muttered. I realized I was shaking my right hand slightly and forced myself to stop. Old nervous habit.

From within the house, I heard a slow, shuffling step, and my hand started twitching again. The door cracked open, revealing a suspicious brown eye. Kitten's jaw dropped when she saw me. "What? How?"

"Surprise." I slipped past her, into the house. It smelled just as bad as it had the first time, but with a faint scent of something...my nostrils twitched...green? Kitten herself looked terrible. Her lean frame had turned gaunt, cheeks hollowed out by grief and hardship, framed by wispy hair that was mostly white.

"You're supposed to be dead!" Kitten finally found her voice. "There was a huge ruckus, then Steve announced that they'd killed some rebels, and I knew it was you!" She began crying, leaning against the wall for support.

"We're not dead. Your niece is alive and well, too." I hastily shut the door, catching it before it could slam. "Is it because you thought we were dead that you didn't leave a message?"

Kitten lowered her eyes, looking slightly embarrassed. "It's a bit silly of me, to encourage a certain behavior against oppressors, and then believe those same oppressors so completely, isn't it?"

I grinned. "It's nice to know we were that big of a thorn in their asses. Anyway, back to business. I've got someone for you to meet. Are you good for a walk?"

"Of course." A hint of testiness entered the older woman's voice. "I may look old, but I'm not dead yet. Where is this person?"

As I led Kitten to River, we chatted casually, as if none of this shit was even happening. "We're growing vegetables in the house. We found a woman who has heirloom seeds," Kitten told me, smiling conspiratorially. "We've got herbs growing too. It's not much yet, but we're getting there."

"Why did you think we were dead?" I asked as I pondered heirlooms seeds.

"I heard about a group of, 'rabble-rousers' was the term used, who randomly started shooting." Kitten leaned on my arm. "I figured that was you. But then Steve said you were all killed, and it's hard to disbelieve them. After all, they're an army, and you're..."

"A bunch of women?"

She shook her head. "Inexperienced. I've got to work on my contacts, find one who will get me the truth next time."

"Next time?" I opened my eyes wide, striving for innocence.

"Hah!" Kitten snorted. "Don't think that whole 'butter wouldn't melt in my mouth' thing will work on me, girl! I've seen the devil in your eyes. Now, who am I meeting?"

I pointed to where River stepped out from behind the tree. "River. She's one of the ones who got out with us last time. She's solid. Got a good head on her shoulders."

After the meet and greet, we moved on, walking slowly around the streets so we wouldn't attract any attention. "Are you ready to hear what I've got?" Kitten asked after a group of Dorothy passed us.

"Hit me."

"I don't know exactly how many troops are here." I grimaced at Kitten's first, bald statement. "This covers the entire West Coast," she continued. "I know there's patrols in eastern Oregon, but I haven't met anyone from there yet. I think those civilians are in Portland." I inhaled deeply, trying not to panic while Kitten consulted a small book. "I've only seen Steve, but I'm finding it very hard to believe they've done everything on their own. However, I have no proof of that. Yet.

"There's an armory at the old prison, west of Lancaster. Good luck getting in there. I don't know anybody who's actually seen it. There's these Hummers." I nodded. The souped-up trucks. She continued. "Also tanks, and a few that are larger. I think they're called 'troop transports.' Nobody in here knows the exact patrol routes." Kitten shrugged. "I know there are patrols outside. Every once in a while, the Steves get switched so everybody can learn the terrain. Portland locks a lot like Salem from what I've heard, and these are the only two holding places in Oregon. Everywhere else that I know of has been destroyed or is being used as a base for Steve. I don't know anything about Washington or California, either."

"Son of a bitch." I made no effort to hide how I felt about this deluge of information. "Right. Shit. What about those structures along the fence? They look like towers or something."

Kitten nodded approvingly. "Good eye." *Not really. Just too many WWII movies.* "The blueprints say twenty feet high, and they'll have two men in them, with a spotlight and a machine gun."

"How do you find all this out?" River stared at the older woman, impressed.

Honestly, I was blown away too by how much she'd learned. Kitten just smiled mysteriously and tapped the side of her nose. What was the deal with that? I never knew what the hell the tapping was supposed to mean.

"And how will they make the spotlight work?" River continued.

Kitten waved that away. "Oh, that, they'll just use a small flame in front of a large mirror, like a lighthouse back in the day. There's nothing in there for the anti-tech thingy to mess with."

"'Anti-tech thingy?'" The corner of my mouth lifted. "What, you haven't learned all about it yet?"

"No." She smacked my arm lightly. "I don't know what it is, or where. There's a general around here somewhere who might, but Steve is very secretive about him." Kitten noticed my poor attempts to hide laughter and she smacked my arm again. "It's not nice to make fun of your elders, Tweedle-dee."

We rounded another corner, and entered a small park, empty at this hour.

"Her name's Captain, now," River informed Kitten. "We decided it was too embarrassing to be led by someone named Tweedle-dee."

"Y'know," I said reflectively, "that's why the name would've been perfect. Steve would never figure it out. Nobody would."

"Before I forget," Kitten said, pulling us to a stop amongst a stand of trees, "Oregon will be farmed. It's meant to support the rest of the coast."

"It'd be easier to hit convoys than having to keep sneaking into Salem," I said after a moment.

"And…" Kitten bit her lip, then squared her shoulders, "you'll hear about it eventually, so better to prepare yourself."

My stomach tightened into a knot. Was it about my family?

"There will be reprisals. After you left last time…Steve said they found people who helped you. Traitors, Steve called them."

"Who…?" My lips were numb as I thought about the man we met first.

"A woman and her son. A Corpsman sleeping with the woman turned them in. The boy…had a story to tell, from what I've been told. All that was officially said is that they were traitors, the woman seduced the Corpsman, who's been punished—"

"But he's still alive?" I interrupted. Mary nodded, and I remembered a little boy that Alex was so reluctant to part with. A tiny, gutsy child. Casey? No. Corey? Yeah, Corey. I turned blindly away from Kitten, and River barely stopped me from running into a tree. I held onto it, wanting to puke. I wanted to sit down and cry my heart out, scream at the injustice. Mostly, I wanted to murder a faceless man, to make him bleed, scream, cry, and die as slowly and painfully as I could manage.

A hand seized my arm, and I knocked it away, barely aware my hand was bleeding, and rounded on the unfortunate soul. Everything was blurry. I saw a white face backing away rapidly, mouth moving, but I heard no words. Another face, closer, terrified but determined.

A few words finally filtered through the roaring in my ears, and I finally recognized the person in front of me. River. "Calm down, Captain! You need to CALM THE FUCK DOWN!"

When I saw she had a gun out, held low down by her side, the fury left as quickly as it came and I slumped down, suddenly exhausted. I dropped my head against my drawn-up knees, shaking like a leaf as color slowly leeched back into the world, and tried to come to grips with the fact that my decisions had an effect on more than just myself. "It's my fault they're dead," I said thickly. "Phoenix wanted to bring them out, but I said no."

Clothing rustled next to me, and a cool, dry hand brushed my hair back. "It's not your fault, girl," Kitten said firmly, composed once more. "It's the North Koreans. They invaded us. They shot those people."

"They'd still be alive if we hadn't come to town," I insisted.

"I hate to be brutal, but the chances are good they'd have been dead inside a year anyway, because *Steve*," she emphasized, "came here to subjugate us. You didn't think all the dying would be on their side, did you?"

"Of course not." I tipped my head back, staring up at the cloudy sky and wished I was at home. River peeked out of the trees, making sure we hadn't been spotted while I had my meltdown. "I didn't expect them to pick people to execute, either. I thought they'd just hunt us. How are we supposed to keep going, knowing that every time we do something, innocents will pay?"

"That," Kitten said, looking at me gravely, "is the wrong question. The question you should be asking is: Can you really stand by and do nothing?" She stood up and held a hand out to me. I took it gingerly, mindful of how frightened she'd looked a few minutes ago. "What will happen if you do nothing at all? People were taken into the streets and shot by the dozens during the first month. Thousands have died from the plague."

"So you're saying keep going, because people die anyway?"

"I'm saying that as of right now, we are as good as dead. You—all of you—are giving us a chance to live." River nodded vigorously.

We walked in thoughtful silence. "'All that's needed for the triumph of evil is for good men to do nothing,'" Kitten softly quoted. "Keep that in mind. Write it down if you have to or else we're dead, one way or another."

Kitten shook off the strange mood first, giving us the last, useful bit of information—some locations where Steve liked to keep soldiers billeted and one spot she suspected of being a brothel. It was thin, and everything could change by the time we next came to town, but it was a start.

We parted ways shortly after, Kitten being very careful not to ask any questions. I watched her walk away, her steps surer now than they'd been when we started.

***

Deciding it was too dangerous to do our shopping (okay, looting) in Salem, and considering it'd probably been picked cleaner than a carcass, we skipped town that night. Getting to a decent location in daylight, loitering and moseying about to deflect attention, and then finding a place to hide until full dark would've been boring beyond belief except for the fact that Dorothy monitored the work crews.

We figured once we got out, we'd check out a few houses just to the north of us. I vaguely recalled driving through an area that resembled a spread-out suburb, and many of the houses were set back from the road, easy to miss from a car.

River had no opinion or knowledge on the matter. "I'm from Grants Pass."

"We ever get down that way, we'll make sure you're there."

Once we had darkness and the timing of the two-man patrols, I sent River through the fence. She emerged dirtier than ever. This spot had a mud puddle, so we didn't have to cut the fence or pull it up. River made the tree line before I began to crawl. I lay half in, half out, braced on my hands, ready to pull my legs through, when a light suddenly appeared on my right.

I froze for a split second, then frantically waved River back and collapsed to the ground. I flipped my hood up to cover my head and buried my face against the ground, extended my right arm forward and sticking my hand alongside a clump of grass. I stretched out my left arm to the side under another bunch of grass and pulled my right leg forward so my foot rested in the puddle.

I could hear the footsteps now, and I kept my eyes open so I could roughly track the progress of the light. The cold water seeped through my clothes as I held my breath. The light swept closer. I tried to not shiver.

Five feet.

Three feet.

The light passed over me...and continued smoothly onward.

I went limp in the mud, exhaling slowly as I listened to the squishing footsteps of a single man receding off to my left. As soon as the light was gone, I was up and running, my wet clothes chafing as I hurried to the safety and shelter of the trees.

"Oh, fuck!" River greeted me as I entered the trees. "I thought that fuckin' sentry had you!"

"And here I thought you only swore during training," I said wryly. "Nice to know you give it more use than that."

"How did he not see you?" She practically vibrated, more animated than I'd ever seen her. "He should've been looking right at you!"

"It's the first rule of hide-and-seek. Don't be people-shaped."

"Is that how you always do so good?"

"I hid in plain sight in a lit backyard, once. Had them going for more than fifteen minutes." I smiled in reminiscence. Those were simpler times, for a while.

***

The moon shone high between clouds before we found a house, and by that time I was shivering uselessly. River, who'd only had a quick dunking, ransacked the house to find clothes while I stripped. She ended up wrapping me in sheets and a couple of towels before doing the same for herself. We huddled together on a mattress after we laid our clothes out. They wouldn't dry completely, but those pants would be drier than they currently were. I absolutely refused to wear denim anymore. These tactical pants—whatever that meant—dried quicker and chafed less when wet.

We rose before dawn, dressed, and decided to do some looting. Only problem was, everything of use in the place was long gone. We had no need for cutlery, couldn't carry the two mattresses in the house, and we'd already ruined the sheets, so we moved on.

Midday found us hunting through our fourth house before we found anything usable. Sure, it'd been gone over, but only by people looking for immediate necessities like canned goods and weapons. The jackpot happened when we found a stash of seeds, carefully stored with paper towels in sealed plastic containers and labelled.

"Heritage seeds!" I held them up, checking the labels through the light from the broken window. My mom had grown everything she could and had brightened our ancient house with flowers. She'd harvested seeds from both vegetables and pretty flowers and replanted the following year. Her and her friends traded seeds like kids traded Marvel figures, so I actually had a vague idea what to do with these.

I used a pillowcase as a sack and dumped them in, then continued the search.

"Hey, Captain," River called. "There's a car in the garage!"

"Ooh, lemme see!" I dodged through the empty house, hefting my bag as if it were Christmas Eve and I was Santa. I deflated at the sight of the two-year-old Kia sedan. "Useless. Dammit."

"Why is it useless? Can't you just take the parts you need from here?"

"No." I sighed. I hated to pop her bubble, but over the years I'd found fewer and fewer people who could find the radiator, much less understand car talk. "Parts are pretty specific. Newer models like this also have tiny computer chips that all talk to each other. They won't work unless they're in a car that also has a chip. Mine doesn't, which is why it still runs. But maybe there's coolant or something."

After a thorough search, we had to admit defeat. Assholes couldn't be bothered keeping any extra fluids on hand. Not that they'd likely work, but still, a girl could dream.

"You know," River said, considering the house once we were outside, her hands on her hips, "places like this are usually subdivided. The original house would be much larger, and richer. Maybe if we found that one?"

"Sounds like a plan."

Yeah, we never did find that house.

Chapter 23

We had maybe thirty minutes of light left and were checking out another small house to the north of the road we were to meet Dereva and Phoenix on. We'd just finished tossing the kitchen, to no avail, and were heading for the living room when the front door opened and two Steves came in, rifles out and held low.

We all stared at each other, shocked, then their rifles came up. I hurled myself backwards, shoving River through the door as I pulled a handgun from a thigh holster. For a moment, I felt like such an Old West gunslinger, until Steve started firing and healthy fear took control instead.

"Go, go, GO!" I screamed, shoving River toward the backdoor. We raced out of the house, the sacks of goods we'd collected abandoned in a corner, heading north towards the hazelnut orchards that covered the land for acres. I heard one of those damn Chimeras roaring to life behind us. "Across the rows," I yelled.

River needed no urging, leaping the low hummock of dirt that marked out a row whilst ducking to avoid the branches of the trees. Our only hope lay in evading them until full dark, roughly an hour away. In bad-guys-are-hunting-you time, that's about a year. In three strides, we leapt another hummock, followed by three more strides. Lights flashed behind us, an engine roared, and crashing sounds signaled the truck entering the orchard.

River glanced back and stumbled. Without pausing I grabbed the back of her jacket, yanked her up and bellowed, "RUN!"

Steve's machine gun fired, an added incentive we really didn't need. We were already running like Tom Carrington waited for us at the finish line. Ahead of us rose a line of taller trees, oak and firs whose roots were sunk in a gully snaking through the farmland. If we could make those trees, our survival rate might rise as high as one in a thousand.

Yay, us. We veered to make directly for the relative safety of the trees.

Behind us, a groaning engine, the sounds of a car in distress, and branches snapping like gunshots had me smiling through the aching lungs and burning breath. The trees were narrow and low, so Steve had to force the truck through too-small gaps if they wanted to keep us in sight. We widened the space, since adrenaline and imminent death are fantastic motivators, and the ground took a slight downward turn. Every step jarred, and my chest heaved like bellows as I leaped the last hummock and exited the orchard.

The machine gun worked overtime, but the poor lighting and the fact that we bobbed around like corks in a stream meant their aim was about as accurate as a stormtrooper's. We'd probably be in more danger if they deliberately aimed five feet to our left. I couldn't hear the sounds of gunfire, not over my own breath, but I saw the damage as twigs and dirt flew, peppered by the spray of bullets.

The land turned sharply downward, giving us a bit of added protection. Ten steps down the slope, ancient sheep fencing blocked the way. River checked her stride, preparing to stop and climb it, but I had a theory, and it'd take a lot less time than climbing a flimsy fence.

"Don't stop!" I increased my speed, and when the fence stood a yard and a half away, the top of it level with my knees (bless those slopes), I jumped, tucking my knees into my chest. I cleared the fence and landed hard, rolling forward to pop straight back to my feet. "Fucking parkour, woman!"

River took two steps back and followed, jumping with more confidence than I'd managed with my theory. It's one thing to see it done on vids and movies, and an entirely different thing to realize you could do it, too. I risked a final glimpse behind us before entering the grove and saw several Steve on foot at the top of the hill.

The grove of trees we'd been aiming for as our salvation was small, one of dozens dotting the landscape, all connected by networks of creeks and gullies. It wasn't ideal, but the trees were tall, the undergrowth thick, and beggars better get out of sight before they become corpses.

Once we were several yards inside the thicket, we paused. I arched my back, hands stacked behind my head, trying to catch my breath.

"We need to hide," River gasped.

I evaluated the trees and shook my head. "Branches too high. Only one of us can get up without leaving signs. I'll boost you. If you think it's safe, bugger off and wait for Phoenix. Then you can bring the cavalry and rescue me."

"What?"

"That tree there," I pointed. A fir tree whose lowest branch would require River to stand on my shoulders should convince Steve not to look too hard. A solid, healthy tree, with thick clusters of needles—enough to hide a person.

We hopped from rock to rock, leaving no tracks. Behind us, Steve's noises grew louder. They were coming down the hill now. At the tree, I balanced on roots and rocks and braced my back against the tree. River climbed me as carefully as she could. I hissed in pain when her boot slipped and slid down my thigh. Her whispered "sorry" was a continuous susurration as she climbed.

Finally, on my shoulders, she hissed, "I can't reach the branch!"

"Jump," I grunted. We didn't have much time. The weight of her on my shoulders made me wonder if muscles could tear from something like this. She gathered herself for the leap. I grunted, clenching my teeth against the pain when she pushed off, and thanked God she made the branch. I wouldn't have survived that twice.

I looked up in time to see River neatly tuck her feet up and hook them around the branch. Before I'd gotten five feet away, she'd disappeared into the tree.

Once I'd left the tree behind, I made a few scuff marks to catch Steve's attention and headed upstream, away from Salem toward our beloved mountains. Steve had spread out, intending to trap us in a net and catch or kill us, but realistically? Six wasn't enough to make a proper search line. A glimpse of the searchers showed a bunch of men kicking through the underbrush, peering around trees and investigating shrubs. They never looked up.

A cry of pain and thrashing bushes made me smile as I skipped over the brushy ground. Somebody met a blackberry bush, and the bush won. The bastards trailing me were noisy, confident I couldn't hurt them. And why shouldn't they be? They'd taken over an entire coastline with barely a shot fired and no serious opposition to speak of.

A thick-trunked oak tree rose tall ahead of me, near the water's edge, barely identifiable in the growing dusk. I ran to it and hid on the far side of the trunk. I looked up at the ancient giant, who hadn't even been middle-aged when the settlers first came. This probably wouldn't be the first round of conflict the oak stood silent witness to.

I carefully turned my head, working my neck slowly. Rolling my shoulders back, I breathed deep, wincing at the new aches and pains, listening for my pursuers. A snapping branch said I'd better get my head back in the game.

The first soldier I shot was young, barely more than twenty. A pang of regret lanced through me, but I ruthlessly shoved the sentiment aside. Who had time to think and feel guilty?

The shot rang out, a beacon, and men shouted, crashing through the underbrush. Any birds that hadn't already fled did so now, their cries and beating wings adding to the din. I took advantage of the racket to run east, stumbling over roots, uncaring of the trail I left behind.

The sun had set, the light fading swiftly, and I knew it would be cold tonight. All I had to do was outlast them. I fired random potshots as I retreated and was rewarded with a cry of pain for my efforts.

At the next spot I stayed put, waiting for the light to fade a little more. The grove was thinning, showing the creek winding through a gully thickly covered with small bushes and brambles. Too hard to get through, impossible to remain unheard. A shiver wracked me, a combination of cold and adrenaline, and I cupped my fingers around my mouth to both warm them and hide the breath becoming more visible as the temperature dropped.

Steve moved in, slow and inexorable, shooting anything that rustled. Assholes.

My shoulders scrunched around my ears and I smiled even as I grimaced. Last time I'd ever let someone jump from my shoulders. Fear had taken a back seat to fun. I'd long since learned that death wasn't the worst thing out there. I might as well enjoy the ride.

Right this moment, I was more afraid of taxes than Steve.

I waited, hugging the steep slope of the gully, hidden by bushes and blackberries, watching the stars and wrapping my scarf around my face. When the gunfire slowed to sporadic shooting, it was my turn. I fired into the bushes, fanning the shots. I emptied two pistols before I stopped, reveling in the pained cries of my enemies, wanting blood, wanting to see their faces as they died, after all the pain they'd caused, and what they did to Corey, the girls—

I stopped short, shaking my head. *No!* That route never ended well, no matter what story you read. I counted backwards from one hundred until I'd calmed, my hands working automatically to switch magazines.

With a better grasp on reality now, I took a couple more shots, then began creeping backwards. Behind me, up the steep slope on my left, the hazelnut orchard ended, and a field of rye began. The grass was short, planted in scrubby rows, but tall enough to hide a belly crawler on a moonless night. My pulse pounded in my neck, my breathing barely muffled by the scarf. As I climbed, a gentle breeze came in from the south, bringing a whiff of moist air. Most importantly, it helped mask my movements.

As I crawled, I holstered the Glock and drew the hunting knife I'd taken to carrying after that incident with the cougar. Theoretically, I knew of some ways to kill a man quietly, but I hadn't stabbed anyone since the creepy bureaucrat. I hoped that if my life was on the line, I could do the job.

I held my breath as I snaked over the edge and into the rye field, praying I wouldn't get shot in the ass. Phoenix would never let me hear the end of it. A branch snapped, the sound subdued by the wind, and I flattened down. I lay two or three yards into the field, and hoped it was far enough.

Two soldiers thrashed through the thick brush in the creek, following it east. I sniggered, listening to the cursing, imagining the blackberry canes catching on exposed skin and rasping over their clothing. I held my breath as more booted feet tramped into the field where I lay.

The only good thing is those assholes didn't dare use a light. They couldn't know where I was, or if there were more of us, not after I'd hit a couple of them. I pressed my face into the mud, resisting the insane urge to look up, and cursing the fact that two nights in a row I was stuck, hiding in mud. I twitched a shrug. Better learn to like it, considering the task I'd set.

Tonight's mud was better than last, at least. Stickier, and not as wet. Most of the damp stayed on the outside, no trickles of water seeping under my clothes yet. I grimaced into the earth. I now had a rating system for mud.

Fan-fucking-tastic.

I cracked one eye open, then risked twisting my head slightly to peer through the short grass just above my head. One man stood maybe fifteen feet away, staring out over the field. Two more were following the edge of the grove, making their way back to the truck. That left one unaccounted for. The one I'd shot earlier?

I forced myself to breathe evenly and deeply, listening to the progress of the two men in the creek as the sounds of their passage slowly faded.

***

I came to my senses quickly, with no idea how long I'd been out. My entire front was cold and wet, the mud and damp oozing through the layers as I'd dozed. My eyes flew open. *Dozed?* Had I really gotten *comfortable?*

Shit.

I rolled one eye, looking for the soldier I'd last seen near me. He was still there, a darker silhouette in front of skeletal branches. He'd moved, standing closer now, and I had the vague memory of him pacing. I'd been bored, listening to him shift and I'd...fallen asleep?

I nearly moaned trying to move. My neck! My *shoulders.* I began flexing muscles slowly, trying to warm them up. I needed to get my ass out of here, and at the rate I was going, I'd fall asleep before a shift change happened.

I still clutched the knife. I'd slept holding it and couldn't put it away without raising my silhouette too much. It was a good knife, meant for survival, with a full tang and a six-inch drop point blade—my favorite style. I'd found it in the Lair's armory while I'd been recuperating from the cougar incident, liked it, and took it. Now, the heavy weight of it in my hand reassured me.

Over the next hour, every time the guard paced, turned, or looked anywhere but in my general direction, I moved. Cautiously, slower than a snail. Easing backward in the row on fingers and toes, then sliding over a hummock of rye into the next one.

I hated shit like this. An eternity later, I lay so close I could have touched his ankle. I clenched my hands repeatedly, pretending they weren't trembling.

The sentry blew on his hands to warm them in their gloves, rubbing them briskly. Idly, he turned, staring up at the sky, and as he moved, so did I, standing abruptly. One hand clamped over his mouth, and the knife in my left hand drove up, under his chin before I even started thinking. There was effort, but only as much as it would take to knock a man down.

My thumb pressed hard against his throat, so tightly I could feel it working spasmodically before his weight became too much and he fell, pulling the knife from my hand. I crouched to retrieve it, grasping the handle and bracing my right hand on his face. His bones were fine, and I realized how young he was, just a kid about Peter's age.

I tugged gently on the knife, and my stomach turned. His cheek dug hard into my hand, his skin cooling rapidly. His jaw moved slightly with the motions of the blade, and—I puked, leaning forward and retching, some of it splashing onto the soldier's body. Steam rose from the meager puddle and I spat, wiping my mouth on my shoulder.

Squeezing my eyes shut, as if that would help at night, I yanked. The knife didn't move, and I panicked, the knife buried in a boy's brain. I jerked on it frantically, finally freeing the blade and drawing it out. My stomach heaved again, and I retreated back towards the grove, away from the still lump that used to be a human being.

I settled just below the rim of the hill, rocking slightly and offering myself all kinds of justifications on why I should live and he shouldn't. They rang hollow, and it all boiled down to one thing; at that moment, I was marginally better off. Luck, skill, who knows? Whatever it was, it was on my side at that moment, but it might not be for long. Not if I stayed in one spot. I had no idea how long until sunrise, and there was no safety here.

I wiped the blade carefully on a clump of grass, drying on my pants. It left a black stain on the grass. I swallowed, sheathed the knife, and turned resolutely away.

Two down, four to go. I stepped carefully, walking parallel to the rim, with my head barely showing over the top. It was slow going. I constantly tested the ground before giving it any weight, terrified I'd step on a stick and give myself away. Once I passed a few hazelnut trees, I crept over the rim and back into the orchard on hands and feet.

At a tiny sound I dropped to my belly, ears straining to fixate on the point. There! Three trees ahead, two to my right, towards Salem, a figure shifted. I muffled my breathing against my arm, grateful the night was too warm for frost.

The clouds shifted briefly, letting moonlight flood the orchard and revealing the sentry I'd spotted, and another one a hundred yards away. My heart thumped painfully, and I buried my head in my arms. Time slipped slowly by, the clouds moved in again, and I was so happy with the darkness that I didn't even mind the light drizzle accompanying it.

Approaching this sentry was easier. The rain hid any noise I made, and he stood with his shoulders hunched, plainly unhappy to be outside. I clamped a hand over this poor sod's mouth and drove the knife in under his chin, just like the last one. Why is it that time slows down in the unpleasant moments? What I wouldn't give to forget the feel of a man dying in my arms, the knowledge that I'd done that to him, the belief that it was necessary.

The knife came out smoothly this time, and though my empty stomach didn't have anything left to reject, it tried. I bit my lip, the pain helping me keep my stomach in place. As I straightened, the clouds parted again, and I quickly whipped the helmet off the soldier and slapped it on my beanied head.

A shout from the Steve to my right had me dropping to a crouch, knife still in hand, the other one pulling a Glock, but the soldier waved towards the rye field, where the other guard should have been. Was he motioning me toward the field, or away?

The choice was taken from me when the man ran over to me, still shouting, and froze thirty feet away. I looked down, then back up at him. My ragtag clothing didn't look anything like a uniform, much less their uniform. I smiled weakly and shot the man before he could raise his rifle. More shouting ahead of me, and I ran towards the noise. After all, it's not something a right thinking person would expect.

I stumbled on the dirt mounded over the row and had to start lifting my knees to avoid tripping, all the while ducking to keep from losing an eye. I paused to get my bearings, breathing heavily. Would I ever get used to this? I lost the helmet to a branch and ducked my head in time to avoid losing an eye, earning myself a long scratch across my face. I hadn't gone a dozen strides before shooting broke out ahead. I hit the ground rolling and came up hard against a tree trunk, expecting to hear bullets peppering around me, but instead I had...nothing?

"Shit!" I hissed. River. It could only be River. Why wasn't she miles away? "Fuck."

Two or three men, depending on whether that kid I shot earlier was dead or wounded. I moved slowly, staying to one side of the muzzle flashes, trying to figure out who was who. Stray bullets whipped past, entirely too close to my head, and I had to seriously contemplate my sanity, or lack thereof, as I ate dirt for the millionth time.

A shriek rent the air, and I heard rage in every note, leaving me simultaneously reassured and concerned. River was reaching legendary status for her mild temperament, the whole reason we considered for our spy run. What set her off? Could anything else go wrong?

Yes. Yes it could.

A giant ball of fire lit up the night sky, entirely too close to me, followed moments later by the deafening *boom* of an exploding vehicle, quickly trailed by a wall of heated air, blasting by at the speed of a fast car. For the first time in months, my nose was dry as a bone, and I hit the ground hard, curling into the fetal position, arms up over my head.

There's no thinking in that situation, no awareness of self, no sight, no sound, just feeling. The vibrations rolled through the earth, smaller ones denoting the shrapnel peppering the ground around me. A large piece of metal buzzed past my head and buried itself in a tree the next row down, causing my stomach to shrivel, and I tried uselessly to burrow into the ground. The heat was intense, and if I'd had much skin exposed it would have burned, until, suddenly—it ended.

The flames shrank, looking like a homely bonfire as they danced merrily around the blackened frame of the truck. I climbed warily to my feet, wondering if the better part of valor in this instance was staying flat. I skulked from tree to tree until the burning truck stood a few yards away. "River?" I called. "Gimme a cough if you're still alive!"

"Here." A waving hand caught my attention. She'd fallen belly down in a tractor rut, coughing.

I stumbled to her, coughing harshly and trying to figure out where all my air went. "You hurt?" I dropped to my knees as she rolled to her back.

"Nope. Just...a little too close."

I checked out our surroundings, looking for the rest of Steve. There were two large-ish lumps on the ground amongst the debris from the truck. "Ain't there a third guy? Or is he dead already?"

"He is now." The glint in her eye made me think this was personal. Very personal.

"Okaaay." I hoped she'd be able to talk about it in the next therapy session Kestrel had. Goodness knows I'm useless. I have a hard time connecting with people. "We should go before Steve sends reinforcements. That blaze is kinda easy to see."

By the time Steve showed up, we'd grabbed our sacks from the house and disappeared into the darkness on the south side of the road.

CHAPTER 24

"'B out time you assholes got here," I growled, crawling into the truck. "Not you, Dereva, you're a sweetheart, but you—" I fixed Phoenix with a glare "—you're an asshole."

Just before dawn, the drizzle grew into outright pouring rain. Unwilling to run the risk of running into Steve again, we'd been huddling under some drippy trees since mid-morning, waiting for our ride out of town.

"Good to see you, too, honey." Phoenix rolled her eyes. "How was your trip?"

"Wet," River grumped, then sneezed.

"What's with all the activity around here?" Dereva asked. "We've been seeing trucks and tanks patrolling all morning."

"Uh. Nothing?" I tried.

"Hah! Nothing my ass." Phoenix turned around in her seat so she could face us. "Talk."

"Fine. But we're not talking about Kitten until we get back to the bunker. I'm not telling that one twice." I glared at Phoenix, wiping my nose on my sleeve.

"Whatever. What happened to you guys?"

"I was nearly jumping out of my skin." River relived the long wait. "How did you survive all those hours?" she asked me.

I shrugged, smiling slightly. "Took a nap."

"Whatever, if you don't want to tell me how you stayed sane."

I merely gave her my best Mona Lisa smile.

When River recounted the explosion, Phoenix grinned widely. "Wicked!" She gave a bemused River a fist bump. "It's your first explosion," Phoenix explained happily. "Did you get any Steve?"

"Three. Two outside. One inside." Phoenix's eyes widened a little at River's tone. So it wasn't just me.

Phoenix arched an eyebrow. "Knew him personally, did you?"

River nodded.

"Eh." I broke the silence, "I'm glad you had the foresight to blow him up, rather than try to attack him with your bare hands like *some* people. I think she'll do just fine as our go-between."

"Though," I added, turning back to River, "why the hell didn't you get out while the getting was good?"

"I recognized that Steve and...I couldn't. So I improvised."

I shrugged and nodded. "Good enough." Improvisation good, dying bad. Since she'd successfully improvised, and I wasn't dead, I decided to call this a win.

Phoenix opened up enough to say that she'd have gone bat-shit crazy, waiting for a chance to make her move. Now I was doubly impressed. Kestrel's sessions were doing wonders if Phoenix could admit a lack in her personality. Maybe we could get her to start up another group for the fighters.

River finally remembered that there were six Steves in the patrol and admitted that she had no idea what happened to them. When they badgered me, I shrugged, uncomfortable. "I happened."

***

I dozed most of the ride back, content to wait until we got back to the Lair to hear how the scavenging went. Once she finished telling her part of the story, River became dead silent. Every time I woke up, I saw her staring out the window, tapping out a little rhythm on her leg.

The moment Dereva turned the truck off, River hopped out and walked straight to Kestrel. She didn't have to say a word—they both headed into the trees. I'd noticed, whenever anyone was stressed, anxious, afraid, we all went into the trees. I had a favorite rock maybe twenty minutes uphill and a little north that gave me a good view that I never told anyone about. I assumed that most of us had a similar place that made them feel safe or helped them put things into perspective. I know they talked about things, but they always stopped when I got too near.

The women slid quietly into the trees, barely making a rustle, and I smiled slightly. Training had finally become habit.

Dereva flung a piece of camouflage over the truck, and we helped pull it over and around. Just because we hadn't seen any planes didn't mean Steve didn't have another way of monitoring from the sky. As soon as her truck was cared for, Dereva went in search of her brother. A routine, now.

First, she cared for the vehicle, then found her brother, then she hunted down a hot meal or something to drink. I think her personal aesthetic was "feminine, with a grease stained rag." She wore it well.

Turning away from the task, I breathed deeply, scenting the fresh air. Some things are forever imprinted on your memory, so ingrained that a single scent can take you back to a specific feeling, place, or time in your life. The scent of pine in freezing air does that for me.

Footsteps and a lack of rustling clothing told me Eleanor approached. The long skirts she favored while at the Lair were so much quieter than our pants. The only times I'd ever seen her in pants was during training.

"How did everything go?" Eleanor asked, looking to the forest.

"River ran into an unpleasant part of her recent past," I said, "but I think she dealt with it rather well."

"Meaning?" Eleanor waited with a raised brow.

"She blew up one of the bastards from the brothel," I explained bluntly.

"Oh!" Eleanor nodded. "I think I know which one. Good."

At that moment Anansi burst from the Lair, trailed by Sirius. "Captain!" he shouted, waving excitedly. I smiled as his kinky mop of hair flew around his head. "You gotta see what we got! I think we can make a better pump now."

"Hold on, short stuff." Sirius neatly collared him. "We've got to go over the mission, find out exactly what happened. If you show her all the cool stuff now, we won't see her for a week. So it'll have to wait until after dinner."

"Can I sit in on the meeting?" His black eyes—partially hidden by hair too long—beseeched her. She sighed, then looked at us.

"It won't be all pretty," I warned him.

"I know." His gaze stayed steady on me. "But how am I supposed to figure out how I can help if I don't know what's going on?"

Phoenix shrugged, Eleanor looked to the heavens for help, and I nodded. "If you get nightmares, I want you to talk to Kestrel, okay?"

"Already got nightmares," the boy fired back.

"Then go find Seahorse and meet us in the Useless Room."

***

"We ended up making several trips," Phoenix recounted, finger tracing the raised map in the Useless Room. "So far, Steve isn't looking too closely at their own trucks, so we just kept on going. Like the kid said, we've got a lot of parts. We cleaned out Silverton's Napa as best we could, then we moved on to Mount Angel."

Mount Angel was a cute German tourist trap, and the next town over from Silverton. Where Silverton had a hundred churches and three bars, Mount Angel had three churches and a hundred bars. Or so the story went.

"...plenty of stuff for pads, and we even found pads and tampons in a couple Mount Angel stores," Phoenix continued.

"We feel," Amana said, looking at Eleanor, then back to the table, "dat de pads and tampons mus' be saved *para misiones,* 'cuz dey are *mucho mas pequena.*"

"Smaller," Eleanor translated. She had a slight smile on her face as she watched Amanacer. "The rest of the time, while at the Lair, everyone will use the larger, bulky pads that we'll make. Everyone will also be regularly scheduled for wash days."

Imparting the news that I brought back from Salem was a lot less pleasant. Phoenix raged when she heard about Corey and gave me a look that said she was two steps away from blaming me for it, but Amana completely derailed her. The younger woman simply put her arms around Phoenix and held her.

"It was no' your fault," she whispered. "There is only one group responsible, and we will make them pay."

After the storm passed, River and me took turns giving out the information. We managed to find the locations Kitten told us about on a detailed map of Salem, marking them with little pins we found nearby. Anansi and Dereva sat quietly, soaking in everything, watching us all. It was a bit unnerving, being the focus of such concentrated attention.

"And what news do you have for us?" I asked Seahorse and Sirius when we finally finished.

"It starts like this," Seahorse got up and gathered a few pins in front of the table map.

***

I holed up on a hillside overlooking—I checked the map—Wilhoit Road with Seahorse and Fox. We monitored one of the routes, pinpointing the best place for an ambush. While we waited for Steve to come back, I pondered the girls' opinions about the news of the retaliations. They were almost unanimous that inaction would be more disastrous than the results of acting. The sole holdout was Jewel, who felt that life, at any cost, was more important than the quality of that life.

I leaned forward, resting my weight against the tree I straddled (and the only thing preventing me from sliding down the hill) and tried to figure it out. For the girls, this issue was black and white, no doubts. I shook my head, irritated. Philosophy was never my strong suit. Best to just deal with the tasks in front of me. At the moment, that meant making an entire patrol disappear without a trace. No smoke, no truck, no bodies.

No sooner had I come to my conclusion than the tree next to me quivered slightly as Fox scrambled down. Steve had just reentered Molalla, the fourth night in a row they'd only done a single day. For three weeks we'd monitored them. They went out for single day patrols for five days, then one overnight.

"See enough?" the teenager asked.

I nodded, then pointed to where the road passed between two shallow slopes dotted with trees. The location was outside the city limits, right before the no man's land of the country. "Right there seems like a good idea." I looked to Seahorse, my eyebrows raised. As the only person in our crew to actually participate in real combat and planning, her opinion mattered most.

"That'll do." I smiled slightly, pleased. Maybe I was figuring things out a little after all. "My advice is to hit them in the evening. We'll have more time to deal with the aftermath, and if there's any smoke, it won't be as visible."

"Tomorrow night, then?"

"Tomorrow, yes sir."

I let the "sir" pass. I got tired of constantly correcting her. I had the sneaking suspicion she did it because she thought it was funny, but I was too afraid to ask.

We felt comfortable enough for a little quiet conversation on our way back to the GMC that Dereva, as always, watched over. Girl never let me drive my own truck anymore.

"Does it seem weird that most of the patrols we've found are in the north?" I asked Seahorse as we walked.

She considered the question. "It's reasonable. They seem to be looking for people who've slipped through the net. As the area north of Salem is the most populated, that would be where most of the patrols should run."

"Either that or we haven't been able to spot the ones in the south!" Fox said brightly, a stray lock of hair peeking out from under her brown beanie. As the one with the most noticeable hair, Fox always kept it covered, lest Steve spot her and us.

"Either way," Seahorse continued, "we have a target, and we need to hit it, hard. Send a message."

"Yes, sir!"

***

Grass and leaves perked up under our first cloudless sky in weeks on the day we hit back.

We'd spent the day placing people, and most of us were out. Amana stayed at the Lair with Moana, Cub, Lightning, and Thunder. The sisters were absolutely banned from further action. For one, they were still too fresh. For another, I'd caught them trying to egg Storm and a couple others into a game of Russian roulette as a way of proving their bravery.

I had a heart attack, the sisters were benched until further notice, and Storm, Hightide, and Jewel had all the shittiest jobs for two weeks for not telling anybody the sisters were that unstable.

Eleanor, strangely, insisted on coming with us. As a Christian woman, I hadn't expected it of her, but she wouldn't hear otherwise. She'd even been training with a handgun and had learned basic hand-to-hand for this occasion. Eschewing her usual skirts, Eleanor donned pants and boots with the rest of us, and, in fact, crouched not ten feet from me.

I stretched my neck and flexed my shoulders, attempting to work out the kinks before shit hit the fan. Across the road, Seahorse and Sirius led the other group. We hid in the grass, and Seahorse showed us the best way to camouflage by picking local vegetation and sticking it through belt loops, into collars and hats, and even in our boot tops. I was festooned with grass and twigs from the mountain ash I crouched under.

We'd positioned Phoenix high up to act as our sniper. Seahorse called her "God," which Phoenix liked and made Eleanor frown. The quivering in the grass that had nothing to do with the breeze caught my attention. The girls were getting antsy.

"Steady, people." I kept my voice low so it didn't carry down the hill but loud enough that the fighters could hear me. "Remember your training. We're all about skill here, not luck."

The ambush went...well, it went.

Watching the truck approach, I tensed up. Seahorse and River were down low with the largest caliber rifles we had, ready to stop that truck in its tracks. "Not yet, wait for it...yesss..."

A fraction of a second later, the booms echoed off the hills around us as the rifles fired a split second apart. The truck rolled to a stop a little bit past where we'd wanted it, but close enough. The higher *crack* of Phoenix's rifle bounced around the hills, and the gunman on top of the truck collapsed, sliding back inside.

Steve, those assholes, didn't send another gunner up, or open the doors and roll out in some formation. No, they had to be clever bastards and launch grenades out the open top.

"Cover!" I shouted as I kissed the dirt. Across the road, Sirius could be heard roaring at her group.

The first explosion went off to my left, and the concussion deafened me. Self-preservation kept my head down as the explosions rocked the ground. A line of fire raced across my lower back, just above my butt, and as suddenly as that, it ended. I popped to my knees and nearly cut myself on the piece of shrapnel sticking out of the tree next to me.

The back of my pants let in a waft of cold air as I lined my sights up on the truck. Steve took advantage of our stunned silence to attack.

"I LIKED these pants!" I bellowed, opening fire.

The sight of bullets kicking up the ground around the truck was the only indication I had for nearly a minute that the others followed suit.

Nobody froze, and that was the important thing. I smiled tightly when my hearing slowly returned, never taking my eyes from my target. The ten of us involved in the fighting had achieved a competency that satisfied Seahorse, who'd set the bar high. We *knew* we could hit our targets, now it was just a matter of learning how to shoot at people who were shooting back.

It was frightening. Terrifying, since we were the ones who'd picked the fight.

The first few times you fight, you're blind, pulling the trigger without knowing exactly where you're aiming, everything a blur as you operate on habit and instinct. Mistakes get made, and you hoped there were enough experienced people to keep the newbies alive long enough to think in the middle of a fight. Eventually, it happened. Eventually, you got used to the adrenaline, enough to be able to think, to make deliberate choices and act quickly enough to make it happen.

Eventually.

Until then, you had to deal with people standing up, screaming and firing, firing until their rifle was empty and continuing to pull the trigger, unaware that they were empty. Then you needed that experienced person nearby to scream "Reload!" until they obeyed, feeling like you'd torn your throat but forging ahead anyway, screaming "Move!" next, because to not give orders, to not get through to them, could mean their deaths, and you don't need more deaths on your conscience.

Slowly, you see reason reenter their eyes, their motions becoming more coordinated, careful, and you finally see the enemy down and know that even as you'd kept an eye on your people, you'd also stayed in the fight.

Once the last enemy was down, it was short work getting through to the rest of the girls. No. They weren't "girls" anymore. They were fighters (maybe not good ones yet), but they deserved to be addressed as such. Eleanor immediately began marshalling the troops, inspecting everyone for injuries, but with everyone on their feet, I wasn't too worried.

Fox went racing back to get Dereva and Hightide to bring the trucks up while the rest of us rolled up our sleeves and got to work, shedding bits of foliage as we did. Sirius took a few people to start hauling away bodies. We'd already found spots where it would be a simple matter to dump the bodies and cave a bank in over them. Some others began sloshing ancient Coca Cola over the blood stains and pulling shrapnel out of trees while I hauled my small toolbox out and got to work under the hood.

I pursed my lips in a soundless whistle. Fifty-cal bullets turn engines into a *big* mess.

Seahorse had a nasty cut from a piece of shrapnel, but a quick bandage later and she was on light duties, which meant pouring Coke. Jewel had the worst injury, because she didn't get her ass down far enough. Eleanor's tweezers didn't have the necessary oomph, so she borrowed a pair of needle-nose pliers and got Phoenix and River to sit on the petite teenager.

"Will she be all right?" I asked quietly when I retrieved my pliers.

"Honestly? I don't know." Eleanor's mouth was pinched at the corners, eyebrows furrowed with worry. "There are some nerve clusters running through there, and I have no idea exactly where they are. I wish we had a doctor..." She turned and glanced at her patient, who was sobbing through the piece of leather clenched between her teeth.

As I turned away, Eleanor caught my arm. "Wait! Your back!"

"It's fine," I assured her, anxious to get back to the truck. In truth, it hurt like a bitch, but less than my period cramps usually did. The only awkward thing was the feel of blood trickling down my butt and legs. It reminded me of sweat running down my back, only thicker. "Just a quick wrap around will do me fine."

Not to be dissuaded, Eleanor turned me around and made me lean forward. The only way to stop her would've been to use force, and I couldn't do that to her. "You're lucky," she said eventually. "An inch closer to the ground and you'd be a paraplegic right now."

My back prickled and my heart stuttered. "Could you do me a favor and not tell me stuff like that? It freaks me out. There's no way I could've gotten lower." As I spoke, Eleanor passed a bandage around my middle.

"You're also running through clothing at an alarming rate."

"Tell me about it," I panted as Eleanor tied it off firmly, finally stopping the warm trickle down my butt. "I hate sewing, and it's what I spend all my spare time doing."

***

Properly dismantling an engine takes both time and an OCD amount of organization. This was worse than chop-shop work. Every bolt went into a bucket, and I flung parts over my shoulder—left for trash, right to keep.

I heard our trucks pull up, and a moment later Anansi squirmed under the engine, giggling as he went to work.

Once the burial crew got back, they began moving the supplies from the truck, transferring everything to ours. Dereva, Fox, and Hightide started squirreling the junk in the woods to my left, chatting as they worked.

The way everything felt normal, but off, crashed over me, and the socket wrench fell from my nerveless fingers as my heart juddered and squeezed. I gasped, leaning against the truck and tried to breathe.

"Captain, you okay?" Anansi's worried face peered up at me.

"Yeah." I gave him a shaky smile. "I'm okay. I just...need to eat."

He nodded, then moved back to a stubborn bolt. To get back into the spirit of things, so the kid didn't need to worry, I began bemoaning the lack of power tools. In a few minutes, the bitching was genuine as I struggled with a stubborn bolt. The wrench slipped off, scraping my knuckles, and I cussed at the truck, clutching my hand. Some of the girls stopped and listened to my diatribe. They still weren't used to the fact that swearing covered more than just "fuck" while Sirius laughed at me.

Bitch.

The light had hit that murky twilight where the sun settled just below the horizon before I got the engine finished. Sirius argued with a door. Anansi moved to help her, wielding a spanner in a business-like manner.

"Here, don't pull on that," he instructed. He moved underneath the hinge. "It works better from here. You just..." He heaved, sinewy muscles standing out in his lean frame, and the metal groaned. The door sagged awkwardly, one hinge loose.

"Damn!" Sirius stood back, admiring his work. "Cap'n teach you that?"

"No. She just told me how car hinges are put together. I figured out the rest."

Sirius looked at me, and I nodded. Once Anansi understood the mechanics of a thing, it didn't take long before he figured out the rest. He said he was better with computers and had never worked on an engine Before. Heaven help me.

Less than two hours later, bloody, grimy, and grinning, we left the area, all signs of our activities wiped away.

"We," Phoenix announced to the women awkwardly sitting on and over parts, "are goddamn *awesome!*"

She got a few cheers, some high-fives were exchanged, and a single snore ripped through the evening. I twisted awkwardly to see Sirius passed out in the back of my GMC. What a legend.

Chapter 25

We set the next ambush near Canby, a large town half an hour northwest of Molalla. It'd been going downhill for years, and at the time of the Invasion looked like a concrete jungle. The north side didn't look too bad, but everything else was just a trashy slum.

We hit Steve a few blocks inside the southern limits. This ambush went much the same as the last, with one notable difference: most of our fighters kept their heads and listened to orders better. It helped that this lot of Steve was less experienced and didn't think to lob grenades at us, too.

The third ambush happened five weeks after the first, halfway to Eugene, and Lightning and Thunder participated. We also sustained our first serious injury, with Kestrel taking a hit low on her side. Despite this, we had the truck dismantled and hidden within four hours while Eleanor tended to Kestrel. We hovered constantly, anxious to hear how she fared.

Another funeral after all the deaths we'd witnessed was more than we could bear to think about, and as a result, Eleanor set Dereva to chase us off and give her some space. When Eleanor proclaimed Kestrel stable enough to be moved, there was a collective sigh of relief. She had a chance now.

During Kestrel's convalescence, we gathered to discuss a bigger job: Salem. Suggestions and arguments flowed through the room, all of us looking for ideas on what to do and how to improve on what thoughts we had.

"We should come in from the north again," Phoenix said. "They won't expect us to go the same way twice."

"Except they would've had to repair the damage from the last time," Seahorse reminded her. "It wouldn't surprise me if they beefed up their security."

We couldn't approach directly from the east. The lack of cover automatically protected Steve. Me and Sirius thought we should come in from the south. "I want to stash the trucks a few miles away and come in slow," I said. "Take our time and leave no tracks."

"Won't we be rescuing anybody?" Phoenix heated up.

"Yeah," I said, keeping my voice mild, "but I want to be quieter about this one. Make it seem like some folks just vanished into thin air. Move only at night. Like we should've done the first time."

"So, who we gonna get?" Hightide asked the big question.

I could see everyone in the room thinking it should be their family first, though most of us had no real clue where our families were.

"That guy," Phoenix said suddenly, "the one we met first. We could help him."

"We should get out the other girls in brothels first!" Storm interjected.

"We made a promise." Phoenix stared at the other girl coldly. Storm bristled, fingers curling into claws.

"Settle down, you idiots!" I snapped, pushing them roughly apart. "We don't do anybody any good if we get huffy. You gotta think of this as a long haul, not a sprint. Anybody we get out is a bonus, and right now we need to aim for what we can get. So you either get your shit together or you can piss off, right?"

"Sorry," Storm muttered.

"'ry." Phoenix looked abashed.

"However, your idiocies did give me a bit of an idea for us to start with." I walked over to the detailed Salem map and snatched up some pins. "So this is what I'm thinking..."

***

I woke to Jewel wildly patting my arm and glanced quickly around, but all seemed as it should be. Sirius slept at my back, River and Phoenix sandwiched next to her. I looked back at the younger woman, who'd been on watch, and her eyes showed wide and panicked above her scarf as she frantically waved for me to follow her.

We'd hid in a sparse grove outside of Salem, waiting for dark to make our entrance into the city. Further north, Eleanor, Seahorse, Storm, Fox, and the sisters Thunder and Lightning had hopefully found a safe place to wait for us. While there'd been some confusion as to why everybody wasn't entering Salem, a bit of logic and a chess board had helped clear that up.

Jewel stopped behind a tree, pointing out at a farmhouse illuminated by the winter sun. I sucked in a breath, hugging the ground tightly. A patrol searched the grounds not twenty feet from us, ransacking the house and barns.

"Wake up the others," I breathed to Jewel. She nodded, white faced, and backed slowly into the grove. Nervous sweat beaded with the drizzle as I watched them move about. We couldn't afford to be seen. Not today.

One motioned in our direction and received a nod. I edged slowly under a bush and prayed the others were awake and ready. The soldier idly poked through the trees, looking at the surface. One foot came down so close I could have reached out and touched him as he stopped and perused the area. My heart beat against the hard earth, thundering away as I held my breath. At last, satisfied, he rejoined the group who had finished their inspection, taking anything useful with them.

I'd barely gathered my shaking self together and crawled out from under the bush when Sirius showed up next to me. "This," she said with a casualness at odds with the trembling of her hands, "is a *nice* grove. Can we stay here longer?"

"I think so." I brushed the leaves and loam from my front, eyeing the others. "Where were you guys at?"

In a tree, under some bushes...Steve looked, but he didn't *see*. Eleanor would feel that her prayer had helped. She'd asked if she could pray for us, and none of us could deny her, though we'd been largely uncomfortable the whole time.

We stood, looking at the lights of the towers. Not all of them were lit yet, but enough to show the perimeter they'd built. "It's sad," I said, staring at those distant lights. "They've barely cleared any ground around the perimeter. Maybe thirty yards? The Nazis had cleared a hundred."

"Those soldiers didn't have their families being held hostage to their good behavior," Eleanor said gently. "They had the Geneva Convention in those days."

"Maybe. I'm just worried that if they've lost that," I clenched a fist over my belly, "*fire*, then how much good can we do?"

"Considering the fact that you've already started something," Eleanor said, amused, "it's a bit late to be worrying about it, don't you think?"

"Yeah, sure. Throw logic at me." This earned me a smile, and I shook my head at the distant lights. "The rest of them can either join us or get out of the way."

***

Outside Salem's fence once more, I could see the cleared ground was wider than I thought, maybe thirty-five yards, the earth still rough where they'd pulled plants up by the roots. River led the way, since she'd been through more than the rest of us—twice since I introduced her to Kitten, and had a few entrances prepared along the line.

When she motioned, we ran, and the hardest part of entering the fence was getting the zip ties fastened in the dark.

Finished, Jewel punched the air. "That was—"

Sirius, closest to her, shut her up by the simple expedient of wrapping an arm around her head, muffling her. "We're not out of the woods yet," Sirius murmured in the girl's ear. "We don't get to make any noises until we're back at the Lair, got it?"

Jewel nodded, eyes so wide the whites showed. River took the lead, moving silently through bushes and eventually into suburban streets, keeping the pace fast. We jogged past a sign I recognized. We were less than five miles from where we'd rescued the girls...was it three...four... months ago? Whatever. Time.

Twice, we hid and watched patrols of Dorothys and Steves go past at leisurely speeds. We passed Kitten's neighborhood shortly before the sky began to lighten, and River peeled off for her next assignment. We'd see her later tonight, if all went well.

***

I shifted, trying unsuccessfully to dislodge the rock when I finally realized it was a tree root. The original owner of the backyard we hid in had been overly fond of trees and bushes, and the evidence of their shallow roots pressed into my front in several places. I buried my head in my arms, trying to catch a moment's sleep with my shoulders hunched to my ears. Not enough to protect me from the fat drop of water that hit me square in the back of the neck.

"Fucking drizzly damn shit freaking..." I muttered into the soil. I closed my eyes, picturing the map, going over the plan again, seeing the little colored flags as they changed position. Entirely too much of this stupid plan was based on wishful thinking and best case scenarios. "I'm a moron." I sighed. At least the plan involved blowing shit up.

***

Shortly after sundown we finally found the right address. Sirius nudged me, encouraging me to knock while she and Jewel went to collect Eleanor, Seahorse, and the others while Phoenix watched the road. I huffed a deep breath, nerving myself to knock on the door. After everything, I still hated having to approach people. You'd think I'd have gotten over that part of my shyness by now.

One more deep breath, and I gripped my rifle—ready to have it up at a moment's notice—and rapped lightly on the back door. Silence. I knocked again. Eventually, I heard footsteps shuffling closer. The door cracked open slightly. "Who's there?" The voice was gruff with fear, and I hoped it belonged to the right man.

I tugged down my scarf. "Your friendly neighborhood spiderman."

"Took your sweet time, didn't you?" He stepped outside slowly, looking like he'd aged twenty years since we last saw him.

"Is your wife...?"

His eyebrows rose with surprise, but grief sat in his eyes. "She's doing better, but our son..." His breath caught, and I saw the source of the recent grief.

"I'm sorry," I said baldly, swallowing hard. "If we'd gotten here sooner...?"

The man shrugged. "We'll never know. Why are you here?"

"Figured you might like a lift out of here. And the rest of the people in this house."

His expression didn't change, then he turned and disappeared into the house. "Check with my wife" drifted back over his shoulder.

"Sure," I muttered, waving my hands, "check with the wife. It's not like we're doing anything dangerous here. Go ahead. Why don't we ask Steve, too—" I cut off when I heard a crackling in the bushes behind me and spun, dropping to one knee as I threw my rifle up—

—in time to see Eleanor exiting the forest, closely followed by Seahorse. "Are you talking to yourself?" Eleanor asked me.

"Yes! I needed to speak to someone with a bit of sense!"

"Where's the man? Aren't they coming?"

"Dunno," I glared at the door. "He's asking his wife."

Eleanor blinked. "Oh."

The rest of the fighters entered the backyard, and I breathed a sigh of relief when I counted. All present and accounted for. "You'll be fine, finding your way back to the trucks?" I asked Storm.

"I know where to go." The young scout's assurance came from someone who'd spent a good deal of time wandering and figuring out how to get home without help.

I nodded, turning back as the shuffling footsteps approached again, and the man stepped out, a thin, pale woman behind him. "We'll go," he said gruffly. "What should we take?"

"Only what you can carry." I gestured to the fighters, who brushed past them, into the house. "You vouch for the others?"

He nodded. "They're good. Getting ready now."

Fighters filed out silently, packs loaded with what useful things they could find, leading children by the hand. The kids were quiet, worried but not scared. "It's because we're women," Eleanor murmured to me. "If it were men here, at this time of night, they'd be terrified."

"I'll take what I can get." Sirius came back around, and I saw the dark band on her arm. It was nearly time. I pulled out a scrap of cloth blacker than the clothes I wore and tied it around my arm.

The parents balked at walking into the night. It had become dangerous, a time when it was best to be locked inside. Hopefully, the kids wouldn't get their parents' fear. Maybe they would see it as I did: a place of safety, and fun, when mischief ran wild—and mischief was me.

"They helped us," I heard Eleanor speaking quietly to the adults. "We were in a brothel." She showed them the brand on her flank. "She helped us."

"Remember," I murmured to Seahorse, "wait for the signal, then run like a bat outta hell." She grinned, and we bumped fists.

My team waited in the backyard as the others slowly made their way into the forest. Five families, seventeen people. As we watched them disappear, a curtain flashed next door, a pale face appearing in the window. Phoenix twisted, showing the band on her arm. The curtain slammed back into place, and the house was silent once more.

A few minutes later, River arrived. "Do you know how hard it is to find shit without phones?" she said, pulling out a piece of paper. "I miss my phone."

We gathered in the emptied house, the others murmuring assent, but I didn't agree. If there was technology, we'd be dead by now. No way to hide from what Steve could bring to bear. "Show us what you got," I said instead.

CHAPTER 26

"Well, there was no alarm," Phoenix whispered as we jogged west, taking advantage of the night. "I think we're getting good at this."

Jewel's sour voice drifted out of the dark. "It was just luck."

"Maybe," I said, picking up the pace, "but we can't rely on luck. We need skills now, people. Keep your head in the game."

We trotted through the streets, heading for the updated location of Steve's whereabouts. Steve had a little building they used as a barracks on the north side. And we...well, we wanted to see what kind of trouble we could cause.

Red armbands were the perfect cover. Anywhere else, covered faces would be a dead giveaway for hinky behavior, but here, if you wrap a scrap of red around your arm, you're fine. Cops gave us a wide berth, and soldiers didn't even look twice.

The site Kitten had noted was in Keizer, not too far from the north gate. Across the street from the west-facing building were the partially demolished remains of offices. They'd been in the process of being torn down when the Invasion happened, and rubble still littered the lot. We crouched behind a crumbling wall, studying the makeshift barracks by the light of two lanterns glowing inside the rooms.

After ten minutes without signs of movement from within, Jewel, impatient, stepped out, ignoring my hissed order. She got three steps when lights flashed over a building to our left as a Chimera truck turned onto the road. I lunged over the wall, wrapping the smaller woman in my arms and collapsed, boneless, taking her down with me. The lights swept over our heads as we lay amongst the tumbled concrete and I desperately pretended to be rubble. Jewel lay rigidly, barely breathing until the truck pulled into the drive next to our target, parking behind the building. When she made to get up, I tightened my grip, warning her to be still. We waited until Sirius and Phoenix came out, and then I knew it was safe.

"You're on toilet duties for a month," I told the younger woman quietly. "If you fuck up like that again, you'll be pumping water, too." Those were the two worst jobs in the Lair, and the ones that most frequently ended up as a punishment. Toilets weren't nasty, but it was time consuming, while pumping water was plain hard work.

Jewel glared at me, petulance rolling off her. Who knows? Maybe she was right to feel it. I'd brought her here, I'd brought everyone here, but she said she wanted to fight and agreed to follow orders. I waited for the tirade, wondering how I was supposed to discipline people when I didn't feel like I had any right to mete out punishment.

"The punishment is fair." River broke her customary silence, cutting Jewel off before she could begin. "You know better. You've done better. We all thought you were ready." River stared at Jewel, implacable certainty rolling off her in waves.

Where did she get it, and could I have some?

Jewel nodded tersely.

Turning back to the task at hand, we perused the barracks once more. "Did Kitten say anything about civilians in the building?" I asked River.

"It's tended during the day by normal people." River closed her eyes, recalling the paper she'd destroyed. "To the best of her knowledge, nobody other than soldiers stays there overnight."

"Okay," I studied the area once more. "You know what to do."

"We're idiots," Phoenix breathed happily. "This is great!"

River and Jewel kept watch. Sirius and Phoenix headed for the south end of the building where the main bulk of it lay. I headed for the driveway. I crept around the building, staying close to the wall, stepping cautiously over broken glass and bits of concrete, grateful for the rubber soled boots. A light flashed in one window, and I hugged the wall next to it, slowly inching my way around to peer through the broken pane. A lone soldier was reading in the corner on a bottom bunk by the light of a single candle. On my side of the room, I caught a glimpse of another bunk bed.

I continued down the drive, passing two more dark windows before I reached the end of the building. The way was blocked by a chain link gate, topped with barbed wire. Beyond that sat the truck the patrol had just brought in. A quick look back showed the light still shining in the window, and nothing else.

I studied the gate carefully. Going over was out but...I took off my pack, jacket, and outer sweatshirt, shoving them underneath the gate, along with my rifle. The gates didn't sit flush and had a chain spanning the gap. Just wide enough that maybe...I eased a leg over, squeezing through, then stopped, caught on the fence. Sliding back out, I removed all my shirts but one.

Left in a long sleeved t-shirt, I continued through, shivering as a fresh gust of wind swirled down the driveway. Working carefully, breathing out in an effort to lose those extra inches, I managed to squeeze through. As I twisted to bring the other leg over the locking chain, the Glock holstered on my thigh caught. I balanced on one leg, awkwardly working the straps off the protruding wires. When it came free, I nearly hit the ground. My training kicked in, and I tucked into a forward roll right before I kissed the pavement.

I waited, barely breathing to see if my acrobatics had alerted anyone, but all was still. The noise must've gotten lost in the wind. Shrugging back into the jacket, I stuffed the rest of my clothes into the pack for later and turned my attention back to the task at hand.

"Hello, baby," I crooned to the truck. "Too bad we can't take you with us." It was, however, the perfect thing to go boom.

With Seahorse's help, we'd shaped some of Anansi's Semtex into small rolls. The detonators were crude, but some experimenting had proved they'd work. Anansi again, playing with dangerous chemicals this time. I blew out a breath, took a roll, molded it to the undercarriage, and set the timer. *His mother will kill me.* I wedged another into the back wall of the building. Squeezing back through the gate took a precious minute, leaving me barely enough time for one more under the lit window.

Subtlety went out the window as I hustled across the street. The problem was that the detonators weren't exactly...accurate. We'd had anywhere from thirty seconds to a minute with the same damn time set. To my left, I saw two other shapes hurtling a low wall maybe ten yards ahead of me. My foot had barely touched the sidewalk on the other side when the first concussion hit.

The movies are wrong. You don't go flying through the air with your arms splayed out, or do a belly flop on the concrete and pop up again in a minute or two looking like a disheveled hero. You go flying like that in real life, you'd break your face. Neither do you have time to think, to plan, or pull your arms in. It's all instinct, fear, terror, and after the first wave of noise, silence.

Ringing in my ears was the first thing I was aware of, then the fact that I had ears. Did I call out? Rough hands grabbed me and yanked me upright, forcefully propelling me...somewhere. I couldn't see. Panic threatened, and

I nearly screamed, until I remembered it was night. Oh, yeah. It finally dawned on me that I wasn't blind. There were shapes around me and I recognized them.

River took the lead, Sirius right behind her, towing me like a tugboat with a barge. The light became better, so we turned north abruptly. I caught a glimpse of the eastern sky and the bright orange glow lighting it. Seahorse wasn't joking about the efficacy of Semtex. We halted and Sirius clamped a hand over my mouth. I realized I'd spoken aloud and pressed my lips together.

My hearing returned slowly as we moved, and by the time we reached the river I had most of it back. River took us down a drive, into—I peered at the sign—the Keizer Rapids Park. I shivered, sweat a cold glaze on my skin. Phoenix hastily gave me my pack back, and after watching me fumble at it with numbed fingers, pushed my hands aside, stripped my wet shirt off, and helped me into more clothes.

"How's she doing?" Sirius asked over my head.

"Not good. She's freezing. We need to stop somewhere and get her warmed up."

"After we cross," I croaked.

Sirius and Phoenix looked at me. "What?"

"We can't be found on this side of the river. We have to cross before we stop." I could barely speak for chattering teeth. "We're in a boat park. Find a boat." I closed my eyes, too cold and exhausted to say more.

"How the hell does she do that?" Phoenix demanded to Sirius as they walked away. "She's in shock, concussed, and half-frozen, and still knows where we are."

Sirius, bless her, sent them off to find a boat, then came and sat behind me, sharing her warmth as best she could.

The sky got noticeably lighter in the east before Jewel came back. "I've got nothing," she said glumly.

From the south, Phoenix and River appeared, hauling an old fiberglass canoe with two oars in it. "That works," Sirius commented.

I fumbled around, finally realizing I'd lost my armband, but Sirius stopped me. "You're our prisoner," she said cheerfully. "After all, you did blow up Steve's building, you naughty girl!" She shook her finger at me.

I gave her one back. "Hope this tub won't dump us in the drink." I eyeballed the canoe skeptically.

"Let's keep her away from the fence," Phoenix said to the others as they unceremoniously loaded me in. "I'd rather not see what kind of security they've got while she's in this condition." I was getting tired of them talking about me as if I were an idiot, or not even there, and I felt utterly useless as I clutched the sides while they launched the canoe and leaped in.

River and Sirius paddled as hard as they could to keep us from getting swept away with the current, steering us for the other side. I watched the water pouring into the canoe, convinced I could see currents and eddies in it before my brain kicked in and I started to bail. The canoe crunched against the far bank and the front caved in, making it quite clear we'd have to find a different way out of town.

"At least she got us here," Phoenix said, looking at the water puddled around her feet. I nearly fell in, tripping over my own two feet as I exited the canoe, and only a desperate grab at a tree branch saved me.

"I think I'm done with boats," I said, wide-eyed, staring at the mud in front of me.

While I stood there, contemplating my close call, the others loaded the canoe down and shoved her back into the river.

She didn't even have time to sink before they were hustling me through the trees. This area looked uninhabited, nothing except a few foot trails meandering through the trees. Sirius found us a spot, and we bedded down in a clump of bushes, packed together like sardines for warmth. We had a couple of lightweight sleeping bags that went under us, and two more to go over the top, then Sirius shoveled fallen leaves over that to give us added warmth and concealment. I ate what was given to me, and slept when that was gone, oblivious to everything else.

***

A slice of watery sunlight trickled through the needles and crawled sluggishly across my eyes, waking me from dreams that were better left alone. A low *moo* sounded close by. I cracked an eye open to see a cow standing several feet away, chewing her cud, mouth moving rhythmically. Crackling in the bushes heralded another cow walking slowly towards the river a hundred feet away. I shifted slightly, wincing as a line across my side fired up at the movement. The weight at my back stirred, and Sirius's grinning face appeared above me.

"So you're finally awake, hmm?"

"Ah!" I raised a hand to shield my eyes. "Warn a girl before you do that! Your ugly mug is *not* the first thing I want to see in the morning."

"It wasn't," she said.

"How would you know?" I groused. "They're my eyes!"

"I heard them open," came her smug reply.

"It's too early for bullshit. Or too late. Whatever."

"Will you guys shut up for once?" Phoenix peered aggrievedly over her shoulder at me. "I was enjoying the sunlight until you two started yapping."

I freed a hand to give her the finger, then gritted my teeth as the movement caused the line of fire in my side to flare. "I think I got hit last night."

"Not too badly," Sirius observed calmly.

"Fuck off! It's my damn side!"

"You're still alive," she pointed out prosaically. "Besides, I'm pretty sure that even with everything, we'd have noticed if you were bleeding like a stuck pig."

"Ah, shut up and check my side, would you?"

"Why is it," Sirius asked the air as she gently pulled up my shirts, "that it's never a hot, muscly guy asking me to look under his shirt?"

"Because you hate everyone," I gasped as she pried the last layer away from my skin. She raised her eyebrows, assessing the damage. Phoenix ignored us, but the ruckus pulled River and Jewel over to observe. To be fair to my cousin, saying she hated everyone wasn't in the least accurate. Sirius is one of those rare few who is happy with herself, and isn't involved in the constant, unconscious search to find someone to "complete" her.

"It's not too bad." The verdict was delivered with a grin. "It looks like a piece of shrapnel hit your back and curved around your side. Congratulations. Your ribs have done their job. Does this hurt?" She poked experimentally while the other two looked on with an abominable lack of sympathy.

"Yes!" I gritted.

"I don't think it's broken," Sirius shrugged. "If it was, you'd probably've screamed."

"You're a psychopath, aren't you?" Sweat bloomed across my skin as I tried to relax into the pain. "How did we not notice this before?"

Phoenix sighed and shifted irritably. "I'm going to get more water, since you two won't let me have any peace." Gathering up the canteens, she left one for Sirius and stalked off.

Sirius used the last canteen to wet my side down and clean the wound, then she started bandaging. River supported me, and Jewel helped my cousin wrap my ribs, ignoring my protests. "You make a sucky doctor," I gasped.

More crackling in the underbrush caused weapons to appear in our hands like magic. When the intruder finally made it through the bushes, I don't know who was more surprised, us or the sheep. It stared at us a moment before *baa*-ing and wandering off again.

Hot on the heels of the sheep leaving, Phoenix returned. "Get this," she said, dropping the canteens. "There's a bunch of patrols out and about, and a hell of a lot more animals around. Goats, sheep, chickens, ducks, the works. Fence is maybe sixty yards that way." She pointed north.

"Map," I said. River fished it out of her belt pouch and smoothed it on the ground. We gathered around the map, heads bent intently, and River traced the city limits before touching the approximate place we currently hid. According to the map, it was unpopulated, which explained the livestock. Following the map to the west, we came to the dot where Kitten had marked a brothel.

"It's right next to the fence," Jewel observed. "Easier to escape."

"Yeah." I examined the area as best I could. "Two of us can watch the building, the other three can find the fence and prep a way out. We need to know how far it is from the building to the fence, and if it's likely that patrols'll hear a fight. We ain't getting caught with our pants down this time, okay?"

When we moved out, Sirius took the lead. In dense undergrowth like this, her poor eyesight didn't matter a bit. Phoenix had the rear, and I wrapped my arm with a strip of red. We hadn't gone far when Sirius let out a warning.

"Fuck! Steve!"

We were trapped, cornered. Any attempt at diving into the bushes would be ruined by the noise of our passage. Only one thing for it.

"Line up, scarves up, keep your mouths shut," I hissed. I stepped to the front as the first soldier rounded the bend, and not knowing what else to do, I saluted. "Sir!"

"Report!"

I bit my lip, feeling the urge to give in to giggles. I always had the urge to laugh at inappropriate moments. Why did that have to show up now?

"Sir, Maxwell of the North Salem Corps, sir," I coughed slightly to add a bit of gruffness and give a reason for my shoulders shaking. "No signs of any people but ourselves, sir."

"Keep looking," he ordered. The care he made enunciating the words made it quite clear that he had no intention of making a mistake and unknowingly becoming a laughingstock. "There are dangerous people loose!"

"Sir, yes, sir!" I saluted again, and the others followed suit.

"'No sign of anyone but us?'" Phoenix hissed when we were clear. "What the hell was that?"

"The truth," I replied, snorting with poorly hidden laughter. "You know I have a hard time lying."

"You were laughing, too?"

I sniggered.

"It's not funny!" Phoenix couldn't let this go. "We still have a mission to complete, and we can't let anything get in the way of that."

I looked away, delighted. Phoenix had a mission and wouldn't compromise? She was concerned about others' lives, and wouldn't throw her own away needlessly? This was the best news I'd had in days. "We'll get the mission done," I promised.

***

Moving out at a quick pace to get away from Steve, we were reminded yet again that traversing areas on foot when we were accustomed to driving takes freaking ages. Meanwhile, we passed various farm animals, and all I could think about was hamburgers and barbecued chicken.

The time passed in a mix between pleasant daydreams where we had enough to eat, and subconsciously noting every tree, animal, and track. Daydream and reality met when Sirius halted, waving us down.

More animals had gathered here, finding shelter from the wind in the run-down buildings that made up this tract of land. Chickens nested under some houses while ducks paddled in an abandoned kiddie pool.

"Keep it tight," I muttered as we quick marched across the bare ground.

Three houses into the new labyrinth and we ran across another patrol of soldiers. I made it through this one without hysterical laughter, at least. "You know," I said, watching them depart, "I'm wondering if they're really that careless, or if it's got more to do with arrogance?"

My statement was met with blank stares.

"What?" I said as we continued on. "From the little we know, North Korea is very regimented, and folks have to conform and never step out of line. Like, they're not used to people being *people,* which is to say, lying, cheating, bastards, and they simply don't expect disobedience on a large scale, 'cuz it's not what their people would do."

"Nice theory," Sirius said, pausing to listen, "but who *cares*? Hasn't got a damn thing to do with what's in front of us."

I shrugged. "True that. River, we need the map again, I can see a road sign up ahead."

Evening settled in, casting long shadows as we examined the map again. By cutting through a few backyards, we could take nearly half a mile off our route and put us at the end of Emerald Drive, just a short walk from our destination at the drive's far end. Kitten had narrowed it down to an area, not a house, and we skulked in the shadows looking for differences.

Phoenix spotted it. Again. All the yards had long, overgrown grass, but only one had a dirt line trampled into it and bars over the small windows. The house was small, rundown at the eaves, with wood rot setting in, though solid enough for the time being.

River and Sirius volunteered to find the fence and prep a way out, so Phoenix watched the back door while Jewel and I had the front.

CHAPTER 27

"There!" I said with satisfaction, peering down my rifle scope through a window.

"I've got one, too," Jewel reported.

We'd only had to wait an hour before we'd finally seen movement, and what I saw wasn't good. A fat man walked through the house, pushing a thin, dirty girl in front of him to the living room.

"Why does this place look so…weird?" Jewel whispered.

"It's subtle," I acknowledged, "but it's a hell of a lot dirtier than where you were held. More remote, too."

"There were…officers," Jewel spoke quietly, more to herself. "Daily bathing, and comfortable beds."

Definitely different from this place. I wrinkled my nose, imagining the smell. A flicker at the corner of my eye showed Phoenix waving for us. I nudged Jewel, and we took the long way round the back. River and Sirius were waiting for us, and Sirius sported an extra cloth sack tied to her pack. When I asked her about it, she just smiled, beatifically.

It rustled occasionally.

"Fence is a thirty-minute careful walk away." River said. She had a stick and doodled aimlessly in the dirt as she talked. "Patrols are fifteen minutes apart, two men each. No sign of Dorothy." At the news that we wouldn't have to deal with the Americans of the Corps, I breathed a sigh of relief. "Found a spot where erosion has left us a hole again. Fence isn't too tight, so we should make it without leaving much trace."

"What's the game here?" Sirius asked.

"It's a shithole," Phoenix said bluntly. "Dirty windows, dirty girl—I saw one—dirty man."

"Sums it up," I nodded. "I'm thinking me and Phoenix go in the front, pretending to be customers. Take down the fat man quickly, then we get everyone out the back. No shots if we can help it. If you need to, kill 'em fast. Sirius and Jewel, you're our backup. River, you're our eyes out here. Everyone who goes in comes out. Got it?"

Nods all around, and we parted, those of us entering the house leaving our rifles with River. Circling wide, Phoenix and I came at the house from the south, and as we approached I tugged my scarf down. I wasn't worried about being ID'd as a woman. Before, wearing casual clothes, I'd frequently been mistaken for a guy. Now, covered in a layer of dirt and five layers of clothes, the fat man would have to have x-ray vision to guess otherwise. Phoenix was to keep her scarf up as long as possible. Unlike me, a single glance and a person could see she was female.

I hesitated at the door for several long seconds. Knocking got harder the more often I did it. It would only take one person shooting through a damn door to give me an outright phobia about it.

The fat man opened the door. Up close, we could see that it wasn't so much dirt as a greasiness of personality that made him look dirty. His eyes immediately lit on our armbands, and he swept an expansive bow hindered by his gut.

I stepped in, clenching my teeth to keep from gagging at the stench. Phoenix followed right on my heels, tension radiating off her.

"We're honored the Corps has decided to visit us this evening," the man boomed with false joviality, eyes flicking over us rapidly, cataloging everything, from our dirty clothes to the quality of our weapons. "I'm Danston, the manager of this establishment. Two of our girls are busy right now." Phoenix's hand clenched. "But we have two other young lovelies to keep you happy!"

He waved to the far side of the room. Two girls, not even in their mid-teens, were draped over a couch. Their glassy eyes and listless forms suggested drugs more than art. Disgust flared into rage at the sight of those children and the bruises not hidden by the flimsy clothes.

"Like them young, do you?" Danston noted my prolonged staring. He started towards them, and I moved abruptly to keep pace with him. I felt awkward, as if my joints had frozen and were barely working, stumping next to the fat man. Danston snatched up the smaller of the two, the girl maybe eleven or twelve years old. A scar from a cleft lip marred her face, nearly hidden as she kept her head tilted down.

"Get your hands off her!" Phoenix snarled. Rough and threatening though she was, there was no hiding the female timbre of her voice.

The fat man moved quickly, pulling the little girl in front of him, but not fast enough. He'd let me get too close.

I sat up from the jumbled pile we created when Danston went down, bracing a hand on his face to yank the knife out of his eye. I spat on him as I got to my feet, lifting the girl with me. This time, there was no remorse.

No fear. No worry.

This time, it was easy.

I set the girl back on the couch while Phoenix went to the hallway to listen and make sure we hadn't been heard. She motioned me over with a quick jerk of her head, finger to her lips. The soldiers hadn't heard anything.

It wasn't hard to tell which rooms they occupied. All we had to do was listen for grunts and the squeaking of beds. Phoenix took one room, I took the other, and I held a hand up, counting. When I hit three, we charged in. The bed stood on the far side of the tiny room, mere steps away. I had an arm around the soldier's throat as I plunged the knife into his back, between the lower ribs and into the lung and heart, just like Seahorse had taught me as a shot rang out next door.

I held him tight while he died, closer than I'd ever held a living person, feeling his heart stop and his life drain away. When I was sure he was dead, I lowered his body, cleaning my knife on the bed sheets.

"You okay?" I called. The girl in here was maybe eighteen, and I only guessed that because of the tattoos that covered her arms. She stared at me dully, unable to function enough to cover herself or cry.

"Yup." Phoenix's voice came clearly through the thin walls as I began wrapping the girl on the bed.

A low whistle followed by footsteps heralded Sirius and Jewel's arrival. "What happened to—oh, never mind." Sirius entered the room and immediately began rifling through the closet. "There's jack shit in here for people to wear, and we've got another cold snap moving in," she complained, emerging from the space with bits of lingerie sticking to the tough fabric of her jacket.

"There's only a knife on the fat man," Jewel said, appearing in the doorway, "and two guns from Steve." She stared in distaste at the dead man on the bed. "You've been killing a lot tonight."

Hauling everything and everyone into the front room, we took stock. We had soldiers' clothing that consisted of pants, shirt, jacket, and overcoat. "Well, we got enough for two," Sirius commented.

"We gotta strip, people." I shrugged my jacket off. "Can't be too much longer before somebody investigates that shot."

Clothes went flying as we found enough under and outer wear for all four girls, who were beginning to shiver and show signs of life. When I finally started putting clothes back on again, I had to strap the double shoulder harness over a sports bra and thin t-shirt with just a jacket over it all. We were all in the same position, with most of our clothing going to the four kids in front of us.

The girl with all the tattoos was the first to move, swatting irritably at Phoenix when she tried to dress the girl. "C'n do i' m'self," she mumbled. Phoenix ignored her and continued putting another pair of pants on her.

It all took too long.

River came racing in, tossing the rifles to their owners. "Steve's on the way, five minutes out!"

Everybody except Sirius grabbed a kid and hustled out the back door, following my cousin as quietly as we could. Phoenix, the shortest of us, ended up hauling the tallest girl, the tattooed one. I traded with her, and we mixed it up until everyone pulled a person they could reasonably manage. As we passed a tree, Sirius leaned over and snagged the pillowcase sack left at the base.

"Seriously, what is it?"

"Talk later," Sirius panted. "Run now!"

Crashing and thumping let us know Steve was searching the house, and we weren't far enough away.

"Keep an eye out for patrols," River hissed. "They might be—"

"Drop!"

No sooner had the word left Sirius' lips than I hit the ground like a sack of potatoes, taking my passenger with me, the others seconds behind. I pushed the girl half under a bush and laid over her, praying there was no exposed skin. Footsteps thundered past, and a boot hit the ground a foot away from my face. We waited more precious minutes after they left, until the vibrations from their passage became distant, then we were up again. Phoenix had the littlest kid over her shoulder in a fireman's carry, hauling ass at an impressive pace.

Mine whimpered as she stumbled, lurching against me. I didn't pause, just turned and scooped her over my right shoulder, leaving my left hand free to carry the rifle, the complaints from my side lost in the moment. Something I've noticed over the years...performing a move in the heat of the moment often works. If I'd tried lifting the girl like this in practice, I'd probably fall on my face. Right now, like this, we were superheroes.

The problem is, bullets don't bounce off of us.

***

Sirius held a bush out of the way and the fence up as we practically slung the drugged girls under before diving through ourselves. Sirius took a moment to tug the fence back down and brush the bush back over the spot, trying to keep it hidden.

We hustled down a deer path, dragging the girls behind. The new surroundings were finally sinking into the girls' brains, and they fought, frightened and disoriented. The tattooed girl pulled back against my hand, trying to escape, and looking back, I saw the others also struggling.

Sirius came up from the rear. "Pick up the pace," she whispered. "Steve's moving fast."

As she spoke, the distant sounds of noobs in the woods filled the air with cracking branches and thrashing through underbrush. Phoenix scooped the kid over her shoulder again, picking her pace up to a fast walk. River followed suit, but Jewel continued to have trouble. Her kid was almost as big as she was and fighting.

"Move!" Sirius headed back to watch the rear.

"She won't...go!" Jewel grunted when the girl landed a lucky blow.

"No time." I stepped closer, leaned my rifle against my leg for a moment and popped the girl on the jaw. Not too hard, but in her condition, it was enough to knock her out. Jewel gaped at me in horror, barely catching the kid. "Well, what are you waiting for? Go!"

Jewel glared but did as ordered. My charge struggled even more, and I finally picked her up again, grunting as I felt the strain in my shoulders and back. Lanterns brightened the night, a shout rang out as they found our track, and the chase was on.

Sirius came up quickly, urging us off the path. River struck out, going north and cutting to the east while my cousin stayed behind to erase our trail. The girl over my shoulder wriggled, nearly causing me to drop her, and I bounced sharply in warning.

Shots were fired behind us, and Sirius came running up. "No good," she panted. "They caught sight of me, so they know."

"Lead the way," I said. "We're too busy keeping hold of these ones."

No good to start a fight right now. Our best bet was to find a place to hole up until the search died down. Sirius was the best equipped to find a spot, as her countless wins at hide-and-seek had proved over the last few months. Behind us, Steve sounded like a herd of elephants to those of us who hunted, a chaotic blend of thrashing and shouting, making it easier to stay ahead.

The night boiled down to putting one foot in front of the other and following the person in front. Jewel had to put her charge down and drag the girl along. While she wrestled with the child, I slid past so they wouldn't hit me and knock us down.

My shoulders were killing me, and when I stepped wrong, jostling my passenger, a line of pain streaked to my ears. Pretty sure that wasn't good. Jewel, behind me again, pushed the girl in front of her as the kid leaned back. It finally dawned on me that to them, this wasn't a rescue but a kidnapping.

Bullets began peppering the trees to our left, slowly fanning across the land. *Lucky bastards, having ammunition to waste.* The reality of that thought brought me up for a moment, until a tree branch over my head cracked with the force of a shot.

"Pick it up," I called to Jewel. "They can't miss us forever."

I had to lower my passenger, agony a constant line from my ear to halfway down my back. Tattoo girl proved herself a badass, because she had enough wits about her now to realize we were trying to help and stopped fighting me. Seeing her move forward convinced Jewel's charge to get moving, too.

Too little, too late.

Jewel grunted, sounding like she'd been punched in the gut, and stumbled into a tree. I turned to yell at her, but she stared at me, bewildered, one hand on her stomach. She reached towards me, her hand black in the dark. I started back, unsure what had happened, when Jewel slumped to her knees.

"It—it hurts," she gasped.

Close enough to see, my blood froze. Shot. She'd been shot in the stomach. I caught her before she hit the ground, slung my rifle over my shoulder and scooped her up, cradling her like I'd last done for my baby brother, Peter. Tattoo girl reached Phoenix and caught her arm, pointing back to me and Jewel.

"She's shot," I ground out. "Keep going."

Phoenix herded the three girls, constantly chivvying them as Sirius took us straight north before slowly curving to the west. River left her charge with the girls, who were now moving forward, if not quickly, and dropped back to cover my ass. Suddenly Phoenix appeared beside me and took part of Jewel's weight. She carried Jewel's legs, one under each arm, and I had my arms wrapped around her chest, stumbling in my haste. Ahead, I saw the rescued girls form a train, the first holding onto Sirius, the second onto her, and so on.

We picked the pace up to a cautious jog, River covering our tracks as Sirius made sharp right turns to throw Steve off our trail. An interminable time later, Sirius cut sideways once more, taking us through some bushes to the towering roots of a downed tree. She parked the girls in the fern-filled hollow at its base, helped us deposit Jewel, then set to with River and Phoenix, carefully pruning more ferns and fir branches for bedding and gathering fallen branches to create a shelter that would hopefully fool passing patrols.

I worked over Jewel, packing clean t-shirts over the wound high up on the right side of her abdomen and trying to make her comfortable, carefully laying my sleeping bag under her. Jewel's pulse was thready. I couldn't believe how much blood she'd lost.

"How is she?" River asked, ducking into the shelter once they finished the outside.

"Not good." I gave them a brief rundown of the younger woman's condition as River helped the newly rescued girls get comfortable. The cold snap had settled fully in; no one was dressed for the weather, and those girls were even less prepared.

"Told them we needed a doctor," Phoenix observed.

"Yes? And how are we supposed to get one?" I snapped. "Steal—" I stopped abruptly, then grinned. "Steal one?"

The fighters broke out into nearly identical grins of evil glee. "Who's babysitting?" Phoenix asked.

"Me," Sirius sighed. "My night vision's shit."

"And me." River looked up from her position by the smallest girl. "They're pretty bad from drugs, and they're coming off their high now."

I nodded and didn't bother asking how she knew so much about drugs. "Where are the doctors?" I asked instead.

"Still at the hospital. It's got a hell of a lot of security."

"Know where the guards are stationed?"

River shook her head, helping a girl sip water. "There's gates that are easy to see and avoid, according to Kitten, but there's also roaming patrols. Just...take your time."

"But hurry." Sirius looked up from Jewel's wound. "I don't know how much time she's got."

Weaving through Steve's patrols to come out on the south side took more time than I liked, but we stretched into a run as soon as we felt safe.

"How're we getting a doctor?" Phoenix said, running easily at my shoulder. "Are we just gonna *ask* them to help and hope they're not on Steve's payroll?" There was a healthy amount of cynicism in her question.

"Uh, I was thinking we'd grab a doctor and ask 'em afterwards. I don't think Jewel's got the time for in-depth interviews." I leaped a log blocking the path, followed moments later by Phoenix. "We can give the doctor back afterwards."

"Catch and release doctors?" Phoenix snorted a laugh.

"What? Like you said, we can't trust them, so we use 'em and let 'em go." I breathed deeply, the muscle between my shoulder and ear still complaining, and hoped we wouldn't have to drag the doctor too much.

"It's been a while since we've seen a patrol," Phoenix said a bit later. We were off the track and taking a road, aiming to get back into the city further south than we'd left it. "We can fire a few shots to take the heat off Sirius and River."

I nodded. "Two to three each do it, you reckon?"

Phoenix grinned and walked a few steps away, drawing a handgun. I selected one of mine, and she fired first. We interspersed them, hoping

Steve could hear the difference in reports. After the shots, we waited a few minutes, then fired off a couple more rounds.

"Aaand that's enough rest." I shrugged, loosening tight muscles, heading south again at an easy jog.

Phoenix fell in behind me, giggling. "Only thing better would be blowing shit up. Can we do that while we're in town?"

"Nah." I ducked to avoid a tree limb, thankful the moon finally came out. If it weren't for this cold snap, we'd've been crawling, unable to see for clouds. The cold air burned my nose and throat, and I hooked my scarf over my nose again. "We don't want them knowing we're back in town. We need this one to be quiet."

Our track intersected with the road, and we followed that, leaving it twice to let trucks pass. To the north, soldiers continued thrashing through the forests, trying to find the poor suckers that got shot.

"Can I shoot people if we get cornered?" Phoenix asked eventually.

"We get cornered, you can shoot me. Truck!"

We ducked off the road, and I stumbled over a tree root and bit the dirt of a deer track. I lay on the ground a moment, dirt and debris digging in. The smell of rich earth, decomposing matter, and brown surrounded me for one long second before I pushed back to my feet.

The track led south and east, so we followed it. The air changed. I inhaled. Moisture, rich and heavy in my throat. Thick forest then. A sudden dip jarred my side, and the line of pain that never completely left flared again. I ached for the chance to curl up in bed until it healed.

The others missed their phones, tablets, and internet. I missed the lazy days. I missed weekends, bookstores, and uninterrupted sleep. I flexed my shoulder as I jogged, hoping it would stop burning, but it continued to vie with my side for attention.

CHAPTER 28

Dawn was breaking when we made the fence. On this side of the city, we saw little more than poles, wire rolls, and stumps of trees. Dodging north a ways, we crawled under a finished section with fewer patrols. Brushing off our red armbands that declared us part of the collaborators we called Dorothy, we pulled our scarves higher over our noses. We trotted down the streets, saluting when we ran across Steve.

We saw few people, and even the civilians didn't want anything to do with Dorothy. At the sight of us, most scurried to the far side of the street. There was one old woman who gave us a disgusted look and shook her head at the sight of the armbands, but she made no move to stop us, just muttered, "God will judge you for this."

Our limited time didn't give me a chance to feel guilty, and walking the streets left me raw, exposed, but we had no idea how much time Jewel had. For all we knew, she was dead already.

How often had I read that all you had to do to be unnoticed was walk with purpose?

***

"Holy shit," I said, leaning against the wall in relief. We'd finally made it to the hospital around mid-afternoon, and now we were hidden from casual observers, protected by low growing bushes and trees. "It actually worked."

"What?" Phoenix, distracted briefly at the sight of a group of Dorothy, glanced at me. "What'd you say?"

"We really made it here in one piece. I wasn't sure walking like we knew what we were doing would work."

Her mouth opened, closed, and opened again before she whacked me. "This was your damned idea, and you didn't know if it would work?"

I sank down slowly, grinning and giddy at finally being off my feet, sheltered by the bushes. "To be honest with you, I never know if anything's gonna work. It's all a crapshoot."

"Well, fuck you, then." Phoenix moved closer to a tree, away from view, and curled up, pillowing her head on her arm. "You can take first watch. Wake me if you see anybody we can grab."

Watching people wearing their clean white coats, I felt like I was grocery shopping. *Too young, might not know their business. Older, won't be able to keep up. Too tall, too noticeable.*

I squirmed, trying to stay awake, as the shadows lengthened across the ground, the chill wind continuing unabated. Movement slowed, but I figured it'd have to pick up again when the shift changed. My stomach roiled when it occurred to me that they might all live in the hospital instead of in houses. I sighed, craning my head around to look up at the windows and idly contemplating what it would take to kidnap a person from a building and get them out through a window. That would have to be a last-ditch attempt, because I just didn't see that ending well.

An eternity later, the shadows moved enough that I could wake Phoenix for her shift. Tears started in my eyes when I lay down, finally—*finally*—able to rest. My exhausted brain couldn't let go, and instead drifted in circles, contemplating any stupid topic that happened to cross its expanse.

I pondered the mysteries of why we never saw any women and thought that maybe they'd been left at home. Perhaps they'd cut their hair short and were indistinguishable from the men? If they were here, what did they think about the things local women suffered? How did these theoretical women perceive the rape and abuse of their white counterparts?

"Hey, hey," Phoenix poked me. "There's people!"

I mumbled something profane and unintelligible, blinking back more tears. It couldn't be time to get up already, could it? I rolled to my side and struggled up, feeling the cut from two nights before pull and stretch, and looked where Phoenix pointed.

"What do you think of that one?" Phoenix pointed to a slender man a few yards away.

I shook my head. "No dice. Skinny guys can surprise you."

Phoenix studied the other people walking across the grounds. "Why don't we take the doc back to the Lair? You know we could use a doctor. We don't have to let them go."

"Because it'd be damn near impossible to keep them." I closed my eyes briefly to relieve the burn. "All they'd have to do is get picked up by a patrol, and next thing we know Steve's not worried anymore because they know they're just up against a dozen women, and they have a guide to our door."

"A dozen kick-ass women," Phoenix said resentfully.

"Don't matter. Once the boogeyman has a face, it ain't that scary any more. We need—ooh, lookit that one!" I needn't have spoken. Phoenix had locked onto the same target.

The woman was small, professional, young, but old enough to have experience. Not threatening, easy to kidnap, and likely a doctor. A touch older would be nice, just so she had more experience, but beggars can't be choosers. And I was back to feeling like I was grocery shopping again. Or slaving.

Not my proudest moment, I'll admit.

We slid further back into the shadows, following the woman.

***

It's a good thing we went for a small woman, because while she's small, she's *damn* scrappy.

We dragged her into the bushes and had to sit on her to get her still enough to listen to us. Apparently, she didn't believe us, or she didn't want to help, so it was Plan B, duct tape and zip ties. I slung her over my shoulders in a fireman's carry, while Phoenix toted the woman's bag and kept watch.

"What happens if she still won't help Jewel?" Phoenix's voice drifted out of the dark. The moon had yet to rise, and Phoenix was little more than a blob against the sidewalk.

"Then we have no need for her." I kept my voice cold. The woman could come to whatever conclusion she wanted, as long as she helped us.

The doctor kicked, muffled screaming working through the gag and guilt tried to worm its way out, but hey, we tried talking to her first. As soon as we cleared the perimeter, we untied her feet and dragged her. While she wasn't exactly willing, she moved.

She fought and pulled, but out in the forest she had little chance of finding her way back to Salem. I found it odd, and sad, that she struggled so hard to escape us and return to the hell she knew. Better the devil you know than the devil you don't.

When we finally approached the hideout, it'd been nearly twenty-four hours since Jewel was shot, and my tension ratcheted with each step. Our captive finally stopped pulling backwards, though that may have something to do with the fact that Phoenix threatened to deck her.

I *know* we were making a bad first impression. Sue me.

Phoenix began whistling "Yankee Doodle," and ahead of us, nearly ten yards beyond where I'd thought. River whistled back. She hustled us off the path, brushing branches and twigs out of the way.

"Is Jewel...?" I hesitated.

"Still breathing. She's in a bad way." River stood back to let us into the shelter, which had become a veritable shrub of its own. A tiny fire burned between Jewel and the girls, and now that we were inside the camp, I finally caught a mouthwatering scent drifting through the air.

As soon as the doctor saw Jewel, she ripped herself away from me and peeled the tape from her mouth with both hands. "Why didn't you tell me she was so bad?" She held her hands out. "Take these off. We don't have much time."

I cut the ties from her hands. "As I recall, we tried. Not our fault you wouldn't listen."

"You were sitting on me!" She took her bag from Phoenix and rifled through it quickly, taking out what she needed.

Sirius glared, ready to let me have it, and I held my hands up, smiling weakly. "So," I tried to distract my cousin, "what's that amazing smell?"

Sirius snorted. "Remember that sack?" Next to us, the doctor cut away the rough bandages and Jewel's clothing, baring the injury. "I might have taken a duck."

"You cheeky beggar!" I eyed her admiringly. Never doubt that Sirius would make time for food, no matter the circumstances.

"And a chicken. Or two."

"You need an emergency room for this, a sterile area, and a surgeon," the woman interrupted us, her gloved hands wet with blood.

We all stared at her. "What do you mean, 'a surgeon?'" I croaked.

"I'm an ER resident, you idiots!"

Phoenix clapped a hand over the resident's mouth, and River and I disappeared into the bushes to run a perimeter check. After fifteen minutes

I returned to the camp, relieved at the silence in the woods. The woman still worked over Jewel, replacing bloodied cloths with fresh, fuming all the while. She had all our first aid kits around her and directed Sirius, too.

I saw River slip into the other side of the camp to sit with the girls, while Phoenix headed out.

The doctor kept muttering to herself, a constant litany of complaints and insecurity. Kneeling next to her, I bent close to see if Jewel still breathed. "Listen," I spoke quietly, checking the injured woman's pulse, "resident or not, you're all she's got. She won't make it back, and turning her in to the soldiers ain't an option. They'll kill her, or worse. So as of right now, she's a dead woman. The only way you can definitely kill her is to do nothing. Anything else is...a chance."

I never looked away from Jewel, but I could see the force of her indecision in the trembling of the resident's hands. I wanted to scream at her to make her choice, to make the choice I wanted, but we'd all been there at one point or another, and she had to make her own decision.

"I need more light, boiling water, and an assistant." Her voice was crisp, with a flutter of nervousness she tried to hide. "We'll also need blood. I hope you know your blood types, and hers."

***

The doctor commanded us like a general with her troops and turned our rude shelter into a makeshift hospital. Phoenix, with the strongest stomach, acted as the doctor's assistant, while Sirius fed the fire and kept the hot water coming. River continued to tend the girls, and I found myself used as a blood bag. We had no idea what Jewel's blood type was, and I was the only type O available, so the doctor said we'd better hope that Jewel was also a positive blood type or this wouldn't end happily.

I opened my eyes to find Sirius standing next to me with a chunk of duck in one hand and a freshly filled canteen in the other. "Here. Doc said to keep you fed and hydrated or else we'll be hauling your fat ass tomorrow."

I stubbornly kept my eyes off what the doctor did while I ate. I'd tried watching at the beginning, but after the second incision I'd nearly passed out, and now I refused to look. Sirius handed over one tiny pot of water and immediately began heating another. Phoenix swabbed, and the woman worked, her concentration intense.

After I finished my dinner, I closed my eyes and tipped my head back, trying to remember what my parents had taught me. Praying never came particularly easy, but I figured now might be a good time to practice.

Eventually, I realized I just couldn't pray. I felt fake. Peace was no longer part of my life. What then? Hope that the overreaching effects of war would only touch the other side? Yeah, that'd be nice. I stared up, wishing I could see the sky, but we'd woven cut branches through the roots to create a smokescreen and shelter.

Near dawn, the doc finally slowed the blood flow. Occasionally, I saw a tiny smile of satisfaction cross her face. Sometimes she'd have Phoenix unclamp the blood line, then clamp it again. Either way, Jewel still lived, so we took it as a good sign.

Noon approached before the doctor finished her work. The north wind still blew, and sunlight leaked through the gaps in our shelter. I was light-headed, the doctor letting my blood flow for as long as she'd deemed safe for me.

The doctor needed Sirius' help to stand and stretch her back and shoulders. Jewel lay still, neatly stitched, a line across her upper abdomen and a small one on her back from the entry wound. "Live or die," the doctor said hoarsely, "I've done all I can."

"That's all we wanted," Sirius replied.

The doctor peered at me. "I hope I haven't taken too much from you," she murmured. I tried to stand, stumbled, and only River being there kept me from hitting the ground. "Don't stand up, you idiot!" The doctor held her hand out, alarmed. River gently lowered me back to my spot. "You don't have as much blood as you think. I had to push it."

"How far?" my cousin asked.

"Let's just say I'd have my license to practice revoked. And you need to eat and drink more," she said to me. "And then sleep."

"We should get out of here," Phoenix murmured. "We can't stay hidden forever."

"She—" the doc pointed at me; I realized we'd never introduced ourselves "—needs at least two days of rest and food before she should be moved. The other one shouldn't be moved for a week."

"Don't matter," I mumbled. "We gotta go. Latest is tomorrow."

Phoenix nodded.

"Do you want her to die?" the doctor cried, exasperated. Everybody shushed her.

"You keep on like that," Phoenix said, glaring up at her, "we'll all be caught and die much slower than we'd like."

The doc stood over her patient, pulling on her lower lip nervously. "What will you do with me now?"

I shrugged. "Catch and release."

"But I know what you look like."

"Yeah, sure. A couple blondes, a couple brunettes, some blue eyes and some kids. Though to be honest, we were hoping you'd forget what we looked like."

"Can-can I make a counter offer?" she asked.

"Shoot."

"I'm guessing that with this rather dangerous line of work you've chosen, a medical professional might be useful to you." She spoke quickly, as if to get it out before she could change her mind.

"Why the hell would you leave your cushy city life?" Phoenix asked. "And your family? Won't they get in trouble?"

"The only family I have here is my husband."

"Sounds like a reason to go back." Phoenix folded her arms.

"My husband currently heads up the "North America Liberation Co rps."" She made the air quotes with a grimace. "He's also...let it go to his head. He's not...I don't recognize him anymore."

I sat back, taking in what she'd said. My head pounded, though she'd already mentioned that would be a side effect of the blood loss. I drank more water. "Well, I'm sold on the idea. We can keep you, I reckon."

Phoenix introduced her to everyone while I ate again, and she looked bewildered by all the names. Phoenix laughed quietly at a question from her, and I fell asleep before they finished talking.

***

When I woke next, it was dark, and the fire had died to coals. I found an MRE and a full canteen lying next to me. Downing both, I collapsed back into sleep, not stirring again until just before dawn, when Phoenix slid into camp. Quietly she woke the others, including the new girls.

"Steve's been busy organizing," she informed us, keeping her voice low. "They've set a perimeter and are closing it. If we leave now, we have a chance at slipping through the net, but it has to be now."

One of the girls whimpered, and all of them looked fevered, shifting restlessly. "Will they be okay?" I nodded at them while I stumbled to my feet, getting our gear together.

"It's like having the worst flu," the doc said. "They can do it, but they'll be miserable."

"Anything you can do for them?"

"No." She paused, tying her hair back, then continued. "There's nothing we could give them even if we had it. They need to get all the drugs out of their systems. Cold turkey is the only way to do it."

"Rendezvous, now," Phoenix ordered.

Me, River, and Phoenix took turns carrying Jewel on a stretcher made from two branches, a bunch of string and rope, and my sleeping bag. Doctor herded the girls, while Sirius walked three miles for every one of ours, back and forth, checking the path and on us.

"Shit, I'm tired," I groaned under the load. Blood loss is exhausting. "Will somebody say something so I can get my mind off this?"

"Are we sure Doctor is a good name for a person?" Phoenix asked seriously. "I mean, there's so much that can be done with it. Like 'Nyaaah, what's up, Doc?'"

Doctor glared daggers at us when we giggled.

"How about 'Hullo, Doctah!'" I waggled my eyebrows at River, who just rolled her eyes, a faint smile on her lips.

"I love that show!" Phoenix exclaimed.

"I hate you all," Doctor announced. "Is it too late to change my mind?"

"Yup. Don't worry, you'll get used to us. Maybe." I shrugged, trying to loosen the muscles. "But we're damn glad to have you."

At the worst point of my exhaustion, I had to leave carrying Jewel to River and Phoenix because if we needed to run for it, I'd fail. Instead, I walked the perimeter.

I stumbled back to the group just before noon, wheezing. The ground swayed under my feet, and my vision swam. I clutched at a tree. "We need to hide," I panted. "They're not far out."

"How do we hide?" Doc stared around at the bare trees and bushes, looking at the fallen leaves under her feet.

My mouth kicked up in a smirk. "Time to take a nap, whether you want to or not."

Soon, I found myself lying near the base of a tree covered in leaves. They'd drifted in the constant wind, and it'd been the work of moments to scoop them out, lay a couple people down and fling the leaves over them before moving on to the next drift. Sirius lurked out there somewhere, watching, circling Steve, ready to create a distraction if we needed it.

I lay with a gun in one hand, hunting knife in the other, trying not to breathe as a soldier slowly walked down the path, holding his rifle at the ready. Rustling in the dead blackberry bramble had him stepping closer to investigate. I kept my eye on him, watching the leaves at his feet. At his approach, the rustling got louder, and I tightened my grip on the weapons, knowing that if I had to use them, we'd never make it out.

Holding his rifle at the ready, shoulders up to his ears, the young soldier poked the bush. He reared back, rifle slamming to his shoulder as two little chickadees shot out of the bramble and away. Letting out a stream of words, he shook his head and continued southeast. He looked back once before laughing and continuing on.

We didn't dare move until Sirius slid into the clearing. Piles of leaves erupted, and people emerged like zombies.

"Are we outside the net?" Phoenix swiped her hat off and beat it against her leg, knocking the dirt off.

"Yeah, but the good times won't last long." Sirius shifted impatiently, anxious to be away. "Steve's all over the place, and I've even seen Dorothy once or twice."

"Well...shit."

"Who's Dorothy?" Doc looked up from Jewel.

"The American assholes who turned traitor," Phoenix elaborated.

Doc paled. "We have to go *now*. If my husband finds us, we're dead."

"Don't worry," I said, helping lift Jewel. "If Steve finds us, we're dead that way, too. As a matter of fact, there's only one way we don't get dead, and it involves walking. Like, now."

At a rest in the late afternoon, we all pulled off our boots to check our feet. The rescued girls' feet needed treating before the blisters got any worse. After the first day, when I'd blistered so badly, we'd learned the importance of checking them often.

Doc noticed them, too, and pointed to my missing toenails. "What happened?" She looked appalled.

"Lost them to blisters," I whispered cheerfully. "But look! Tiny little nails are growing back!" And they were, though slowly. I still only had half nails on four toes. What gave me the most discomfort were the calluses that my little toes had turned into. They were always peeling, and if my feet were dry, then the skin was tough. Most days, the pressure of my boots was enough to make them throb. The blister scars were fading, though. The other fighters' feet looked much like mine, minus the scarring.

Doc lifted one of my feet. "So this is what we have to look forward to." She felt the calluses stretching in lines up my toes and the thick peeling skin on the bottoms of my feet.

"'Fraid so," I smiled. "You get used to it, 'specially when everyone's feet are the same." I raised my voice. "And it's time."

Groans rose from the group, but everyone hauled themselves to their feet, including the new girls. The oldest one, the tattooed girl, was nearly clear-eyed and helped Doc keep them moving. From their looks, despite the fact that they were cold, hungry, footsore, and suffering from withdrawal, they were happy to be out of that disgusting hellhole.

CHAPTER 29

"Cap'n! Hey, Cap!" The words barely preceded Seahorse, who stepped from the trees to our left. It'd taken us two more grueling days to get here, and we'd been afraid that our ride had given up on us. Seahorse's sudden appearance brought glad cries from our throats, and two of the girls broke down in tears.

"We don't have time for 'hellos,'" Phoenix snapped, red-faced and exhausted. She and River had carried Jewel today after I'd passed out while carrying the stretcher, and now they were wiped. The inked girl and Doc had half-carried me since, and while my mind worked okay, the rest of me was failing miserably.

In all the bustle of loading people into the Chimera that Seahorse and Dereva brought, we managed to fill them in on Jewel's shooting and my subsequent use as a blood bag. Doc, in the back, watched over Jewel and the two littler ones who'd been harder hit by the withdrawal as Dereva hauled ass out of town.

I rested my pounding head against the window and let Phoenix and Sirius fill Seahorse in on the highlights of our misadventures. We'd get into the dirty details back at the Lair. I fell asleep listening to them, and I woke when my head was jarred off Phoenix's shoulder.

"Contact, two!" Seahorse was shouting.

"Fuck!"

Screams erupted from the new girls.

"Sirius, decoy!" I shouted, throwing a helmet her way. It bounced off Dereva's seat and hit Sirius in the chest as she lurched up, angling for the gun hole in the roof. From a distance, Sirius was capable of passing as Korean, with her dark hair. No sooner had her head disappeared through the gun port than I found myself shoved to the floor so Phoenix could get her rifle set up.

"Ease up, kiddo," I advised from my cramped location. Dereva's foot lifted off the gas slightly. "We're out on patrol, same as them, bored and arrogant, remember? Hey, anybody got any water? I'm out, and dying of dehydration, here."

"Now?" Seahorse hissed, tensely watching the other car.

"What? I'm thirsty."

While I looked for a canteen, Steve rolled past us, though nobody relaxed until several minutes had passed. Sirius' re-entry was the signal that the coast was clear. Back on the seat, filled with water, danger gone for now, I started to doze once more.

"I shouldn't have taken so much," Doc murmured behind me, apologetic.

"Meh," I yawned, and blackness closed in as sleep swallowed me once more.

***

Arriving back at the Lair by a roundabout route took us well into the night. As always, Eleanor met us in the clearing around the Lair. She took one look at my pale face and Jewel in the stretcher and whistled sharply. Within moments, people poured out of the bunker. Some gathered the new people, minus Doc, hustling them inside. Anansi joined his sister, holding me upright, and we moved slowly, a six-legged beast with two legs that weren't working properly.

Jewel whisked past, carried by fresh hands, followed closely by Doc and Kestrel, who still used a cane.

"We need..." I paused to catch my breath, relief at being back so great I had to blink back tears. "We need to go over the job...everything...go okay for you?"

"Other people can rehash the mission," Eleanor said as she appeared in front of me. "You need a bath, water, and rest. Amana!"

"*Si?*" The young woman shouted from inside the doorway.

Eleanor began calling orders in rapid Spanish. Amana came out of the Lair, handed her mother a steaming cup, and responded tersely, then left at a run.

"Here, set her down for a minute." Eleanor helped the kids lower me and pressed the cup into my hands. I wrinkled my nose at the smell and tried to hand it back.

"No," Eleanor said firmly. "Doctor said you're suffering from blood loss. You will drink this. Now."

There was no arguing with that tone. I took the cup, gagging after the first sip. Eleanor glared until I downed all of it. I swallowed the last, then closed my eyes to keep my tears in check. I wanted sleep, and to cry, and to be clean, and at this moment, all of it was too much work.

Hands levered me upright and led me along, and I followed obediently, eyelids too heavy to lift.

"Is she okay?" Dereva's voice echoed down a tunnel. Weird.

"She'll be fine." Eleanor didn't sound any closer. "She needs extra care for the next few days, that's all."

The heady smell of food wafted around me. Kitchen. Warmth. I swayed.

"Whoops! Steady there," said an unfamiliar woman. I frowned, one hand dropping to my gun, but Eleanor responded without fear.

"Do you have the bath ready?"

I heard splashing, then they led me forward. Eleanor ushered everyone away, then I heard a door shut with a click. She began pulling my clothes off, but when she tried to lift my bra I flinched back, hands lifted in feeble protest.

"Don't be difficult, Captain." Eleanor took my hands gently in her own. "You'll sleep better if you're clean, and we need to warm you up. It's okay. You can open your eyes. You're safe."

I obeyed, and everything slowly swam into focus. We stood in the little mop room just off the kitchen. A half barrel filled with steaming water sat in one corner, propped up with cinder blocks. Eleanor waited patiently for me to get my bearings before reaching for my bra again. I raised my arms compliantly, bending over so the shorter woman could pull it off. Once I stood naked, she helped me into the tub, propping my head and neck on a folded towel, my legs hanging over the end.

Eleanor soaped up a cloth, and once she had a good lather, began washing me gently, as if I were a newborn. Everything from the past few days, the fear, pain, worry, rose up in my throat, and I put a hand over my eyes. Eleanor said nothing when the tears ran down my cheeks, the slow, soothing rhythm of the washcloth never wavering.

At a soft knock on the door, she left briefly. When she returned, she pressed another cup into my hand, this concoction smelling and tasting better than the first. Another knock some minutes later, and a bundle of my clothing was placed on a chair.

Through it all, the tears never stopped, though exhaustion had such a grip on me I didn't have the energy to sob, no matter how much I wanted to. When I was cleaned to Eleanor's satisfaction, she helped me out, dried me off and dressed me. Then, she sat me down and held me.

Finally. Finally, the sobs came, all the hard emotions pouring out as I wept.

***

I slept for three days.

***

"Doc hopes Jewel will wake up in a day or two," I informed Phoenix as we went over our gear. It was another post-mission thing that quickly became a ritual. Go over your gear and weapons, clean everything, and make sure it was still operational. Necessary but boring. "As long as she doesn't get an infection, anyway. The new girls should be better by the end of the week, though who knows exactly how the drugs will affect them long term."

Phoenix grunted, working on her rifle. "Keep an eye on them?"

"Shit yeah. We don't need another Thunder and Lightning happening." Those girls had tried egging others into playing Russian roulette to prove their bravery. The memory still pissed me off, so I turned my attention back to the stupid sleeping bag on the table in front of me.

"Fuck me!" I snarled.

"Thanks, but no," Phoenix said dryly without looking up. I gave her the finger, which she ignored. "Why'd you offer?"

"It's my damn sleeping bag," I said, holding up the offending item. "It's got *three* more freaking holes in it and a nice, long tear. On top of the shit I've already patched! It's holier than the fucking pope!"

"I only got one more hole. What are you doing in that thing?"

"The horizontal tango, what d'you think? Sleeping, dammit! I keep snagging it on branches or some shit."

"Blankets." We turned and saw Eleanor had joined us in the common room. "Woolen blankets. They're far sturdier, warm when wet, and they can double as outerwear in a pinch. Just look at the Scots."

"Meh." I turned back to the bag in front of me. "I'm allergic to the stuff. Using one would drive me crazy."

"Like you're not already," Phoenix snorted.

"There aren't enough rude words in the world to cover what I want to say to you," I informed her primly.

"We can sew a liner on yours, and anyone else who needs it." Eleanor, well used to us by now, simply ignored our childishness. "Easy enough, and we have plenty here. They're bulkier than your bags, so I'm thinking we'll just replace them as they wear out. Make the blankets the measure of last resort."

I looked at Phoenix. She raised her eyebrows and shrugged. *Why not?* I nodded and we turned to Eleanor. "Yeah, sure."

They gave me the first woolen blanket, and I didn't shiver at all my first night out. I'd forgotten what it was like to sleep under the open sky and not have a cold ass.

***

A few days after the conversation with Eleanor, Doc showed up at the gym during training. We were split into groups doing strength training, hand to hand, and tumbling—everything we could think to throw at them. Doc watched us, then waited until my wobbly match with Phoenix finished to wave me over. She had a towel and water waiting, and I took them gratefully.

I wiped my face and swiped the towel between my breasts before taking a long drink of water. "So, what's up, Doc?" I asked, grinning.

Phoenix cracked up while Doc just rolled her eyes, exasperated. "This is getting real old, real fast," she sighed.

I sniggered. "Couldn't help it. Anyway, you summoned?"

"Jewel woke up," Doc smiled. "Properly woke up, I mean, not just to eat, drink, and fall asleep again. She'd like to see you."

"Me?" I was taken aback. "Does she want to yell at me?" On my left, not even hiding her interest, Phoenix grimaced.

"Just talk to her. Oh, and then you can visit the new girls. They're finally over the worst of it and are ready to pick names."

"Okay..." Not really sure why they need me to pick names, but I figured it couldn't hurt to humor them. Lord knows those kids had been through enough.

Jewel must've painted her door sometime, and I'd never paid attention. I vaguely remembered seeing a similar sight, and it was called...impressionism? I shook my head and opened the door slowly, in case Jewel slept again, but she sat up, propped in place by pillows.

"How's it going?" I asked, taking the chair left next to the bed.

"Okay." Jewel seemed unusually subdued, thought that likely has something to do with the bullet. "I just...wanted to thank you. Doc and Eleanor told me everything you guys did. Even after..."

"Ah, no problem." I waved it away, ducking my head. "We all get out, y'know."

"Yeah," she sighed, leaning her head back.

"I should let you get some rest." I stood up.

"No!" Her hand shot out, gripping my wrist. "I had one more thing. We need... we're not all making it out of this." I grimaced, although it was true. "I realized that if I hadn't made it, nobody could've told my parents someday, because nobody knows who I am. We need some kind of record. We need it."

Jewel shifted in the bed, agitated, hands plucking at the blankets as if she'd storm out of bed in an instant. I did the only thing I could and assured her I'd get right on it, then hurried to call Doc.

My next stop was the small barracks Doc had converted into a sick room, and the girls in it.

They sat on the floor, a pile of cards in the middle with a few more held in their hands. Crazy eights. I wondered who taught them. My parents had showed me, but I hadn't played since I was a kid.

"Can I join?" I gestured to the floor, then plopped down when they made no protest. They just stared at me, mouths open. "What?" I asked.

"I just never seen an adult sit on the floor before!" the little one whispered.

"You saw me sitting and sleeping on dirt," I reminded her.

"That's different! We didn't have no chairs!"

"Stick around, kiddo, and you'll see me do lots of other things you never seen adults do before, I promise." I grinned at her awed face. "Doc tells me you guys want to pick names?"

"Yes, but..." The oldest, the one with tattoos, hesitated. "We're not sure what's acceptable."

I considered that. "Well, I wouldn't choose Ice Cream, but that's because too many of us would cry at the reminder." They giggled. "So other than that, anything goes. Some have been named for their pasts, or stuff they like, so, y'know...go nuts."

Abandoning their game, they discussed it, sometimes laughing, sometimes serious, as they tried to decide what name they'd be known by. I gathered the cards and shuffled them, setting up a game of solitaire while I waited, and offering an opinion if they asked. In the end, the tattooed girl settled on Ink. "It's short, it's sweet, and it's to the point."

Feisty was the girl I'd had to punch, and she remained proud of the fact that even being out of her mind on drugs, she'd been that much trouble. Next was Squirrel. I don't know where she got it, something about a TV show. The girl looked to be the same age as Feisty and Dereva, about fifteen. Last, but definitely not least, we had Mouse. Small, nimble, and, it turned out, actually thirteen years old, though she could easily pass for ten. Both she and Squirrel had braces, and I worried how we were going to remove those things.

Once their names were selected, the nervous energy that kept them moving lulled, and soon they were yawning. I helped them back into bed and headed off to find Eleanor. I couldn't think who else might figure out how to put Jewel's wish into action.

<h1 style="text-align:center">CHAPTER 30</h1>

Over the weeks, our routine changed yet again, expanding to take in all the new people. We began putting pins into a map, marking out common routes Steve would take and then hitting them one at a time. Depressing as it was, seeing all those pins, then taking them out left me feeling...content, if not happy.

Steve stepped up their patrols, but rarely ventured into the mountains. The few times they did, we let them pass unmolested so as not to draw their attention.

Inside the Lair, just as Hightide experimented with hides, trying to figure out how to tan them properly, Ink began experimenting with plant dyes. Not only for clothes, but for skin, too.

One day, Anansi found me under the GMC draining the oil. "Look!" he shouted, kicking my feet and bouncing excitedly. "You gotta see this!"

I squirmed out to find him standing in a t-shirt, snow crunching underfoot, just to show me his arm. He sported a stylized mask inked onto his arm in white. "Ink designed a tattoo for me, based loosely on my heritage." His face fell. "It's only temporary, but she's hoping we can find a tattoo kit sometime. I gotta show Dereva!"

I watched dumbfounded, as he bounded away, curly hair flying. I closed my, slumped back, and whimpered. "I'm dead. She'll kill me."

I was still lying there, arm across my eyes, slowly freezing and thinking this would be a more peaceful way to go than what Kioni Blake would inflict, when Seahorse brought the girls back from a run through the forest. She sent them into the Lair, and I listened to her crunching lightly through the snow until the sound stopped next to me. I peeked out from under my elbow as she paused, feet apart, hands on her hips, breathing evenly.

"What's wrong with you?"

"Anansi has a temporary tattoo," I said glumly. "His mother will kill me. Slowly. Painfully."

Seahorse burst out laughing. "Look on the bright side. Steve will probably kill you first." She jogged off, still laughing as I cowered on the ground. "Almost time for dinner," she called over her shoulder as she went to continue the reign of terror we called training.

When I made it into the common room, I walked in on Eleanor and Lavender talking with another rescue, Evenstar, about the kids with braces. Lavender was married to the very first man we'd ever met in Salem, a fella who'd chosen the name Driver.

I hadn't gotten to know her or Evenstar very well, but that didn't stop Lavender turning to me mid-sentence and asking, "Is there any way you can go to Salem and find a dentist or orthodontist? I'm not sure how long those braces can stay on without adjustment before it affects the girls' health."

"It's not like we can just waltz in and ask for one," I said, taken aback. "Every time we go in, it's a huge risk for us, and we can't take the time to pick and choose. We have to have a target already in mind, and a plan set up. But tell you what," I said on a sudden inspiration, "every time we do pull people out, you should interview them, and find out what useful skill sets they have, and between you and Amana, give them jobs that make the most of those skills."

Lavender thought about it a moment before nodding. "Fine. Now, if you'll excuse me, I need to find the children."

As she left, I looked to Eleanor. "'Children?' As in, plural?" Lavender had had three children, but two were lost to famine and plague. There was just a little girl left. Beth.

"She's taken Moana and Cub under her wing. Cub is about the same age as Beth," Eleanor told me quietly as the triangle rang for dinner and everybody lined up to grab a bite.

"She'll be okay?"

"As good as the rest of us." Eleanor smiled sadly. "She's having sessions with Kestrel. Poor thing has more patients than she'd ever thought."

Once we were seated and took the edge off, I kept talking. "What's your take on the lot?"

We had Driver, the first person we'd talked to in Salem, his wife Lavender, and their daughter, Beth. They weren't inclined to be a part of the fight, though Driver had joined another, Dry Eyes, in doing wide sweeps of the area, and tracking Steve's movements. They'd given us warning twice when patrols rolled past. The only problem with Lavender is she kept butting heads with Amana.

The older woman tried to take over the running of the Lair, but Amana refused, first polite, then in a heated argument that finished with Lavender storming away, shrieking about "today's youth."

"Don't worry," Eleanor told me, "I'll speak to her. There shouldn't be any need for your brand of 'convincing.'"

"You make it sound like I beat them up in dark alleys," I said dryly. Lavender had a problem with everything except kids and the dogs, and all things considered, I was happy to leave her to Eleanor and Kestrel.

Eleanor laughed and continued the rundown.

Dry Eyes himself was a recent widower with three kids, all of them younger than ten. Then we had our Tolkien fans—Thrain, his wife Evenstar, and their son Thorin. ("They do know how it ended for Thrain and Thorin, right?") That family decided to join the fight, and we were happy to have them. The final two families were just kids, the oldest 12 if she was lucky.

"Thorin did try flirting with Amana the other day," Eleanor finished.

I winced. "You want to take him, or shall I?"

"I spoke to him already. He's a decent boy who just needed a bit of help understanding, though we should keep an eye on him, make sure he doesn't say the wrong thing—"

"And get himself shot," I finished, sighing. "Adding guys to the mix makes this all the more complicated, as if it wasn't bad enough."

"We need to sit down soon and come up with some ground rules," Eleanor pointed out.

"I know, it's just with the car crisis, the meat crisis, the bra crisis, and spring coming on, life's a little busy these days." I scratched my neck and stretched the muscles in my shoulder. "We'll need more than you and me, too. Everybody, actually."

***

The winter passed without another major raid into Salem. Both Kitten and River advised against it, as Steve took new security measures after the disappearance of the beloved doctor wife of the leader of the American Liberation Corps.

"'Beloved wife' my ass," Doc said when she heard. "If they didn't need doctors, he'd probably have broken my neck and called it an accident."

Instead, we kept busy hitting patrols, and even found three more women, all old enough to join us fighters after training and counselling.

Kestrel never came on raids anymore—she had a constant stream of people through her room, though she made sure to join us for training daily.

"I have to acknowledge that being killing fit makes me feel more secure, and helps me deal with the nightmares," she observed when Seahorse pointed out she didn't have to train so rigorously anymore.

I had enough parts to keep the vehicles in decent shape. After I repaired the hoses, the GMC should be good for another month. If we had oil, anti-freeze, and sufficient spare parts. Every raid, we hit stores for car supplies, feminine products, and medicine.

In between, small parties went out to scavenge. Always accompanied by two fighters, but with instructions to avoid Steve if at all possible. Scavenging became a good way for new fighters to get a bit of seasoning and learn to deal with the adrenaline rush of being in dangerous territory.

***

Winter was finished even in the mountains when I lay on a low hilltop with Sirius, watching work crews head into the field below us. The warm spring sun countered the chill wind, leaving me pleasantly drowsy.

There would be no rescue attempt today. The one time we'd tried to save a work crew, half the workers tried to leave while the other half held them back. Workers attacked us and each other to prevent anyone leaving. It turned out Steve had wised up and held the families as hostages. If even one person went missing, all would suffer. Then Fox, on lookout, shouted that troops were approaching, so we buggered off.

Ink, Feisty, and Squirrel had joined us for the first time, hoping for a fight. Phoenix nearly had to deck Feisty again before she'd stand down.

My mouth quirked when Mouse crossed my mind. I couldn't think of Squirrel without Mouse joining in. The littlest of the big girls, she was pissed at not being allowed into the field. I told her if she survived to fifteen, she could come, and in the meantime she could train. At this rate, she'd be the best-trained fighter. She was in the gym every day, taking on people twice her size, her baby face set with grim determination.

I sighed, rolling onto my back, enjoying the new spring grass, and stared again at the Cascade Mountains, both our home and our prison. "Passes are clearing," I commented. Sirius grunted. "After we get those buses, I need you to do something for us." And with as much confidence as I could muster, I laid it out for her.

"You want me to *what*?" She turned onto her side, glaring at me furiously. "You have some fucking hare-brained ideas, you know that?"

"What? Can't walk that far?" I taunted. "Getting old?"

"Oh, fuck you. I can walk to Idaho. I just don't know if I'd want to come back. Asshole."

"Jerk."

"How many people can I have?" Sirius's ability to go from "hell no!" to "okay" could make your head spin.

"Three? Just not Storm or River." Storm could run circles around the rest of the girls through the forest, while the others struggled to remember if they'd been walking uphill or down.

"Can I have Anansi?" she asked slyly.

I laughed. "You know the boy can't walk fifteen miles. Besides, kid's working on stuff all the time. Maybe I should just give you your blankie. You'll be fine with that, right?"

It'd gotten to the point that nobody even wanted the lightweight sleeping bags anymore. Useless without a tent, and even the synthetic ones left you a bit chilled when they got wet. Instead, the lined wool blankets were the hottest item for anybody leaving the Lair. On a scavenging run two weeks ago, we'd had a particularly cold night, so they'd doubled and tripled up, a blanket on the ground, one over the top, and two to three people huddled underneath. Any sleeping bags were added to the piles, but those who had three woolen blankets to work with fared better.

That had been a particularly fruitful raid, I mused. The scavengers returned with a couple books, one of which Hightide said had the information she needed to produce good tanned leather. I sighed, contentment stealing through me like warm honey.

In the field on the other side of the hill, Steve cracked the whip, and a faint cry drifted up to us, dispelling the warmth. Sirius winced for the poor bastard.

"Come on." I sat up. "It's too depressing to listen to that. Besides, I need a bath." We'd camped next to a creek, and while the water chilled us to our bones, it wasn't frozen, making it warm by our new standards.

"You are particularly fragrant today," my cousin agreed, following me. "I think you're worse than those guys in Poor Town."

River told us that's what the inhabitants of the eastern side of Salem called their slum, and it stuck. Jewel, still the good advocate for the oppressed, berated her for "putting down those poor, deprived persons." River informed that the name had come from those "deprived persons," and besides, as far as cleanliness went, we were worse off than them.

"And you smell like what? Roses?"

"Dogs, which is still better than you."

"Whatever." I brushed it off. "You all ready for tonight?"

We'd combined some information from Kitten with River's observations, along with knowledge taken from our newest members, and concocted our boldest—and stupidest—plan to date. Just last week we'd stood around the map table in the Useless Room, solemnly trying to find faults, when Sirius chuckled.

"I like it."

CHAPTER 31

For some reason (I blame Anansi) this particular idea had been dubbed the Great Bus-capade, and the night found me crouching in bushes, which turned out to be stinging nettle, along with Fox near the south gate of Salem. Barely ten feet from the base of the completed guard tower, which was fifteen feet from the fence and fifty feet east of the gate, we crept incrementally closer. River and Ink should be as close to the tower to the west of the gate. All the towers were two hundred yards apart and the .50-caliber guns at the tops were more than enough to cover the distance. Despite the darkness, I still wished for more space between us.

In the trees behind, Phoenix and Storm, our other long-range shooter, got into position. The wind moved the nettle, brushing it over my cheek and eye, and I hissed, but we moved forward nonetheless. Every bit of breeze meant another few inches gained. During the lulls we froze and cursed the stings.

I will fucking eat every single last one of you! I thought furiously as another line of nettle fire started at my ear. *I swear, I'll dig you up, take to you Amana and have you cooked in soup, you son of a bitching piece of shit plants!*

Once we made it to the tower, we stayed flat next to the pillars. Fox was nothing more than a lump at the base of the tower, her bright hair hidden under a dull hood. The exposed skin on my neck, face, and wrists burned and itched, and I found myself obsessively going over the plan as an attempted distraction. I grumbled softly. Going over the plan kept me from sleep last night, despite the fact that we'd hashed and re-hashed the plan, trying to work out the kinks ahead of time. Our lack of military strategy and tactics worried me because I felt like there must be a step we missed. This constantly gnawed at the back of my mind.

Everything changed when a flare shot into the sky. Fired from a moving vehicle, the spotlights zeroed in on that point, and we burst into action. The sliver of moon played peek-a-boo through the clouds and provided the cover of piss-poor lighting as we scaled the tower. Fox had the ladder, hugging the shadows and keeping pace with me as I climbed the pole itself. I'd worn moccasins tonight, and they gripped the wooden poles better than boots ever could.

A burst of excited chatter covered my grunt as I strong-armed myself up the next level, and Steve got *really* animated when a series of explosions lit the north, unsure whether they should try to figure out who shot the flare, or abandon all for the explosions. The tower floor loomed three feet above me when I heard a stumble followed by a thud, then another. I heaved upward, levering myself over the side in time to see Fox launch herself in a slide across the floor.

Before the light had time to sag, she'd set herself up with the dead soldier's helmet, keeping the light moving in the same ragged zig-zag they'd used. I swept up the other helmet, clapped it on, and took up position at the gun. I glanced to my right in time to see River take up the other gun and stand as casually as if she did this every day.

"That was a bit sooner than I expected," Fox commented. Phoenix and Storm were supposed to wait until I was at the railing. She divested the soldier at her feet of his jacket while I held the light, then did the same so I could get my own jacket.

I checked to my left. All quiet. "I don't think I care, as long as our neighbors don't notice the change." This particular plan involved multiple groups moving independently, improvising along the way. I didn't like it, but as my cousin pointed out, "We can't be everywhere, now, can we?"

I liked to be in the middle of the fight, not on the outskirts, waiting. My only comfort lay in the fact that in another fifteen-ish minutes, this should be the middle of the party. A light swept over the tower to our right, and at the signal, they turned their light towards us, then Fox swept ours over the tower to our left. River had informed us that this stood for "all's well" and allowed them to check on each other.

Abruptly, the light from the tower to our left flashed over us, catching me squarely in the face. It continued, then doubled back, concentrating on us. My pasty white face that's seen no real sun for months gave us away.

"Son of a bitch!" I snarled. I turned our gun towards them, as they shouted and turned toward us.

As suddenly as that, they jerked and fell. Snipers one, Steve zero. Fox whooped. "The gate!" I shouted, shifting the gun back.

The gun nest at the gate hadn't been oblivious to what happened above their heads and was currently turning its two guns on us. Fox killed the light as I began firing, and River joined in from the other side. All along the line, lights at the other towers leaned at crazy angles as Storm and Phoenix continued sniping. They stopped three towers to either side of the gate, giving us a little breathing room.

As the snipers fired, the towers cleared the gate, and Fox readied her bolt action rifle, the one with an inscription from Lucy, now known by the same name.

"Chimeras coming from the east!" Fox called, bellied down and ready.

As good as her rifle was, it couldn't handle the bulletproofing on the trucks, not at this range. Firing from the east told me River and Ink were already engaging, and a quick glance showed that they had two trucks. I stopped our truck in its tracks, and Fox took the opportunity to let the air out of its tires, keeping them clear of the gate.

I picked a point on the truck and sent round after round to the spot until the glass shattered and Steve poured out. We never got a chance to deal with all of them before two more trucks came screeching around corners.

"We're screwed, aren't we?" Fox gripped her rifle tighter, barely a quaver to her voice.

Pride welled in me that this girl could face odds that made grown men quake in their boots. "We all came in, we're all getting' out, y'hear me? We don't run on luck or numbers, we got skill, so give 'em hell!"

I gave up picking shots and sprayed the area, letting Fox mop up the edges. Across the way, Ink's light shut off, and I risked a look, but the sight of two muzzle flashes reassured me both still fought. Chaos reigned as bullets flew, and more soldiers kept pulling up. My entire goal narrowed down to keeping the main road clear. As long as the trucks stopped before it, I did my job. Fox kept stubbornly picking at soldiers, but there were too many. Occasionally, a man fell when neither of us aimed at him.

Not enough, though. Not enough.

Fox suddenly whooped, making me jump, and a stray bullet created a puff of dust halfway up a building. "They're coming," she screeched.

A large, yellow school bus, driving with its lights off, barreled down the road heading directly for the gate. Hot on its bumper came a second, then a third. Pale blobs in the window disappeared as their passengers hit the floor when the buses entered our range. I opened fire on a fresh Chimera, while below, Sirius never slowed, hitting the gate like a battering ram and blowing it off its hinges.

"She's getting good at this, isn't she?" Fox yelled, grinning madly.

When the third bus cleared the gates, Fox fired a flare. As it sank, she slung her rifle and slid back, heading down the same pole I'd climbed earlier. Across the way, River and Ink abandoned their tower so fast you'd think it was on fire, while I raked the ground, spraying large caliber bullets everywhere.

A cry from below had me ditching my post, and I fell as much as climbed down, nearly landing on Fox at the base. She whimpered as I accidentally stepped on her hand, and I yelled "Time to go!"

No movement.

Running out of time, with Steve making moves to come after us, I scooped her up in a fireman's carry and started running after the others. Warmth seeped down my back as I sweated through my sweatshirt, and I lifted my knees high so as not to trip on the uneven ground.

Realizing we were lagging behind, River and Ink dropped back, providing cover, and my heart nearly burst with pride that I should be fighting beside such dedicated women. Over my harsh breathing I heard them alternately yelling "Go!" "Go!" as they took turns covering us.

The last bus waited for us, as arranged, Evenstar white-knuckled behind the wheel. "I need Doc!" I bellowed hoarsely as I stumbled in, laying Fox in the aisle. As soon as Ink and River made it in, Evenstar hit the gas, though she adjusted her mirror to display the aisle.

"All in, all out?" Fox whispered, gripping my hand weakly.

"Yeah, we all made it out," I assured her, squeezing. "Don't talk, Doc's here, she'll get you sorted."

"Not-no luck" Blood bubbled from the girl's mouth as the corner twitched up. "we...all...skill."

"Hush, now." Doc knelt over the girl, hands busy cutting away her clothes. I pulled and stretched fabric as needed, ignoring the faces peering at us from between the seats and the two fighters hovering behind me.

But the blood had stopped flowing, and the brown eyes were open, fixed, and there was nothing Doctor could do. Our bright little redhead who loved climbing trees and acting as a lookout was gone.

"She-she's..." Doc tried.

My hands trembled as I leaned over the young woman's body. "It's all right," I whispered thickly. "You're okay, now. No one can hurt you." I stretched over and pressed my lips to her forehead, a mother tucking a child in to sleep as tears dropped from my eyes, hitting her still cheeks. "Rest now, little one. You've done enough."

Rising, I tugged her hood off, letting her hair free, and Doc and I arranged it neatly around her face. Behind me, Ink kept insisting we stop making her look pretty and *do something* to help her. Gaining my feet, I stepped carefully past Fox and Doc and walked to the back to keep an eye out for Steve.

***

Pursuit was fierce, and Sirius kept up a grueling pace until Seahorse and Dereva found us and began picking soldiers off one truck at a time. We didn't try to destroy the trucks, just get them off our tails. Sirius drove with lights, but the buses behind kept them off, until we hit a town, then Sirius shut her lights off, too, driving dark.

In the hills, on the gravel roads, the fight came onto our turf, where side roads appeared out of nowhere, difficult to spot with the encroaching forest that we only encouraged. Sirius took every advantage, finally turning the buses off and shutting everything down. Our faster vehicles barreled past as if they still followed us, and Steve chased them.

I worked my way down the line, letting Thrain, who drove the middle bus, Eleanor, Sirius and the others know that Fox had fallen. Hightide collapsed when she heard, inconsolable, so I brought Eleanor to her.

It was a red dawn that greeted us at the Lair, and those who stayed home came running, to be met by sober faces and red eyes. Newly rescued people poured out of the buses, confused, jubilant, or silent. The Great Bus-capade had been a success, loosely speaking, though after bringing out the still, young woman, it didn't feel like one.

As Amana and Lavender got the newbies inside and settled, we grabbed shovels and headed into the meadow just down the hill. Two at a time, we dug the grave, while the others scoured the surrounds for rocks to build a cairn. We could never dig deep enough to ensure animals wouldn't disturb the bodies, and soon a large pile of rocks grew next to the smaller pile of dirt.

Later, all the fighters assembled. Around the edges were a few of the newly rescued, pale, thin, but clean, and in better clothing. Once the last stone was placed, Eleanor, who stood on my left, nudged me.

"Say a few words," she murmured.

I stared down at the churned earth, exhausted, hands trembling and dirty, and tried to come up with something, anything. I looked to my right, where the graves for Leo and Jasmine lay, remembered that day, and spoke the only words that came to mind.

"Hail the victorious dead." Ignoring the puzzled looks, I continued. "Hail, all those who fall fighting for what's right, for freedom."

"All in, all out," River told the air. "That's what Fox said."

"Hail the victorious dead," I whispered, "who learned the skills, but didn't make it anyway."

Bottles and cups were passed throughout the group. A bottle found its way into my hand.

"No luck," Ink choked out. "All of us are skilled."

"Hail the victorious dead!"

"Hail!"

I raised my bottle high, then carefully poured a bit on Fox's mound before taking a long swig.

***

I woke with a start, heart pounding, and froze, trying to remember where I was. I slowly relaxed as I realized I was in my bed in the Lair. Gradually, my breathing evened out as I tried to sort through the nightmare, but I gave it up as a jumbled, terrifying mess. Every time I closed my eyes, I slid back into the dream, back into blood and screams and monstrous faces. Shaking, I clambered up off the mattress, wincing when my feet touched the cold concrete. Standing there, I let the cold anchor me in the now, let it pull me awake and keep me out of my head.

Looked like it was time for another midnight walk. They happened more and more frequently, mostly when I slept in the Lair. I walked through the halls, listening to snoring, footsteps heading down the hall to the bathroom, a light flashed on the wall as someone lit a candle. With all the new refugees, the Lair was never truly silent, not like it had been.

I paced through the halls, past the barracks so recently filled. Three busloads of people, totaling two hundred and forty-seven escaped souls, and we didn't have the full count on families yet, though the estimate was roughly eighty.

I walked out the front door, the cold night hit me in a blast of fresh air, and I breathed deep, turning to climb the mound. I didn't expect to see another person perched up there and was surprised to see Lavender dimly illuminated by the stars. I'd thought she'd be the one sleeping the deep sleep of the terminally exhausted, but there she sat.

"You, too, huh?" I said quietly.

She whirled around, nearly toppling over. "What the—! Oh, oh, my God!" She put a hand to her chest. "You scared me half to death! I never heard the door open."

"Anansi found some WD-40 the other day and oiled every hinge he could find. I think he was having fun. May I join you?"

She waved me down, and I sat next to her in the dew-laden grass, the cold and damp seeping through the lightweight pants I wore, making me grateful I'd had the sense to put on a heavy sweater.

"It's so eerie, not having any city lights," Lavender said eventually, breaking the silence. During the day, all you could see were trees and hills, but at night, you were aware of the lack of lights. There should've been a glow to the north for Portland, and a slightly brighter one to the west, for Salem. "It's frightening, seeing all this *black*."

I rocked gently on the grass, "I kinda like the dark."

"Are you insane?" Her head turned my way, and now I could make out more of her features. "How can you not be scared, never knowing what's out there, and you in it all the time?"

"'A witch ought never to be frightened in the darkest forest...because she should be sure to her soul that the most terrifying thing in the forest was her,'" I quoted, smiling into the night. "Words to live by, those."

Lavender laughed. "So what? Now you're a witch?"

"We all have our life goals, now, don't we?" Amana told me they'd finally hit an equilibrium, once the older woman realized that young didn't mean stupid, so I sat, happy that I didn't need to do anything for a while.

We enjoyed the night, and I lifted my head, feeling the breeze kicking up. In the dark, with nothing to distract me, I smelled the rich browns of thawing earth, and the deep greens of spring growth, though there was still a hint of ice in the air. Why didn't I take the time to notice these things in daylight?

"What brings you out on this brisk night?" Lavender asked.

"Oh, the usual," I waved airily. She waited. My lips twisted. "Nightmares. Helps to walk it off. You?"

"Memories," she sighed. "My babies." She and Driver had lost two children to the plague and famine that swept through, and only their youngest survived, a bright little girl named Beth who'd already become fast friends with Moana and Cub. "Actually, I'd wanted to talk to you." I tensed. Those words never really boded well.

"After we were brought out, Driver told me he'd met you months ago." Lavender shook her head, hair whispering over her jacket. "I remember the morning after you'd met him because he'd been so...nervous. Excited. Afraid. I didn't understand. Then, when he did tell me, I was hurt, at first. That he hadn't told me sooner. The more I thought about it, though, I was glad." She shrugged, searching for the words. "It must have been so hard for him, keeping it secret. When there was that big chase, he must have thought it was you."

"It was us," I murmured.

Her mouth dropped open. I guess nobody'd thought to mention it. "He just shrank into himself, and any time more people disappeared, he seemed like he was trying to hide in plain sight, but at the same time he was, well, *thrilled*. I just hadn't understood. And, I guess, I just wanted to know, how do you deal with all those emotions? It's absolutely exhausting."

"Therapy," I said, nodding firmly. "I don't know if you've noticed, but Kestrel has a constant stream of people into her room."

"But not you."

"Oh, I need to, I just need a moment where both of us are free." I needed to get this conversation away from me and the emotions I was not dealing with. "Speaking of people, how are you handling the new lot?"

"Well, most of them are lovely folks, pitching right in to help, but there's a small core of people who so far look to be a bunch of entitled, self-righteous pricks—"

"Lavender!" I interrupted, laughing. "I didn't know you swore!"

"—who may yet settle down," she finished.

"Well, if you need anybody shot, maimed, or disappeared, let us know," I said, only half joking. "And keep those pricks out of any positions of power. This is currently a dictatorship, not a democracy. Also, if Amana didn't tell you, they don't work, they don't eat, excepting the sick and the too young. We don't have the luxury of feeding idle mouths."

Lavender nodded slowly. "That's a hard stance."

I smiled, finally tired and ready for more sleep. "You may have noticed it's a hard life we have here. We don't have time or energy to coddle them. If they don't want to stay, we'll blindfold them, take them a sufficient distance away, and let them go with food and supplies to get across the border. Something to keep in mind if they do try to give you trouble." I stood slowly and stretched, yawning. "Back to bed for me."

"You know what really makes you frightening?" Lavender asked when I reached the bottom of the mound. I looked back. "It's the fact that not only do you mean what you say, but that you can back it up. It's both reassuring and scary."

How do you respond to that? "Good night," I said, and walked back into the Lair.

CHAPTER 32

The next days were insane.

We'd freed nearly two hundred and fifty people, and none of us had realized what a logistical nightmare it would be, feeding and clothing that many. Even with the leather Hightide finally managed to make, things were tight. The clothing stores were distributed, but sparsely. As Amana pointed out, we had no idea how long we'd be here and how many other people we'd need to clothe.

Every hunting trip brought back the entire animal now, not just meat, and the animal was parceled out accordingly—meat, bones, and innards to the kitchen, head and hide to Hightide. That young woman had been particularly affected by Fox's death and flung herself into her work as a result. She recruited the least squeamish people available and set up shop in the farthest corner of the Lair, Section 8, right next to the greatest concentration of vents.

While bras for the fighters were of the highest priority for the leather-workers, that tiny core of entitled pricks kept attempting to demand leather clothing. I only found out after the fact that Kestrel and Storm had to forcefully keep Hightide from beating one of them, sitting on her until she calmed down.

Mouse and Squirrel, the two with braces, managed to find six other people with braces, and they formed a small band with a single goal.

"We'd like your permission," Mouse informed me gravely, "to enter Salem and find an orthodontist to remove our braces. We don't need any other fighters. We're willing to go alone."

"I see." I rubbed a hand over my mouth, trying not to smile. "You understand I have to refuse you at this time?" The little girl frowned. "However, I can give you permission to question everybody here, and see if you can either find an orthodontist, or if anybody knows one. Once we have a location, we can discuss it further. In the meantime, you have duties in the gym to attend to."

Mouse reluctantly turned away and dragged her gang after her to the gym, where the girl helped Seahorse train the children and provided water and cloths for the adults.

Other adults volunteered to patrol, scavenge, and hunt, and a few more joined our band of fighters. Training intensified, with all of us who had experience pressed into service to get the newbies fit for duty.

One woman, Wildwood, had been an herbalist before and now began running classes, teaching people about edible and medicinal plants. She worked closely with Doc, making decoctions and various other brews. I turned around one day and discovered we had both a doctor and an apothecary. They set up shop in the unoccupied room next to the Useless Room.

Even with all the running around and the wealth of new people, three women stood out. Ranging from their mid-thirties to forty, they'd all been beauticians for years Before and had worked their trade in the brothels since. A few days before Sirius left, they broke out chairs and scissors and offered haircuts all around.

Such a simple thing, a haircut, but it makes such a difference. After more than six months without, we were all in desperate need of a trim at least. The opportunity to shorten, and in many instances, remove a bad case of two-tone hair, was too good to pass up. The Three Fates, as they were called, assured us that having well-cut hair would enable us to walk through Steve-controlled Salem much easier, and that well-styled hair helped a girl's confidence to no end.

"How can a woman possibly be ready to take on the world with hair that looks like a mouse nest?" one said.

"Yes, and with the right shoes, she can conquer the world," another declared. I looked down at my bare feet and figured that if those shoes were hiking or combat boots, the lady did have a point.

So we all had our hair cut in nice styles, and it turned out that most people in our part of the world didn't have yellow hair, but actually light brown to black. I hadn't realized that many people dyed their hair.

When the Fates saw Eleanor, the First Fate screamed, "We thought you were dead, *cheri*! But we are so happy to see that you are not!"

"And that you are doing so well," the Second murmured. "Though I do wish you'd taken care of your nails sooner, dear. Your hands are appalling."

"Are you, like, sisters or something?" Anansi looked up from where he was getting his long curls trimmed by the Third Fate. She smiled.

"Bless you, no!" exclaimed the First Fate. "Do we look anything alike?"

"No," the boy admitted.

"Aren't you a handsome one," the Second interjected. "Look at those eyes, that skin." She sighed.

The black eyes she so admired hid as Anansi looked down, blushing. The Third finished with him and he hopped up, hesitated, and said, "So what are you to each other, if it's okay for me to ask?"

The First Fate tapped her chin with the scissors. "We are...happy friends," she said coyly,

Anansi just looked around, bewildered.

"A *menage a trois*?" the Second suggested. The Fates giggled.

"Do you have to keep messing with me?" Anansi hated not understanding.

I hooked an arm around his shoulders. "They're all lovers together," I said into his ear.

He digested this silently, then laughed. "I get it now. Happy!" He eyed them speculatively. "I didn't even know three was an option."

I cringed as he bounded off, followed by cheerful farewells and invitations back from the Fates. "His mother will kill me," I confided to Eleanor, who watched everything with patient amusement.

***

Two weeks after the Bus-capade, Sirius was finally ready to leave. She'd chosen her band, selecting the sisters Lightning and Thunder. Sirius had taken to them, and they to her. I suspected her favor had something to do with them trying to blow my head off. Sirius is adorably precocious like that. She also took Thorin, the sixteen-year-old son of Thrain and Evenstar.

His parents couldn't decide whether to be glad their son would be heading into the unknown, away from Steve's armies, or worried that he'd be out of their sight. I'm not sure why Sirius chose him, since he barely had a couple months training, but she was confident that everything he needed to know could be taught on the trail. The young man stood straight, proud to have been selected.

Eleanor ended up taking his parents aside to explain their new life. I didn't stick around to listen to the entirety of her speech. While the descriptions she gave were true enough, they were still high-minded euphemisms for bloody work.

***

"Well isn't this just fan-fucking-tastic," Sirius grumbled at dinner, the day before they were due to leave.

"What?" I sipped my cup of tea. Amana had informed me that since it was made entirely of local plants and herbs, with no tea leaves whatsoever, it was technically an herbal infusion. Showoff.

"I started," Sirius shifted on the bench. "Of all the shitty luck."

"Do you have cramps?" Seahorse asked.

"Uh...not really." Sirius sounded surprised. "I used to, every period, but they've been manageable lately."

Doc looked up from her stew, elbow resting on the table, supporting her drooping head. "I've been asking the women as they come in for checkups, and most say something similar. On average their flows are lighter, too."

"Really?" I frowned. "I'd swear mine are getting heavier."

An older woman passed by and gave me a disgusted look. "At dinner? Really?" She turned her nose up. "Disgusting savages."

"Hmmm." Amana busily pulled out a notebook. "She may work *los banos* for now."

Giggles broke out around the table. "Is that how you decide who works where?" Sirius snickered. "Whoever pisses you off does the toilets?"

The woman shrugged. "*Si.* Or deeshes."

***

"Did we find you guys enough pads and tampons to last you?" I asked Sirius the next morning.

"Yeah." Sirius knelt on the ground, hands buried in Cin's ruff. The old dog knew something was up, and that he wasn't invited, so he attempted to ignore his human, but she wouldn't let him. Obelix danced nearby, excited in his little pack and harness as he waited for them to leave.

The sisters said their goodbyes and waited by the trail out. That just left Thorin and Sirius. The boy held tight to his parents before tearing himself away, wiping his eyes on his sleeve. When Sirius finally stood, we hugged, fist bumped, and left it at that. Everything else had been said, and if the worst happened to either of us, the other knew what to do.

"You know," I said to Eleanor, watching them disappear down the trail, "I envy her. I've never seen Eastern Oregon."

"Not to mention the general lack of responsibility," she replied dryly.

"That, too." I smiled. Dealing with the refugees was exhausting, more akin to herding cats than managing people, and I didn't know the half of it.

I turned slowly back to the Lair and the training session I needed to start, my eyes lingering on the trailhead. "Footloose and fancy free," I whispered. "Hah!"

***

Turned out the Fates knew of a couple more brothels in Salem, though they'd always been blindfolded when they were taken to them to doll the women up.

River, who by this time had gotten pretty comfortable with Salem, began working with them, slowly going over every detail, how many turns, in what direction, what they heard. The next time River went to Salem, she passed the word to Kitten, then worked along the route the Fates mentioned until she got to a point that confused her. Armed with a better understanding of the area, she'd return, and they'd go to work in the Useless Room again.

Meanwhile, we hit another two patrols and actually managed to take a Chimera, whole and working. The pickup and the first truck were getting entirely too crowded and overworked between raids and scavenging. Then we stumbled across a little town, barely more than a single street well north of Salem, whose signs had been removed.

It harbored a recreation center for Steve.

It was full of young women and girls. They ranged from fourteen to nineteen, an even dozen of them.

"Let's fucking kill them all!" Ink lunged at Steve, teeth bared.

"Please, no," Eleanor pleaded, barring her way. "Not like this. This is...wrong."

"Did you look at them?" Ink screamed, pointing back at the girls.

"Captain." Storm looked my way, fingers dancing over her pistols. "We can't just let them walk. We've ambushed men. How is this any different?"

Eleanor stared at her daughter, the corners of her mouth pulling down. "Oh, Storm. This is in cold blood. This can hurt you—"

"So did rape." Storm's even tone was harder to deal with than Ink's rage and screams.

"Captain." Eleanor turned to me, but I held a hand up. I needed a moment.

"Right." I turned back from my pacing, "I think I've got it. We've been making men disappear for a while now, no trace. I think it's about time we did give them a trace."

"You're going to let them *go?*" Storm stared at me, betrayal stark on her face.

"Let me finish." I resumed pacing.

***

"I changed my mind," Eleanor said faintly an hour later. "Killing them would have been kinder."

"I don't know." Storm shook her head. "We don't want to be kind. We want Steve afraid."

The soldiers huddled together, naked and bloody, many of them crying, broken messes. I closed my eyes and lifted my blood-spattered face to the sky and dreamed of cold water sluicing away the memory of the last hour. The rescued girls had been given the chance for revenge, and many had taken it by taking the balls of the men who'd hurt them. I'd guided their hands, or taken their place if they felt unable, and now...I shuddered.

"Release them," I rasped.

"What?"

"Turn them loose. Let the enemy know who we are."

***

The trucks ferried the rescued girls back to the Lair while we headed south in an old minivan I had hotwired. The crew only numbered eight: Eleanor, Phoenix, Storm, Ink, and me from the original group, and two women and a man from the bus escape who'd shown promise—Hawk, Oak, and Porkpie.

These three had learned the quickest of all those who'd volunteered right after their escape. Oak, a solidly built, stocky woman who reminded me of Sirius, was a human tank. Hawk, short, petite, in her late thirties, had previous experience camping and was one of the few people who didn't get lost ten feet into the forest. Porkpie...well, he loved his pies, and claimed the only reason he'd joined was to kick Steve out so he, Porkpie, could have his preferred dinners back.

Thrain and Evenstar rode with the trucks as guards, and our good-byes were quick. Fist bumps, and, strangely, clasping forearms had quickly become the standard greetings and goodbyes, leaving us milling together, touching everyone we parted from, just in case someone didn't make it back.

***

It was a crowded van that set off, and we made some stops along the way. We ran across a work crew and started a firefight with the guards, taking at least two of them down before we split.

The next day, we spotted a Chimera truck sitting on the side of the road while the patrol was off somewhere, so we stole that and left the van in its place. When it ran out of gas, we ditched it and headed across country. Along the way, we surprised another patrol, got into a fight, lured them into an ambush, then circled around and stole *their* truck. It seems with the advent of spring, Steve was setting foot outside Salem's gates more, which meant we didn't have to look as far to cause a bit of trouble.

It also rained for several hours a day, every day.

Damn *beautiful* Oregon.

The second day out, I developed a hole in my boot that let water pour in just walking over broken concrete. So I broke out the moccasins again. Two days after that we holed up in a barn with barely enough roof to keep us dry, and I examined my feet by the light of a small fire.

I rubbed my thumbs over my feet, feeling the callused ridges and thick, peeling skin, looking for sore spots. "Y'know," I said, squinting down at a spot, "I think my toes are actually better for being in moccasins. Weird."

"You're leaving fewer and harder-to-read tracks, too." Phoenix looked up from her own feet, frowning. "I've got a callus here that's really hurting."

Everybody immediately began digging through tiny packs, looking for anything to help, when Oak and Hawk also chimed in, citing blisters. I found a half-full pot of pawpaw ointment at the bottom of mine, while Eleanor produced a few forlorn Band-Aids in a side pocket of hers. Storm then pulled out blister pads, offering them to the newbies.

"You should have told us your feet were hurting," Storm said sternly, looking utterly adorable with her golden hair peeking out from the blanket covering her head. "Infections are really hard to fight off, so it's better to get to things early."

"No new blisters for you?" Eleanor asked. I shook my head. "Maybe we should have some moccasins done up, if it reduces the chance of blisters."

"It's not painful, having no thick soles to protect your feet?" Porkpie inquired.

I flexed my foot experimentally. "Feels pretty good. Though if people had to carry really heavy packs, or had foot issues, they'd still need good boots. Besides, we don't have any spare leather yet." Hightide and her team were working on bras. While those without finally had something to hold their breasts down, feedback said they weren't the most comfortable.

I sneezed, rubbed my dripping nose, and accepted the mug of stew offered by Eleanor.

I'm so done with this rain.

***

We spent three weeks running around the Valley, sleeping in every weather and finding shelter when we could and going without when we couldn't, before returning to the Lair in another stolen vehicle. In the last fight, Oak caught a bullet, though we managed to bring her body home.

Porkpie, that idiot, had gotten an infected blister he'd decided not to tell anyone about until the red lines were streaking up his leg.

Now, we just hoped we'd save his life by getting him to Doc in time.

"You know," Phoenix grunted as she stumbled on a root, weighted down by the front of Porkpie's stretcher, "now may not have been the best time to let the blackberries cover the driveway."

"Yes," I groaned, straining with the back, "because I knew Porkpie would ignore everything we'd told him about infection. I planned this."

Hawk and Storm carried Oak, and we were preceded by Ink, who ran to tell Doc to gear up. Soon enough, civilians led by Doc and Lavender arrived, and more hands helped us get the sick man inside.

"Can you save him?" I asked Doc back in the infirmary.

"Maybe." She surveyed his leg, cutting his pants leg even higher, trying to find where the red lines ended. "Why didn't you bring him in sooner?"

"I had no idea it was a problem, and it didn't occur to me to tell him to get naked," I grunted, rolling Porkpie onto his side in her direction. "Idiot never said he was having problems with a blister, he just limped for an hour and then collapsed."

Squirrel, who'd taken up the post as Doc's assistant, directed two people with a pot of boiling water, set some rolled cloths out, and organizing a tray of instruments I decided not to examine too closely.

Doc looked up. "I need a—"

"Here." Dry Eyes thrust a wood saw under her nose. "It's not cleaned yet, but it's the best I could find this fast."

"Squirrel." Doc gestured, and the girl leaped forward, taking the saw and getting busy.

"What else do you need?" Amana asked from the doorway. Porkpie moaned on the gurney, nearly insensible.

"I need…" Doc consulted a notebook, "Thrain, Edmond, and Evelyn. They're all type O-positive. Here." She handed the notebook to Amana. "Make sure everybody else on this page eats and is hydrated in case I need them."

"I'm an O," I reminded Doc.

She shook her head, staring at the leg, mentally preparing herself. "You've been through enough, and you may be more worn down than you think. I can't risk him getting sick or anemic. Rest. You've done enough. Now it's our turn."

I stepped back as she lifted a scalpel from the tray. Squirrel positioned herself opposite and nodded to Dry Eyes. "If you could prepare the patient?"

Dry Eyes stepped forward and delivered a solid, precise punch to Porkpie's jaw, and the injured man slumped immediately. Dry Eyes stayed close, keeping two fingers on the man's jugular to monitor his pulse.

"He's out," Dry Eyes reported, and I hastily left before Doc made her first cut.

I made my way slowly to the common room and the ever-warm pot of stew that Amana had taken to leaving on. With people constantly coming and going, it was impossible to keep strict eating times, so the pot lived on a corner of the gas stove, perpetually hot.

"Dereva." I greeted the young woman who'd just sat down with her own bowl, ignoring the pool game happening in the corner. "How's it going?"

"Just got back from a scavenging run," she yawned. "Played a little game of hide-and-seek, but we won. Got some more antifreeze and oil, too."

"Nice! How's my baby running? Wait—should you even be that active yet?" I sat down next to her, then paused. Something was off. I looked at my bowl, at the wall, at her, down at the bench. "Are you taller? Or am I getting shorter?"

The small crowd around the pool table cheered. Bits of paper changed hands. It looked like Feisty was taking a newcomer to the cleaners.

She looked down. "Uh, I grew a bit. I remember my mom saying she kept growing until she was seventeen, so I think I have a couple more years. Hightide pointed it out. Truck's fine, by the way, though I'm worried about pressure damage on the hoses, so we've been keeping an eye out for more."

"Good." I continued shoveling stew into my mouth. "How is Hightide, anyway? I never saw her much, and since she's gotten those books, I see her even less. Just...I know her and Fox were friends, and I wondered how she's handling it."

A small group of men and women who worked patrols sat down at the next table over, setting up cleaning supplies for their weapons, and gave us a casual greeting.

We returned it before Dereva gave me a sideways look. "Honestly, when it comes to people, you are so dense."

"Hey!"

"Her and Fox were *dating.*" Dereva said bluntly. I thumped my head onto the table. "So she's working through the stages. Kestrel's been giving her exercises to do, but it's still really rough for her. I think she's stuck on bargaining right now. Or depression. It's hard to tell."

"I am *such* an *idiot!*" I moaned into the table. "I can figure out where Steve's going, but can't see what's right under my nose. That poor kid, losing her girlfriend after everything else."

"Captain! I've been looking for you!" Anansi raced into the common room, hair flying wildly. "You gotta see what we did! You can come, too, Der."

"Thanks," Dereva said dryly.

I smiled. Trust the boy to come when I needed cheering. Anansi didn't take us far, leading us into the back of the kitchen where he'd taken over a small pantry. Inside, a confusing tangle of glass and copper that looked like it belonged in a chemistry lab dominated the tiny space.

"What?"

"Here." Anansi handed me a glass of water. "Try this."

Confused but trusting, I took a gulp and choked, coughing. My eyes watered. "Is that alcohol?" I finally managed to wheeze.

"Yup," he said proudly. "The potatoes were starting to go off, so Eleanor asked me to make something with them!"

"This is what you came up with? What is it?" I asked hoarsely, backing slowly out of the room.

"Vodka!"

His sister leaned against the wall, laughing so hard she cried at the expression on my face.

"Wonderful." First a temporary tattoo, now alcohol distillation. I wondered if it was me or him that led us to these situations. Was I failing as a pseudo-parent figure? "I should lock you in a room and throw away the key," I informed him, my throat rasping painfully.

He laughed. "You can use it on open wounds to stop infections, stuff like that. I'm actually taking some to Doc right now."

I wiped my watering eyes. "What, like if Porkpie survives having that put on him, he's indestructible?"

"I see your protégé has shown you his latest creation," Eleanor said dryly from behind, handing me a cup of water when I turned.

I took it with a grateful nod. "It'll make a mean Molotov cocktail." I sipped the water slowly, soothing the burn from what had to be one hundred proof vodka. "Keep the door locked. Last thing we need is some idiot trying to get drunk on that stuff. They'd probably die. We're having enough funerals."

Phoenix walked into the kitchen, took one look at my face, and collapsed against the doorframe, laughing hysterically. "Anansi showed you the vodka, didn't he?"

"You knew about this?" She nodded, unable to breathe, tears streaming down her face. "And you didn't warn me?" She shook her head. "Asshole."

***

Walking across the meadow after a quick dunking in the creek in my underwear, I was contemplating the vagaries of life while toweling myself dry when a burly man flagged me down.

"Captain!" he called. "Do you have a minute?"

I shrugged. "Sure. What can I do you for?"

"I've been thinking, talked to my kids, and I have a proposition for you." I guessed him for his mid-forties, with a confident stance that said he'd seen trouble before.

"Go for it." I gestured for him to join me on my way back to the Lair.

"I'd like to help train the new recruits." He didn't beat around the bush. "I spent years as a sergeant major, training Special Forces. I'd offer to hit the field with you," he added, shooting me a quick glance, "but my kids have already lost their mother. I'd rather they didn't lose their father, too. It'll free up the soldier you already have in there. I know she'd like to spend more time in the field."

"You talked to Seahorse?"

"Just casually. After she mentioned she'd like to see more action, I came up with this." He grinned a little. "The position comes with a name, too. Sarge."

I thought about it a little. "We'll need to assess you, see if you can handle what we've got."

He tensed, then forced himself to relax. "I wish I could give you references, but I'm more than happy to get onto the mats with you, prove I'm competent to train."

"Oh, I'm confident you can train the recruits you were given," I waved that away, "but these girls aren't them. I've seen some movies, talked to some people, and I believe your usual training methods involve a lot of yelling, minor cruelties, all in the name of toughening them up, yes?"

He nodded. We stopped outside the Lair. Interruptions happened less often outside.

"These girls don't need to be toughened up. They've been beaten so hard they've broken. You do your normal training routine on them, you'll wake up some night tied upside down to a tree. It's anybody's guess whether you'll still have your balls." I grinned when he paled and cupped himself reflexively. "Still want the job?" I asked brightly.

He never hesitated but nodded firmly. "I do want to contribute, and I feel this is the best way I can do that. Plus, my kids can help, collecting towels, keeping fresh water coming, cleaning after training sessions, all that."

"Fine. You're on probation until we're absolutely sure the girls are okay with you." I stuck my hand out, and his huge palm engulfed mine. "Besides, they'll get experience tangling with a guy three times their size. It'll be good for them."

As we turned back to the door, little things scattered all over the ground finally registered. "That's sheep poop," I said intelligently.

"How do you know that?"

"Ex-farm girl. Phoenix!" I bellowed. "I know you're out here somewhere!"

"Yo!" Phoenix tumbled agilely down from a tree, landing lightly on her feet with her rifle ready to fire.

"What you know 'bout sheep shit?"

"They come from sheep."

I waited.

"One of the raids found a dozen of 'em a couple weeks ago," she admitted.

"Where are they hiding the smelly things?" I looked around, half expecting one to appear in a tree.

"Pretty well, if you have to ask that," she smirked, turning back to her tree and her practice.

"I'm totally gonna work on that with the recruits," Sarge said.

"Uh, huh."

That night we had mutton in our stew, so now I knew where one of them was.

CHAPTER 33

I snarled, punched a soldier in the face and spun, whipping my knife out in time to meet another one. Catching his rifle on my arm, I thrust. Turning away before he even fell, I kicked the first soldier in the groin and kneed him in the face when he bent.

I spun in a complete circle before I realized that all the soldiers were down and my people were the only ones still standing. We'd followed a patrol into Canby only to find them waiting for us. Fortunately, Phoenix had arrived in the Chimera, giving us a chance in a hairy hand-to-hand encounter.

"How is everybody?" I called, walking through the group.

We suffered cuts, bruises, two creases from bullets, and Ink had been hit in the side, a through and through. Fortunately, we'd brought Doc with us this time. She'd barely managed to save Porkpie's life and decided that the best way to prevent something like that happening again would be to come out with us.

She immediately got to work on Ink, assisted by Squirrel, delving into her pack and producing an odd combination of thread, scalpel, needle, and pots and unguents made by Wildwood. Doc also pulled out packets of dried herbs and someone got a pot of water boiling.

I left Ink to Doc's excellent care and joined the fighters in exploring the area Steve had chosen. We gathered outside of a laundromat.

"I didn't think they'd set up shop in Canby again." Phoenix looked around at the dilapidated buildings. "We made that last lot disappear, after all."

"Maybe we have to make two lots vanish before they get worried," Dereva said. "I thought I heard something, coming from back there." She pointed down the narrow alley.

"Fantastic," I muttered as I walked cautiously down the alley, rifle at the ready, making sure to look up. "The very places we were warned to never go, that's where we're heading. I'm S-M-R-T smart."

"Quit your bitching and pay attention," Phoenix hissed from behind me. "We do tons of shit we were told to never do."

"Easy for you to say. You're short and behind me."

The alley yielded onto a small courtyard, completely surrounded. There were two different paint jobs, so at least two businesses. The only openings were three windows high up the walls and a single door, ahead and to my left. I could hear a noise, now, metal on metal, clashing and jerking. It was barely audible from the courtyard.

We might've misnamed Dereva with hearing like that.

After a few minutes without seeing any movement except some birds, we started towards the door, keeping to the walls. When I tried the knob, it opened with a faint creak, and I stopped immediately.

"Phoenix," I muttered. "In the largest pocket I've got a small can of WD-40. Pull it out for me, will ya?"

She shouldered her rifle and worked the zipper of my small pack, which opened smoothly. I regularly doctored the zippers with WD-40, too. When the can appeared over my shoulder, I grabbed it and liberally oiled the hinges.

As soon as she tucked the can safely back in my bag we moved in, stepping lightly and waiting inside the door until our eyes adjusted to the dim light. The metallic clinking sounded louder, somewhere above our heads, and a faint rustling accompanied by the occasional thump drifted down.

We cleared the ground floor quickly and found three large rooms bisected by a hall. The front door looked like it had seen plenty of traffic, scuff marks and footprints blurring together. To our left, the stairs rose straight up, ending at the back wall and a blind corner. I loosened the straps holding the handguns on my thighs down before shouldering the rifle again. Phoenix knelt on the bottom step, covering me as I climbed the stairs.

At the top I waited for her to join me and we checked these rooms, too. This floor had obvious signs of life, with cots, bedrolls, and dishes in a small kitchen. Steve may be neat and tidy on the parade ground, they may keep it clean around their commanders, but when left to their own devices, most of these guys were absolute *slobs*.

"It looks like the guys' dorm rooms when I went to college," Phoenix whispered, staring around, appalled. "Like, the first time they found out their mom wasn't there to check on them, and make sure their beds were made, they just let it all go."

"To hell," I agreed, making a wide berth around the overflowing trash can.

As I climbed the next set of stairs I tensed, my breath sounding loud as I waited to see if guards lurked above.

I cleared the stairs, and when Phoenix joined me, we moved through the first room, which only had a large mattress on the floor in one corner, covered in dirty blankets. Sick to my stomach, we entered the other half to see a woman cuffed to handrails next to a toilet. Bedraggled, her hair made indeterminate by filth, the woman appeared in her late twenties and sported a black eye, along with a series of other bruises and contusions.

A direct approach didn't work as she struggled like a rabbit with its foot caught in a trap. I watched the door as Phoenix set her rifle down, got onto her hands and knees, and slowly crawled over to the woman, whispering soothing nonsense the whole time.

A soft thud from the floor below had my head whipping around, and in the middle of her sing-song, Phoenix said, "Go on and check it out. I've got this. You're okay, now. Those men are gone. You're okay."

I swiped my hands quickly over my pants and took a fresh grip on my rifle, crossing the empty space to the stairs quickly. If I could get them while they were trapped on the stairwell, I'd have a chance.

Please let it only be two people. Just because I had multiple shots in my rifle didn't mean I wanted to see who'd win in a showdown.

A faint squeak and a loaded pause told me the first person had nearly reached the top. I breathed out slowly, aiming where the body should be. A flicker, and I leaped forward—nearly blowing Thrain's head off.

I let out an explosive breath and hastily pointed the barrel towards the ceiling while the man stared at me, white as a sheet and shaking like a leaf. "Fucking hell, Captain," he whispered as his wife, guarding the bottom of the stairs, ran up to help her husband lean against the wall, both of them trembling.

"Everything okay out there?" Phoenix's voice drifted out, supernaturally calm.

"Yeah, we're good," I leaned over, resting my hands on my knees as I caught my breath. "It's friendlies. Evenstar and Thrain. C'mon," I said to them. "We've found a captive cuffed, and I have no idea how to get her out without a saw."

The poor woman nearly tore her arm off in a panic when she saw Thrain walk through the door. "Sshhh." Phoenix rested a hand on the woman's ankle soothingly. "They're friends. He won't hurt you. He doesn't want to, and we'll shoot anyone who tries."

Thrain had to stand in the other room before we could get her calmed, and then he walked in slowly. "I actually know how to pick handcuffs," he confessed quietly. "I need to come over there, though," he informed the woman. "Is it okay if I walk over? I just need to reach the handcuffs."

"Keep the cuffs," I told him as he worked over the woman's hand while she strained away, pressing hard against Phoenix. "I want to learn how to do that."

His hands blocked what he was doing, but the cuff was off the woman's wrist in a moment. "Sure." He smiled over his shoulder at me, pretending not to see how the woman scrambled away from him, secure with Phoenix and Evenstar. "And you can teach me how to hotwire a car."

"Done deal." He had the other cuff off the bar, folded and tucked into his pocket. "Let's ditch this shithole."

"N-no," the woman spoke up, voice raspy and hoarse, surprising all of us. "I need—" She coughed, clutching the other two to keep upright. "I need to find my family. I'm not going anywhere."

"They're not here," I informed her.

"You won't be able to find anyone until you're healthy," Evenstar told the woman firmly. "If we let you run off now, you wouldn't get ten feet. Come with us, we'll get you better, then we'll help you find your family."

"Why should I trust you?"

"Because we just broke you out." I scratched my head and scooped up my rifle. People are weird. "Listen, you may not trust us, but there are people downstairs who've been where you are now, and maybe they can help you more."

She continued to stare at me, shaking, terrified, with an edge of belligerence that I couldn't help but admire.

"Thrain," I called.

"Yo!"

"Can you get Eleanor up here, please? It seems freeing our new friend isn't enough to make us trustworthy, and we really need to leave now."

"On it, Cap'n."

Footsteps thudded softly down the stairs and I looked at Phoenix. "You see that?" I demanded. "I asked, nicely, and he did it! Why can't you ever do that?"

"Because your 'requests' are usually more along the lines of 'Phoenix, can you train all these new people who've never seen two trees together to find their way through a forest?' If you just asked me to get Eleanor, I'd say sure, no problem, too!"

I stuck my tongue out at her and she grinned while Evenstar rolled her eyes and the new woman stared back and forth between us, wariness replaced by confusion. "You people are weird."

"Thank you!" I turned to Evenstar. "That's the reaction we keep trying for, but do we get that? Noooo! Instead we get told to behave like grownups. You do know we're not paying rent, taxes, or for food, all those things you're supposed to do when you're adulting, so why do we have to act proper and stodgy?"

"Because you're at an age where you are grown up, maybe?" Evenstar's lips twitched.

"Age is just a number," Phoenix said, nose in the air.

I sniggered.

Footsteps coming up the stairs forestalled further banter and Eleanor entered the tiled room. "Captain? What are...oh."

"If you will?" I bowed arm extended towards the woman. "She doesn't trust us, and you're our best bet until we get back to Kestrel. I want to be out of here within the hour."

"Boom?" Phoenix asked.

"Boom," I confirmed. "This shithole's going down."

We left Evenstar and Thrain upstairs with Eleanor, the couple whispering to each other in the secret way long-time lovers have, and headed downstairs to finish ransacking the place.

"I wonder if we'll ever have that?" Phoenix asked.

"What?"

"That." She jerked her head up. "What Thrain and Evenstar have. Love. Commitment."

"You didn't before, with...?" *Dylan's father* remained unsaid between us. Her young son, murdered by soldiers during the very first weekend of occupation, was rarely mentioned. Memories of him were still too raw and made her sad.

"No. No, it wasn't like that with him. That was just...stupidity."

Once outside, we joined the small swarm of people, some loading supplies into the trucks, others standing guard, tending injuries, the busyness that happens after a battle, appropriated some explosives and headed back inside. It took some time to locate the trap door, and when we did, we stopped, surveying the black hole, torn cobwebs at the corners, the perfect Halloween decor.

"You go down," I nudged Phoenix. "I went up the stairs first."

"I crawled on the bathroom floor."

I winced. That was pretty bad. "Flip a coin?"

"Do you even have a coin?" Phoenix arched a disbelieving brow at me.

"No."

"What are you arguing about?" Thrain called from the bottom of the stairs. Footsteps sounded closer until he wandered through the doorway. "Were you going to just let me get lost?"

"Yes. We were debating who's going down there." I pointed to our feet.

He cringed back. "Ugh." He leaned forward again, peering cautiously. "I-I guess...I could go?"

My eyebrows shot up. "You're comfortable setting charges?"

"Uh...no?"

In the end, he picked a number and we had to guess. I lost, so I took three charges down with me while Phoenix would set the rest on this and the second floor.

"Have you guys ever dropped a building before?" Thrain asked, looking over my shoulder as I prepared.

"I read an article, once," I said seriously.

"We've blown up a few cars, too!" Phoenix smiled brightly.

He nodded, lips pursed. "I think I'm gonna tell everyone to move a little faster. Just in case."

It took a while, figuring out which beams were the most load bearing, and even then, I guessed. Thickest beams first? Space was tight under the floor, and I wriggled and squirmed my way through. I wedged the charges between beams and floors as we had only one hand drill, and Phoenix had that. Once out, I found Phoenix still on the first floor, red faced and sweating while Storm took her place manning the drill.

"This shit's exhausting," Phoenix wiped her forehead, then snickered. "I never knew you could make those kinds of noises. All that squealing and squeaking. It was kinda cute."

Storm's shoulders shook and she lost her grip on the drill while Phoenix stared at me blandly. I flipped them both off, then screeched as something fluttered down my back.

"Get it off, get it off!" I ripped my jacket off, turned and smashed my back against the wall, rubbing frantically. When I felt sure it was dead, I turned back to the other two who'd given up all pretense of sophistry and had collapsed to the floor with hilarity. "The least you can do is get the remains off!"

Phoenix kept pausing to wipe her eyes, giggling as I stripped off the harness and she pulled up the back of my shirt. A fresh cackle had me craning my head around. "What the fuck is so funny?"

She held up a nearly invisible thread of golden brown. "It'sa-it'sa haaai-irr!" she howled.

I snarled, then tugged my shirt down and got the harness back on. "Fuck you," I enunciated with as much dignity as I could muster. "You have thirty minutes." I stalked off, leaving them screeching like banshees behind me.

***

A dozen miles and two hours later, I watched the flames rising above the trees. That night, tiny scattered campfires dotted the ground, all of them invisible from thirty yards, a few people gathered around each one.

"This is Bear," Eleanor introduced us to the woman. "She was taken from her family three weeks ago."

"So you got to experience the plague, famine, and Steve?" Seahorse grimaced. "I'm so sorry."

"Keep your sympathy." Bear stared into the flames. "I just need to get better so I can get into Salem to find my family." She paused for a moment, then looked up. "Who's Steve?"

CHAPTER 34

I abandoned the group and jogged ahead. We'd sent Doc, Ink, Bear, and a small guard back to the Lair ahead of us and had taken some detours again, arriving a week after they should have gotten back, and now I worried. We should've seen patrols by now.

"Where are they?" Phoenix spoke a few feet behind me on the trail. I hadn't asked her to come, but I'd begun to expect her presence.

"Damned—"

"Captain!" The high voice barely preceded Mouse tumbling out of a tree. "You're back!"

"Where is everyone?"

"Trouble at the Lair! Sarge had a bunch of us positioned all around because we didn't know where you'd be coming from. Amana's in trouble, they're trying to hurt her, and we can't make them stop!" Tears stood out in the girl's eyes, skinny frame trembling.

"Slow down, and breathe," I commanded, setting a pace slow enough that she could just keep up. "Details."

Mouse took a deep breath, then another. "Okay. Some boys tried to hurt Amana, but she hurt them instead. Killed one."

"Holy shit," Phoenix murmured.

"Windrunner killed herself." I sucked in a breath, heard a low cry from Phoenix. "Now all the civilian types say Amana's guilty of murder and they want to hang her! Driver, Dry Eyes, Sarge, Lavender, Doc, that couple that was with you, they're all trying to stop it, but there's too many of 'em! So Sarge says we gotta go watch for you. I think he's trying to keep us out of the way," Mouse finished sullenly. "I think it's gonna be a riot, soon."

"Right." I had to take a few breaths myself. "Good job. Tell Eleanor and the others what's happening, then go around the line and tell 'em we're back, but you guys are our perimeter now. Steve may come looking and we need you to watch for him."

"But I wanna see!"

"No!" I shouted, breaking into a run. "I need a perimeter watch, and you're the commander, so see to it!"

"Kid's just about floating," Phoenix commented. "You making her a commander."

"She's got a good head on her shoulders. If adults reported as quickly and concisely as her, we'd get shit done a lot faster."

Neither of us mentioned Windrunner. She'd been one of the twelve girls found in Steve's recreation town the other month. Quiet, hurting, but working on herself. Ahead, the susurration grew into the roar of a mob. I ran faster, bursting into the small meadow to find utter chaos.

Bodies filled the meadow from one side to the other, an angry, shouting mess. Barely visible over their heads, I saw Amana attached to a tree, rope around her neck. In a tiny semi-circle in front of her stood Lavender, Driver, Dry Eyes, Sarge, Doc and every other person who'd decided to fight. I'd thought our numbers were pretty good, but compared to the crowd of civilians between us and them...

I plunged into the mob, throwing elbows and knees, breaking a trail for us while Phoenix kept them off my back. Open mouths and wild eyes filled my view, feral, snarling faces that dropped back when I shoved past.

As we neared the edge, I heard a pompous voice rising with anger. "Step back! Free our children! That little bitch hurt my son and killed one of his friends. We will have justice!"

"Whoops," I snarled as my elbow clipped his head. "Coming through."

In the tiny clearing, I noticed Anansi behind Amana, frantically working on the manacles that'd been put on her. *Where the fuck did they get manacles?* A long cut showed, starting on his jaw, running up the right side of his face and disappearing into his curly hair.

"What the fuck is going on?" I demanded.

Phoenix brushed past me, heading straight for Amana.

"We want justice!" a woman screamed, red faced and red eyed. "That-that *whore* killed our son! Hang her!"

"Hang her! Hang her! Hang her!" the crowd chanted.

"Did they get into the armory?" I muttered to Sarge.

"No," he whispered. "I managed to lose the key. For now."

I tried to speak, but the noise levels kept rising in pitch. They were wild, frenzied...Impatiently, I yanked a handgun out and fired it into the air, then lowered it to point directly at the pompous ass in front of me.

Silence spread.

"Right." I said into the growing quiet. "This ain't how I want to run things, but seeing as how you're all behaving like assholes, I'll treat you like ones, yeah?"

"We want—" a man began.

"Shut the fuck up!" I snarled. "I've had it up to here—" I held a hand above my head "—with the demands people have been making. Now to find out that women here were raped and harassed...You can keep your damn mouth shut. You say you want justice? Fine! We'll have justice. The same justice we've already shown to rapists!"

"*Capitan.*" A gentle hand rested on my shoulder. "I can speak."

A stirring on the far side of the clearing got my attention, and I saw Eleanor, Storm, Seahorse, and the rest of the fighters. I bared my teeth at the mob. "First witness against the boys, Amanacer, has the floor. Anybody who don't like it or who tries to talk over her's gonna get their ass kicked. If you'll look behind you, you'll see the rest of the fighters. They're acting as peacekeepers. Talk in peace, stay in one piece. Got it?"

The fighters spread out, staying in pairs, looking like they'd love an excuse to fight. Heads swiveled back and forth, unsure where to go. The cowards who like to live at the back of mobs, keeping them alive, now had nowhere to hide.

Once the rumblings settled, Amana spoke. She kept it clear and concise, and I realized she'd been messing with us all these months, for she spoke without a trace of an accent or a word of Spanish.

"Those boys have been harassing girls on the quiet for weeks," she began.

"Lies!" a woman at the front cried.

I held up my handgun, barrel straight up and tick-tocked it, shaking my head *no.* The woman subsided.

"At this moment, I know of two girls who have been raped," Amana continued.

"Fucking cunts asked for it!" a man at the back shouted. Seahorse slugged him neatly.

"What did I just say about interruptions?" I eyed the crowd. "Let the woman speak. Don't make me regret pulling your sorry asses out of Salem any more than I already do."

"Arkansas was the first," Amana spoke quickly. "She told me she'd been afraid to speak, she thought it was normal. With Windrunner, they'd gotten rougher. Hurt her. Windrunner even spoke to a parent." Amana pointed to the mother of the slain boy. "She got laughed away for her troubles."

"How do you know?" I asked.

"She left a note." Amana gestured to Sarge, who produced a folded letter from his breast pocket. "She killed herself just three days ago. We haven't even had time to bury her. Then they came for me." Amana faced the crowd, jaw tight. "Those *pendejos* thought that a girl who doesn't fight can't fight. They'd gotten used to hurting girls who were barely healed. If I could, I'd have killed them all."

"Fuck yeah!"

"You tell 'em, Amana!"

I smiled, seeing the uneasy glances from the crowd as it subsided, confusion and insecurity spreading. The parentals at the front stirred uneasily as the crowd slid back, leaving them in a tiny clearing all their own.

"For fairness' sake, let's bring out the boys," I spoke over the crowd's muttering. Nobody got out of control. I reckon they didn't much fancy a hard nap and a headache later. "Where do you have them?"

"Evenstar and Thrain have them out in the woods," Sarge rumbled. "This lot," he gestured scornfully to the mob, "kept trying to free them."

One of the fighters detached from our group and disappeared into the trees.

"Morons," Phoenix spat contemptuously.

An older man at the front, fairly fit and reeking of privilege, straightened himself. "I," he announced, "am a judge, and the only one here—"

"Your son is one of the rapists," Amana spat.

Unused to being interrupted, the man reddened. "I am the only one here with knowledge of the law, and we'll give you the death sentence, you wetbacked cunt!"

I hit him like a freight train, slamming him down and pressing the pistol against his mouth before the crowd's collective gasp had time to finish.

Phoenix stood straight next to me, gun drawn, keeping the rest of the crowd away, but the man had crossed a line and the gap between him and them widened.

"I'd like it very much if you repeated that," I said pleasantly. "You have repeatedly called one I trust a liar, now you resort to slurs? *Tsk, tsk, tsk.* That's not nice."

The man lay there, pasty white, a dark stain spreading on his pants as I smiled into his eyes, pistol still pressed firmly to his mouth.

"No? You don't want to repeat that? Then perhaps you'd better apologize." He nodded and I moved the barrel enough for him to speak.

"'m sn'ry," he mumbled, snuffling and snorting around the broken nose I'd inadvertently given him. "Sn'ry!"

"I accept your apology, but I do not forget." Amana stared down at him, pitying. "Let him up, *Capitan*. It is time to hear from the rapists."

I stood, shoving back from him. As soon as there was distance between us, he glared hatred at me. He hated us all, but me the most. I could see it in his eyes. I'd humiliated him, and he'd never forgive me.

I could live with that.

Phoenix stayed toward the front, taking the first line of defense as the two remaining boys were brought forward. Late high school, I guessed, of a similar age to most of the fighters. I vaguely recalled seeing a few other boys their age around, but it seemed only three had been involved.

"Got anything to say?" I asked them. Seeing Kestrel enter the clearing after them, I waved her forward.

"Why should we?" one of the boys said, looking around. "They're sluts! We all know it. They were fucking the enemy."

Phoenix and a few of the women around him started forward, but I waved them back. At the rate this kid was going, we wouldn't have to do a damn thing to convince the rest of the mob he was guilty. One of the younger girls wouldn't stop until Driver and Lavender stopped her.

"They were probably happy to have an honest white guy between their legs," the boy continued, oblivious. "Except for her." He waved to Amana contemptuously. "But what does she know, she probably can't even read. Stupid bitch."

"Your son, is he?" I asked the man with the hate-filled eyes. "You must be so proud."

"Hey!" a woman in the crowd yelled. "Don't you be calling Amana that! She's the one who helped find clothes for us!"

"She brought my daughter soup last week when she was sick," a man called out.

Praise for Amana now rained out from the crowd, while the parents at the front looked around like animals caught in a trap.

"That was...fast," Amana looked taken aback. "They were just calling for my death."

"The crowd that cheers your coronation is the same crowd that will laugh at your beheading," I murmured. "Or something like that."

"You come up with that?" Driver appeared next to me.

"No, she reads," Anansi said dryly. "A lot."

"That's my line, kid," I ruffled his hair. "How's your face feel?"

"Hurts," he admitted. "What now?"

Looking over the crowd, it appeared the boy had hit the nail on the head. *What now?* "Punishment," I decided. "Kestrel, is there any hope of, I don't know, rehabilitation?"

"It would take years of therapy, and even then..." Kestrel shook her head. "Neither boy has shown any signs of guilt, and they actually laughed about Windrunner's death. Called her weak."

Angry murmurs from the women around us.

"Captain!" One of the younger women, a light blonde called the Celt, stepped forward. "You mentioned justice, the same as we gave out at the center." I remembered now that she was one of the twelve. "We call for that justice!"

"Justice! Jus-tice, jus-tice!" It became a chant amongst the fighters.

Finally, the two boys began to look worried, realized their parents weren't stepping forward as expected.

"What does this justice entail?" a woman asked shrilly.

"Castration and exile," I said, "which is the same punishment given to the last lot of rapists we dealt with."

"You CAN'T DO THIS!" the same woman shrieked, pushing forward. "You have NO RIGHT, you're not a judge, you're no—"

"Right now," I pitched my voice louder, "this is not a democracy, it's a benevolent dictatorship. The boys confessed. It's either this or execution. We have no use for prisoners, and no way to keep them. We can send you away with your boys."

"How will we survive?"

"You can't do this to us!"

"We will, of course, provide you with some food, enough for a couple weeks, which should get you to the Idaho border," I announced. "But neither these boys nor their enabling parents are welcome here. You're too dangerous. We promised these women safety, and you have broken that promise. We aim to make sure their safety here is never challenged again."

"And there you go," Phoenix spoke to the deathly silent crowd. "Justice."

CHAPTER 35

Midnight again, only this time I hadn't managed to fall asleep. Instead, I lay in bed, cursing my shoulder—which had developed into a line of fire from my shoulder blade to my neck—Steve, and the state of the world in general. Finally giving up, I wandered down the hallway, through the gym, and back to the front. I headed topside, only to find Eleanor on top of the Lair.

"Couldn't sleep," she said. She'd thought ahead and brought a blanket to sit on. She patted the space next to her, and I climbed up.

"Me neither." I settled down, crossing my legs and tucking bare feet under me. She sighed, then said, "How on earth did you decide what to do with them? I've been thinking about it all evening, and I'd probably still be waffling on about it if the decision had been left to me."

I rubbed my eyes. "What was I supposed to do? Can't keep 'em here, can't release them scot-free. And we've done the castration thing before. As for the families. I dunno. I just kept talking and hoped it'd make sense."

Eleanor looped her arm with mine, leaning against me in companionable silence as we watched the stars turn.

"I'm tired," I said eventually. "I'm tired of this whole administration thing. The fighting stuff is mostly all right, crazy as it sounds. At least I know who's on what side. Here, all this damn backbiting, the mob sways this way, the mob sways that way. Most of 'em aren't fit to be anywhere near a fight, they're emotional wrecks and a hindrance, and they don't have a clue." I sighed heavily. "And now I'm whining. Don't tell anyone, will you?" I pleaded.

"As if I were a priest in the confessional," she promised. "Though you're right, we can't keep all these civilians here indefinitely. They need a more settled place. Maybe something they can farm and keep a few animals. It'd be rough, but it wouldn't be the fight."

"Right. I think this is a problem for tomorrow. Maybe next week." I yawned. "But we gotta start looking."

"We'll also settle some rules of interaction between the men and women, especially singles." Eleanor yawned, too. "Write it down, then post it in the common room, barracks, and gym. Tomorrow."

"C'mon." I pulled her to her feet. "Let's get to bed. It's gonna be a long day, and Moana and Cub want to show me a play they came up with."

"How come I never get invited to the plays?" Eleanor griped good naturedly as I helped her over a slippery spot.

"Because you're always in them," I said dryly. "Good night, Eleanor."

"'Night, Captain."

***

As predicted, it was a full day, though in a strange way, normal too.

We'd decided to castrate the young men in the early morning, before the little ones were up, and to keep the males away from the Lair. On getting to their holding pen, we found each one had the word 'rapist' carved into his forehead, and the guards, a mix of women and older men, all had no idea how it could possibly have happened.

I snorted at the too-innocent looks on their faces, but let the lie slide.

Afterward, I washed in the creek, scrubbing blood from my hands and trying to drown the pitiful screams and pleadings of those who hadn't appreciate the consequences of their actions until directly confronted with them.

I applauded loudly after Moana and Cub's play, joined by Phoenix. The girls had done an adorable, jumbled mixture of kids' films and songs, enthusiastically.

Then it was fight training in the gym, and Sarge gave me a good workout, followed by lunch.

"Is it just me, or have we hit a routine?" I asked.

Eleanor looked up from her tea. "We've found a new normal. Contrary to what the movies like to show, people manage to find a routine and make life 'normal' under most circumstances. It's subjective to each person, really. Oh, and on the matter of normal, don't forget to check on Porkpie. You haven't seen him since we left, and he's doing quite well, physically. I think he's worried about how he'll fit in without a leg, though."

"And Bear," Amana interjected. "She is...*muy enojado*." The young woman watched me expectantly.

"Are we seriously going back to this?" I glared at her. "We know you don't need to throw around all this Spanish, and I have no idea what '*eno-enojado*' means."

"*Si.*"

"I hate you."

In the background, Windrunner's friends entered, wet and dirty from digging her grave. The funeral would be in the evening, after stones for a cairn were collected. The girls insisted on doing all the preparations themselves, though they did allow Eleanor to help prepare Windrunner's body.

After lunch we headed into the meadow for archery, which I still struggled with. Storm, Phoenix, Seahorse, and I taught a group of newer women and two boys when wagering began on shots. I had my allotment of canned fruit for the next month riding on Phoenix when Seahorse nudged me and tipped her head, indicating a woman walking toward us.

In her mid-thirties, the woman had the fit look of a person who'd spent a good deal of her life in a gym, maybe playing sports. Wealthy, then, and she looked like a model. Though we'd learned the hard way that being too thin could make life in the hills difficult. Now, the fitness freaks had a hard time keeping enough fat on their bones to have the energy to run all day. Turns out, a bit of thickness could be a good thing.

"May I speak to you privately?" she asked me softly.

I stepped back and held out a hand, indicating she should lead the way. She chose to sit on top of the bunker, and I plopped down next to her, making sure I could keep an eye on the shooting and my wager.

"What can I do for you?"

"I don't know if you recognize me, but it was my husband's nose and pride you broke yesterday."

"Oh. Uh, I remember the incident, not the face." This woman was a good deal younger than her husband, and less than twenty years older than the boy, so...I eyed her speculatively. Trophy wife, I bet.

"Yes, well." The woman smoothed her hands over her thighs. "I've come to ask a favor, though I realize I don't have the right to do so."

"Ask." I sat up straighter. Phoenix stepped to the mark for the deciding shot.

"I've come to ask to not be exiled with my husband. I would rather volunteer to be a fighter, if you find me suitable."

My jaw dropped, and I stared at her. Over by the tree, I heard screaming and groaning, but ignored it. The thought of this obviously well-educated woman from a wealthy marriage wanting to join the fighters...

"I'm sorry." She brushed her hair back from her face, embarrassed. "I shouldn't have asked. I'm too old, and I have no experience. I'm sorry." She rolled to her knees, preparing to stand.

"No!" I exclaimed, putting out a hand. "It's not that at all. Most folks with kids aren't exactly lining up to join the fighters. And it's not that we don't accept your age. After all, we have Eleanor. I'm just...surprised."

She watched me anxiously, and I blew out a breath. Right. Let's try this again. "You're right, you will have to prove yourself. We'll put you through your paces, and you'll have to pass a lot of physical tests before you're accepted. You'll sweat, bleed, and cry, but plenty of girls make it. We do it to reduce the number of deaths we suffer."

"I heard." She licked her lips. "I understand, and I want to help. I'd rather stay here and work. I'm not...I don't want to go with my husband!"

"Ah." That explained it. "We won't force you to go with them. You don't need to become a fighter. And you'll need a name. Honestly, I don't actually know what your name is. And you'll fill out a page in the Book, too."

The Book was Jewel's idea. After nearly dying, she realized nobody knew who her family was, and we'd never be able to contact them. Eleanor and Amana worked out a binder with plastic sleeves, and every person connected to us filled out a page with their name, alias, a list of their family members, Social Security number, and last known address. Amana was the keeper of the Book and the one who filled out information about the person's death.

It became a ritual, filling your page in the Book, one that approached making a Last Will and Testament.

"That easily?" The woman stared, surprised. "I thought you would need to know about me a bit more."

"Nah. We'll know everything we need to over the next few weeks."

"Then I would still like to become a fighter, please."

***

That evening, shortly before sundown we laid Windrunner to rest.

"Hail the victorious dead," Arkansas intoned over the cairn piled over the girl's resting place.

"All in, all out," sighed the fighters.

"Hail the victorious dead." The Celt raised her bottle high, and we copied her.

"Windrunner!" we bellowed

After the funeral, the trophy wife approached me as I drank with my small circle.

"Captain?" she asked.

"Yeah." I stepped away to meet her.

"I'd like to be called Sparrow."

"Sparrow. A plain little bird."

"I've always dreamed of being plain." Sparrow tried smiling at me. "Beauty can be a burden."

"We'll do you one better." I rested a hand on her arm. "We don't give a rat's ass what a person looks like, just if they can fight. You'll be woken early. We're starting you on strength training first. Sarge!" I waved the man over. "This is Sparrow." I introduced them. "She's joining the recruits, starting tomorrow. You'll also need to move into the fighter's barracks. Sarge, will you?"

I let Sarge make arrangements, giving her a partner who would show her the ropes for the next couple weeks, then got back to the business of mourning a young life and planning the next step.

∗∗∗

The second morning after Windrunner's funeral, we sent the exiles on their way. The two boys, Sparrow's ex, and the dead boy's mother were given small packs with enough food for a week, canteens, and a knife each. Sparrow watched with a blank face as her husband ordered her to stand beside him and turned away when he began screaming abuse at her.

Phoenix smacked him across the mouth, then gagged the man. After blindfolding the exiled, Seahorse and a small band led them into the trees. They'd head east-ish for a couple days before setting the exiles free.

That evening I lay in bed exhausted in body and mind, wishing sleep would find me, wishing my shoulder would stop screaming in agony, when a knock sounded at my door. I rolled to my side, wincing as the line of pain shot up to my ear.

"What?" I snarled.

The door swung open, revealing a tiny little Cub, dressed in a cut-down nightgown, gazing at me, her large brown eyes showing hurt and a gathering of tears. Before I could apologize, say anything, she disappeared down the hall. I heard the pattering of her bare little feet and above that, a sob.

"Fuck." I rolled out of bed, limping down the hallway after her, wincing every time my right foot hit the ground. That rock I'd landed on had given me a deeper bruise than I'd thought.

I followed the sounds of Cub's cries, finally tracking her down to a storage closet of all places. She huddled amongst the sheets and blankets, knees tucked to her chest, arms wrapped around them and head down, making the smallest bundle possible.

"Cub, Cub. Baby." I reached out to her tentatively, on my knees in the doorway. The little girl flinched away, sobbing now. "Oh, honey, I'm sorry. I didn't mean to snap at you."

She curled tighter.

"I thought it was Kestrel or Phoenix. You know they always piss me off." I peered down, trying to see her face. The sobs quieted to little sniffles. "What did you want?"

"I-I wanted you to tell me a story," she whispered, barely raising her head.

"A story?" All these months, and she'd never asked for one before.

"Bethy's mommy was holding her and telling her a story." Her breath hitched. "I wanted my, my mommy. I wanted to be held, and mommy's not here, so I went to you, and you were mad..."

Tears pricked my eyes. I reached out and gathered the girl up, shifting so my back was against the blankets in the bottom of the closet with Cub cuddled close.

"Oh, baby," I whispered into her herb-scented hair. "I'm so sorry I sounded mad. But do you know what?" I tried looking at her face again. Cub tipped her head to the side, just enough that I could catch a glimpse of one eye. "Even if I'm mad, seeing you makes me feel better. So you can come in any time you want, and my mad will go right away."

"Really?" She treated me to wide-eyed incredulity.

"Really." I leaned in closer to murmur, "But don't tell anybody that, because then any time I'm mad at Phoenix, she'll just send you in, and I think it's funny being mad at Phoenix."

The child let out a watery giggle, then stretched up to whisper, her hot breath puffing in my ear, "I promise."

"Good." I smiled. "Now, what story do you want to hear?"

So it was that when Phoenix tracked me down an hour later, I was in the middle of telling the story of Robin Hood, who stole from the rich and gave to the poor. Not just any version, but the Disney telling where Robin was a fox, rings were stolen right off fingers, and sadness never lasted long.

***

I woke to scratching and a whine at my door and found myself on my feet, gun in hand before it registered. I yawned, rubbing my eyes. Cin had decided to sleep in my room, and now needed to be let out.

Awesome.

"You do realize that I was finally sleeping past the midnight mark, don't you?" I grumbled to the dog as I let him outside the Lair. I frowned when I saw how slowly he moved, as if his hips pained him. Sirius had had the old boy booked in to see the vet, and she'd worried her dog might have arthritis. I think I could safely say he definitely had arthritis.

As we made our slow way back down the stairs, a light caught my attention, and I slipped ahead, worried about more trouble from assholes. I lunged around the corner to come to a screeching halt, face to face with a surprised Amana clutching the Book.

"*Que mierda, Capitan?*" Amana reared backward.

"Oh, fuck!" I paused awkwardly, one hand in the air. "I, uh, didn't know it was you." I sheepishly tucked the offending limb behind my back.

I studiously avoided looking at the Book. We'd decided Amana should be the only one to know where it was kept to prevent anybody taking it to Steve, and now I'd gone and surprised her while in the process of hiding it again.

"Well, erm, goodnight." I smiled and determinedly turned away, back to my room.

"*Buenas noches,*" she said softly to my retreating back.

***

"What is it that has you so upset?" Eleanor asked me gently. She'd finally cornered me in my room when I had no ready excuse to escape her gentle interrogation. "Ever since I said that prayer yesterday, in fact."

"I haven't been grumpy," I said, crossing my arms.

"Oh, no?" She raised her eyebrows and nodded at my arms.

I uncrossed them hurriedly. "What? I always cross my arms. Keeps my shoulder from hurting."

"Hah! You only talk about your shoulder when you're avoiding. Talk."

I spun away, raking my hands through my hair, annoyed when they caught in tangles, tugging painfully. "It's that whole thing where you prayed for our deliverance, and for us to know God." I finally gave in. "I always thought He wanted peace and was full of love and all that. But I'm a fighter. I've killed, and I'll do it again, many more times. According to what I remember of the New Testament, I'm virtually antithetical to everything Jesus taught. So how am I supposed to reconcile the two? Be a peaceful person of God while our world burns? Or reject everything and fight back? I don't see a happy medium here.

"And what about the way people are being treated?" I spun, pacing the room. "The Invasion, the rapes, the murders. I heard a lot, Before, about how can we say God is good if He allows all this suffering? How's this supposed to make sense?"

"Captain." Eleanor stepped forward, sympathy shining bright. "Sit down before you wear a trench in the concrete." I couldn't, but I did lean against the wall, wary in a way I never was in the field. "First off, it was very rare for physical freedom to happen as a result of direct interventions like fire, brimstone, or miracles. It seemed that most of God's rescues involved Him empowering and blessing a few people who fought impossible odds."

I snorted. "So what? Now we're blessed?" I couldn't keep the bitterness out of my voice. "Yeah, we're doing great, with all the innocents killed, ain't we?"

"You are doing very well." Steel laced Eleanor's tone. "How many people are living here in safety?"

"Two weeks ago there were four more."

"And we dealt with it as soon as we knew. You are not responsible for the behaviors of others. Neither is God." She walked forward, long skirts swirling around her legs. "One thing people tend to overlook about the Bible is that Adam and Eve were given knowledge of good and evil. Knowing the difference means you can *choose*. So if there's evil done, it's because a human *chose* to do it. Those young men had every advantage in life, knew better, and chose their path. Steve *chose* to come here. the soldiers continue to *choose* to follow orders. *They* chose this. They did. Not you.

"Now you have a choice to make, too. To keep fighting, to keep struggling in the direction you know is right, or to give up. If you choose to give up, would that be on God, or on you?" Eleanor rested a hand on my arm gently. "Think about it. Just because you're not sure you believe in God anymore doesn't mean He doesn't continue to believe in you."

I stayed against the wall, staring blindly, unaware she'd left until the door clicked shut behind her.

CHAPTER 36

Two weeks after my conversation with Eleanor, I was in the field again. I lay behind a downed tree on the edge of a hayfield, waiting, waxing mentally philosophical.

Or bullshitting myself. Take your pick.

The lookouts had noticed a routine of three trucks heading north to Portland every other week, and a dispatch of scouts confirmed the road used as well as the regularity. Deciding where to ambush the trucks had been a conundrum as there were several likely spots, so we picked the most unlikely spot we could find, an open hayfield on either side of snake curves.

The trucks needed to slow considerably to make it around the corners, and in the meantime, the grass grew just long enough to hide a person or ten.

Phoenix, lying to my right, rolled to her back, basking in the sun. "How's it going, Cap'n?"

"Oh, you know," I scratched my side, "enjoying the whole sensitive skin and grass thing. Thinking of taking a nap."

Phoenix yawned. "Nap sounds nice. Bastards better hurry up or else we'll all be asleep before they get here."

I squinted up the road, wishing I had a pair of sunglasses. You only needed them once or twice a year, and when you did there was never a pair to be found. "Maybe Steve's already taking a nap?"

"Maybe. The homeland's pretty warm, ain't it? Humid, too, right?"

I squirmed in the grass, irritated by the tiny abrasions. I hated hay. Just as I opened my mouth to continue complaining, River, on lookout, cawed.

"Shit's going down, people, so look alive!" I called in a low voice. Metallic snicks and clicks sounded through the warm air as fighters readied weapons.

***

"Well," I panted, Thrain's body a heavy, limp bundle over my shoulders in a fireman's carry, "at least we know we've got Steve's attention."

"Ya think?" Phoenix growled behind me.

Ahead of Eleanor, Evenstar pulled weakly against the women towing her, trying to join me. Half of us were loaded down with bodies while Storm led the front, taking any trail that took us deeper into the hills, and Phoenix guarded our rear.

"I can't believe Steve actually ambushed us," Phoenix snarled.

"They had to get smart sometime," Eleanor gasped.

"Yes, but...in the trucks? We've seen those trucks heading north for weeks, and they just so happen to have soldiers in them the one time we stop those damn things?"

We'd ambushed the trucks as planned. The nail-riddled strips across the road doing their job only to have a dozen or more soldiers hidden in each truck ambush us.

Three fighters never got up. Thrain died hurling his wife out of a bullet's path, amazingly firing twice and taking a soldier down with each shot. Now,

I carried him over my shoulders. Our numbers were down to twelve and more trucks had arrived, disgorging soldiers like clowns from a tiny car. My best estimate had us outnumbered four or five to one.

"It had to happen sometime," I grunted as my foot slipped and I nearly went down. Regaining my feet, I powered up the slope. "This just means we need to get more creative, too."

At least we'd picked a spot Steve hadn't expected an ambush from, and a few hurled grenades gave us just enough time to get out of sight with our dead. Those who weren't carrying a body lugged weapons and doubled up with the small packs. A sticky, warm dampness spread down my back, mingling with sweat.

Phoenix planted a hand on my butt to boost me up a steep point in the trail then patted my rump. "All in, all out," she encouraged before dropping back.

***

Dark had settled fully before we felt safe enough to stop. I groaned as helping hands relieved me of my burden, and then I flopped to the ground, stretching my back in relief. But we were unable to rest long. We needed a secure camp and some sleep.

A strange rustling had me sitting up, and I gasped in horror at the sight confronting me.

"I am not sleeping in that thing!" I stalked over to the women working.

"Why not?" Phoenix asked, offended. "We went to a lot of trouble to get it!"

"You did not," I said crossly. "You stole it from some house."

"So what? We needed something big enough to meet in when it rains, go over maps, shit like that, and there's no reason it should be empty during the night. Since you're the only one we may need to find in a hurry, you should sleep in it."

The object of our disagreement was a green and gray camping tent, big enough to sleep four, according to the label, and rising like a fungus. Phoenix decided we should use it as a command tent.

"Ever think that if you can find me, so can Steve?"

"What makes you think they'll find it?"

"I don't know! Maybe because those colors practically glow at night? And the forest is literally crawling with Steve?" I waved my hands, feeling a little dramatic. "Although...heh." A thought flitted across my mind. "Guys! Over here..."

***

I woke the instant a hand closed over my mouth, holding my Glock like a child clutches her teddy bear. Phoenix leaned in. "They're here," she breathed.

I sat up, groaning silently as strained muscles complained with every movement, easing the blanket back and pulling my holsters out of my pack, which doubled as a pillow. Strapping the holsters on took mere moments and then I stood, ready to go. This night we hadn't even removed our boots. All around me, fighters awakened from where we'd scattered throughout the thin underbrush.

The muffled sounds of people trying to be stealthy filtered up the hill to us. I smiled. The bastards should've spent some time hunting, then maybe they'd have learned what it really means to stalk prey. Crouching stretched my legs and hips as I carefully poured water over the dirt, mixing it to make a mud paste that I then smeared over my face and exposed skin.

Stealthy movements in the shadows and pale skin disappearing told me the others followed suit. As soon as everybody covered up, we were ready to go.

Seahorse took Legs, a track runner we'd rescued in the Bus-capades, and Hawk to the left, and River went to the right with Feisty and Storm. Phoenix followed at my right shoulder down the middle while Dionysius, a young man who'd also volunteered as soon as he was freed in the Bus-ca-pades, followed behind. Dionysius had proven to have a quick, capable mind in training, and he hadn't lost his cool during the failed ambush, so he showed promise.

Eleanor and Doc stayed at the camp, mostly to keep an eye on Evenstar. We didn't want her going suicidal on us, for her son's sake as well as ours.

Heading down the hill, we shifted from tree to tree, shadow to shadow. The moon had nearly set and the shadows it cast concealed rather than re-vealed, allowing us to move more quickly than we'd originally anticipated. At a rough estimate, ten soldiers surrounded the tent, left like an offering in a shrouded clearing. A few bundles on the ground each had another soldier standing over it, so twenty in all.

I'd barely felt Dionysius tap my shoulder, telling me he'd caught up when Steve moved. They didn't shoot—instead, the men tried taking the bundles at their feet prisoner while three men slashed the tent open, leaping inside, ostensibly to take us by surprise. The swearing had just begun when it became our turn.

I did *not* leap out and yell, "Now!" In my opinion, doing so would have ruined the element of surprise. I simply opened fire from behind my tree while my world broadened to see the other flashes all around the camp and narrowed to each target in front of me. Screams and shouts rang out from the soldiers while my fighters stayed deadly silent.

Then Steve took the initiative and charged.

"Gang up on 'em!" I bellowed, dropping the rifle to bring up a handgun. The first soldier was nearly on me when I shot him. Air puffed past my face and the next soldier rose up, mouth open in a silent scream. My world narrowed further to become the people immediately around me. Screams, shots, the hot splash of blood, the numb thud of a blow landing, it all blurred in the dark.

Don't let them hit you. They hit you too hard, you won't recover in time, you're dead.

The litany repeated over and over, as I spun, suddenly finding a knife in my free hand. My gun emptied, so I holstered it and drew another, never stopping my forward motion. A couple strained in front of me, shrieks of rage from the one on the bottom. I drove forward, knocking a man back, and we fell. I twisted, landing on top of him, knife tip first. Rolling to my feet, I aimed at the first body in front of me, only to realize my people were the last ones standing.

"Everybody okay?" I said harshly. My left hand twitched involuntarily and I realized I still clutched a bloody knife. I cleaned it on a body and sheathed it in the small of my back again, ignoring the blood coating my hand and sleeve. It blended well with everything else I could see.

We mostly suffered scrapes and bruises, though River'd taken a blow to the stomach bad enough she needed help to walk.

"Some of these bastards are still alive," Phoenix called from where she knelt next to a soldier. "Are we killing them?"

The soldier nearest her scrabbled weakly, trying to escape. Before I could respond, Storm hailed me from the trail downhill.

"Captain! We got incoming, maybe two miles out!"

I spun back to Phoenix. "Leave them, leave all of them!"

"But—"

I ignored her. "Load up and move out."

Catching my urgency, everybody raced up the hill to collect our people. I slung my gear belt around my hips, fastened the canteen snugly, and slung on the small pack. Evenstar still knelt at Thrain's body.

I rested a hand on her shoulder. "We need to go. Steve's coming," I said to her and Eleanor, standing right behind her.

"Thrain—" Evenstar clutched my hand.

"All in, all out," I assured her. Kneeling, I took one cold hand and wrestled him up. Rigor mortis had set in, so I needed help to get his body over my shoulders. The others also carrying bodies came over and took up their smaller burdens.

"How much time do we have?" I asked Storm.

"A little over an hour," she responded. "They don't do too well at higher altitudes, especially on foot."

"Good. Keep us moving up. Let's hope the kids made it to Bastard." The lack of ready communication meant planning out alternative meeting points. For some reason, everybody liked to name these points after swear words. "Phoenix!"

"Yo."

"Take Hawk, watch our back trail. Slow 'em down. Don't get caught and don't lose us."

I saw Phoenix punch the air and head downhill with Hawk while the rest of us made our slow way after Storm. Eleanor and Evenstar assisted those of us loaded with the bodies of our dead, and Doc helped River along.

We climbed, the time marked only by the stars turning in the heavens. Every step became agony, and my back and shoulders screamed in pain with every jarring motion. Maybe two hours after the fight I heard a series of evenly spaced shots downhill, too high to be rifles, but the event was swiftly forgotten under the trial of putting one foot in front of the other.

By the tilt of the Big Dipper, four a.m. had come and gone before we made the gravel road. Dereva, Hightide, and Wilder—a young woman from the Bus-capade—were waiting for us, hiding in the bushes. Storm whistled shrilly to tell Hawk and Phoenix to move their asses, then we loaded the trucks. All the bodies went in with Wilder, who also had Doc, Evenstar, and Legs.

"Take them back to the Lair by the most direct route you can," I told Wilder, stretching my back and shoulders while everybody else picked a vehicle. "Hightide, go with them as a guard. Dereva," I put a hand on the girl's shoulder, "we're the distractions. Remember the locators Anansi planted?"

The kid had been busy as all hell these last few months, and this would be the first time we implemented an idea of his. All trials had been successful, but adrenaline and fear changed the parameters in ways we couldn't predict.

"Oregon grapes!" the three drivers chorused.

I gave them a thumbs up and leaped into the back of my old GMC. Dereva preferred driving her, and I preferred riding in that truck, though I discovered that the girl had made an addition. I'd bought the truck with a toolbox in the bed, just behind the cab. Dereva had added another one right by the tailgate. A quick peek showed a jumble of boots, clothing, and blankets, while the one at the cab was loaded with weapons and ammunition.

Phoenix jogged out of the trees, followed by Hawk. Phoenix immediately veered toward me and the pickup while Hawk jumped in with Wilder.

We all formed small groups within the whole, even during the end of our world.

"Hey, Cap'n." Phoenix rolled into the bed of the truck, keeping her rifle clear. "Did you know Steve would do that?"

"Do what?"

"They executed their wounded." The words dropped into the early morning air, rocks in a still pond. Those gunshots earlier suddenly sprung to mind and dread settled in my gut.

"Oh." I shook my head. "I thought Steve would stop to care for them, give us a bit more time." River retched out the window, but that might be due to the blow to the stomach and all the jogging.

"Yeah," Phoenix snorted, carefully pulling out the huge Barrett sniper rifle she'd finally gotten proficient with from the toolbox and assembling it. "They slowed down."

"Not as much as they should've," I muttered. Raising my voice to carry over the murmurs rolling around the trucks I called, "You heard what they do to their own. So don't get caught!"

"Yo!"

"No problem!"

Wilder's truck, loaded with dead and wounded, left first, followed closely by Hightide, who had the majority of the able-bodied fighters to guard them. My truck pulled onto the road last, and we split off at the first turn, hunting Steve.

***

Anansi and his people had only just gotten his idea situated, and I looked forward to disappearing off Steve's radar. Or dying abruptly. At this point, it was a toss-up. Finding an enemy truck didn't take long, and getting their attention look even less effort. Then our insane, underage driver took off like a bat out of hell, spraying gravel as she took corners too fast.

As soon as we had enough of a lead to drop out of sight periodically, Dereva and the Celt, her navigator, spotted an Oregon grape and screeched to a stop. Me and Phoenix piled out and rustled the bushes lining the road. The kid was thorough, I'll give him that. Three of the bushes were removable, lifting easily out of holes barely large enough to fit the burlap wrapped roots.

As soon as the truck could fit, Dereva drove through and we dropped the plants back in, holding onto them to keep it steady until Steve passed. A quick check of the road showed us this truck patrolled alone, so we moved the plants out again and got the truck back on the road. It took barely a moment to wedge the boards Anansi left back in. My little genius thought of everything.

"You know," I frowned at the road behind us, "we should've planted a couple landmines first. If Steve ran over one, great. If not, dig 'em up again."

Phoenix laughed. "Remember when we used to feel bad about ambushes?"

"Seems like ages." Was it really only a few months ago? I had no idea what month we were in, but I guessed May or June. The first ambush would've been roughly January-ish, when I'd been so reluctant.

Huh.

"Sirius should be home soon," I said irrelevantly. Dereva accelerated and we knelt down to brace as we opened the weapons box to get ready.

We caught up to Steve quickly, just a glimpse around a corner, and Phoenix braced the bi-pod of her sniper rifle on the cab of the truck while I stood, legs spread and knees bent slightly, one foot in front of the other to keep my balance. We came to a straight stretch of gravel, the trees opening enough to give us a good field of view, and a better one of the patrol truck roughly seventy-five meters ahead of us.

I bent, swinging the large metal tubed we'd just assembled up, resting it on my shoulder, swaying like a drunken sailor.

Phoenix craned her head around to squint up at me. "You sure that's the front?"

"No."

"Oh. Okay." She turned back to her rifle, tucking stray bits of hair under the bandana tied around her head and clearing her line of sight. "I'll just get ready to shoot, then, shall I?"

"Yeah, you do that." I squinted through the scope, aiming.

***

Eleanor walked barefoot across the grass in the meadow around the Lair's door to greet us. Dereva and the Celt must've told her we were coming when we'd stopped to check in with the perimeter guards. "So. Did the rocket launcher go how you expected?"

"Uh…" Phoenix and me gave each other sideways glances. "Not exactly," Phoenix admitted. She had a red mark like a sunburn on the right side of her face, and the exposed skin of her forearm showed more of the same. "There was a lot of kick. Lot of boom, too."

"Don't forget the fire," I added.

"Some screaming."

"A little falling." I arched my back and rolled my head around. I'd feel it in the morning.

"I see," Eleanor said evenly. "And will you be playing with such danger-ous toys again?"

"Hell yeah!" we chorused.

Technically speaking, our first outing with the rocket launcher was a success in that Steve's truck blew up, leaving a smoking crater in the gravel road, a burning hulk, and more bits scattered around. It also knocked me on my ass, slamming me into the clothing box. Ironically, if the box hadn't been there, I'd've broken my neck, landing with my head on the tailgate (in between enemy contact we'd tested the theory).

We'd also been jarred just as I squeezed the trigger, so the barrel of the launcher had pointed slightly downward while Phoenix bounced up, which is what led to her looking like she'd gotten a bit too much sun.

Also interesting, I'd've missed the truck completely if not for that pothole.

The rest of the day and part of the evening had been spent tearing over the countryside, shooting trucks and leading Steve on a merry chase and generally causing havoc and chaos.

Anansi bounded out of the Lair. "You're back!" He ran over to me, wrapping an arm around my waist as I wrapped one around his shoulders. "How'd my idea work?"

"We'd be dead if it wasn't for you," I told him honestly. "There were so many soldiers out there. You have everything really nicely spread out, too." I hugged him. "Thanks. This almost makes up for the vodka."

The boy sighed, unusually somber. "We have the graves ready." My smile died. "We'll have the funeral in the morning. We have a lot of funerals, don't we?" He sounded like a lost little boy, and I remembered he was only thirteen.

"At least we brought them home." Small comfort, but it was all I had.

***

I surveyed the small meadow. Four new cairns laid in a row, the people surrounding those forming small clusters, with a tiny divide between fighters and civilians. The civilian families or friends of the fallen looked at the fighters with a degree of blame in their eyes, while the fighters looked back with defiance and grief.

"B-birch loved to dance," an older woman choked out, wiping her eyes.

"Hail the victorious dead," the fighters intoned as one.

People who'd never seen a funeral yet, Bear among them, looked about, wide eyed at the solemn men and women.

"My niece was an artist in her spare time." A man rubbed a trembling hand over his mouth. "You—she...called herself Foxglove."

"Hail the victorious dead." The fighters spoke louder, as if to drive away the fear that lived in each of us.

"I didn't know Thestral well," the Celt spoke up. "She didn't know what happened to her family, but I know she had a wicked memory for stories, and she could hustle pool like nobody's business."

"Hail the victorious dead."

Evenstar stepped forward now, laying a small flower on Thrain's cairn. "He was a wonderful man," she whispered thickly. "A good father and husband. I am so," she swallowed, tears falling, "so fortunate to have known him."

"Hail the victorious dead!"

Death found us all. The best we could hope for was to die with purpose.

CHAPTER 37

The next morning found me in the common room nursing a hangover, unable to decide which was worse, the disease or the cure. Eleanor had a nasty smelling concoction to help with hangovers that she called "An old family recipe."

The rest of us called it "Barely Better Than Suffering All Day."

What can I say? The name's a work in progress.

My holsters, guns, rags, oil, and soap lay in a heap on the table in front of me as I propped my head on my hand, an elbow resting on the table. I desperately wanted to crawl back into bed, but after the exertions of the last few days I really needed to clean my gear.

Plus, Eleanor banged on my door until I got up.

I perused the contents of my mug, trying to work up the courage to drink it, when Phoenix wobbled into the room and gingerly sat down across from me, glaring blearily through hanks of hair when I sniggered.

"Are you gonna die on me?" I asked, peering at her through my fingers without raising my head.

"Not so loud," she complained, clutching her head. "I wish I was. Then maybe Eleanor would let me sleep."

"Eleanor's sludge is in the pot." I rolled my head to the left, toward the kitchen. "Help yourself."

Phoenix sighed, levering herself up and shuffling to the counter where the pot rested. "My bra is wearing thin, and the scavengers haven't been finding enough replacements." After filling her cup, she brought it to her mouth, tossing the drink back quickly, grimacing as she swallowed. "God! That shit's disgusting!" Wiping her mouth, she refilled the mug and came back to the table. "We need more bras."

I finally drained my mug, clenching my teeth to keep myself from gagging. After a moment to recover I opened my eyes. "Dunno. Hightide said most of the fighters have got something. They're still working on finding a good style, but we should be able to replace yours with a proper bra. It's only the civilians who are hit and miss, and Lavender says walking around without a bra won't hurt 'em."

I sighed. No point putting it off any longer. I refilled my own cup and sat back down, getting to work cleaning gear. In truth, I like mindless tasks. Your brain can go for a wander while your hands do the work.

As I scrubbed another set of straps, Phoenix wandered away, then came back with all her guns. Like me, she carried four handguns and a smaller, maneuverable rifle for distance shooting, but she also had the huge sniper rifle that sat on a bipod. She laid all six out on the table next to me, beginning the never-ending round of cleaning.

The experienced fighters were constantly armed, first to be prepared, and secondly because we insisted the trainees always be armed and it'd be hypocritical of us not to. The only exception to this rule was during cleaning, and I found it disturbing how I relaxed the moment I re-armed myself.

Others filtered through, some just finishing a round in the gym, some learning how to care for their gear, others heading to the kitchen to take over the next cooking shift. Amanacer brought out a cutting board, knife, and a whole bunch of weeds. Doc and Wildwood, our herbalist, decreed that we all needed to eat as many greens as possible, so once a week the kitchen made a green soup out of whatever could be gathered from the forest. This meant dandelion, skunk weed, and nettles, with whatever else they had thrown in the mix.

"Are jou going to do training today, or just polish dat all day?" Amana nodded to my holsters.

"I'm gonna do as little as possible until I'm sure my head won't fall off."

Amana organized her board and bowls and began chopping dandelion roots for the soup. "*Si?*" She raised an eyebrow, index finger and thumb steadying the knife blade while the rest of her fingers gripped the handle. The fingers of her left hand curved slightly so the blade could rest against her knuckles as she chopped quickly.

I heaved an aggrieved sigh. "I'll take a run and hit the gym after I've cared for my gear. Me and Phoenix are the last ones, I think." We worked in companionable silence for a while, watching the rest of the people as they went about their days. "How's the tannery coming along? Phoenix almost lost her bra the other day."

"Hightide, she has *cinco ayudantes,*" (that's five something), "and a man trained *muy bien.* Maybe she will *daselo a el.*"

"What?" I glared at her over the table.

"Why?" Phoenix moaned. "Why does she do this to us?"

"Dere... are... five... people... helping... in... de... *curtiduria,*" Amana spoke slowly, maintaining eye contact. "One... man... bery... good. Maybe... she... will... gib... heem... control... of... production."

"I hate you," I said clearly. "Who's in there? Are they any good at it?"

"Nobody ees de man who works good tanning. Wisteeria ees making bras. Only okay," Amana interjected when I opened my mouth. "No' bery good ones. Al is...*inutil.*" I sighed, doing my best to give her the evil eye. The corner of her mouth twitched while her hands never stopped. "He cannot fight, he cannot cook, and he keel eb'ryt'ing he plant. So, he go to *curtiduria*. Ruby *no trabajo*, Lavender send her to *curtiduria*. Dere is *un ninita* who also *trabaja en la curtiembre*. Optimus Prime."

"Optimus Prime?" I snorted a quick breath of laughter, stopping when the motion threatened my stomach's equilibrium. "I need-need to meet the girl who-who-who," I gasped, trying to keep still, "decided to be called Optimus *Prime*!"

"Jou've seen her," Amana informed me, moving on to the leafy greens. She put on a pair of lightweight gardening gloves to shred the stinging nettle.

"She's in the gym when she isn't in the tannery," Phoenix rolled her eyes. "You are so oblivious, it's scary."

I snorted some giggles, hands immediately going back to my gear as I thought. "The really short one with the black eyes and light hair?"

"*Sí.*"

"How about the other girls? The ones who got attacked?" I went still and looked down to realize I'd finished with the holsters and belts already. "Huh." I went to work on the handguns.

The handguns were relatively simple to care for now and happened on autopilot. My pump action rifle had more moving parts than Phoenix's bolt action, but less than her massive semi-auto, so I hoped I'd be done faster than her.

As we worked, Amana continued to fill me in on the people she encountered every day (which was nearly everyone) and all the little tidbits that she thought interesting or important.

A crash startled me, and I slammed the magazine into place, racking the slide as I leaped to my feet, pistol in hand, ready to shoot...a pot? The lid on the soup pot had jumped with the force of the escaping steam, creating the noise. I gave a shaky little laugh, looking around the room to find Phoenix lowering her rifle while the rest of the room stared at us, mouths open.

"Whoops."

***

"We need to change something!" Phoenix exploded, pacing around the table in the Useless Room, where we were joined by Seahorse, Eleanor, and Driver. While we may have been sitting at the table, we were far from calm, all of us twitchy with cabin fever. "It's been two weeks since that travesty of an ambush. Steve's been all over these hills ever since."

Every patrol we'd spotted had a minimum of two vehicles, and numerous foot patrols scoured the hills. Scavenging, hunting, and raiding had ground to a screeching halt.

"What if we change the way we ambush?" Seahorse asked.

I looked up, eyebrows raised. I kept trying to only raise one, but it never worked. I simply didn't have independently working eyebrows. My brother Sean could go full Spock, but my best option was looking terminally surprised. Can't whistle, can't raise a single eyebrow...

"Whatcha got in mind?" I asked.

Seahorse sat forward, gathering up the Risk army pieces we used for visuals. "Right, so what we gotta do is this..."

We all piled together, examining the board as she laid out her plan.

***

The preparations went slowly, since everything had to be low-key enough that Steve's patrols didn't catch us, requiring long hours and plenty of detours for those leaving the Lair.

Eleanor somehow still found time to check in on each of us who'd stepped foot inside the brothel, though. When I asked her how she kept up with everything, she gave the most elegant shrug I'd ever seen.

"I don't deal with everyone. Lavender monitors the kids and civilians, Sarge has all the trainees, Seahorse helps him, and Amana oversees everything. I only have you girls. All the ones we started with. It gives me time for the rest of my duties."

Eleanor's chosen duties were a long list, from occasionally acting as a nurse for Doc to helping in the kitchen, being a willing ear for hurting hearts, and a never-ending load of mending.

"You know," I said, looking up from sharpening my knife for the umpteenth time, surrounded by branches, leaves, and rope, "I talked with Amana the other week, and I have no idea how that woman keeps track of so many people. I had to keep asking her for descriptions, because I had *no* idea who she was talking about half the time. How bad is that?"

"I'd hardly call it bad." Eleanor sat down and fished a bit of mending out of her shoulder bag. That thing went with her everywhere, and she constantly put little bits and bobs in it, usually finding a use for each one later. "You're an introvert, dear, and suddenly finding yourself at the head of a mob won't change that. I'd say this is the healthiest way for you to manage. If you're not crazy yet, then I'd say it's working. Now, have you heard about..."

As she talked, I realized this conversation had the exact same flavor as the one with Amana. She filled me in about the people inside the Lair, particularly the fighters, about the issues they dealt with, whether or not they were physically or mentally able to go into the field-

"Are you listening?" Eleanor looked up from her mending, eyebrow raised. Dammit.

"Yes, Mother." I grinned, setting down the whetstone, a warm glow filling my stomach at the look of surprise and delight on her face.

***

I lay still, breathing shallowly as I watched soldiers walk past the bush I hid under. I wore a jacket and cargo pants under a blanket made of rope and string, carefully decorated with plants to help me blend in with the scenery.

This was our second ambush using Seahorse's proposed plan and style, and each one required careful preparation. We'd meticulously chosen this site, well south of the Lair and on the edge of Steve's southern patrol range, and it'd taken us four days just to get here, two driving, two on foot. Fighters dotted the steep hillside, concealed under handmade camouflage net cloaks. We'd brought everyone Sarge deemed ready to fight, and this was Jewel's first fighting mission after her shooting last winter.

Leaving the Lair is…different, now. With the deaths from the failed raid still hanging over our heads, apprehension created a bad taste at the back of my tongue. The first time we left, fighters and civilians stood about awkwardly, unsure how to say good-bye without feeling superstitious about it.

Eleanor nudged me.

"Why do I always have to say something?" I hissed.

"Because you're the closest thing we have to a leader," she murmured. "Sucks to be you."

"Bane of my existence," I muttered. A few people noticed us talking and a growing circle of quiet surrounded us as people stopped to stare. Faced by all those eyes, I panicked and blurted, "All in, all out!" then closed my eyes in despair. We'd only used these at funerals.

"Hoo-rah!" Fighters punched the air.

My eyes popped open. Okay. Go with that, then.

"One shot, one kill!"

"Hoo-rah!"

"No luck, all skill!"

The fighters roared.

Guess it hadn't been the wrong thing to say after all.

***

Returning to the present as a foot fell dangerously near me, I watched the black boots continue on. We'd dug trenches, loosened and moved stones, piled rocks, and moved downed trees. I'd learned more about ropes and knots than I'd known existed. We all sported blisters, splinters, and one guy managed to get himself a herniated disk. Phoenix had offered to help him, but *noooo*, he was a big, strong *man*. Idiot.

Not three feet away from me, one of the soldiers sprouted an arrow, accompanied by screaming, and I bared my teeth. Time to start.

The soldiers fell into a crouch, hiding as best they could in the surrounding shrubs. The one unfortunate enough to choose my bush was met with a knife in the eye, and I grunted as I rolled, dragging the body with me to dump him out of my way. Upslope, the people Steve had chased into this mess, Storm and Legs, paused long enough to fire an arrow each before running again.

More cries erupted, and the ones that were too loud were abruptly silenced. Fear, shock, pain, all these could be heard in our enemies' voices. Even hiding in bushes wasn't enough to save those men. An arrow flickered past overhead, followed by a short cry down the slope. The second half of the patrol finally joined us.

I grinned, gathering the rope as everything went still.

I waited, panting lightly, watching the boots march past. When one pair of feet straddled it, I rolled, pulling the rope taut. The man yelled and went down, legs hopelessly tangled. He grasped desperately at the soldier in front, pulling the man off balance and tripping up the soldier behind.

In that confusion, a flat patch of leaves and pine needles burst up as two fighters leaped out, fired a crossbow bolt each and raced away up the slope, abandoning the cover they'd hidden under. I scrambled out of my rope, tripping as my foot caught in it before skidding around the tree, hiding behind the trunk as shots were fired. I strung my own bow and took up a quiver of arrows before running to change position. Both patrols scattered throughout the forest as careful shots from above forced them apart.

Crashing sounded to the north, accompanied by screams. The rockslide we'd carefully built. I fired at a soldier, missed, ducked around a bush, ran behind a carefully constructed screen of ropes simulating a solid wall of bushes with four other fighters. A second later it dropped, and we fired three fast shots before scattering, all heading uphill.

Barely leaping a covered pit in time, I slammed into a tree and felt the impact of a bullet next to my cheek before pushing off. At every bit of cover, we fired, always, always running uphill. A short scream behind me as the soldier didn't make the leap and met the stakes at the bottom of the pit.

Steve...didn't do so good at hills. They tended to rely on guns to reach people, and in all the chaos, trees, and plants that really shouldn't have been Plan A. A crunching, booming rumble gave scant warning, and I threw myself down, huddling against a tree.

"Oi!" I bellowed up the hill, through the dust.

When the logs passed, I couldn't find my bow. Abandoning it, I kept running and found myself next to a soldier. I lunged, right hand whipping out the hunting knife in the small of my back as I stabbed. I don't know where I hit. I heard a grunt and ran again.

I couldn't breathe...the uphill, the altitude...

Ink streaked past wearing a camouflage cloak of leaves. "Now you're making me look bad," I mumbled.

Four men were in hot pursuit. The one closest slowed, shock etched in his face as my knife entered his belly, and I shoved him away, hot on the heels of the other three. The second in line tripped, a rope tangling his legs. The third jumped him, and I fell on the downed man, knees first, thrusting twice before gaining my feet and running once more. River, also wearing a cloak, shot the third man with a crossbow just as the first tripped a wire, taking a branch and stake through the chest.

Cutting to the north, I saw Hawk go down and Feisty raced out, dragging the injured woman back to safety. Screams echoed over mountains, cracks, snaps, more rocks and logs tumbling down, and in the center, I stood, listening.

A woman cackled uphill from me. Phoenix. She'd made it down from her tree. Fresh shouting down the hill. More troops.

I hauled ass up the hill, skidding down behind the low rampart we'd built, finding myself next to Phoenix. "More are coming," I rasped, unable to catch my breath.

"You're the last," Phoenix grinned at me through the mud coating her face and the leaves and twigs in her hair and clothes.

"Sure?"

"I'm sure." I looked over to see Eleanor. "I counted. You are definitely the last."

"Time for the grand finale, then."

***

Hawk was in bad shape.

We split into groups, and Legs and Feisty carried the woman. We also had a broken leg, two more gunshots that Doc stabilized, and a slew of bruises, cuts, nicks, and sprains. Doc stayed with Hawk as everyone split into prearranged groups with instructions to make their way off the paths through the trees, while staying in contact. A few of us would remain behind to give them cover and a head start.

Pain, fear, and grim determination were visible on everyone's faces.

"All in, all out," I said quietly.

"Hoo-rah," Phoenix punched the air.

"No luck, all skill."

"Hoo-rah!" More joined in.

"One shot, one kill."

"Hoo-rah!" Teeth were bared in jubilation.

"Let's show these assholes what Oregonians are really like." I grinned around the circle, finding answering smiles on most faces. "Move out, cause havoc when you need to, disappear when you can."

The fighters began filing out, heading toward a rock face with a slight cleft in it. The hunters had found this area, and we'd deepened the cleft to provide more cover. From ten feet away you'd never know it was there. You had to be looking at it from the right angle. The trail dropped off on the other side of the ridge into a steep mountain valley, and a taller ridge rose up behind that. In between, ranks of evergreen trees formed waves of green, crisscrossed with deer trails.

This was our territory, and we would take advantage of every inch of it.

***

Phoenix and Seahorse stayed behind with me, and we pulled out the rifles we'd stashed for the occasion. The psychological effects of arrows finally gave way to the necessity of bullets against greater numbers.

"Anybody else notice how we went from, like, ten soldiers to a hundred?" Phoenix asked as she settled in with her smaller rifle, snuggling her cheek against the stock. "We're killing these ones, right?"

"Yes." I rolled my eyes. "If you can find one." This lot showed a healthy level of self-preservation, keeping their heads low as they made their way up the slope.

"Yay," Phoenix mumbled, already sighting down the scope.

"I really can't say I expected this many to show up." Seahorse said. She also had a bolt action, though hers had a small box magazine that carried five rounds, and she took her first shot. A small rustle in a bush and a limp hand falling out said she'd made her shot. "Honestly, I thought we'd have fifty at the most. You know wipe them out, disappear, all that stuff."

"The family motto won out." I watched a bush I thought moved, waiting for another sign. Next to me, Phoenix's rifle boomed again. I winced and dug through my jacket pocket, hoping. I grinned when my fingers met earplugs and I pulled them out and sighed in relief as the sound was partially blocked.

"You have a motto?" Phoenix eyed me.

"Well, no." There *was* movement in the bush. As soon as I decided on the location, I squeezed the trigger gently, absorbing the recoil and working the slide on the pump. A body fell from the bush I'd been watching. "But if we did, it's 'Expect the worst, hope for the best, prepare for the ridiculous.'"

"Words to live by." Seahorse's laughing eyes belied her solemn face. She pulled the trigger. I didn't see where it went, but a faint cry drifted up.

"I hope Dereva and Wilder found lots of their cars." I tracked over the ground, looking for a new target. "We really need the parts. Or new cars. I'm not picky."

"Watch the sides." Seahorse shifted suddenly, aiming to her left. "They're trying to circle around."

Phoenix took the north while I kept firing down the middle. "Okay, I'm not really sure," I said, adjusting the scope to try for a clearer image, "but I think they have one of those things where you drop the bomb thing in a tube and it shoots it a hell of a long way."

"A mortar?" Seahorse took her shot and rolled back, face white.

"Is that what it is?" I tried, but my rifle couldn't touch the men working it. "Phoenix? Never mind! Huddle!"

The mortar men dropped a bomb thing down the tube and within seconds I knew nothing.

CHAPTER 38

The incessant ringing in my ears drove me crazy, and I shook my head, trying to clear it. All that accomplished was to make my head swim and I rolled, wondering why were rocks on my bed? And when did my bed get so hard?

My hand scrabbled for purchase and I realized I had something in it. I tried, but I couldn't see anything in the dark, then it occurred to me that my eyes were closed. Opening them took effort, so much effort...I raised my free hand and found dust on my face...

The thing in my hand coalesced into my rifle and the dust...

"Phoenix! Seahorse!" My lips moved, my throat hurt, but I heard nothing except the ringing in my ears. I crawled forward, rifle thumping down until I found Seahorse stirring, nearly indistinguishable from the rock because of the dust. As soon as I saw her moving I headed the other direction, toward Phoenix and where the mortar fell, Seahorse at my heels.

"We need to get out of here!" Seahorse sounded like she was miles away. "They should be heading up the hill now!"

I shook Phoenix and growled when I got no response. "Grab her and let's go," I snarled, tears pricking my eyes. I slung my rifle and Phoenix's over my shoulder and got her arm around me and scooped up our packs. Seahorse took the other side and we staggered through the crack, making it around the corner as another mortar shook the ground behind us. As we wobbled through the crest Phoenix stirred, groggily moving her head.

"You're gonna be fine," Seahorse choked, tears running down her cheeks.

We set Phoenix down and I ditched the gear before staggering back to the trail, tripping the last trap we had—a rockslide to block the trail and make crossing the ridge more difficult. When I made it back to the other two, more dust rising in the air behind me, Phoenix finished downing a canteen of water and looked...well, like I couldn't tell. Dust caked all three of us, and I took a drink from my own canteen, swirling water around my mouth, trying to wash out the grit.

"We don't have long," I rasped. "If we head to the second point, we can slow Steve down a little more."

"No, we can't," Seahorse said grimly. I looked at her, confused, and she continued, "The rifles are blocked. We won't get a shot out of any of them until they're cleaned."

I looked, and sure enough, there was almost as much dust on the rifle as there was on me. "Well, fuck me," I said mildly. "That's damn inconvenient."

Phoenix entered the conversation. "Guess we better start running."

"Run, my ass." I shouldered the rifles again. "I'll be lucky if I don't fall down the damn hill."

Seahorse chuckled hoarsely. "C'mon," she said as we boosted Phoenix up. "Let's go, O fearless leader."

"Fuck off."

***

We headed south, crossing to the other ridge and leaving enough signs to keep Steve's attention. The day ended fine, and I breathed deep, enjoying the sharp scent of pine and dry earth. We continued into the night, following a barely discernible deer trail over the ridge before camping in a hollow left by a downed tree.

By the light of the moon I worked to clean my rifle, setting out the pieces on a blanket spread neatly on the ground. In between pieces I snacked on homemade pemmican, jaws aching from the stress of the day.

"Get some sleep," Phoenix murmured drowsily.

"Can't." I rubbed my eyes, feeling like they were full of sand. "We might need a rifle later. You nearly got blown up, though, so stay put," I ordered when the stubborn woman tried to get up.

"Whatever," she yawned.

Seahorse came back to the hollow and joined me in cleaning her rifle. "We all survived today, didn't we?" she asked eventually.

"I think so." I coughed and drank a bit of water to soothe it. "Nice change from the last one."

The rest of the time passed in silence, all of us too tired to maintain a conversation. As soon as I had my rifle reassembled, I rolled into my blanket, asleep before I settled my head onto my pack.

The next day began before dawn, with Phoenix nudging us awake with her boot. We set out, still glimpsing Steve in on our back trail. Phoenix slowly disassembled her own rifle on every break. Just after noon we paused, waiting for Steve to get close enough to mess with them. While Seahorse and me took potshots at the soldiers Phoenix finished giving her rifle just enough of a clean to get it functioning again.

In the confusion we took off at a run, and at the first breakaway heading east we turned, careful to erase as much as we could of our exit from the trail. I hid behind a tree, breathing shallowly, while Steve continued south, creeping through the brush. The slope rose steeply enough that my feet were level with the men's heads as they passed our hiding place.

After they'd gone, we crossed the ridge, leaving the soldiers far behind us. This high up we could still see the sun. It made a stark contrast to the shadowed valley below us.

"Did you see how many?"

Phoenix shook her head, breathing heavily.

"Counted fifty" Seahorse said, resting her hands on her knees, taking a breather and stretching her back.

"There, see?" I copied Seahorse's pose, my spine popping as I exhaled. "We only had...fifty on our tails...just like you were hoping, Seahorse."

Seahorse moaned indistinctly.

In the trees once more, we swung north, heading back to our home turf. Water was scarce at this altitude, so we drank sparingly until we'd find good water, then we'd drink as much as possible after filling our canteens. We were crossing a creek with clear, fast water when an odd, crackling sound had us scattering before the noise properly registered.

Seahorse and Phoenix disappeared off the trail with barely a whisper, and I stepped sideways around a huge pine, clutching it to keep from slipping down the slope, holding my breath to hear if the sound repeated.

"Yeah, close but no cigar," drawled a familiar voice. "I can still see your hip. Idiot."

I swung out from behind the tree, grinning. "'snot my fault my mama gave me wide-ass hips. Sirius!"

Sirius stood, hands on her hips in the middle of the trail, her blocky form taking up the entire, narrow space, grinning so wide I could see the gap from her missing tooth. She had a new scar on her jaw but the rest of her looked as familiar as home. I lunged toward her and she met me halfway, clutching each other tightly. When we finally let go, the rest of our teams had arrived.

Seahorse checked in with the sisters first, while Phoenix ruffled Thorin's hair. The boy ducked away, swatting her hand playfully. The corner of my mouth pulled down. We'd have to tell him about his father at some point.

"What brings you this far out?" Sirius asked.

"Oh, you know." I shrugged. "We felt like a little walk. Figured we might stretch our legs a bit."

Sirius snorted. "You're still full of shit," she observed.

We laughed and Phoenix and Seahorse filled them in on our latest escapade.

"How are my parents?" Thorin asked eagerly when the tale was finished.

Silence dropped and I grimaced, wishing we'd made it back to the Lair before he'd asked. He took one look at me and swallowed convulsively, tears starting in his eyes.

"Mom? Dad?"

"Your dad, Thorin," I said quietly. "He died saving your mom." His face crumpled.

Sirius stepped forward, wrapping the kid in her arms. Lightning and Thunder engulfed the two of them and the rest of us gave them space. The boy pressed his face against my cousin's shoulder, his muffled sobs heartbreaking.

Too soon, I had to break them up. Steve could come around the corner at any moment and we needed to be gone.

Sirius shifted slightly as her crew looked shifty. "Uh, we've brought...help?"

"Soldiers?" Seahorse whispered, hope shining in her eyes.

"No. Think more along the lines of inside information." Sirius whistled sharply and a small shape stepped hesitantly out from behind a tree and walked cautiously down the slope, accompanied by the pup, Obelix.

A second later, Thunder and Lightning blocked the path, stilling our hands when we tried to draw weapons.

The girl walking oh so carefully down the hill was Korean.

***

"What the hell are you doing, traipsing around with Steve?" Phoenix was nose to nose with Sirius, spitting mad and ready to break my cousin's neck.

"She's not the enemy," Sirius repeated, losing her patience after so many repetitions. "Sung Ki is another person who needed help. We found her being hurt by her own side."

I pinched the bridge of my nose, hoping it would help ease the headache. We'd long since found a hidey-hole for the night, inside a thick copse of cedar trees. This was one of several hiding places we'd found and equipped with canned goods and spare ammunition. The excuse for a discussion had been going ever since we'd stopped.

"How long has she been with you?" I finally asked.

Sirius looked gratified to have a different question. "Three weeks. We found her on our way back."

"Right. And what's your assessment?"

"Sung Ki was sent east for punishment." Sirius glared at Phoenix. "She'd actually spoken out against the treatment of people here."

"How do you know she wasn't sent to find us and be a mole?" argued Phoenix.

"Because we found her being gang raped!" Thorin shouted, unable to bear it any more.

Phoenix, silenced at last, held up her hands in surrender, bowing her head slightly to Sung Ki. In the ensuing silence Sirius and the others gave us the short story, since the long version would have to wait until we were back at the Lair.

The walk back to the Lair could have been accomplished in a few days, but happily, such was not the case. There were numerous small groups of soldiers hunting us through our mountains, trying to be sneaky. Some we made vanish completely, on others we practiced "catch and release." Any group of five or less disappeared, while the others we just messed with a little, shooting them up and running away.

Chapter 39

Sung Ki's introduction to the Lair was...tumultuous, at best. Civilians shouted and called for blood, but the fighters...oh, they were thinking. Against the woman at first, but the assessment from those of us who'd gotten to know Sung Ki made them willing to reserve judgement and give her a place within the gym.

The civilians might not be willing to trust a North Korean, but most of the fighters had run across American collaborators, so it made sense to us. We couldn't possibly be the only ones to have people willing to switch sides.

Ignoring all the surrounding fuss, Thorin went straight into his mother's arms. Evenstar gave a strangled cry then sobbed as she held him close. The young man cried and Evenstar murmured to him, stroking his unkempt hair and face, checking his limbs.

Sirius, Lighting, and Thunder were greeted by the rest of the old guard while Sung Ki stood awkwardly to the side, me and Phoenix nearby, unsure how to make her feel welcome. Amanacer had no such issues, walking up to the foreigner, taking the other woman's arm and leading her into the Lair. I followed close behind, ignoring the people trying to snatch at my arm and make demands of me. Sung Ki gawked as she walked down the steps into the bunker, eyes like saucers, head twisting to see everything at once. She smiled at the sight of children, who hid when they saw her.

They'd learned not to trust anyone who looked like her, though I hoped that in time, the kids might change their minds. It wouldn't help them to grow up hating an entire ethnicity for what a few did.

The moment we entered the Lair, Cin, Sirius' old dog, mobbed his human, whining and barking, leaning hard against her. Sirius knelt down, tears in her eyes as she cuddled him.

***

After everyone had time to clean up and grab a bite, we met in the Useless Room, most of us bringing our stew with us.

Sirius looked around at all the people who participated in our meetings now. Driver, Sarge, Lavender, Dry Eyes, Amana, Seahorse, Eleanor, and Phoenix, as well as myself and the rest of her crew. "Well, well, well, aren't we coming up in the world?"

"Silence in the peanut gallery," I commanded, grinning. Then I thumped the table. "No, dammit! I actually need you to talk. Dammit."

Sirius laughed, the motion puckering the new scar running along her jaw to her ear.

"When did you get that, anyway?" Phoenix asked, motioning to her face.

"Oh, 'bout a month after we left," Sirius replied, rubbing the scar. "Lemme run through this all together. It'll help me remember and make it less confusing all 'round. So save the questions for after, all right?"

Eleanor smiled at her. "Very well. Welcome home, by the way. You as well, dear," she said to Sung Ki, taking her hand gently. The small Korean woman smiled timidly back. She'd been much surer of herself on the trail.

Can't be easy, being surrounded by those who were warring with your old comrades. "This is your home, too."

The young woman regarded her hand in Eleanor's. "Thank. You," she said softly. "Sorry, my English ver' bad. Sir'us teach, but I is ver..." She paused, mouth working silently, forehead furrowed. "What is word for not good here?" She pointed to her head.

"Crazy?" Thunder guessed.

A pause. "No."

"Stupid?" Lightning supplied.

"Yes!" Sung Ki cried triumphantly. "I am stupid!"

Eleanor rounded on the sisters, furious. "What are you teaching her? You are *not* stupid, my dear, never think that," she said to Sung Ki before swinging back to the sisters. I realized with a spurt of amusement that all of our heads were turning with Eleanor, watching her scold them and their attempts to placate her.

I smothered a snigger, but Eleanor, with cat-like reflexes, spun on me. "Do you think this is funny?" she demanded.

"No, ma'am," I replied promptly. "Just happy that Sung Ki has you to protect her. She won't need nobody else."

Eleanor eyed me another moment, radiating matronly sternness, then nodded, satisfied with my words if nothing else. "Very well. You may continue with the meeting, then," she informed the group at large.

"You smooth motherfucker," Phoenix murmured.

We clustered around the detailed map of Oregon on the wall, Sirius at the front. Cheeky asshole even found a pen to use as a pointer.

While my cousin gathered her thoughts, one apparently passed through Lavender's mind. "Why didn't Sung Ki get a new name?" the older woman asked.

Sirius looked around, slightly distracted. "Sung Ki doesn't mind if her countrymen know she switched sides. She hasn't got any family left in

North Korea, so no fear there. We're all hoping that Sung Ki might be a catalyst to get Steve independently thinking."

While Lavender digested that, Sirius went back to contemplating the map before putting her finger on Bull of the Woods Wilderness, where the Lair was located. "Crossing the Cascades was fun. Near death experiences and all that shit. We came out here." She moved her finger to a dot marked Madras. "Not that it matters. Every town we found looked like a bomb had been dropped on it."

"No effort was made to stop any fires, either," Thunder added.

"The bodies were left lying around." Lightning looked sick.

"How the fuck did they explain doing that?" Seahorse exclaimed. Sirius jerked, staring at Seahorse. The former army woman rarely cussed, letting us know just how thrown she was by this information.

Sung Ki nodded wearily to Sirius, who explained. "They were told Eastern Oregon was a prison colony. That murderers and rapists were sent there instead of being given the death penalty, as they might've been in North Korea. As far as the soldiers are concerned, they did us a big favor."

Quiet swearing from the men and stunned looks all around. Many people would have family over there. I frowned. Now that I thought about it, I'd had relatives there on Mom's side, though we'd rarely seen them. Guess that chance was gone forever now.

"Patrols are rarer than here," Sirius continued, tracing her finger over the map, following their route. "We were able to find enough game to live off of, and you really have to watch the horizon. There are some wide open spaces in Eastern Oregon." She trailed off, staring at nothing for a few moments before shaking herself out of it. "We had to fuck with a few patrols, of course. Got these." She rubbed the bridge of her nose, which had a lump from being broken, and the scar on her jaw.

"Anyhow, with patrols and finding food, it took us thirty days. Reckon people can make across in less than, but they'll either have to be small enough groups to avoid patrols, or big enough to wipe 'em out."

"Yeah, that's all well and good," Driver interrupted, leaning forward, "but what about our army? Did you ever find them?"

Lightning snorted and rolled her eyes, and Thorin grimaced. I winced. This wouldn't be good for us.

"Oh, yeah, we found 'em. About here." Sirius jabbed a finger at the map, clearly in Idaho. "We found a ginormous-ass fence. Think rolls of barbed wire, ditches, mines, the whole nine. Assholes took us prisoner, basically. We were separated, locked up, and interrogated. When they moved us, we were blindfolded. Fuckers."

Seahorse's compressed lips showed white at the corners as she shook her head.

"There was this one guy who was decent." Sirius got a faraway look in her eyes. "Don't know what branch, but he didn't let them shoot Obelix and took care of him for me."

"What did they want to know?" I asked quietly, breaking the silence.

"The usual," Thunder sneered. "Our names, ranks, and all the info on our associates."

Lightning laughed. "It was kinda fun, sometimes. They even hooked me up to a polygraph and it drove them crazy, especially when they asked my name. I told them Lightning, and it came out as true!"

"Sometimes," Sirius allowed. "Others..."

Grim looks from everyone on her team.

I closed my eyes. How often had they nearly died? I sighed. "Nice to know our own side won't be any help."

"Let me put it like this." Sirius folded her arms. "With friends like those, who needs enemies?"

Seahorse winced.

"So what happened after that?" Lavender asked.

"Oh, they said they were shipping us back east." Sirius waved a hand. "Something about being tried for war crimes, since we did admit to fighting back."

"What?" The room exploded, everyone asking questions at once.

I tried getting their attention, to no avail. Finally, I took a deep breath. "QUIET!!" I bellowed in my best farm voice. People settled down slowly. "Let her finish. We don't have to worry about the whole war crimes thing right now. That'll only apply if we actually live."

A giggle escaped Sarge, and we turned to stare at him. Now that I thought about it, I'd never heard the man laugh before. How did someone so big have such a cute little laugh?

Grinning, Sirius returned to the story. "All that aside, it was Lightning who opened the door to my wannabe cell."

All eyes turned to the petite woman, who gave us an evil smile. "Let's just say they thought 'small' meant 'weak,' and they tried to break me by giving me solitary confinement." She examined her nails casually. "Problem is, they were keeping us in a school, you know, the kind that has those movable ceiling tiles? Anyway, I'm small enough to fit in the gap. Once I was out, I stole some keys and unlocked every door I came across until we had everyone."

I narrowed my eyes. No way in hell it was that easy. We'd probably have a collective heart attack if they told us the truth.

"Breaking out of there was easier than Salem," Sirius continued, "though I think that's more because the army underestimated us. In a nutshell, if we want to get civilians out that way, they'll probably be okay as long as they're not armed and say they've never fought, but Eastern Oregon is a crapshoot to get across, especially since we were seen coming back. Steve'll probably have more patrols running now."

"Why would they punish us for fighting against Steve, though?" Driver looked up. "It doesn't make any sense."

"Why hasn't the army gotten its ass in here and kicked Steve out?" I countered. "Steve must have something else going on. I mean, we don't even know what's being said about us out there. History is told by the winners, or by those who have phones and internet." I turned to Sirius. "Did the army happen to tell you guys anything about the state of the world in general? Or why they decided to sit this one out?"

"Nope," my cousin shook her head, "and we decided not to stick around and find out. As soon as we found my puppy, we ran for the border. Who'da thunk we'd actually run back *into* this mess?"

"That's probably what made it so easy to get back into Oregon," Thunder commented dryly. "Nobody in their right mind would voluntarily come back here."

"Nobody in their right mind, and anybody who wanted to avoid being waterboarded again," Sirius muttered, not quite low enough.

I growled, and the others looked at me curiously, being a little too far away to hear Sirius. My cousin looked at me and shook her head. No need to tell everyone just how bad it was over there. I snarled, then nodded shortly.

"We did leave them a message," Lightning said, grinning, "after we made it through the fence, just to tell them we'd left Idaho."

"What was it?" several people pressed.

"Oh," Lightning waved a hand carelessly, "just a review of their hospitality. Nothing much." Thunder and Thorin ducked their heads, avoiding Eleanor's gaze.

"Must have been pretty foul language, then." Eleanor also noticed those two squirming. "Still, there are times when it's appropriate, as I'm sure it was then. Now, where did you find Sung Ki?"

The Korean woman turned away, refusing to look at the group. Amana stood and went to her speaking too quietly for us to hear.

"We found her in New Princeton," Sirius said shortly. "You can guess the circumstances." She shook her head. "It's the worst I've ever seen."

Phoenix whistled soundlessly and Lavender gasped, tears filling her eyes.

Sirius ticked each item off on her fingers. "We killed a bunch of men, burned the place down, stole a truck, ran into another patrol, broke their truck, then had to run for it."

"Ah," I said dryly, "there's my degenerates. You realize we are exactly what our parents warned us against when we were kids?"

"The thought crossed my mind," Sirius replied, eyes sad. "We ended up running south, taking out as many patrols as we could, but not as many as we wanted." She looked at Sung Ki, still standing with her back to us. "We ended up on the Pacific Crest Trail, took it all the way back here."

"No shit?" I rocked back. "I always wanted to do that trail."

Sung Ki and Amana returned to the group, the Korean woman looking a little better.

"I wonder how the higher ups are feeling about losing so many cars?" Phoenix laughed.

"He ver' angry," Sung Ki replied. "We lose more cars and mans than beloved leader says."

"And if that doesn't give you a warm, fuzzy feeling I don't know what will." I smiled, then turned to Sung Ki. "C'mon, let's introduce you to the other fighters. I don't want any bullying from them. Sarge?"

"Right behind you," the big man rumbled.

CHAPTER 40

"Kitten's finally narrowed down the locations for those two brothels the Fates told us about." River paced around the Useless Room, where we were gathered. The Fates, three beauticians who'd been forced to doll up the women kept at various brothels, had been working with River, and by extension Kitten, to give us two more locations by means of memory and mapping. Now, they finally had something for us to work with.

"One of them is here, in southeast Salem, and the other is north, near Keizer." River circled the locations on a detailed paper map of the cities.

"Shit." Phoenix peered at the one near Keizer. "This area is at least three blocks."

"It gets worse." River turned to face us. "Kitten's daughter was taken the day before I got there. She's been in Steve's hands for four days. Kitten's got reliable information that her daughter is in the south Salem location."

At least that one had been narrowed to a specific street. I peered at the map. Stonehaven Drive.

"Does she expect us to mount a rescue for just one woman?" The speaker was a newcomer, Sophie. The civilians wanted a person in on the meetings who had their best interests at heart, fair enough, but Sophie, an aging woman who dreamed of the glory days of her youth, wouldn't be my choice for this role. A career politician and Oregon's representative in Congress, Sophie won the position through lobbying, manipulation, and, I suspected, bribery.

On seeing the looks of distaste around the table, I decided this would be Sophie's only time at a meeting. Being a dictatorial tyrant had to be useful sometime. Driver and Lavender could tell the rest all the nitty-gritty details, which I thought they'd been doing anyway.

"Kitten put her family in danger by spying for us." Phoenix got in Sophie's face, then cast a look over her shoulder at me, pleading. "We won't hang them out to dry now that they're in trouble!"

"Yes, we're going to mount a rescue for the one woman we know," I said quietly, "and for the other ones we don't." Sophie opened her mouth to protest, but I didn't give her a chance. "It's what we do. If we didn't, you'd still be starving in Poor Town."

"She's got you there," Driver murmured. "When do we leave?"

I raised an eyebrow, surprised, while Phoenix whooped.

"What?" he asked. "You'll need every hand you've got. I'll drive."

"Now that's what I'm talking about!" Phoenix cried, pointing triumphantly.

Once again Sophie tried to protest but we simply ignored her. "You're here to observe and inform the others," I said tersely. "Unless you've got something useful to say, zip it." Damn politics anyway. If we left it up to her, we'd be cowering in the Lair with the fighters working to protect and supply her and her "constituents."

"Oh, one more thing," River interjected. "Kitten thinks someone in her house is spying for Steve. Probably trying to get put in a better neighborhood or more food."

"Goddammit." I sighed, sitting back in my chair. Around me, people voiced their anger and outrage or looked defeated. "Does she know who it is?" I cut through the chatter.

"Mmmmina?" River asked rather than stated, staring at her feet. "Mary?" she tried again. I hoped nobody noticed the little starts from me, Sirius, and Phoenix at that. "No, Mina is closer. Muna? Mana? Mona? Mona!" River looked up triumphantly. "Mona! What should we do about her?"

"Kill her?" Phoenix suggested.

I shrugged, and a moral debate nearly broke out, but Eleanor overruled them all, saying that we'd cross that bridge when we got there, and it should be Kitten's decision, anyway.

"We don't have time for this!" River slammed a hand down on the table, startling everyone to silence. "We need to get in there ASAP before they do any more damage to another woman! So can we please plan this sucker?"

In the ensuing silence, I studied the map. "We'll need at least four groups," I announced. "One each for the brothels, one to get the rest of the family out, and a spare to make some noise when we need it."

"I want the one for Kitten's family," River volunteered.

I nodded. "You got it. You know the area and patrols best. Sirius, I want you and your team on standby. We'll figure out where in a minute. Seahorse." The soldier sat up. "You've got the northern location, I've got the south. Pick your people."

***

I stared around in the cold pre-dawn light at the meadow full of people. Those staying behind had turned out to see us off, and it caught me, seeing the differences between the groups. The fighters were hard, sharply defined, all angles and violence. Their ragged clothing, much mended and patched, did nothing to detract from the aura of danger. Weapons, holsters, quivers, bandoliers, and small packs jockeyed for space on every person, yet not one looked unbalanced or uncomfortable.

Nervous, yes. Uncomfortable, no.

The ones staying behind were split into more groups still, with hunters and guards having a similar feel to the fighters, minus the violent edge, while the civilians looked far more reputable. Thin, but without the patches, holes, and stains that everyone else here sported, many of them developing calluses suited to farmers and tradespeople.

I walked through the civilians, who parted to let me pass, to the fighters, and breathed deep, taking comfort in the scent of evergreens and damp. Warm days and cool nights meant a good chance of mist for cover.

Another step and I could smell the clean, cold scent of the creek, riding on the slight breeze. Reaching the fighters, I walked through them, clasping shoulders and circling around until I climbed on top of the Lair.

"Y'all know what's at stake," I announced.

"All in, all out."

"One shot, one kill."

"No luck, all skill!" We shouted. Our cries echoed from the hills as the determined group of men and women disappeared into the trees, heading for the vehicles.

***

I stretched out on the grass in a patch of sunshine, resting my hands loosely on my belly. It'd been a long two days to get here, and we were finally going into Salem tonight. We'd come in from the north looking like a work convoy, splitting up before we got to Salem's north gate, each group making their way to a predetermined spot to wait for nightfall.

"Here" was a clearing south of Salem in the middle of a bunch of trees. A tiny dirt road cut through the north side of the clearing, and a little creek burbled happily on the far side of the bushes to the west. The sunlight shone on the leaves, turning the air golden and green with rich life. It felt good in the warm valley, thawing the cold from my bones.

My team had gotten to our location just after noon, and by my reckoning we were the last ones to do so, coming at the city from the southeast. Every group consisted of five fighters and a single driver to stay with the car, while Driver and Doc stayed at the bus, hidden in a centralized location. All of us would simply have to load up to overflowing or steal an extra car. We'd already brought every working vehicle we had—four trucks and a bus, the last one left running from the Bus-capade.

Eyes closed, my lips twisted as I recalled people's protests at Sung Ki's inclusion as part of Sirius' team and her acerbic response. "She's killed more soldiers than most of you."

I listened to my team moving around, idly thinking about the people I'd be risking my life with in a few short hours. Phoenix, small, fierce, and dedicated, her short, sandy colored hair kept hidden under a ball cap when we were in the field. Sparrow, the woman who would be beautiful even in a potato sack, had a lot of nervous energy about her, though the moment she got called on to work, her hands were rock steady. She still looked uncomfortable in the cargo pants, combat boots, and t-shirt that was practically a standard uniform for our lot.

My lips curved as I thought of Dereva. My rock in the field, the unflappable driver who always thought of a way to go, no matter who pursued us. She was almost as tall as Eleanor now, maybe five foot eight, and she kept her curly hair long, pulling it back from her face with little clips. Every time I saw her, those brilliant blue eyes of hers gave me a shock. She and her brother were favorites of the Fates, who spoiled them at every opportunity.

My mind wandered to Legs next. Long and lean, the young woman won every footrace we had, over any terrain. She'd blushed red as a beet when we told her she'd be a part of my team, and she'd spent most of the time since then staring at me with worshipful hazel eyes. I found it very disconcerting.

Finally, the Celt, whose long, curly white/blonde hair and green eyes made her look like a Celtic princess. She enhanced the look by wearing a few tiny, beaded braids in her hair. In many ways, she reminded me of Phoenix when we'd first met her. Tiny, angry, reckless. This woman, though, had eleven others who'd shared her same misery, and had a weekly appointment with Kestrel that she had to keep if she wanted to stay in the field.

I didn't twitch at the footsteps nearby as Sparrow paced. Sparrow—who'd walked away from her stepson when he'd raped some of the girls in our care, and his father when the father defended the young man—was on her first mission and unable to stop pacing. The Celt hummed a tune I couldn't make out as she whittled, throwing all her concentration into the task.

Dereva tried to convince Phoenix to let her accompany us on the mission, backed up by Legs, who'd done brilliantly on the last mission as bait to draw in Steve.

I heard the smirk in Phoenix's voice as she told Dereva, "We should've named you Captain America."

"Nope," I announced, without opening my eyes. "With my luck, we'd run into your mother, who'd kill me. I'd tell her it's all your fault, Dereva, but she'd never believe me."

"You'd tell on a kid?" Phoenix's voice was thick with mock disbelief. "Very mature."

I cracked open an eye. Dereva stood near me and Phoenix had her back to us both as she set up her large rifle to have it ready in the truck. I snatched up a pinecone and flung it at the back of her head, scoring a direct hit. Phoenix whipped around and I widened my eyes, striving to look innocent as I pointed at the younger girl. Phoenix shook her head, slowly drawing a finger across her throat, then pointed at me.

A snort of laughter surprised me, and I sat up to watch Sparrow slowly lose it at our antics. I got up and ambled over to her, patting her on the back. "That's it," I soothed. "Let it all out now."

Her laughter took on a hysteric edge before slowly subsiding. "I'm-I'm sorry," she gasped, wiping her eyes. "I don't know what came over me."

"Nerves," I said cheerfully. "We all deal with shit differently." I forced myself to lie down again, closing my eyes and breathing deep to keep calm. As stupid as it sounds, I looked forward to these times, to the chaos, the mayhem...I took a shuddering breath. "I can't believe I'm a fucking adrenaline junkie," I murmured, shaking my head.

"You only just figured that out?" Phoenix said wryly from a few feet away.

"When the hell did you get over here?"

"Apparently while you were having an epiphany."

"Ah, fuck off. Stop listening in to people's private conversations."

She extended her middle finger. "One, if you don't want people to hear, don't say it out loud." She extended her index finger. "Two, I don't think you qualify as 'people.' You're weird."

"Pot. Kettle."

As the afternoon wore on, the three teenagers took to the creek to play. Able to recognize a great idea when I saw one, I moved my lounging upstream from the girls, who finally looked their ages as they splashed and laughed. Wiggling my toes in the cool water, I stared up at the sky, contented, until an inadvertent movement rubbed a thick callus the wrong way.

"Motherfucker!" I walked gingerly to my pack, digging around for a small pot of salve. Wildwood, the herbalist, had concocted the salve to deal with most things, from calluses to rashes to small cuts, and even minor infections. Plopping onto the ground, I rubbed both feet thoroughly. When I finished, Phoenix clapped her hands and cupped them, so I tossed her the jar which she neatly caught, then propped my feet up on my pack to give the salve time to do its work.

Stretching a bit, I hauled my rifle over to give it another look, just to make sure there'd be no issues tonight. Phoenix had the same idea, checking her scope's sights and ensuring the zero was set, wiggling her toes in the grass as she worked.

Sparrow had fallen into a light doze until a shriek of laughter tore the air and the woman sat up with a start.

"Oi!" I yelled. "Keep it down! You wanna tell Steve we're here and ruin the surprise?"

"Sorry, Captain!" the girls chorused.

Shaking my head, I laid back down, stretching my arms over my head and arching my back, groaning in pleasure as all the muscles stretched. I missed being in a small group and actually being able to remember the right name the first or second time. Is it good or bad, or neither, to not know much about the individual?

With so many of us, I felt like I knew them best as a skill set rather than an individual. Tracker, sniper, driver, scout, gutter fighter.

I cut my eyes to Sparrow. Explosives.

"Hah!" I snorted a laugh, looking at Sparrow again. Who'd've thought the woman raised in privilege would be so damn cool under the pressure of creating and setting charges? She did pretty good at disarming them, too.

Finally tired, the girls left their play in the water, flopping down in the sun to dry. I smiled at Dereva's sleeping bag. I'd gone through two different sleeping bags before finally getting the blanket, but somehow that girl still had the one she'd started with, which had a huge cartoonish picture of Wonder Woman across the front. Not exactly subtle.

The Celt began humming, then sang softly.

I haven't done all that I could
I haven't been all that I should
Always told myself I'd do better
Never believed I could

I rolled my head carefully to see Phoenix, afraid that if I moved too quickly I'd startle the Celt to silence. Phoenix had her face tipped to the sun, a smile dancing on her lips. During the chorus, Dereva joined in, harmonizing. When I turned toward the girl, I also saw Sparrow, curled on her side, watching the girls in wonder.

I say my lines, I play my roles
I play my part, I say I'm fine
But in the end, I always long for
The home I never knew

My eyes stung and I laid back down, tossing an arm over my eyes so the others couldn't see the memories of home on my face. I pulled them out, holding each one up in my mind like precious gems in the sunlight. Grace's smile and the smell of her homemade pizza and how she looked in her wedding dress. Sean's teasing and laughter. Peter hugging me before he deployed. Papa's strength and the smell of grease that I couldn't help but associate with him.

I ride the rails, I see the world
Every part a beautiful piece
Now I see how it's all connected
I am already home

Thinking about them made it so much harder to do what we did. Remembering who I was and the person I'd been. The person I'd never be again. Thinking about them made me want to tear Salem apart to find Papa and Sean or die trying. I always got stuck on the dying part.

The only option I'd found that worked was not thinking about my family at all, and hope that one of these missions I'd turn around and find that we'd accidentally pulled them out of the frying pan. But today...with that song drifting through the air...I left my arm over my face and hoped nobody noticed the tears.

CHAPTER 41

We jogged silently through the sleeping city, keeping close to the buildings and staying off the main roads. Getting inside Salem had been a cinch, the ground here far more level than what we'd become used to, and all of it forested. East of us lay newly cleared ground, the ploughed earth already showing signs of crops.

We'd entered the city using a shallow gully. Steve had concreted it, but all the rain that we took for granted caused it to shift, giving us enough space to slip around it.

A sudden gust had me blinking furiously to dislodge a speck and I rubbed it cautiously, feeling the sweet relief when my vision cleared. And then I sighed. Sparrow and the Celt were ducking and diving for the ground every other step, twisting constantly to look over their shoulders.

"Guys," I murmured to them, waving a hand in front of their faces. "You gotta trust the person watching your back. Besides, if we do see Steve or Dorothy, your behavior is gonna send up so many red flags we'll be fucked."

The two straightened slowly, Sparrow looking shame-faced.

"Just...trust your training, all right?" I rubbed my irritated eye one more time, and they nodded.

Phoenix had gotten a little ahead of us, but we soon caught up and resumed our pace. Stonehaven Drive was our destination, a mere three miles away from the perimeter fence. The street was lined with apartment-type homes, large buildings, very comfortable looking. Kitten knew for a fact her daughter was in there because an officer, a Dorothy, had mentioned to a friend, who told another friend, who told Kitten, that this location was for officers only and the girls here were pretty and well treated.

I think he meant to reassure Kitten in some weird way, like, "Yes, your daughter will be raped repeatedly, but at least she won't be chained or smacked around!" as if being here were a good thing.

Kitten passed on the man's name and description, with the request that if we ever ran into him, we should cut his balls off for implying that rape wasn't harmful. We would accommodate her request.

As we continued, little alarm bells went off in my head and I ran faster to catch up with Phoenix. "Why the fuck are the streets so quiet?"

"River did say the fences between Poor Town and here are as tight as the perimeter," Phoenix murmured.

"You reckon they...they don't expect trouble?" I grunted softly. "Idiots. Sirius'll chew them up and spit them out."

We paused at a corner and I reached out and snagged the Celt's collar before she wandered out. Phoenix cautiously poked her head around, checking, then led the way across the street. We went across one at a time, when she gave us the all-clear.

Dawn was the barest blush over the mountains when Phoenix led us to Stonehaven Drive. Bushes and small trees sheltered the entire lane, inadvertently giving us cover. We slid into the safety of the plants, finding a location that gave us a good view of the first building's entryway as well as both ends of the lane.

"Dawn's the signal, right?" Sparrow asked again, nervously fingering her holstered gun.

"Yes," I repeated. "The last of the men leave roughly this time, so we shouldn't have to deal with a full house."

Along the drive stood four two-story houses, each building showing two doors. The buildings were mirrored, so two homes per building. Even the flower beds were echoed, paths laid out in perfect symmetry. As we watched, two men stepped out of the second building from the entrance, each towing a pair of near-naked girls. The girls stumbled in the men's wake as they were taken to the last house in the line, where the drive formed a cul-de-sac.

Around me the fighters snarled, and Phoenix adjusted her grip on her rifle, taking aim when I reached out and tapped her head. "I need you thinking."

She relaxed slowly. "Yeah, yeah," she muttered.

As the sky slowly brightened, the scene repeated itself several times. By the finish, I'd counted twenty-four women herded into that single building through both doors, with two men staying inside each one. The last man out stood for a time, fiddling with the door before walking back to the first house in the line.

"One stop shopping," I muttered, crawling deeper into the shrubs.

Sparrow gave a horrified gasp and I turned to see her staring at me, mouth open in shock.

Phoenix patted her companionably. "We know."

I shrugged, and Phoenix smacked me. "Be nice," she hissed.

"Oh, that's rich, coming from you," I murmured, crawling on my elbows and toes, cradling my rifle. "Let's get moving before it gets too light, yeah?"

"I should've made Sirius go with you," Phoenix complained lightly. "Then I could've taken her place with nice, normal people." She scrunched around a rhododendron.

"Lightning and Thunder are normal?" I sniggered. "You're crazier than I thought."

Once we got further from the entrance, we dared stand, moving more quickly between the bushes to reach our target. The second-floor windows had bars over the windows, but not the ground floor. So all the captives locked upstairs, probably guards downstairs. We made our way around to the back of the house, checking the windows till we found one that let into a small living room with a closed door to cut our noise off from the rest of the house.

I braced my back against the wall, legs bent in front of me in a wall-sit. Phoenix stepped lightly onto my bent knees to pop the screen off. Legs caught it neatly and stuffed it under a bush.

"What's taking so long?" I grunted. "This ain't easy, y'know."

"It's locked." Phoenix pulled out her knife, trying to work the tip under the sill.

The Celt hissed from where she lay in a flower bed, keeping watch, and waved for us to duck. Phoenix jumped hastily off my knees and I bit my hand to keep from screaming when her hiking boots slid over the tender skin of my legs, clamping my other hand over one knee as I collapsed, screaming silently. Phoenix squished me behind the meager shelter of the flower beds, Sparrow lay near us with her hands up helplessly, looking like she desperately wanted to do *something*, while Phoenix silently mouthed "Sorry, sorry, sorrysorrysorry!" over and over.

"Okay, clear," the Celt whispered.

I braced myself against the wall again, and Phoenix hesitated. "Just do it," I muttered, wiping my sleeve over my face to clear the sweat. The rough fabric of my jacket didn't do much except smear the moisture around, however.

Phoenix stepped up again, grimacing the whole way, but wasted no time being gentle on the lock. She grunted, shifting her weight and I opened my mouth in silent agony, her legs flexing as she leaned in on the knife. With a sudden *crack*, the window gave way and Phoenix lurched forward, her feet slipping again as she crashed down on top of me.

I buckled under her, gripping my legs, my screams muffled in her jacket.

By the time I caught my breath, Phoenix and Legs had hauled me to my feet, and a bunch of faces hovered around me anxiously.

"Are you okay?" Legs reached out to touch me then changed her mind, tucking the hand self-consciously behind her back.

I unclenched my teeth. "Holy Mary, Mother of God!"

Phoenix chuckled at that response, relief evident in her tone. "She'll be fine," she announced. To me: "Don't let Eleanor hear you say that. Her Presbyterian soul would be scandalized to find out you're Catholic."

"I'm not." I leaned forward, gingerly pulling up one pant leg to check the damage. "But better that than an atheist in her mind, right?"

"Nah, atheists don't require tons of retraining, she says." Phoenix knelt to help me, her hands gentle, revealing skin torn in a few places, scraped off in others, the remainder already changing colors. "You'll live. We should doctor you up now."

"No." I shook my head. "We don't have the time, or the gear." We'd left our packs with Dereva, bringing only what we could carry in pockets and belt pouches. "You wanna get me help, let's do the job and get the hell out before it gets any lighter."

"Actually," Sparrow said, holding up a small glass bottle, "I have some of Anansi's vodka we could put on your legs."

We stared at her, Phoenix's face showing the horror I felt. "That stuff's gotta be more volatile than the landmines," I said, aghast. "What the hell do you have it for?"

"Molotov cocktail," the woman explained with a shy smile.

Mine wasn't the only jaw that dropped at the thought of this sophisti-cated woman planning such a move.

"That is so *gangsta*," Legs breathed.

"We're idiots." I raised my hands helplessly. "Final and incontrovertible proof of our low intellectual status."

The Celt made her way back to us. "What are you waiting for? Coast is clear, and the sky's only gonna get lighter."

"Okay." I looked around the small group. "Do it fast." I took a hefty bite of my sleeve and nodded. Sparrow hesitated a second, but an impatient scowl from the Celt got her moving. Sparrow poured a healthy blob on each leg and I hissed, squeezing my eyes shut as tears leaked out. Phoenix quickly wrapped clean cloth around my knees, just trapping the fire against my skin.

Phoenix waited for me to recover with false patience, the Celt's eyes glittered, anger leeching from every pore, while Sparrow looked nervous and Legs watched my face intently.

Once I got my breath back, I could finally lay it out for them. "In and out, quiet as possible. I'd rather not alert the boys next door. Too many chances for noise and mistakes. We'll take care of the ones in this house. Go upstairs and figure it out from there."

I had an idea to get the women from the other house out, sparked by my brother Sean's time working in construction. It should work. The others nodded and Phoenix dropped the mask, grinning tightly.

I bared my teeth in a parody of a smile and boosted a sniggering Phoenix into the room, Sparrow passing the rifles up to her next. I boosted the other three through while Phoenix helped them, then backed up a few steps, eyeing the window sill, the bottom of which was at my eye level.

The people inside moved away from the window to give me a clear space and I ran the short distance, feeling the skin over the thick muscles around my knees tear and protest at the activity. I used the bottom of the wall to give myself a boost and leaped, slamming my hands on the sill to propel myself over the edge. Phoenix neatly snagged my belt to help me get the rest of the way into the room. I tucked my head and hit the floor in a neat roll, popping straight back to my feet. A trickle of blood made its way down my shin, but for lack of time I decided not to mention that just yet.

When I checked out the room, I found the Celt guarding the door, listening carefully. She nodded and waved us forward, one hand on the door knob, ready to fling the door open and jump out of the way. I retrieved my rifle, slung it over my shoulder, and pulled a knife while the rest stood behind me.

As the best—and dirtiest—hand-to-hand fighter present, I got to be the first one through the door. I nodded, and the Celt's free hand began a countdown. When she reached *one,* she swung the door inward, stepping back to give me a clear path.

Right on the other side, a surprised soldier stood in a short hallway. Steve opened his mouth to yell, one hand slapping his hip and the handgun holstered there. I lunged through the door and grabbed him with my left hand while my right slammed the knife under his chin, straight up. We held that position for a moment, standing eye to eye. The light in his eyes went out, while his throat worked, pressing against my knuckles.

I let him down slowly but didn't withdraw the knife until I'd dragged him back into the room. Legs, Sparrow, and the Celt stared at me, pale faced and wide eyed, as I wiped the blade clean on the dead man's clothes. Phoenix took up position in the doorway.

She bared her teeth in a grin as I straightened, green eyes wicked. "Another one bites the dust."

I shook my head, huffing a breath because she just *has* to mess with the newbies.

We moved cautiously down the hall, two doors visible on the left. A quick check of the first door revealed a closet filled with jackets and shoes as well as a vacuum cleaner. At the next door I heard clothes rustling inside, and I held a hand up. Sparrow tapped my shoulder, telling me everybody stopped. A moment later a toilet flushed, and I raised my head, surprised. Bastards still have flushing toilets?

A splashing warned me to get ready, and I crouched. The doorknob was on the opposite side from me, so when Steve opened it, I'd have a straight shot to him. The knob started to turn, and I braced against the opposite wall. When the door began to swing, I hit it like a freight train. The hollow interior door splintered in large chunks, breaking away in jagged sheets. I barreled into the soldier and we fell into the small space, careening off the toilet before hitting the floor, the knife between us and the point aimed straight at him.

I lay still for a moment until I recovered enough to remember what the soft thing under me was. I scrambled to my feet, pulling the knife free, and had to stop there to catch my breath. When we fell, the hilt of my knife slammed into my sternum, and I rubbed the spot.

"Well," I wheezed, "that'll leave a bruise." Still bemused, I turned to the sink and had a moment of shock when water actually poured from the faucet.

"You okay there?" Phoenix leaned against the door jam. "Having fun?" She nodded to my hands, where I splashed as I washed them.

"Piss off," I grinned, then grimaced. "Dammit, this hurts."

"What hurts?" Sparrow examined me over Phoenix's shoulder.

"Everything."

"I'm taking point." Phoenix stepped up, not giving me a chance to protest. Sagging with relief, I followed her into the hall, waving her on.

The Celt spun to the side, allowing Phoenix to pass, braids swinging as she moved. The rest of the house was simply the kitchen/dining area to our left and the stairs rising from the entryway to our right. Phoenix led the way up the stairs, walking lightly, close to the wall to reduce any noise. The upstairs was simply a landing, the bathroom, and two closed doors leading to rooms that should share a wall with the neighboring house. Both those rooms had padlocks on the doors to prevent any escape.

"So what now?" Sparrow whispered, looking at the closed doors. "Do we break them down?"

Phoenix and me shared a look, shrugged, then Phoenix stepped forward and knocked lightly on the first door. "Hello?" she called softly. "Anybody awake in there?"

No answer.

She knocked again, a little harder. "I don't know how to reassure you through the door. We're not soldiers. Will somebody answer?" We heard rustling from inside the room while those of us outside held our breaths to hear better.

"Who are you, then?" a light, feminine voice asked.

Phoenix turned her head to look at me, shrugging wildly. "What do I say?" she mouthed.

I shrugged, then remembered our first rescue. I put my mouth close to the door. "We're the rebellion," I said clearly. "And we're here to get you out."

A long pause, then "Good enough."

"We need you all to stand back from the door, and please, don't scream."

I stepped back, and motioned Phoenix to the door. "Why me?" she complained.

"Because your boots broke my legs. Suck it up, buttercup."

She sighed. "Fair enough."

We moved back to give her room. Phoenix had her back pressed against the railing, concentrating on the lock. She took a quick step forward and slammed her right foot into the door next to the padlock, punching her foot through the door without moving it, getting her foot stuck in the process.

Phoenix balanced precariously on one leg, holding onto the bannister, and gave me a helpless *What now?* look.

I laughed quietly at her expression. "Yeah, ain't so easy, is it?"

"Will you just..." she said, gesturing to her foot, "get me out of it?"

Sparrow supported Phoenix while Legs and the Celt carefully pulled her foot out of the door, keeping their faces turned away from Phoenix, but I could see their shoulders shaking. While they worked, I pulled out one of the handguns holstered at my thigh. These ones were a touch heavier than the ones in the shoulder harnesses, and I figured it'd work a bit better. I removed the magazine, ejected the cartridge and stepped up to the door once Phoenix's leg was freed.

I carefully placed the butt against the door just above the lock. Making sure the barrel didn't point toward anybody was second nature by now. Then I slammed the palm of my hand against the gun, breaking another small chunk of door away. I worked my way around until the lock was attached to the door by a small strip underneath. Turning the handle, I hit the door with my shoulder, knocking the last remaining bits off and entered the room in a rush.

The smell hit me like a living thing, and I reared back, bringing a hand to my face. It was a standard sized room, roughly fifteen by fifteen feet, with three mattresses on the floor and a bucket in the corner that appeared to be the source of the smell. Six women in bits of nothing clustered together against the wall, watching me warily.

"Captain, couldn't you have done that before—" Phoenix cut off abruptly as she came in behind me. "Fuckin'...*Fuck!*"

"Yes, Phoenix." I turned my head to address her without looking away from the six. "How about you break into the other room while we make a start on getting the women next door?"

Phoenix huffed out a breath but left the room. I smiled reassuringly at the women against the wall, and they huddled together even more.

"Tell you ladies what." I took a few more steps into the room, "I'm just gonna have a look at the wall back here, okay? Celt, can you and Sparrow see if there's anything these women can wear?"

"There's nothing here." I recognized the voice as the one I'd spoken with through the door. Nearly my height, the woman was quite noticeable, with black hair hanging halfway down her back, dark eyes, and full, pink lips. "This is all we have to wear."

I nodded. "Search and destroy," was all I said. Sarge had introduced us to the phrase, and he'd learned it from a cook in the military. The cook had used it whenever they'd needed an item and the kitchen was nearly out. Basically, you took anything and everything you needed that remotely fit the criteria. Our scavengers used the term most often, and people who graduated from scavenging to fighting brought it with them.

Sparrow and the Celt disappeared back downstairs. After a minute, faint thumps and rustles drifted up the stairs, while I pressed my ear to the back wall, knocking on the drywall.

CHAPTER 42

"It's absolutely disgraceful, the way builders separate homes with nothing more than two thin sheets of drywall and some insulation," I said gleefully as I helped the last woman through the hole in the wall, then sent her downstairs.

"Bless our greedy builders," Phoenix agreed, crawling through last. "Good riddance to that shithole."

We joined the rest of the team downstairs. The entryway was crowded with twenty-four women in varying stages of undress, but the one we wanted, Olivia, was not here.

Phoenix surveyed the disheveled women, frowning. "There must be more women in the other houses."

"Some of the favorites have their own rooms in the second and third buildings," the black-haired woman volunteered. She'd stepped forward as the spokeswoman, and now I dealt with just her.

"What about new girls?" Phoenix edged closer. "Have you seen a woman about this high?" She held a hand up a couple inches above her own head. "Dark brown eyes, light brown hair, maybe thirty?"

The woman shook her head. "No. Give me a minute." She left us to circulate through the crowd.

"At least we'll have a chance to get more shoes and pants," I said, trying to figure out how we'd get all the women to the bus. Might have to steal a car.

The woman returned. "New women are kept in isolation in the second building, the one closest to the guards. Private apartments are in the third."

"You know how many of both there are?" Phoenix asked her.

The woman shook her head. "We don't really get a chance to socialize with them. They're kept in their rooms. The men who see them head right up."

"What's in the first building?" I inquired.

"Guards. Lots."

"What, exactly, is 'lots' to you?"

"Like, six to ten."

I turned back to the room at large, one hand raised to get their attention. "Okay! Ground rules! Everybody listens and we have a better chance of living, all right? Good! Now, no noise. If you have a question that isn't directly connected to our survival, keep it to yourself until we're safe. If you have an observation about the location of a soldier, please, let someone who's carrying a gun know! Second, follow orders as if your life depends on it, because it does. Phoenix, am I missing anything?"

The women stared at me. From their general expressions, I guessed most of them were nonplussed. Maybe even a bit bemused.

Phoenix ticked items off on her fingers "Uh, be quiet, listen to us...nope, I think you've got it."

"Okay, kids! Follow the people in front of you. Me and Phoenix got the front, Sparrow has the back, Celt, you've got the left, Legs, the right." I clapped my hands, feeling a bit manic. "Right, off we go, and let's not lose anyone!"

I wish the Fates had told us there were so many women here. I cracked the door open and cautiously stuck my head out. It'd grown light enough that I could see clearly, though the sun hadn't quite made it over the mountains yet.

Walking quickly, we moved around to the back of the house. Legs checked the windows of the house next door. When she gave us the all-clear, we hustled women past. Leaving the women hiding in the shrubs around the third building, Phoenix and me went to the window.

This house turned out to be the easiest, as the soldiers were either asleep or keeping a slack watch. I had counted five women leaving the building when Phoenix crept halfway down the stairs and waved me over.

"I got a problem," she hissed.

I waited. "Well? Don't leave me hangin'! Is this problem gonna get me killed?"

"Get up here and have a look."

I stuck my head in to find a room like every other in the building: a plush, comfortable, queen-sized bed against one wall, rich cloth hanging from the walls, and feminine bits of frippery draped over most surfaces. The only way you could say it differed was the woman still in the room. She had masses of honey-colored hair piled on her head and wide, dark blue eyes

"I am not going anywhere with you!" the nearly naked lady whisper-shouted. "I see the condition your skin and hair is in. I am not having any of that!"

Phoenix had flattened her back against the wall next to the door, hands up defensively. "I just don't see why you'd want to stay here and get raped by any asshole who walks through that door."

"Listen," the woman continued fiercely, "I like to eat on a daily basis, and more than the twigs and leaves you people look like you live on. I like to be clean, and I happen to enjoy sex on a comfortable bed. So you can take your 'offer' and shove it up your ass!" She folded her arms, glaring at us.

"Um," I said, cautiously bringing the rest of me into the room, "what's going on?"

"You heard her!" Phoenix jabbed a finger at the recalcitrant woman. "She *likes* it here and doesn't want to leave. I think she's been brainwashed."

"Hah!" The woman leaned forward, fury vibrating through her. "I know perfectly well what's happening, and I'll do what's necessary to take care of myself."

"Yeah, but you don't have to screw Steve to do it," I pointed out, a heavy weight in my chest. "You don't have to fight, and we're the only ones who get really grubby. You'd have easy access to plenty of water."

The woman showed the first signs of humor, her lips quirking into a sad smile. "Don't say anything else. While I won't tell, I'd still rather not know anything more about you, to prevent accidents. After all, my clients have times where they just can't keep their mouths shut."

"I'm sorry that you feel you should stay here."

She gave me a genuine smile. "Thank you, but it's not necessary. I do well enough."

"Maybe you do," Phoenix glared, "but what about the rest of the women who don't want to be here? What about the little girls? You okay with all these child rapists?"

That comment struck a chord. "What are you talking about? No one here is under eighteen!"

"Oh, yeah, what a miracle." Sarcasm dripped from Phoenix's words. "Tell that to the twelve-year-old we found. Or that little thirteen-year-old. Hey, how old is Mouse?"

"Thirteen," I replied, watching the woman closely, gauging her reaction, "but she says her birthday was sometime this spring, well after we got her out, and she's small enough the pimp thought she was ten."

The woman's eyes blazed, and her manicured nails curved into claws. "They *told* me... They reassured me..." She choked, tears of rage in her eyes. "What do you want? What do you need? I *told* them I wouldn't put up with children being hurt. They promised me!"

"And they lied," I nodded. "So you're saying you want to help?"

"Oh, yes."

"Can we trust her?" Phoenix murmured.

I shrugged.

"Here, give me a moment." The woman went to her little desk and pulled out a pad of paper and a pen and sat down, scribbling busily. "Ambrose Sutter is the leader of the American Corps." My eyes widened and I bit my tongue. This woman knows *Doc's husband*? "A mean son of a bitch, a fascist and a bully. He hides it well, but he hates women. His wife even left him somehow. He won't go into details, but one of my other clients said she up and disappeared. He lives at the university by the Capitol building."

I concentrated on not choking, rocking back on my heels. *Shit!* Didn't know Dorothy was quartered there, too, and Sirius should be near that damn building. Anxiety built up, spurred by her comments. This was all taking too long. We still had two houses and needed to get everyone the hell out of Dodge.

The woman stood up, holding out several sheets of paper torn from the notebook. "Here's everything I know about the occupation. Hopefully, you've heard it from other sources to corroborate."

I pursed my lips in a soundless whistle, scanning the papers. "Would you be willing...to do this regularly?"

"You want me to meet with someone?" She shook her head forcefully. "No. Too dangerous."

"How about a drop point where you leave stuff like this and we have a courier pick it up?"

"How do we go about this?"

I thought quickly. "As a favorite, can you ever leave this place?"

She nodded. "Every afternoon I go for a run."

"We'll send someone to meet you, some afternoon. The contact's name is River, and they'll find you."

"Who are you, then? And your angry friend?"

I grinned. "I'm Captain. My angry friend is Phoenix."

"And who will I be?"

"Nightingale?" Phoenix threw out. "I think that's a songbird. Pretty standard."

"Do I look like the usual?"

"Bluebird? Robin? Chickadee? Tit, shrike, butcherbird..." I threw the names out desperately, needing to be done. The woman narrowed her eyes, contemplating. "...kinglet, warbler, lyrebird..."

"Nope" She shook her head. "Shrike. I like that one."

"Now we just have to figure out how to explain you surviving," Phoenix put in.

"Surviving what?" Shrike asked.

"We're gonna blow this shit to Kingdom Come shortly," I explained. "So you probably shouldn't be here."

"I'll tell them I was out for my run." Shrike went briskly to the closet and pulled out running clothes, stripping unselfconsciously.

"Will they believe you?" I cocked my head, listening. Silence. I breathed out, some of my anxiety leaving me.

"I'll make them." Shrike looked sure of her ability.

I shrugged. "Okay. You sure we can't interest you in leaving with us?"

Shrike's brows drew together. "You're willing to lose all the information I could give you?"

"I'd rather you were safe," I informed the woman, leading the way down the stairs once she finished dressing.

"Pffft." She waved a hand airily.

"Whatever," Phoenix snapped. "We've got other people who need our help, and we still have soldiers to finish."

"Fuck me." Shrike looked at us, her blue eyes wide. "You're going next door?"

"Eventually. Everything in its time." I smiled tightly. "Oh, and better not come back here until you hear a boom and see a big cloud of smoke, okay?"

***

We found an unlocked window on the ground floor of the second building, and I boosted Phoenix through, then I overturned an abandoned bucket and used that to get into the room. I let Phoenix lead, and we only encountered one guard on the ground floor. I closed my eyes, gingerly rubbing my legs while she dealt with him. We climbed the stairs cautiously, but the entire upstairs was empty. There were signs that it saw frequent use, and a bad, permeating smell of sex and fear, but no Olivia.

I tilted my head toward the wall. Did we want to go through upstairs? Phoenix nodded. It only took a moment to find a hollow point, and even less to cut through the drywall. I pulled my sleeves over my hands to protect them from the damn insulation. Nasty stuff.

Like the house we'd just left, the upstairs rooms were unlocked and empty. I bit my lip, heart starting to pound and sweat prickling on the back of my neck at the onset of panic. Where was Olivia? She should be here, and we needed to get moving.

Phoenix paced next to me, rubbing her hands on her legs and muttering indistinctly.

My eyes widened at a sudden realization. "The closets! We need to check the closets!"

"What?"

"The women are kept isolated, and in the dark. There's too many windows, no curtains, and it's all soft beds." I pointed back at the rooms. "The closets are perfect, though I don't recall anything unusual about the one we saw."

"Downstairs, then." Phoenix firmed her jaw, taking the lead.

On our way down the stairs, we heard movement. We peeked and saw a soldier walking toward the stairs, concentrating on something in his hand. Phoenix took a deep breath, then leaped—one hand on the railing, the other holding a knife—lightly over the bannister, dropping like a hundred and thirty pound rock on the unsuspecting man's head.

She stood victoriously over the man, waiting for me to join her at the bottom. Sure enough, the closet here had a padlock on the door. Phoenix prepared to break the door down, but I stopped her, pointing silently to the hinges on the outside.

"Oh."

I walked back to the downed man, kneeling slowly next to him to rifle his pockets for keys. I'd never spent much time next to the body of a soldier, and it hurt to see how young he was. We killed and we moved on, to survive. That had been the way for months now, but the man looked my age, mid-twenties.

My questing fingers found a metal ring in his pocket, and I pulled it out to the jangling of keys. "Catch." I tossed the keys to Phoenix and went back to the man. The item in his hand caught my eye and I pulled it out for a better look. "Oh. Oh, fuck." I sat down hard.

"What?" snapped Phoenix, already on the third key.

I held up the item, a photo of the soldier with a woman and a little girl.

Phoenix swallowed. "We always knew it," she said hoarsely, as much to convince herself.

"Yeah. It's just...rough to have it thrown in your face, y'know?"

She shook her head like she was shaking off water or waking from a dream. "We don't have time for this. It's getting later all the time. It's already full light."

I swallowed and gave her a sickly smile. "Nag, nag, nag. Get the door open, woman!"

The last key on the ring worked. Finally. Opening the door revealed the pale, dirty face of Kitten's lost daughter squinting in the sudden light. She huddled against the back wall, using it to brace herself as she kicked out.

"Olivia!" Phoenix exclaimed, jumping back. "It's me, Alex!"

"A-Alex?" Olivia croaked, peering out. When she realized it really was her cousin, she collapsed in Phoenix's arms, sobbing.

I gave them a moment, but no more. We simply didn't have time. "I'm sorry," I interrupted, "but we really have to go. She's Phoenix now, by the way."

While I led them briskly to the heavily locked and fortified back door, Phoenix hurriedly explained the basics of our survival to the bewildered Olivia. By the time I got the door open, Olivia had begun to fill us in. That Steve never touched her was the first piece of information she gave us, repeating it over and over, like a mantra. She had no idea how long she'd been locked up, but each time a soldier opened the door she did her best to kick the man's balls into his throat.

She told us that last as we reached the rest of the women, and the awed looks given to her far outweighed anything the rescued women showed us.

I smiled grimly. "We've still got one more house, and...Legs?"

Legs waved from the side, a fresh bruise showing on the side of her face. "Sorry, we ended up having to take care of the two soldiers in the other half of house four anyway."

I nodded. "Good. Okay. Whoever did it all right?" Taking a man's life was never easy, particularly the first time or twenty. We just...shoved it into a box, after a while.

"I'm fine," the Celt said stoutly. "We should get moving."

"Right, last house and all. Wish us luck." Phoenix nodded, turning quickly away from her cousin.

"Wait!" the raven haired spokeswoman stopped me before I could leave. "What do we do if you don't come back?"

I grinned. "Run. That way." I pointed south.

"Nah," Phoenix disagreed, still facing the last house. "Somebody always comes back. We're like the cockroach that survived a nuclear bomb."

"Besides, this one's staying with you." I gestured to Legs. "Got that, Raven?" The newly named woman nodded numbly, eyes huge. "Good. Sparrow, you got everything you need for the houses?"

The older woman looked up from her pack. "I have enough."

I flipped the women the peace sign over my shoulder as I walked away, following Phoenix and the Celt. I could barely hear the woman say "Raven?" but by that point I needed to concentrate on the job in front of us.

***

Water splashed on the dry ground around my knees as I knelt in the thirsty grass, allowing Sparrow to dump another bucket of water over my head. The water sluiced the blood from me, and I scrubbed my hands over my face and through my hair, trying to rinse it all out. Phoenix stood a little ways away being rinsed off herself, eyes closed and jaw clenched tight.

Olivia hovered around her, gently pouring water over the fighter's head and wiping the blood from her face. I swallowed, seeing the love in her eyes as she tended her cousin. It was worth it, everything we went through, if it meant women like Olivia didn't have the light erased from their eyes and hearts.

I tipped my head back for the final bucket, closing my eyes. When I opened them, the new rescues still gave us a wide berth, watching with a mix of horror and satisfaction. I felt fairly confident in who would join the fighters and who would prefer to stay at the Lair.

As I climbed to my feet, the women nearest me edged back and the pang in my chest surprised me. For a moment, I wished I could go home. My home, to find Papa and the kids all there.

I sighed, scrubbing my hands over my face one last time to remove the tears. I had no time for emotions right now. Curse yesterday for making me sentimental.

Shrike strolled up, ignoring the women who glared at her. "You definitely got all of them?"

"Yeah." I blew out a breath, trying to banish the scent of blood and the memory of it splashing on my face. Phoenix shook her head, spraying water from her short hair.

"Good," Shrike said. "You even gave them a better than even chance, only three of you going in. More than they ever gave anybody else." She folded her arms, one hip cocked out.

I gathered my hair up, wringing it out. "We need to get moving, and so do you."

"I'm gone. Tell River I usually run around Berger Lake there." She gestured to the west of us. "If I'm not there, I'm at Hillview Park over there." She pointed south. I nodded again, and without another word, she turned and jogged off to the lake.

"You sure we can trust her?" the Celt murmured.

I shrugged. "Damned if I know, but she won't know when River shows up, so setting up an ambush would be a bit difficult. Besides, we saw her face when she found out Steve takes kids. I think she's solid, and River won't take any chances."

"Mmhm," Phoenix nodded. "Plus, you shoulda seen her when Cap'n said she'd prefer Shrike safe than useful. She's good."

***

I ran to the right of the group, needing to draw off the soldiers Legs had spotted ahead before they saw us. The sun showed mid-afternoon, and while it wasn't the heat of summer, it was a damn sight warmer than anything else this year. I ran across the road, but the buggers didn't even see me. I had to run over it twice more before I caught their attention, then they took off after me like dogs after a rabbit.

Once they caught my scent, Steve stayed in pursuit and I took them on a merry chase, running until my breath came short. A chest-high, off-white picket fence blocked the path I wanted. Timing my strides, I went over it in a sweet forward roll, popping back to my feet without missing a beat. As I hurdled the remains of a swing set, a piece of cloth slithered down my chest and back, and pressures changed oddly.

Everything around my chest felt...freer, than usual, and my breasts bounced entirely too much as I ran. I dived under a hedge, scrambling the rest of the way through and taking off to the left, then I booked it through the broken picture window of an abandoned store.

Not so abandoned, after all. I raced past a small group of people, their pale, scared faces barely more than a blur as I hurdled the coffee table in their midst and wondered, incongruously, how large-breasted women managed to do anything. Another left, jump the chain link fence as high as I can...swing the legs over...and as quickly as that, I saw Steve's backs in front of me. Turning back to the south, I slowed to a jog, my abused lungs struggling to bring in air.

I caught up to Phoenix, who turned with her rifle leading, relaxing only when she saw it was me.

"It's pretty quiet, now." She gestured down the road.

"That's nice." I bent over, hands on my knees, breathing heavily. "Why the fuck was I the one who was the damn decoy again?"

"Because you can't shoot for shit, and the others would never find us again."

"Oh. Right. Fuck you."

"Asshole."

"Jerk. Where are the others at, anyway?"

Phoenix led me around a corner, ducking quickly between two buildings. Behind a high fence, the women sat resting while the fighters stood guard.

"Can you check something for me?" I asked Phoenix, pulling up the back of my shirt.

"Are you hurt?" Anxiety and fear spiked her voice, making it sharp.

"What? No! It's just…" I twisted, pulling my shirt higher to reveal my bra. "Can it be saved?"

Phoenix smothered a relieved laugh. "Nothing a needle, thread, and a whole new bra can't fix."

"Dammit! I've had this bra longer than anything else I'm wearing." I sat down and kept going until I was lying on my back, looking up at the sky. "I'm tired. How long have we been awake?"

"Less than twenty-four hours." Phoenix made herself comfortable next to me, patting my shoulder companionably. "You'll be fine. We have a bit of time."

"We don't have time." I struggled up. "We gotta coach the women on where to go and how to get there. Then you and me gotta go make some noise. Then, we gotta—I gotta—"

"We have time," Phoenix said firmly. "The morning, at least, and every-one needs a nap. Rest. Sparrow has first watch."

CHAPTER 43

It was early evening when I stood in the middle of a group of women who were wearing a mish-mash of clothing and staring at me like I was their only hope of salvation while trying to coach them on staying calm in the middle of a firefight. Lord save me.

A sudden explosion a couple miles behind us, in the general direction of Stonehaven Drive, ending my attempts at speech. The women crouched, hiding their heads in their arms, some crying out in fear.

I caught Sparrow's eye and gave her a thumbs up. "Nice! Though I have to say, I'm surprised it's taken them this long to check any of the houses."

"What are you talking about?" Raven cried.

"We may have set some explosives on the doors, rigged to go off when they were opened." I grinned. "Surprise!"

In the distance we heard men shouting, running, and some vehicles racing toward the scene of the fire.

"Well!" I dusted my hands off. "Looks like it's time for us to go."

"Shouldn't need another fire now." Phoenix looked despondent, even going so far as to kick the ground, digging her toe into the grass.

"Okay, ladies, remember what we told you, and stick with your groups." We'd have to spread out to avoid notice. A nagging finally surface. "Wait! Hang on, I gotta pee first. Go now or forever hold your pee!"

Turned out I wasn't the only one with a full bladder, though the rescued women were so used to going without privacy that they squatted anywhere.

Our run to the fence was direct...until we saw the fence. I ducked down beside the Celt, cursing Steve. They'd finally gotten wise and had the fence fully manned, both towers and foot patrols.

Crawling back to the main lot I found Phoenix coming in from the rear. "You get your wish." I rolled my eyes. "Damn Steve stayed put."

"How do we know this one'll work?" she asked.

I shrugged. "Don't. What else are we gonna do?"

"Okay." She crawled rapidly over. "Let's go make some noise!"

We slid over the fence, ready to do something incredibly, amazingly...stupid.

***

"Small fire! I said to start a small fire! That is not small!" I yelled at Phoenix as we raced back to the women. Shadows stretched longer, though the impending sunset was now overshadowed by the raging fire to the west of us.

Phoenix waved her hands helplessly, then laughed. "You said we needed to distract them," she protested. "Guess what? They're distracted!"

The blaze behind us loomed far bigger than the one set off by the explosions at the brothel, and the south breeze threatened the entire north. When we got back to the group, we found Legs, the Celt, and Raven leading the women out of the shelter of the yard, heading for the serious gap in security at the fence. The soldiers weren't all gone, but they'd reduced their numbers enough that we might actually make it.

Phoenix put on a burst of speed, passing me up and leading the way to the left of the group. I took the right while Sparrow chivvied everyone forward, herding them like a flock of sheep.

Phoenix threw her rifle to her shoulder, firing a round and dropping a man with barely a pause. Show-off. I skidded to a halt, hearing her rifle speak again, then I shot a man on the machine gun in the nearest tower. I didn't stop to watch him fall, since the shooting drew their attention back to us. I worked the pump and ran forward a few more steps, kneeling quickly to steady myself. Peering through the scope, I saw my target fall, then I glanced at Phoenix to see her waving at me.

"Are you shitting me?" I bellowed.

Time didn't slow, rather it all sped up. Running, leaping, firing as we could, keeping the women moving, the Celt, Sparrow, and Legs all joining in the action. Screaming, in pain, in fear, in exultation. The next tower over, also in range, began firing at us. My quick shot produced yelling and cursing, but the bullets still came. I took a knee, shooting the soldier as he brought a large-bore rifle to bear.

"Teach you to stand near a light!" a woman behind me shrieked.

"Keep running!" a panicked Legs yelled.

We created a narrow corridor free of soldiers, and Legs sprinted into the lead, wire cutters in hand. The landscape took on a hellish bent, distorted light, ash drifting down, and the fire an audible roar over the sounds of gunfire.

As soon as Legs made an opening large enough, Phoenix dived through, racing ahead. Sparrow and Raven began shoving women through while Legs picked up the space. It didn't take long for Phoenix's rifle to begin speaking again, and her rifle had better range and accuracy than the towers.

Just over half the women had gone through when a group of civilians appeared from the east, chivvied at a run toward the fire, soldiers pushing them along, presumably to fight the blaze. Poor bastards.

"What are you doing?" Raven screamed at me. "Shoot them, free those people!"

I shook my head. "No point!" I shot a soldier aiming a gun at us. "Those people won't come."

"How could you possibly know that?"

"Been there, done that. Move!"

Sparrow shoved the woman through the fence, though she screamed and fought. Sparrow, better trained and taller, bundled Raven along as gently as possible, always keeping her moving. Eventually, Raven stopped fighting and started moving under her own steam, but every chance she got, she threw me hateful looks.

Farther north, past the now minor blaze of the brothel, another explosion rent the air.

"Whelp, that's Sirius and company," I muttered, ducking through the fence myself. I found myself trotting at the rear of the group, next to Phoenix. "You know, I'd half thought we'd steal a car. As it is, I'm not really sure how we're gonna get out."

"Why don't we worry about that when the time comes?"

"What do you mean, 'when the time comes'?" I demanded, speeding up. "The damn time is now!"

Chapter 44

F*UCK!*

Fuck, fuck, fuckfuckfuckfuck!!

Sure, my team had gotten out in one piece. Sure, we'd managed to find a car we could jack, but not everybody in the four teams had gotten out. Not everybody we'd intended to retrieve had made it. Kitten died in the extraction, shot by the woman she'd suspected of spying for Steve, Mona. Three of the women in my own group had died, though all the bodies had been recovered, carried out by their friends.

And at this moment, three days after we escaped the city, I stared through a scope at the other two people who hadn't made it out, Thunder and Lightning. Steve didn't know exactly where we hid, but they knew we were in the Cascade Mountains. To that end, they'd brought what looked like the entire damn army into the foothills, making no effort to hide themselves.

They'd set up in a huge, open field, the army standing in a cluster with a small clearing in the center. Inside the clearing I saw a slim, dignified soldier of medium height, a huge white man with the sleeves torn off his shirt, a lovely young woman, and next to these three, Lightning and Thunder hung, crucified on rough logs.

The young women barely moved, and I found it difficult to focus on them, tears constantly forming. I wiped them away angrily. Crying wouldn't help them now.

While we'd sent all the newly rescued on to the Lair in the bus with an escort, the majority of the fighters, nearly thirty strong, lay in a row along a tree-covered ridge, half with me and half with Seahorse a little ways to the north. Despite the fact that we had roughly two miles between us and the soldiers, we kept our heads down.

Close enough to see, but not to shoot.

Three people to my right, Sung Ki got her hands on a scope, and she tried scrambling to her feet, hissing angrily. Sirius grabbed the hem of her jacket, dragging her down easily.

Sung Ki, normally so calm, turned on my cousin, teeth bared. "Is him!"

"Him?" Sirius pointed, disbelief evident in her tone.

"Ye!"

"Who is this 'him' you're talking about?" Phoenix asked.

"Go Kwan-Jae," Sung Ki gritted. "He is man who, who—"

"That's the sadistic bastard who sent her east," Sirius finished bluntly.

That got my full attention. "What do you know about him?"

"He is control here."

Holy shit. So that non-descript man down below was the distant enemy we'd been facing for roughly nine months. All of us went back to the scopes, finally putting a face to our foe.

To my left, Doc hissed a curse. "You see that big white bastard with Go Kwan-Jae?" she asked. "That's my husband."

"Motherfucker." I gave him more of my attention. He stood a good deal taller than Steve, his brown hair in a crew cut. With the torn shirt, we could easily see the muscles in his arms. He looked a hard man, one who'd let cruelty have free rein. This thought was borne out a moment later when he reached over and casually pinched Thunder's nipple, twisting until she arched in pain. Her scream reached us long seconds later as Doc wept, then the girl slumped against her bonds.

"And her!" Sung Ki whispered. The young woman with Go shone in the bright spring sun, mahogany hair and slim form set off by the exquisite dress she wore. She stood as painful contrast, in her manicured perfection, to the sisters, bloody and torn next to her.

"Who the hell's that bitch?" asked Phoenix, tense and angry next to me.

"She belong Go Kwan-Jae. She tell Go Kwan-Jae where send me." I glimpsed the woman passing her scope to Eleanor, who'd crawled up to see, too.

The young woman looked vaguely familiar, though I couldn't place her. Eleanor moaned, slumping to the ground.

"Eleanor!" A scuffle ensued as we all tried to see to Eleanor, our rock and moral compass. When the dust died, Storm held her mother closely, staring across the distance to the army with red-rimmed eyes.

"That's Eleanor's daughter, Anna," she said tonelessly.

"Oh, fuck." I rubbed my face, feeling suddenly ancient. Just one thing after the other. Why did we never have any time? Still, time to pretend to be a leader. "Doc." She didn't respond. "Doc!"

"Yes?" She looked at me like she'd just woken up.

"Can you tell how bad the girls are? Can they walk?"

"Are you thinking of a rescue?" Phoenix stared at me, a grim smile stretching her lips but never touching her eyes.

"No. Yes. Maybe. Dammit! Doc, what do you think?" I looked to the doctor desperately, hoping for a good verdict and afraid we wouldn't get one.

She stared through the scope for long minutes, fingers tapping on the ground as if she were counting. Finally, Doc put the scope down, scrubbing a hand over her face. Lines stood out sharply, making her look older than her years. "No good. I can see bone in at least three places on Lightning. Thunder has either two or five, it's really hard to tell. Their legs are definitely shattered, even if the bone is still under the skin." She delivered this to us in a dull monotone, but for the last bit her voice trembled just a little. "Thunder... Thunder looks like she's been partially skinned. One breast, and her hip, leading down toward her vulva."

Blood roared in my ears, gasps sounded all around us, and Dereva turned away, vomiting into the grass. Eleanor let out a sharp cry.

"My daughter...?"

"Storm, could you?" I gestured for her to take Eleanor away, where she couldn't hear any more. "So, Doc, they definitely can't walk? Can we build stretchers?" I knew stretchers was a long shot. Steve had brought what looked like his entire damn army in the hopes we'd come storming in to save those girls in a suicide run. I wanted to. God knows, I wanted to, but I also figured Doc would be giving me a really good reason not to.

The woman didn't disappoint, shaking her head decisively. "I'm honestly not sure how they're still breathing. Even with a fully equipped hospital I don't think we'd be able to save them. Maybe if we had everything we needed, from blood to organs, magically on hand." Her mouth turned down at the corners. "Whoever did this was...skillful, to do this much damage while keeping them alive."

My arms prickled as I remembered what Shrike, our new informant, had told us about Doc's husband, Ambrose Sutter. He hates women, he's cruel...I looked at the crucified girls. That kind of cruel?

Maybe.

"Captain." Sirius appeared at my side, tears on her cheeks, her lips trembling. "We can't leave them like this." Her voice was rock steady. "Please. We don't leave anyone behind."

I nodded once. Steve had come out in force, hoping to flush us out, track us back to the Lair, and finish us all for good.

Fuck 'em.

"Once upon a time," Doc said quietly, drained of life, "we'd have viewed death as the worst thing that could possibly happen. How sad that we know better now."

"Cap'n!" Legs called quietly. "Lightning's talking."

I squirmed back to the top of the hill. Phoenix passed me her huge Barrett, the scope already calibrated for the distance. We could hear the faint sounds of her voice drifting on the breeze, though we lay too far away to make out anything.

I watched her lips, blood forming on them even as she screamed her defiance. I could see plainly what she said. *Kill us. Please, kill us.* A stray breeze lifted a lock of hair that wasn't matted to her skin with blood.

I wanted to wail my heart out. To curl into a ball and pretend this whole thing was a bad dream, that I'd wake from it if I tried hard enough. I took a deep breath. Discovered that wasn't enough, and took another, ignoring the babble of voices, some talking about storming the army, others all for running back to the Lair and never stepping foot outside it again.

I had no good options. Steve would be coming for us the moment they saw movement, but I couldn't leave the girls like that. I sat back on my heels, the sudden motion stilling the voices around me.

"Phoenix?" I looked over at my friend. She watched me silently, waiting. "Can I borrow yours? Mine doesn't have enough range."

"I can do it," she rasped. "I'll take the big one."

I shook my head. "You'll never get in and out with that thing. I'll use your smaller rifle."

"I should do it," Sirius put in. "I owe them this much."

"I shoot long range better than you," I pointed out ruthlessly. We didn't have time to coddle egos. "And I sneak better than you," I added, forestalling Phoenix's next argument. "You guys need to get back to the Lair and start getting ready for visitors."

"What? You think they *told*?" Thorin shouted, red-faced, hands clenched.

I grabbed the boy, dragging him close and pointing his head in their direction. "*Look at them!*" I hissed. "In that condition, I'd've said anything to get them to stop! We have to assume the worst and prepare for it."

He gagged, tears welling in his eyes, but he looked ready to fight me on it.

"She's right," Sirius said heavily, holding up a hand to halt Thorin. "We need to think about guarding the Lair and meeting Steve before they get to us."

"I need Seahorse." I looked to Legs. "Please."

She nodded and raced off to find the ex-soldier, a hundred yards north of our position. When she arrived back with Seahorse, filling her in on everything we knew, I looked up from my preparations.

"Booby-trap everything between us and them," I said without preamble. "After that, fall back to Opal Creek. Let the traps slow them down while you get gone. Everybody knows what needs doing. Give 'em hell."

We had a plan. Sort of. The plan was to stop Steve before they made it to our wilderness. Most of the ways in were hiking paths, and the road we'd first come in on. We had Opal Creek to the west, Detroit to the south, and Bagby Hot Springs to the north. Miles of nearly trackless land, steep slopes, and thick, old-growth forests.

If we couldn't stop Steve before he made it in, we'd never stop him at all. Divide and conquer, that was the aim. I looked out at the mass of soldiers on the hills below us. God knew we'd never be able to face them in full-on classical battle.

"What about you?" Eleanor had returned unnoticed, gray faced and haggard from the emotional blows. Storm stayed staunchly at her foster-mother's side, though the look she turned toward Steve—and Anna—contained so much rage and hate that it amazed me she didn't try for a suicide run.

"I'm heading north, then west." I took the extra pouch of pemmican Sirius offered and the bandolier Phoenix had recently taken to carrying. A single shot rifle's disadvantages could be mitigated by bringing a ton of spare ammo. My pockets were already packed with spare magazines, protein bars, and a folding knife. I had my larger knife in the small of my back, all four handguns...I looked around, searching for the last thing I needed to change. Right! My boots.

I left the boots behind, pulling on a pair of knee-high moccasins, then refilled my canteen and made sure the flap holding it down was closed tightly. Seahorse had the fighters heading into the trees downslope of us, putting to use all the skills we'd learned over the last months. Some carried shovels, others had coils of paracord slung over their shoulders, flitting into the underbrush with barely a rustle.

Finally, I stood, ready to leave. "All in, all out," I offered, trying to smile. The corners of my mouth turned down, no matter how I tried to stop it. Before another word could be said, I turned and jogged into the trees.

"Hail the victorious dead!" Sirius cried behind me.

"Hail!" yelled every person in hearing.

CHAPTER 45

I found a deer track heading in the direction I needed and followed it. I had just over two miles to go, maybe an hour, if I could keep to trails. As I ran, I stuffed every piece of emotion I could find into a little box in my chest. I had no time for them. I swallowed a sob, then stuffed that in the box, too.

We'd looked while the army was setting up but hadn't seen any unusual movement in the trees between us and them. Trusting to our earlier findings, I didn't slack. Less than a mile. Plenty of distance. That's all I needed.

I leapt a fallen branch and felt a twinge in my knee. No time. I breathed deeply, and I concentrated on it, feeling my lungs working. Running was such an easy effort these days. We ran everywhere; to a fight, away from it, to evade the enemy, hunting...

I changed course mid-stride to avoid a clump of shrubs, leaped from rock to rock over a narrow creek, climbed up out of the gully, and paused just before the top to peer over the edge. Almost there. Almost to the grove of trees I'd sighted earlier. I swung north a little more. Didn't want to come toward Steve directly. Slower now, creeping through blackberries on a narrow game track, last year's canes brittle and prone to snagging on every little thing, including skin.

Bushes replaced the blackberries, letting me know I'd found it. The grove of trees. I sighed, craning my head back, walking carefully through the grove to spot a good tree. I stood at the base of one, a huge fir. The tree stood about three rows back from the edge, giving me cover while allowing me to see.

Slowly, slowly, so as not to rustle a branch or a needle, waiting for every gust of wind, I inched my way up the tree, pausing with the breeze and taking care not to hook the rifle on any branches. I stopped nearly two-thirds of the way up, straddling a branch barely strong enough to support me. I had both feet braced on lower branches and peered out around the trunk. I looked just over the oval, light green leaves on top of a walnut tree. The edge of the trees was packed with plants taking every advantage of the excess sunlight, predominantly blackberries.

Positioning my feet and knees so I'd be secure, I carefully unslung Phoenix's rifle. The sap on my hands made the rifle sticky, and I unconsciously wiped them on my pants, trying to dislodge the sap but picking up more dirt instead.

Sighting down the rifle, I could see the girls clearly if the leaves of the walnut moved just right. Moving in millimeters, I found the giant that Doc had pointed out as her husband. Anna and Go Kwan-Jae remained out of sight.

Just as well. This was a mission of mercy. Thunder and Lightning came first.

This close, I realized Doc had been generous in her assessment of their condition. My heart thumped heavily and saliva gathered at the back of my throat. I swallowed the bile back as my stomach tried to rebel at the sight of the burns, lacerations, and blood, trying desperately not to count the number of visible bones.

At least the cool day and good breeze spared them the irritation of flies, allowing me to see them clearly. Thunder had tears running unchecked down her face, head thrown back to the sun, mouth moving soundlessly. Lightning...I swallowed convulsively. Her eyes were missing. The blood ran freely down her face, mixing with that on her body. Her mouth was open in a silent scream, agony written deeply in the lines of her face.

I squeezed my eyes shut, resting my cheek on the warm, wooden rifle stock, breathing deeply. I rubbed my cheeks on my shoulders, telling myself those weren't tears. I was just sweaty.

Liar.

I inhaled and held it, opening my eyes and sighting down the scope once more, ignoring Steve, Anna, Go Kwan-Jae, Sutton. I focused the scope on Lightning.

"Hail," I whispered and exhaled slowly.

***

After the first crack of the rifle, Steve began swarming like ants, spreading out over the ground, trying to discover where the shot came from. Before the sound of the first shot faded, I'd moved the rifle a fraction and fired again. I caught a glimpse of Thunder sagging against her bonds before I lowered the rifle and pressed my face against the rough bark, crying silently.

I hugged the tree, the rifle awkwardly squished between me and it, listening to the shouts, whistles, and hastily fired shots from the army a stone's throw away. I stayed in my tree until darkness crept over the land, hiding against the rough bark and coming to grips with my new reality.

The reality of being a person who could commit a mercy killing.

I heard the soldiers come into contact with the thorny brambles near my tree, rifle shots to the east, a few scattered explosions, and screaming. Lots of screaming. I fell into a light doze, and after a while I couldn't tell what was reality and what was nightmare.

One voice pulled me out of my haze, a lone scream of agony, the sound rising and falling before a thick bubbling note entered. How long could a person scream? Thunder and Lightning knew. Eventually, he fell silent, just like them.

When I estimated it had been dark for three hours, and I hadn't heard any other movement for a while, I began warming up my muscles, flexing one group at a time. While I'd tried to keep them warmed, the tree was pretty damn uncomfortable, and moving now brought shooting pains to...everything. I nearly fell out of the tree when I unhooked my leg from its branch.

I stuffed the collar of my jacket into my mouth, biting down as joints and muscles shrieked in protest at what they'd been put through. Gravity aided my descent from the tree more than any ability of mine, and my legs folded neatly as my feet touched the ground. Lying prone, I stretched everything, shifting uncomfortably on the rifle under my back. At least now I could move without needing to worry about a forty foot drop.

Retracing my steps out of the grove took barely a minute, and I took the first path south, pausing often to listen for Steve. Yes, the concentration of soldiers was greatest to the south, but I hadn't brought much in the way of supplies, and they'd pissed me off. I had no idea how wide a net of traps the fighters had set, but by the number of screams I thought it likely that Steve had found many of them, though hopefully not all.

Even before the thought passed through my mind, another scream started, almost directly east of me. I paused, listening, pursing my lips as I gauged the distance. Maybe a mile and a half. I kept looking for Orion, my favorite constellation, before I remembered that he wouldn't be visible again until fall. My mouth pulled down and tears welled. Crying at the drop of a hat would be a standard thing for a while, I knew, but I really wanted to see the Hunter. I felt less alone when he strode across the night sky.

The breeze we had all day had ushered clouds in, obscuring any moonlight and forcing me to slow almost to a crawl. Creeping through some shrubs, I heard a cough and froze. I listened, straining my ears to place the person who'd coughed. Rustling to my left, along with the man quietly clearing his throat showed me where the bastard hid. I finally found him as a darker shadow against the moving leaves.

I dropped slowly to my belly, smearing all exposed skin with dirt. Steve paced a slow circle, once passing right in front of me before returning to the more sheltered location. He look like…I looked slowly around the space in front of me. Was he guarding someone? A bit more time and careful listening showed a small patrol scattered in the clearing in front of me.

I bared my teeth, snarling, because these men slept peacefully while women worth a hundred of them lay dead. The snarl turned into a grin. I needed supplies anyway.

***

The thing about being on your own is all the extra time to think. Evading patrols, rifling houses, and hotwiring cars had long since become second nature to us. Sure, you pay more attention at the moment of being exposed, but most of the time a tiny space was left for random thoughts. Like, why couldn't Steve figure out they all sounded like a herd of schoolchildren? They really couldn't grasp the concept of walking silently.

I ran through a neglected orchard as I pondered this thought. Weren't army guys supposed to be silent and deadly? My best guess, as I clambered carefully over a barbed wire fence, was that they *were* quiet. We'd just learned to be quieter, courtesy of our current status as prey.

I slept part of that night in a maple tree, lying along a thick branch, tied loosely to the trunk. I watched the sky darken, enjoying the contrast of new, green leaves against a dark blue sky. I woke with a start, listening, and heard a clattering close by. I untied myself and hitched around until I could peer around the trunk. There, barely twenty feet away, a group of three soldiers set up camp.

I snorted softly. Making a big fire. What a bunch of idiots.

Too bad they'd never learn.

***

The next day had scattered shots sounding through the mountains to my left, and I decided that this was the perfect time to turn east. Two nights and one day of heading south should've put me in the general vicinity of the ridge we'd long since equipped to take on an invasion. The idea was to keep all fighting as far from the Lair as possible. All the fighters would've been slowly retreating in front of any soldiers, making their way to this ridge, leaving a trail just clear enough to be visible, but concealed enough for Steve to think he had us.

A single road led to the wilderness point, which was crisscrossed with trails barely wide enough to walk single file. Before the road reached the parking lot giving access to these trails, however, a tall ridge rose next to the gravel road. Its slopes were lightly forested with ancient trees that were unable to grow too large, and the crown of the ridge sported a nest of boulders.

Now I just had to find the damn thing.

***

I lay in a field in the early morning, exhausted, landmarks obscured by a light mist. I could still hear the shots. I'd barely slept and had been walking since just before first light, continually hitting dead-ends and having to retrace my steps and start fresh.

The final straw happened when I walked over a patch of grass barely covering slick mud. My feet ended in a puddle, my back and ass in the mud, and I hit my head on a small rock nearly covered by grass. Moving again was too much effort. I lay there, staring at the sky and wondered why I should get up.

The girls would be fine without me. Seahorse and Phoenix could lead. Tears welled up, and I saw Thunder slumping against her bonds again, face finally relaxing in death. Lightning's agonized, silent screams, slacking only when my bullet tore through her heart.

"What's the point?" I whispered brokenly to the clouds. "They're better off without a murderer anyway."

Tears trickled down the sides of my face, and I couldn't find the energy to wipe them away. I just...I wanted to *sleep*. Maybe forever. I didn't want this stupid war. I didn't want the time to contemplate who I was becoming in fighting it. The tears came faster, and I writhed in an agony that didn't have a physical source. My fingers clawed at the ground and my jaw hurt, but no matter how hard I tried I couldn't pull them apart to let out the scream building in my throat.

I don't know how long I lay there, grunting and struggling against myself, when suddenly, warm air rushed over my face, and a soft, velvety *something* pressed against my forehead. It didn't move, it just held the spot, warmth pressed just above my eyes, and slowly, I relaxed, slumping to the ground.

I opened my eyes to see a horse looming over me, a lovely black and white—I twisted my head to check—gelding, whose feet were barely more than a foot from my head. Noticing movement, he lipped my hair gently, nosing me until I rolled onto my hands and knees. From my new position I saw he'd approached me with a purpose.

He had orange bailing twine tangled around one rear and one front leg. Recently enough that he was still healthy with no apparent signs of swelling, but enough to limit his movements. I pulled up a handful of grass to wipe the worst of the snot from my face, then finished the job with my cuff.

"Hey, buddy," I croaked, voice raw from crying. "Need a hand?"

I stood slowly, using the horse to get to my feet, and he waited patiently, sniffing me. I pulled out a small pocket knife, flipping it open, keeping my free hand on his side to reassure him and let him know exactly where I stood. It took only a moment to cut the twine, and a bit more time to unwind it.

I blew out a breath of relief when I saw he definitely didn't have any infections, though the hair was rubbed thin in a few places.

"Looks like I came along just in time, didn't I." I gave a watery chuckle, rubbing his nose. He nudged me, hard and I paused. I came along, just in time for him. Who's to say...maybe the fighters could use a hand, too? He pushed me again. "All right! I get it." I sighed, rubbing his ears. "Wanna come?"

The horse shook his head but followed when I took a few steps. I went back to fetch the lengths of twine and held them up, assessing them. I shrugged. Couldn't hurt to try. It took several minutes, but I finally had a working hackamore, with enough left to give me a single rein.

"I hope you know neck reining, boy," I muttered, finding a low rock to give me a slight boost. It'd been years since I've ridden, and I wasn't particularly good to begin with, but I couldn't pass up a fresh set of legs. It took a few tries before I found my balance, and what do you know? That horse found a small track that soon led us to the very road I'd been trying to find for hours. "You beauty!"

I leaned forward to hug the horse, and lurched, sliding abruptly down his side. I only prevented myself from falling off by grabbing his neck and mane before edging myself cautiously upright. This time, I settled for patting him carefully, then nudged him up the road.

***

I couldn't be sure how far I had to go before we reached the ridge, and after a few minutes we tried trotting. Trotting with a broken bra feels almost as good as running. Still, we kept a steady pace, and I heard gunshots more frequently. Not enough for me to think they'd joined in outright combat. More like the fighters were still drawing groups of Steve in.

A sudden wetness between my legs had me sitting rigidly on the horse's back, and he halted. I popped a squat against a rock and discovered red slime in my trousers. Shark Week had struck again. I sighed, reaching for the pocket where I kept an emergency tampon. All of the female fighters carried one or two, and this looked like my last.

"Motherfucking period," I muttered. Damn thing had been getting even harder to predict, and by my best guess, it'd been nearly two months since my last one. Doc reckoned hard exercise and a lack of fats were to blame, and who was I to argue with a medical professional? "Ugh," I grimaced as I inserted the damn thing and hoped I wouldn't get sepsis from my poorly-cleaned hands.

I'd just bent over to get my pants up when a rapid exchange of gunfire sounded to the east, the direction I needed to go. I craned my head around so fast my neck crackled.

"Fuck!" I put one hand to my neck, testing the movement while the other kept my pants from falling. I rolled my head around, and to my surprise, all the pain I'd been experiencing over the last few weeks in my neck and shoulders had vanished. "Hot damn!"

I pulled my pants up the rest of the way and hustled to the horse, only to have to stop and concentrate on unsticking my zipper and doing the belt up properly. We tried a canter this time, and the horse had less trouble than I did. Between sensitive boobs, a sore groin, and early onset cramps, I was pissed off.

"Fucking sonuvabitchin' assholes, invading our fucking miserable country, can't keep to themselves. *Nooo*, they have to come here and bother us." The horse's ears flicked back periodically, listening to my litany, but he obediently kept up the pace.

When I pulled the horse up, the shots sounded so close that my ears hurt. I stashed him down a side track that led to a small pool in the passing creek. He'd be safe there. Joining the fight, I didn't even come close to the first soldier. I saw a helmet, I shot it. Moving slowly from one point to another, shooting anything not me, pausing with increasing frequency as the cramps steadily worsened.

I bent over, leaning against a tree, breathing slowly until the cramps eased. From that position, I saw another soldier, this one climbing the ridge. I knelt, unslung the rifle and shot him, moving on without watching him fall. I curled up again, breathing slowly to stop the pain tremors that sometimes happened on bad cramps. I saw another soldier and shot him, too, not caring if he were dead or wounded.

You know what? Wounded worked just fine. I hurt, and I wanted them to hurt, too.

I still hadn't seen any of my people, and I hoped all of them were safely inside the nest of boulders. I only saw an occasional flash of movement up there as they fired shots, harrying the enemy, but plenty of soldiers on the slopes. A sudden rockslide took out a thickly clustered group who'd found the path, and I laughed, seeing the fighters ducking out of sight at the top.

There they were. Fucking shit up and making me proud.

I made my way to a new spot, pressing gently on my belly until I needed a fresh cartridge. This new position granted me an even better view of the men on the ridge, and best of all, I could keep kneeling. "Assholes picked the wrong fucking week to mess with us," I muttered, glaring through the scope. One man after another tumbled down, my own shots blending into the general cacophony.

I curled a little tighter, moaning as the pain radiated out to my ovaries, everything feeling like it was twisting in on itself. Stubbornly, I reached for another cartridge, but an empty leather loop met my questing fingers.

"Fuck."

A shout from my left told me I'd been seen, and I lurched to my feet to meet the new threat, tripped, and grunted as I slammed my left arm into a tree. Seeing me off balance, he charged me with a *sword*. I groaned, snatching out the first handgun, the one under my right arm, and shot him with less than six feet to spare.

"Fuck you, Steve," I spat, struggling to my feet. Another shout (why did people always shout when they spotted an enemy?) and a new guy slammed a fist into my head, barely rocking me. I laughed, jerked my elbow into his ribs, then turned and kneed him in the balls. I said, "Fuck you, too, asshole," and left him puking and holding his crotch.

I had exactly one magazine in each handgun, so I scooped up the sword as I went past. It had a nice balance, with a medium-length blade that looked more like a katana.

A female scream from above had me twisting around in time to see a girl with dark, curly hair and blonde streaks—Dereva—get pulled back from the edge by two others and into the shelter of the rocks. My breath stopped as I stared for long seconds, trying to see what happened to the girl and when I couldn't...

Everything went red.

CHAPTER 46

I fired, and my last handgun's slide locked back. I shoved it into its holster and then spun, flicking the sword out and down, slashing the closest soldier. *Don't stop moving. Never stop moving.* I dimly heard maniacal howling echoing off the ridge, sounding vaguely familiar. I plowed through the soldiers in front of me, continuing between two trees, forcing the rest of the soldiers to scramble around.

Dodging left, I surprised a soldier, cutting him down while his mouth gaped in a round 'O' of surprise. Two shots sounded nearby, and my last two targets dropped. I turned to meet the new threat, teeth bared.

"Captain!" the voice. I should know that voice. I shook away the distraction, hunting for another enemy.

A twig cracked on my blind side and I spun, lashing out as I dropped to one knee.

"Watch out!"

"Keep clear of her. Captain!"

I blinked, trying to clear my eyes. What was wrong with the left one? I shook my head, like a dog shaking water from its fur. No improvement.

"Captain! Oi, snap out of it, woman!"

I snarled, lunging.

"Eleanor!" it cried—no, *she* cried. "Can you—?"

A new voice joined the lot, soothing, mellow, calm. The voice spoke in a low, slow voice, gradually coming closer. I finally made her out through the blurring in my eyes to see a woman in her late forties, with mahogany hair and fine features, leaning close with concern in her hazel eyes.

"El-Eleanor?" My voice cracked, and I sat down hard.

"It's me, honey." She nodded, crouching and stroking my hair gently back from my face. "Can somebody bring me some water and a cloth?"

I squinted up to see Phoenix standing just out of reach. "Huh," she said. "Seems more like you should just shove her in the creek." Despite her words, concern furrowed her brow.

"Phoenix." This time the name was a statement. The precipice receded a little more.

"Not gonna try to take a chunk off again?"

"No promises," I rasped. "Try not to be such a. Pain in the ass. Then maybe." I slumped, suddenly exhausted, and rested my head against my drawn-up knees. A sudden memory had me struggling to lift the two-ton weight that was my head. "How's Dereva? I saw her fall."

"She's fine," Eleanor soothed. She had a wet cloth in her hand, and she was using it to clean my face. Where had that come from? "Doc got to her quick. The bullet was a through and through. A bit of rest, a couple stitches, and she'll be fine. You're the one we're worried about right now."

"Report." I looked to Phoenix, stubbornness the only thing keeping my head up.

Around us, fighters gathered the dead soldiers into a pile, tossing the bodies on unceremoniously, restoring a semblance of normalcy to the ancient wood. The major signs left were scuffs through the loam and blood spattered over leaves and bark.

"A broken ankle, another bullet hole, a variety of scrapes, burns, and bruises, some small breaks, and two dead." She answered the question written all over my face. "Both of them are from the scavengers, Paisley and Gull. Sarge caught a bullet, too, but he's fine. Gonna need a sling for a while, is all."

"Well," Eleanor commented, working her way down my arms. "Somehow, by some miracle, very little of this blood is yours."

"Oh, there's more here." I gestured to my legs. When she felt my pants, Eleanor gasped when her hand came away red. "Oh, it's not that bad. I started." I squinted up. The sun still shone on the top of the ridge, but down in the valley shadows reigned. "This morning, sometime. I only had one tampon and no time to change it out even if I did have more."

Eleanor left us, flagging down a person hidden from view.

The people working on clearing took care to give us a wide berth. I looked after them curiously. "Are they...okay? Am I?"

"Uh, yeah." Phoenix rocked back and forth on her heels. "You were just...a little out of it, when we got here. You might've freaked some of the kids out. They'll calm down once they see you're back."

I winced at that, then took a moment to give her a longer look. She had a couple visible bandages herself, dirt and soot on her face, and more on the bandana tied around her hair.

"Nothing broken?" I asked. She shook her head. "Then sit your ass down. My neck hurts, trying to look up at you."

"Now you know how it feels," Phoenix gibed, lowering herself carefully next to me with a groan.

"I don't know how they're still going." I gestured to the men, women, and older kids organizing and helping the wounded.

"They're probably part of the reserves," she replied. "The ridge worked out pretty well. We were able to hold a lot of people back. Once you turned into a human wrecking ball, we were able to get more people down on the side paths to give you a hand. That's actually where most of our injuries came from."

"Helping me?"

"No, getting down the paths. Those things are steep."

At that moment, Eleanor returned with Sirius in tow, loaded down with cleaner clothes.

"Here." Eleanor set down the sturdy clothes and tampon before helping me out of most of my gear. "Go change and wash up. We can talk once that's done. I'll watch your things." I set the sword down with my guns and reached out a hand. I'd never make it to my feet on my own.

"Cousin." Sirius grabbed my hand and pulled me effortlessly to my feet. "We need to talk when you have a minute."

"Come with me, then." I struggled out of my beat up jacket and dropped it on the pile at my feet before accepting the bundle from Eleanor, being careful to keep hold of the tampon. I looked at the blood-spattered jacket. Sure, it had a couple new tears, a hole, and it was hella filthy, but it was still salvageable. Kinda like me.

I could work with that.

We started slowly out, heading for the road, passing people trying not to stare at the blood on my clothes, particularly my pants. "Relax," I heard Phoenix say. "It's just her period." A couple shocked masculine gasps made me hope the few idiots left in the Lair might start taking female troubles seriously.

Sirius waited until we crossed the road before she broached the subject weighing her down. "Thunder and Lightning...?"

"Hail the victorious dead," I said quietly. "And they truly were victorious. After the damage I saw on them, and the fact that Steve didn't head straight to the Lair..." I still couldn't believe they hadn't given us up. Normal people would've spilled their guts at the first sign of danger.

"How bad were they, really?" came her next, hesitant question.

"Doc was right. They had hours to live at best. I saw their faces. They were peaceful, in the end." And they had been, after they'd died. Everything relaxed in death. No more pain. No more suffering. I refused to tell her the additional details I'd seen. No need for her to carry those nightmares.

"I want to know!" Sirius insisted. "They were like sisters, especially after eastern Oregon and Idaho."

"Then remember them as they were." I hardened my voice. "You know they suffered, and you know they didn't break. I'd bet one in a million couldn't say the same."

As we neared the creek, an equine snort greeted us. Sirius, alarmed, whipped her rifle off her shoulder, aiming it before she saw my horse, then she froze.

"A horse?" she whispered, face crumpling. The horse whickered, taking a few steps closer. Sirius stumbled forward, holding her hand low for him to sniff. Tears tracked slowly down her cheeks as she moved closer, ending with her wrapping her arms around his neck, leaning her full body against him. The horse bore her weight patiently, even leaning into her embrace.

Sirius had had a horse once, though he'd died of old age a few years before the invasion. Her sister, Toni, still had a horse, stabled near her boyfriend's house, and Sirius occasionally went over to ride her. I mean, she'd had a horse *Before*. The corners of my mouth turned down at the reminder.

While my cousin stayed with the horse, I stripped off moccasins, shirt, and pants, grimacing at the streaks of red down my thighs. I walked gingerly to the creek, every muscle aching, and sat on a rock at the edge to rinse off. I hissed as the cold water hit my legs, combining with the cold rock under my butt to chill me thoroughly. I hurried through the wash, taking the opportunity to insert the tampon as I sat.

My lips twisted and I couldn't stop my face contorting. Tampons are just so uncomfortable, and I hated using them. Freaking periods.

As soon as I washed, I pulled the clean clothes on, sighing as a measure of warmth seeped into my legs, then I went to rejoin Sirius. She still leant against the horse and I rubbed her shoulder. "Would you ride him back to the Lair for me?" I asked. "I'm not straddling anything right now, and I don't want to leave him for Steve to find."

Sirius straightened, sniffing and wiping her eyes. "Yeah, I can get him back. What're we gonna do with him?"

"I dunno. Feed him, let him give the kids rides. What else can we do with a horse up there?"

Sirius shrugged. "Scout? Steve's looking for human prints, not horse."

I thought about it. "Maybe. First, we need to get gone." Steve would be all over these hills by nightfall, and I was amazed no additional patrols or small armies had shown up in the meantime.

***

Once at the top of the ridge, the horse was fussed over while Seahorse signaled, then two avalanches were released, sealing the easiest routes to the top. After all the traffic, Steve would've found them regardless, so best to seal it up now. I was surprised to see kids at the top. Mouse, the little girl with braces we'd rescued months ago, was a frequent figure around the fighters, but a few of the girls were unknown to me.

Eleanor squeezed the shoulders of a familiar child, a little sandy-haired tyke who'd just finished stuffing used bandages in a backpack. "Thank you, Prime," Eleanor praised. "I don't know what Doc and the rest of us would've done without you."

The little girl's black eyes lit up at the warmth and love Eleanor shared so easily. "It's okay," she replied. "I'm too scared to fight," the child confessed in the tones of one sharing a deadly sin, a red flush creeping over her cheeks.

"Fighting ain't all there is to the world, little one," I told her, kneeling to look her in the eyes. "You're Optimus Prime, in the tannery, right?" The kid's eyes widened at being recognized. "You're learning a trade, making something. Creating. The world would be a better place if more people were like you. Don't you ever let someone tell you that you should fight, kiddo."

At that, the child's eyes lit up, and she straightened her shoulders before donning a small pack and trotting off to her group.

I watched her leave with Eleanor. "What the hell's happening that we've got kids out here?" I demanded, tears threatening again.

"Everybody's out somewhere," Eleanor said quietly. "You know the plans."

"The plan's to have all the damn *adults* out! The kids were supposed to stay at the Lair with Lavender!"

"We ended up short-handed. There were a number of smaller fights, and not everyone made it here. I don't like it either," Eleanor said sharply, "but don't you dare say anything to demean their contributions. They need to feel needed, to feel like they belong. We're the only family most of these kids have left."

I scrubbed my hands over my face. "I know. I know, I'm just... I'm so fucking tired. I need to sleep for a year, and I'll be lucky if I get two hours. This damn filthy war, and it's not even as bad as I can imagine. Fuck. Let's get out of here."

CHAPTER 47

"Hope." I looked up, shocked to hear my name, even from my cousin, as she walked into my room and closed the door. "I need to get away for a while," Sirius continued. "I can't..." She shook her head. "I can't concentrate. I just keep seeing...them."

"Okay." She looked surprised at my quick agreement. "Got anywhere you want to go?" It'd been a week since the battle, a week and two days since the girls died, and the ground to the south, the site of the battle, had a damned army camped on it, while patrols scoured the ground, even going so far as to burn old growth forest.

We'd talked about the raid on Salem, trying to figure out what went wrong, how the girls got caught, and what we could do to prevent it ever happening again. What we came up with was that we needed fighters to have a modicum of self-preservation, and to follow orders. Sirius had given them instructions, but the girls had disobeyed in order to plant a bomb in the University that Dorothy used as a barracks.

"Anywhere that isn't here," Sirius replied, walking restlessly around my room. "I just need...out."

"Well, I was thinking about doing a quick run into the Valley, get some supplies, truck stuff, maybe blow up a patrol to get the army out of the mountains. Small shit. Me, a driver, and you, if you want, and if you're not gonna do something stupid."

She thought about it, cocking her head to the side. "Yeah. I could do that. When you wanna leave? We bringing Phoenix?"

"Tomorrow works. I'm hoping I can find a few more bras, too, since the tannery's offerings aren't frequent or too comfortable yet." I scratched under my arms and between my breasts for the umpteenth time. "And no, Phoenix ain't comin'. She's sticking around to help Olivia, Sam, and the kids. They're having a private funeral for Kitten tomorrow." I still found it hard to believe that dynamic woman was gone.

"Then bring it."

***

"I cannot *believe* you're going without me." Dereva glared up at me from her bed, her purple bandage visible through her white shirt. "You don't go anywhere without me!" She barely held back tears glittered through the fury, one fist clenched at her side.

"Eleanor would kick my ass if I tried to take you with me right now," I explained again.

"So wait until I'm better. The hills are crawling with Steve right now, anyway."

I grimaced, shaking my head. "They're pretty sure we're in these hills somewhere. I wanna distract 'em. Plus, you know the damage the vehicles took last week. I need stuff."

"But-"

I shook my head. "Nope. I'm not getting on Eleanor's bad side for anything. And your mama, when we find her, will kill me. For all the things Anansi's done, at least."

"So what's dying one more time?" the girl wheedled.

I laughed. "No. And if you keep this up, I'm gonna send Eleanor in."

"Bah!" The girl waved her uninjured arm irritably. She was cute, with her face all scrunched and grumpy and her hair a wild halo around her head. She'd make my life hell if I told her so, though. "Send her in, then. I need help brushing my hair, anyway. Brat," she mumbled under her breath.

***

"Oh, my God," Sirius groaned one evening three days later. "Why did I let you talk me into this?"

"Because we need bras. Yours must be about ready to break." Mine had broken over a week ago, in Salem, and now I had to use bandages to keep my tits under control. To say that finding another bra was approaching an obsession would be an understatement, and we got to do this while dodging Steve. We had taken the time earlier to drop a landmine and got Steve to drive over it. Even though it meant we'd spent the rest of the day running, it pulled patrols out of the mountains and away from the Lair.

I reclined on my blanket and a foam pad, staring up at the patchy clouds through the leaves of a cherry tree. Ripe cherries dangled from in branches, which meant my birthday had passed. I closed my eyes, drifting off to sleep after the exertions of the day.

***

A noise had my eyes snapping open without me moving another muscle. I carefully eased my blanket aside, grateful the heavy wool didn't make a sound and laid a hand on my rifle, lying next to me. The noise sounded again, a faint rustle, far more than we expected from wild animals. A few feet away, at the base of a tree, I saw a tiny movement as Sirius turned over, getting a hand on her own weapons.

In this situation, Sirius was the best possible person to have on your side. At night, her poor eyesight didn't matter, while all the skills she'd developed to be a quality scout became even more valuable. After all, she had the best ears in the Lair, even down to identifying how far away a person was. She disappeared to the left, I went right, and Hightide, our driver for the week, found a safe spot by rolling under the truck.

The rustling continued, moving slowly toward the last place I saw Sirius. I followed the sounds, slipping through the night, holding the rifle with the barrel pointing to the ground, ready to come into action. I made out darker shadows, their faces paler blobs against the irregularities of the bushes. Two taller shapes, three shorter ones, looking about the size of children.

Moving slowly, I slung my rifle over my shoulder, then crept up to the closest adult-sized shape. Breathing out in preparation for a fight, I stepped up suddenly, looping my right arm underneath his, and my left around his throat. With a quick heave I straightened, tightening my arms so that my victim dangled haplessly, right arm flailing in the air, the left struggling futilely to get a grip on me. The person let out a strangled shout, and Sirius leaped out at the other tall figure, dropping it handily by stomping its foot and punching it in the face.

The kids hit the ground immediately, arms covering their heads, whimpers filling the night.

"Who are you?" I growled. "What're you doing here?" I loosened the grip on my captive's throat.

"You're not *them*?" The man at Sirius' feet sounded confused. "The Liberation Army? Or the Corps?"

"Nope," Sirius said cheerfully. She put her foot on the man's back and leaned on it. "We're their worst nightmare."

"Very melodramatic, thank you." I rolled my eyes, unseen in the dark, and tightened my grip. "Still waiting!"

"We-we're from Salem," my captive, a man, gasped. "We escaped, I swear!"

"There we go," I grinned. "One problem. Why should we believe you?"

"Have the soldiers ever brought kids out of Salem?" my captive asked.

I looked down at the kids, crying a little louder now. "Very good," I said approvingly. "Very quick thinking. What do you think, Sirius?"

"Sounds good enough to give 'em a chance, Captain." Sirius stepped back. "While we keep a damn close eye on 'em, at least."

Once back at our camp, I got a tiny fire going in the cook stove, just enough to heat some water. The poor kids were freezing, and the men asked if we could give them something to warm the kids up. The dim light from the stove showed us the gaunt, hungry faces of two men in their mid- to late twenties and three kids, a boy and two girls. The men had enough similarities that I figured them for brothers or cousins, and the kids obviously belonged to one or the other of them.

"Is that...*chocolate?*" a young voice asked in awe.

"Yes, it is." I looked up from the tin mug and handed it to the kid. "Be careful, it's hot."

The girl accepted the mug reverently, holding the handle with one hand and pulling her sleeve over the other to protect it from the mug. I estimated her age at seven or eight, though the dirt and poor lighting made it hard to tell.

"Thank the nice lady, Lina," one of the men croaked. He swiped a quick hand over his eyes while the girl blurted out a hasty "Thank you!"

before putting her nose back to the mug. Hightide, who'd managed to find enough mugs for everyone, as well as blankets and warmer clothes from the second box in the truck bed, got another stove working.

I passed out mugs of chocolate to the other two kids, maybe three and five, and tea for the men. I flashed them a grin. "Sorry, we run out of coffee as fast as we can get it."

Taking a page from Hightide's book, I got more water on to heat. Might as well feed these poor suckers. While we waited for the pots to boil and Sirius to get back from scouting, I looked to the men.

"Twenty questions time." They didn't try to avoid me, didn't cringe, though one looked desperate.

"Maybe we want to know some things about you, first," one man said belligerently.

"Doesn't work like that. Not yet." I stared the man down. "We found you, and we're your best hope right now, but we need to know if we can even remotely trust you."

The man sighed heavily, then nodded, looking at the kids. "My name—"

"Not that." I held up my hand. "We don't do names, in case you didn't notice. I wanna know how you got out, who you're trying to avenge or whatever, whose kids these are, and while you're telling me all that, I'm also gonna try to decide if you're lying. So go."

"Okay." The man drew the word out, thinking. "This is my younger brother," he said, gesturing to the man I'd collared, "the munchkins are mine. As for how we got out..." He shook his head. "I don't know if you noticed, but there was a fire in Salem, nearly two weeks ago."

I nodded, and Hightide very carefully didn't look at either man.

"We managed to sneak out in all the commotion. My kids were playing near the fence about a month ago and found a section that'd been cut. It was only held to the pole with zip ties." I pursed my lips and tried to look innocent. "We didn't have anything strong enough to cut through the fence, but zip ties? Yeah, we could manage that. We'd already been collecting a bit of food, packing it away, hoping for an opportunity. Though we've kinda run out of food." This last he said wryly, as his stomach rumbled on cue.

The pots came to a boil, and Hightide and me began dumping broken pieces of spaghetti into them before putting the lids back on for it all to cook.

"I'm...looking for my wife," he admitted. His brother began to protest, only to be hushed "We don't really have a whole lot of options here," he muttered to him. Then back to us, "She was taken by soldiers months ago. I saw them take her out of Salem in a truck, heading north, so we decided to go that way, too. Until..."He waved a hand around, indicating us, and everything.

"Could you...describe your wife?" Hightide asked carefully, stirring her pot. "Just so we know who we're looking for?"

"She's about my age." The man leaned forward eagerly. "She had dyed blonde hair, but it's been growing out, so it'd probably be browner now. Hazel eyes. Cute little nose and a great ass."

"And the disposition of an angry bear," the brother mumbled.

I choked, then coughed into my elbow. "Holy fucking shit," I giggled, staring from one man to the other. Hightide had a hand to her mouth, eyes moist, as if she were watching a romantic part in a dramatic movie.

"What? What!" the man demanded, looking back and forth between me and Hightide. His tone and actions dragged the kids' attention away from their hot chocolate, and now they watched, interest in their little faces. "What do you know?"

"Has she, maybe, got a tattoo?" Hightide sounded like she was being strangled.

"A paw print. A bear's paw print, on her left shoulder blade. It's a family joke. Have you seen her? Have you heard of her?" Desperation shone on his face, even in the dim light of the stoves.

At that moment, Sirius walked out of the trees to the south, hands relaxed at her sides, and jerked a thumb behind her. "All clear."

Hightide and the man ignored her, and I watched them both, waving a hand for Sirius to hush. This was better than a movie. I wished I had popcorn.

Hightide leaned forward, ignoring her bubbling pot. "Well, the thing is..."

I whipped the lids off and poured powdered soup inside each, darting glances at them to make sure I didn't miss anything.

"...we do know her," Hightide continued. The man gasped, looking ready to leap up and run to find her. "We...rescued her, a couple months back, and she's been looking for you. We call her Bear."

The man gave a strangled laugh, tears shining in his eyes, and the oldest kid whispered, "Daddy, do they know mommy?"

He hugged her tightly. "Yes, they do," he choked out. "And they'll take us to her."

Hightide had tears tracking down her cheeks that she mopped away with both hands.

"Soooo...we don't care that we're safe?" Sirius interjected. "Anybody wanna fill me in?"

"Sirius," I said, switching between the pots, stirring irregularly, "meet Bear's family."

"Holy shit! Fuck, yeah!"

***

"You're back!" Eleanor exclaimed, rushing out of the Lair to meet us. "I was beginning to get worried. Did you have much trouble with Steve? Where's

Sirius?" She stopped in front of us abruptly, skirts swirling around her legs. "How are you, Hightide? Why are you looking like that?"

"Oh, never mind me!" Hightide waved her hand impatiently. "Where's Bear?" Without waiting for an answer she strode to the open bunker door and bellowed "BEAR!"

I raised my eyebrows, impressed. I'd never heard anything louder than, well, loud talk from her. Seems she'd been learning from Sarge. In answer to Hightides's summons, Bear exited the Lair at the head of a train.

She looked about the clearing, arms crossed, clearly unimpressed with the cloudy spring day. "What's so important, then?" she snapped.

"B-babe!" a male voice called, choking. Bear looked again, and saw the man, her husband, rushing from the trees uphill.

She made an incoherent sound and raced to him. They collided close enough to the Lair for everyone to get a good view, clutching each other tightly. Behind them, at a more sedate pace, Sirius and the brother-in-law, Gummy, brought the kids. When Bear's kids saw her, they broke free and raced over, sobbing fitfully.

I turned away from the reunion then and helped Eleanor chivvy the rest into the Lair to give the long-separated family a little privacy. I did notice we didn't have a single adult with a dry eye.

"So," Phoenix dropped back to walk with me, "boring trip, then?"

"Yup."

"Tell me."

I jerked a thumb behind us as we walked down the stairs. "Aside from that, I now have a freaking garden hose in my truck."

Her mouth dropped open. "What?"

"Yeah. I had to perform emergency surgery on my baby. I didn't think it'd actually work!" I wailed a little. "I don't know how long it'll last, and we never found time to find bras, and this thing is killing me!" I scratched at the bandages tying my boobs down.

"Why did you need a hose?"

"Because Steve blew a fucking big hole in my truck!" I was definitely wailing now.

"Language!" snapped Eleanor.

"Sorry." I lowered my voice.

"And you don't have to worry about the bras anymore," Phoenix piped up. "The tannery finally has a *comfortable* working bra."

While the rest of the crowd went back to whatever they'd been doing, Phoenix, Eleanor, and me walked the twisting tunnels to the tannery.

I pulled the leather lacing tight and tied it closed. The bra looked like a crop top with crossed straps on the back and lacing on the front. I'd shrugged it on easier than a shirt, while the metal grommets on the front provided easy lacing. I bounced around, did some jumping jacks and a sloppy handstand. I looked down to make sure the girls were firmly in place and snorted in amusement.

"Amana, darling," I called through the curtain to the group waiting outside.

"*Si, mi Capitan?*"

I turned to face her as she entered and watched her eyes fasten on my boobs, lips pursed in a soundless whistle. "Yes. About that. Who designed the bra?"

She passed the query back. "Al," she returned. I stared at the ceiling, trying to remember Al. "Baneeshed *de la cocina*," she whispered.

Right! The guy who broke or killed everything we didn't want broken or dead. So clumsy he'd sprained an ankle twice just walking outside the Lair. Fell down three steps last month. Man had talent at this, though, I had to give him that.

Phoenix stepped impatiently around Amana. "What's taking so...long." She looked me up and down and gave me a wolf whistle with a little leer.

"Oh, yeah," I grinned. "Al did it. He made a bra that keeps the girls in place, feels like Tom Carrington is personally holding my boobs, and will give even the flattest chested girl some cleavage."

"From the looks of you, you were never flat." Phoenix grinned, eyes never leaving my boobs.

I looked down, too, and my hands automatically came up to cup the girls. "This thing is so freaking comfortable…" I shook my head, squeezing gently, the leather smooth and soft under my rough skin. "A-fucking-plus, Al!" I shouted through the doorway.

"Thank you!" the young man shouted back.

Amana giggled, still standing in the doorway, looking back and forth from room to hallway. I shared a significant look with Phoenix, but neither of us mentioned the uncharacteristic giggle. Relationships fell under Eleanor and Lavender's purview. I didn't worry about those things until Eleanor sicced me on some poor bastard.

Phoenix wiggled her eyebrows. "So, Tom Carrington *personally* holding your boobs, huh? Maybe I should get me one of those."

"He is such a freaking dreamboat, isn't he?" We sighed, staring into space as we contemplated the British actor rocketing his way to stardom. The man was gorgeous, and if even half of what they said about him was true, the man's character was almost as good as his looks.

"While I'd never wish this shit on anyone, if I were to suddenly meet him, I wouldn't complain." Phoenix grinned wickedly.

"Hey!" The shout came from the hallway. "Are you done yet? We got work to do!"

"Yeah!" I shouted back, scooping up my shirt and sliding it on.

Hightide led the team in, and I noticed Al, a thin young man with pleasant features, pause in the doorway to exchange a few words with Amana before approaching me.

"Do you, uh," he swallowed nervously, "do you want us to fix the, uh…" He cupped his hands in front of his chest. "…cleavage?" he squeaked.

"Nah," I laughed. "Who cares? Not like anyone's ever gonna see it."

CHAPTER 48

"So, Shrike had a few interesting things to add," River said casually, after giving us the most recent report. We had the usual Useless Room lineup of Phoenix, Eleanor, Driver, Lavender, Sarge, and me. The only one missing was Sirius, but she was out, dealing with her grief and running an errand for me.

River had already given us the latest about troops, but Shrike's privileged position gave us a wealth of new information. Like the fact that the guy running the entire West Coast operation was pissed that Go Kwan-Jae hadn't wiped us off the board yet. If this was the quality of information that Shrike had on our first contact, I couldn't wait to hear what else she'd learn.

"She said it's not essential to any of our usual stuff," River continued. "She just thought we'd like to know."

"Well!" Phoenix urged. "Don't keep us in the dark. Spill!"

River took her time, enjoying this. Interesting. She didn't usually make a fuss, just delivering the news and telling us her observations. I wondered what had her looking so gleeful. She walked over to lean casually against the table.

"There's a few rumors in Salem," she began. "The soldiers think a demon's been raised against them." We laughed. A demon. Sure. "Apparently, the same night Thunder and Lightning died, they experienced losses that had nothing to do with our traps."

My smile died and I turned my head away, looking at the wall, biting my cheek.

"A patrol was miles away from the trapped ground," River continued, relishing the story, "camping out to continue hunting us the next day. The first night, a patrol never reported in. Their bodies were found, a single, clean stab wound in each man, supplies ransacked, and no sign of an intruder. The next night, two more patrols were taken out. In one case, the guard was left alive. Apparently, the men were killed while he was on watch. The day after that was the Battle at the Ridge. All they have to go on is the words 'Courtesy of Captain' carved into the ground at one site."

River sat back, and I could feel the eyes of everyone present boring into me. I refused to look up, tears welling, and my shoulders began to shake. From a distance, I heard Eleanor ushering everyone else out of the room, shutting the door behind Driver, the last one out.

"Do you want to talk about it?" Eleanor asked gently. She rested a hand on my shoulder, but that only made me cry harder. Eleanor bent, wrapping her arms around me, and I turned into her, sobbing against her shoulder.

"I didn't even think at the time," I cried. "I just... Lightning, and Thunder, and I was so *mad*. I killed them, like they were nothing, and—"

Eleanor held me as I cried like a child.

EPILOGUE: THE PRESENT

"**I** found out later that Shrike also knew how much Thunder and Lightning had told, which was everything." Hope paced across the stage, paying little attention to the crowd beyond the lights now. Lost in the past, words tumbled out, eager to be spoken now that she'd given them an outlet.

"The thing is, they didn't actually know where the Lair was on a map. The soldiers were too hasty. If they'd left the girls able to walk..." Hope broke off abruptly, realizing the topic should go no further. Her lips twisted in a pained smile. "The best part is, they all assumed we were men. I wonder what they'd've done differently, if they knew."

Hope turned and stared blindly out, seeing mountains, valleys, trees, and the faces of the dead marching past. "In the end, it didn't matter. It was too late. For all of us."

T hank you for reading *The Rebels*. If you enjoyed this and want to stay up to date on new releases and get sneak peeks, sign up to my newsletter and ALSO GRAB the first 2 chapters of *The Stillness Within the Storm*, Book 1 of *The Dragon Queen Cycle*.

The Stillness Within the Storm:

The event that broke Jen's soul happened in another life. The curse has followed her for centuries. Now, the sorceress who cursed her is trying to return to the land of the living.

Will Jen finally break free? Or will she die too young once more?

If you enjoyed The Rebels, I would love it if you let your friends know so they can experience the thrills of life with Hope, Sirius, and Phoenix, too!

And as always, please leave a review! It helps other readers find or avoid my books. Thank you!

As a special Thank You for making it this far, intrepid reader, turn the page for a sneak peek of **The Northwest Uprising Book 2: The Irregulars**

THE IRREGULARS CHAPTER 1

"Fuck those fucking assholes who can't walk into a fucking occupied fucking valley without getting fucking captured. Fucking twats." I stalked back and forth just outside our camp on the edge of the foothills near Eugene. I'd been fuming for over a day, and my mood wasn't made any better by the dreary day in late fall. The sky hadn't let loose yet, but in Oregon, all you had to do was think of rain to summon it.

For over a year, I'd been running around with my cousin Sonya—everyone knew her as Sirius—Phoenix, and a pair of siblings, Dereva and Anansi, fanning the flames of a rebellion. We'd been invaded by the North Korean Liberation Army, who had taken over the entire West Coast.

After disabling our technology (we still didn't know how), they'd rounded up the inhabitants of California, Oregon, and Washington, turning them into slaves. Oregon had been turned into a giant farm, with animals and crops all over the Willamette, everything and everyone heavily guarded. We couldn't even rescue anyone because the families of the enslaved were kept separate as hostages so the enslaved would return each day.

Motherfuckers.

In all this time, the only thing we'd wanted was the US Army, riding to our rescue. We were less than a hundred fighters holed up in the Bull Run Wilderness, with nearly three times that in non-combatants stashed in the mountains. Sirius had come back from mourning her friends with the location of a cave system large enough to hide all our non-coms with room to spare in the Jefferson wilderness.

Just us, against an entire army.

Then, last week, a man showed up on the edge of our camp, telling us the army had arrived. He was an advance scout, and he'd stood in the middle of a camp full of angry, armed women while keeping an admirable level of respect and calm. I could work with that, and it didn't hurt that he was easy on the eyes.

Well, handsome as fuck was more accurate, but I conveniently forgot the way my heart jumped when I'd seen him.

Then I met his commander. A more self-righteous son of a bitch I'd never met. He'd taken one look at us, said "Collaborators and unimportant," and fucked off on some secret mission to the Valley. The asshole in charge, Major Hendricks, refused to tell us anything.

"Your...*fighters*," he'd managed to say as he looked down his thin, autocratic nose at me, despite being a couple inches shorter, "have...fraternized...with the enemy. We simply can't trust them. Or you." Then they'd promptly gotten captured.

Morons.

Based on how much I trusted Hendricks (not at all), we packed up and moved camp as soon as they were out of sight. Then, I'd sent my cousin to take a few scouts and follow them. I found out they'd been captured the day after it happened.

Normally, I'd be inclined to leave them, but my baby brother, Peter, was one of the idiots who got his ass caught. Now, four of us risked death, or worse, to spring these dumbasses from prison. I'd even had to send a vehicle back to the Lair, our home base and a former secret military outpost, to get additional support.

Who's the idiot now? my inner asshole taunted. *Fuck you, too*, I told it.

Taking five slow, deliberate breaths, I headed back into camp. "All right. I'm ready," I announced.

As Seahorse had predicted all those months ago, the girls weren't overly thrilled with the plan. Who could blame them? One thing goes wrong, and we're all either sex slaves or on the torture rack. To give ourselves our best chance of blending in, we'd brought the Fates—non-combatants who hadn't left the area around the Lair in months—into the field.

The Three Fates, former beauticians who'd been freed in one of our earlier rescues, circled me, plucking at my clothing and clucking. Going by the noises, they didn't approve of my fatigues, plain T-shirt, boots, sweatshirt, and plethora of weaponry that passed as our uniforms.

The First Fate, a woman who neither confirmed nor denied when I asked her if she was from Europe, snorted. "You aren't ready yet, but you will be."

Around us, fighters—mostly women but a scattering of men—prepped for the coming fight, giving their weapons a final check, tightening laces, and making sure they had plenty of ammo. I wished desperately to be a part of their number, but instead I faced the Fates, who were armed with the tools of their trade—makeup, scissors, hair dye, and...clothing.

Calling the tiny slip of cloth *clothing* was being generous. Sirius, Phoenix, and I had gone into Salem nearly a year ago, just to see what the hell was happening. While there, we broke into a brothel, killed a bunch of soldiers, stole a bus, and rescued some women who had been forced into prostitution. On our way out, we'd sacked the place, taking anything that might be useful, including the clothes.

That piece of foresight finally came in handy. I now sat on a tree stump in my bra and underwear while the three women worked over and around me, patting, trimming, primping, and coloring to make me look presentable.

Occasionally, they called for another bucket of water. Then they called in another fighter, Ink. The teen had a keen eye for art and tattooing. She drew designs over my scars with henna.

When they'd all finished and got me into the slip of a dress, I surveyed the expanse of visible skin, and how much of it was covered in henna tattoos, including around my left eye, where a cougar had given me a memento.

I stood and twisted experimentally, the cold wind blowing up my nether regions. "You know, I don't think I've been this naked in public since I was born."

They laughed, then the Second Fate brought over a pair of six-inch platform heels. "Your shoes, my dear."

I eyed them dubiously, but obediently sat down on the stump to pull the shoes on. "When did we get shoes?" I grunted, struggling to get a foot into the strappy contraption of torture.

"They came in an hour ago." Phoenix folded her arms, scowling down at the shoes she already wore. "They suck."

The First, seeing me struggle, knelt and brushed my hands aside to work the shoe on herself. "It won't fit?" She sat back, surprised.

I held up the other shoe, squinting at the text on the bottom. "Heh. It's a normal width shoe. It'll never fit," I informed the nonplussed beautician.

She looked at my trapped foot, my toes not even passing the halfway mark, her lips compressed in a thin line. "This was the only pair they found in your size. Now what?"

"I go barefoot." I wrenched the wretched thing off and flexed my foot, stretching my toes before standing. "If I walk right, I should be okay. I'm doing a natural thing." I wrinkled my nose, grimacing.

The First stood up, dusting off her knees. "It will have to do. We do not have shoes for another girl, so we cannot replace you. You must make the best of it. Now, you learn to walk!"

This declaration received some notice from the fighters surrounding us.

"But I already know how to walk!" I said. Women huddled around Dereva, who had a pad and pencil out, swirling apart and coming together again, their grins swiftly hidden at my glances.

"Hah!" The First brought my attention back. "No. You stride. Every move conveys violent intent. Now, you must learn to *seduce* with a step."

"Fuck me." More than one person had to hide a reddening face or outright laughter. I scowled. "Whose dumbass idea was this, anyway?" I asked the air.

"We only have one person who could come up with something as *bold* as this," Dereva piped up. The word *stupid* hung unspoken in the air. She looked like all she needed was a bowl of popcorn to be all set. Her pencil hovered over the pad. "You."

"The peanut gallery can shut up," I groused.

Nobody tried to hide their laughter anymore.

"You realize I'm about as seductive as a pineapple, right?" I looked at the Fates as if they would save me.

"Spiky on the outside, sweet and tart on the inside, and will dissolve you in acid if given enough time," Phoenix chortled, happy now that someone was more uncomfortable than her.

"...Okay. I'll give you that one. Asshole."

"Now, Captain." The First Fate interrupted our Roast The Captain session. "What you must do is this..."

***

Sung Ki's black eyes met mine as the truck slowed at the last checkpoint before town. Steep hills covered in fir trees held the mist barely above our heads, revealing the town at the last minute. *Only four of us.* I pressed my lips together, then remembered the lipstick and immediately softened them. Phoenix, Storm, and me sat in the back, dressed in tiny bits of nothing. In front, Sung Ki drove the only military truck we'd stolen that didn't have bullet holes in it.

"Lucky you, avoiding the shoes," Storm whispered.

"Big feet." I grinned.

"Shit." Phoenix pulled our attention around to see the compound. "Look at the security here."

"Well, at least we're in the right place."

Out of the whole town, only the industrial area had tall chain link fencing and curled barbed wire with guards walking their rounds. It was a small section, maybe a square mile. Steve even included a few houses from the neighboring suburbs inside their compound.

We were silent, conscious of our lack of weapons and clothing. "Not like we didn't know about this," I muttered, shifting in my excuse for a dress.

Sirius had brought word back that the place was like Fort Knox, which is why we'd brought the Fates in to tart us up like high-priced call girls, ready for a day or three's worth of debauchery. The Fates had assured me that women were often sent out to one of these bases for "entertainment" and that getting in wasn't the problem. What straight man is going to complain about scantily clad women showing up?

Leaving would be difficult, which is why we had friends on the outside.

The truck rolled to a stop at the gate and Steve whisked the door open for us. I was last out, and my eyes widened when the other two wobbled on the uneven asphalt. I let out a slow breath when they caught their balance.

Around us, Steve broke into excited chatter, and three stepped forward to frisk us, groping and fondling where they could. We gripped each other's hands in a mixture of courage and "we can't kill them yet" as we stood in a row. One Steve hiked up my skirt, but Sung Ki bulled through the soldiers, snapping and pushing them away.

They settled in a loose ring around us, several of them eyeing the sleeve work Ink had done on my leg to hide the scars that that mountain lion had given me.

Impatiently, Sung Ki waved at them to unload the bags and lead the way. Before moving out, the soldiers searched each bag. All they found were short lengths of solid steel pipes, meant to be fitted together, bases and ceiling attachments, wooden sticks, and a few more costumes as well as curtains and rope. Grunting, they finally led the way into a building a couple hundred yards away.

Sung Ki turned away from the men, and I saw her hands tremble until she clenched them into fists. Catching her eye, I nodded. Squaring her shoulders, she took a deep breath and followed Steve towards what looked like the offices for the warehouse complex, brusquely waving us after her.

I checked out the buildings we passed, hissing and hitching my stride when I stepped on a sharp rock. Grunting, I remembered what the Fates had said about walking. Rising onto my toes, I stepped carefully, my hips automatically swaying from side to side. *Fuck this shit.*

Once inside, Steve led us to a large central room with doors and interior windows along two walls. Sung Ki shooed them out, snapping orders at their retreating backs. With no time to lose, we ransacked the bags, pulling out the pipes, cloth, and ropes Steve just checked.

I stood on a chair to attach the ropes to the ceiling, stringing the cloth on it to make a curtain and stage area. The others began assembling the pipes into floor to ceiling poles, carefully setting aside a few extra pieces.

I flipped a ratchet out and started tensioning the first pole to the floor near the center of the room while Storm held it steady. We needed to make this look good.

"All set?" Sung Ki asked.

Glancing around, I nodded. "All set. Good luck."

She left through the only door that led to the outside, laughing quietly with the guard stationed there.

"Hey." Phoenix jolted me back into the room. "Where's the piece with the hooky thing?"

"Um..." I flailed around behind me, my questing fingers finally latching onto it. "Here." I held it out gingerly.

Phoenix took it and carefully peeled back the layers to reveal a gray center. Sparrow had spent hours disguising bits of explosives as pipes. Though she assured us they shouldn't go off on their own, I didn't find *shouldn't* particularly comforting.

She bustled around the main room, setting out the chairs stacked against the wall into neat rows. Some of the chairs had a bit of the soft explosive molded to the bottoms. Others had the extra pipes taped to them. We used the only stuff Sparrow could find that was moldable: some old, volatile acetone triperoxide putty.

"Here." Storm set the slightly curved wooden sticks at my side and shook small components out of a bag. I didn't know how they worked, but Seahorse, our former beauty queen and resident explosives expert, assured us they would form not only operable but semi-reliable timers.

I took a screwdriver and scraped out the (non-exploding) putty we'd used to keep extra items inside the pipes in the second bag. Mostly throwing daggers and a couple of disassembled handguns. Phoenix, done with the chairs, slipped all the knives into a bandolier and set it by Storm, then began putting the guns together.

"I wish it was more than just us to start," Phoenix muttered.

"Not a snowball's chance in hell," I grunted, jerking the wrench to ensure the connection was as tight as possible. The Fates had been clear. The fewer women who went in, the better chance we had of not being raped by the common soldiers. We were entertainment for the officers first.

Once they were done, the usual was for the girls to be passed around to the soldiers.

A soldier opened the door, whistling appreciatively. Storm raced over, shooing him out, blowing kisses as she shut the door. "Impatient bastards," she snorted, coming back to help place the third, and last, pole.

***

The curtains were drawn, and the room began to fill with officers. The murmur of their conversation was broken with the clink of glasses, slurping drinks, and the scrape of chairs against linoleum. Every time a slurping noise carried over the other sounds, I growled. Each noise piled on top of the others, fogging my mind until I was ready to walk out there and slaughter the lot.

Someone began shouting, then more joined in, whistling and catcalling in their native tongue. I didn't speak much of it, but catcalling sounds the same in every language. I braced my back against the wall while Phoenix used me as a ladder to get into the air duct near the ceiling. Storm pulled the curtain back and posed seductively in the narrow gap.

"Coming soon!" She blew kisses and flipped the curtain closed again.

Phoenix, finally in the damn duct, held her hands out. I passed her the bags and waved urgently to Storm. She snatched up her bandolier and slung it over her head and practically ran up me, her bare feet flexing as they pushed off my limbs. Their discarded shoes littered the floor, thankfully.

After passing my sticks to Storm, she scooted further into the duct to give me room. Sweat gathered in my armpits and upper lip despite the cool day. Sparrow had been quite clear that her timers had a good five-minute window to go off, and we were already too close. The damn officers had begun gathering earlier than we'd thought, and the last of our preparations had been hounded and plagued by them, slowing our exit.

Taking three fast steps, I ran up the side of the wall, barely catching the edge of the duct. As soon as I had a grip, Storm wriggled forward, grabbing the harness I'd added to my ridiculous outfit. We'd planned on putting on sensible clothes before shit hit the fan. The officers' early arrival screwed that. Now, the only thing she could grab was the harness.

As soon as I got my upper body in, Storm reeled backwards. I pulled my legs up—and the world exploded, everything turning red, then black.

***

I floated, randomly back in the foothills. It'd been a bit of work getting Peter alone without anyone noticing. I'd had to wait until he left the camp to find a tree, then I had to wait until he finished peeing before I could ambush him and drag him away. I'd cried. He'd tried to be manly before putting his head on my shoulder and sobbing. Sirius found us and we sat down to talk.

Peter, naturally, wanted to know if I'd found Papa and Sean, my younger brother. I hadn't. I asked him if he'd heard from Grace, and his news nearly gave me a heart attack.

"Grace and Charlie decided they're sneaking into occupied territory to get people out." He'd hunched his shoulders, waiting for my outburst, but I was so stunned I couldn't even move. "They're only going to Washington, though," he hastily reassured me. "Because that's the only place they can find soldiers to let them through."

I whimpered. Sirius snorted. "What? Now I know she's your sister. I sometimes wondered, considering she's so sweet and you're an asshole, but it turns out you guys have flaming recklessness in common." She shook her head, pointing at Peter. "All three of you."

"Pot, kettle," I taunted her.

***

"Fuck. Fuck." I coughed, rolling over, slowly returning to the present. I was on...what? I looked around groggily, my ears ringing. Crawling forward, I crossed over a low broken wall. What? Further in, I narrowly missed a piece of metal sticking up in front of me. Feeling it, half blinded by dust, I followed it up until it ended in jagged shards. Ah. Right. A pole

Twisting around, I barely made out Storm's head and arms reaching down. The conduit hung tenuously from the ceiling, shaking every time her or Phoenix shifted. Her mouth moved and she stretched her hand down urgently. Light finally dawned. The explosives had gone off early.

I think.

Time was relative when you didn't have any working timepieces. I don't know why we kept using hours and minutes. Habit, maybe.

"Captain! You idiot, get moving!" Storm's voice finally made it through the ringing in my ears.

I shook my head. The dust settled enough for me to see the bits and chunks scattered around. Staggering to my feet, something squished underfoot. Taking a deep breath, I resolutely did not look down and went to the fighters.

"Keep going," I said, my voice swimming as if through water. "We'll meet up at the pickup. Just...find some folks along the way, yeah?"

Storm disappeared briefly, then her head reappeared, her blonde hair hanging over her eyes. Shoving it back with one hand, she dropped my sticks and a pair of moccasins with the other. "You'll need these."

Nodding, I flexed my jaw, trying to pop my ears. Goddamn explosives.

I pulled the moccasins on before I had a chance to step on anything even more objectionable than I already had, grabbed the sticks, and staggered to the doors. Well, to the doorway. There was a large, gaping hole where the doors had been. Their remains littered the room beyond.

My ears cleared enough to hear the moans and weak cries of the wounded. The soldiers rushing in weren't interested in a filthy woman, no matter how little she wore, so I made it out unmolested. Exiting the building was as simple as stepping over the windowsill, making sure I didn't cut myself on the broken glass stubbornly clinging to the frame.

I lurched, slamming into a wall and bouncing off it in a moment of dizziness, weaving my way along. Sirius had given us a decent idea where the soldiers would be, and I made my slow way there. I passed a barrel filled to the top with rainwater and took a moment to dunk my head, trying to clear the dust from my eyes and ears. Seeing the difference in color between my hands and arms, I practically climbed in to wash off. By the time I finished, my slip was soaked but I didn't have dust filling various crevices anymore.

Scooping my sticks up, I pondered my dress as I walked. Which did I want to cover, my boobs or my crotch? This dress didn't give me an option for both. Sighing, I tugged it down. I felt a bit more secure that way.

Every building I passed, I checked the windows for occupants. After the third one, I hissed impatiently. Where were they?

At the fourth, I peeked through the widow perfunctorily, prepared to pass as quickly as I had the others. Ducking under the window, I paused, frowning. Edging back, I looked again. A dim red glow deep inside a nearly black interior. Nothing else had been quite so dark. And that glow...a fire?

Seizing it as my best option, I circled the building, passing huge loading docks until I found a people-sized door on the far side, then went up a narrow set of stairs. At the top, I was high enough to see another billow of black smoke, followed by reaching flames. A second later, the concussion from the explosion hit me, and I smiled.

Trying the doorknob gave me no results. Locked. Pounding on the door, I screamed. "Help! Help me! Please let me in."

I sobbed loudly, my mouth pressed to the crack. Coughing, I spat some dust and sobbed hysterically. *How long can we do this?* I wondered. Acting panicky was hard work, and every second that passed left me sounding less like a scared woman and more like a pissed off bitch.

The door cracked open, and a suspicious eye glared at me. I sniffed and wiped my hands over my face to hide the lack of tears. The eye looked down, up, and down again. Then the door opened wide, and a leering soldier gestured me in. Like a lamb to slaughter, I gave him a trembling smile and stepped in.

Four guards lounged around the former office, which stank of unwashed people, fear, and blood. Any doubts I had about this being the right building disappeared. The office looked out over the warehouse, and now I could clearly see a sullen fire smoldering in a brazier set in the middle of the warehouse floor next to a table.

Cages lined the walls, filled with listless men in ragged clothing. I couldn't see how many men were in there. They wouldn't be able to move very fast. Doc would have her hands full with this lot. Turning, I smiled at the soldiers eyeing me hungrily, ignoring their predatory gazes.

"What those for?" one man asked, pointing to the sticks in my hand.

"It's part of my routine." I smiled brightly through clenched teeth. "I'm an entertainer." I used a sideways glance the Third Fate had spent half a frustrating hour teaching me just this morning with a shard of mirror. I got it right, if the rise in his pants was any indication. "Would you like me to show you?"

Enthusiastic nods all around. Smiling slightly, I stepped lightly into the middle of the room. This wasn't something I'd learned from the Fates. This, I'd learned from Sarge. Holding a stick in each hand, I spun them around, to the side, in a figure eight. Still spinning the sticks, I moved into the beginning steps of a dance, flowing high, then low, never stopping, always moving.

Giving the sticks an extra flick, I spun, whacking a soldier across the face, knocking the lower three-quarters of the stick loose, which was what I wanted. He cried out in shock as he fell, and the others scrambled to get their hands out of their pants. Another twist, then the blade was completely revealed. I slashed a man, opening a gash across his torso while the sheath flew off the second blade.

It was over quickly, and none of the enemy had gotten off a shot. Cleaning the blades took a moment, then I sheathed them and clipped the sticks onto the harness so their hilts protruded over my shoulders. It was the best place for them when I needed to run. Going to the desk, a quick search revealed three bunches of keys. I checked Steve's pants next, hoping for *something* to cover my legs, but they were all fouled by the men's deaths.

"Fuck. Oh, well." Snatching the keys up, I ran to the stairs, skipping down to the warehouse floor. Down here, the stench was even worse, and I gagged. An unwashed person in the wild doesn't really smell much. More like our scents blended into the forest. We smelled of dirt, leaves, and leather. Animals scarcely paid attention to us, and we barely noticed each other.

This was different. If despair had a scent, this was it.

The table had straps hanging from it and was marked with black blotches. From it rose a stale, metallic tang that clashed with the sweet smell of death. I didn't care to look more closely than that. Instead, I focused on the cages. What if Peter were already...?

Biting my lip to keep from shouting for my brother, I went to the closest cage, trying keys. They shivered and clanked in my hand while I tried key after key. Caged soldiers struggled to their feet, some limping to the bars. While some had less damage than others, none of the prisoners were uninjured.

"Hi!" I smiled and nodded. "Um...is this all of you?"

"All that's left." The man's voice was hoarse, raw, but when he walked over to me, he seemed steady enough. "Do we know you?"

"Last time you saw me, I had more clothes on." Moving onto the next keyring, I started fresh. "I'm Captain."

"Well, at the risk of sounding sexist, I can honestly say you're the best thing any of us have seen all week." I glanced up at him, startled. His eyes moved down my dress to my moccasined feet and back up. I blushed, glad it was hidden by the darkness. "But shouldn't you have brought stuff to shoot the bad guys with?"

I couldn't hold back a grin when the lock clicked open and I moved to the next. "What, you think this dress isn't enough to blind the enemy?" I looked down quickly at my legs, which shone like a beacon. "And if the dress doesn't, my glow-in-the-dark legs should. There's some extra guns up there." I jerked my head to the office, my hands already busy with the new lock.

Some of the men limped up the stairs, but the one talking followed me. "I spoke to you, back at your camp."

I made a non-committal noise. "Talked to a lot of people there." A quick glance from the corner of my eye caught his eyes at the right angle. Deep blue, they were the same shade as an early fall sky. Memory dawned. He was blond under the dirt, sweat, and blood.

He'd been the first one to walk into our camp. Storm had found him scouting for his unit, and he'd managed to convince her to not kill him. He'd stood in the center of a circle of armed women, cool as a cucumber. He didn't threaten, posture, or impress us with how great he was. He'd just stood there, his hands out to the side, fascinated by us.

The second cage's lock gave way under a key, and I moved to the last lock. Deciding to risk it, since it was too dark for him to see if I turned red. "I remember you, you know. Pretty Boy."

He groaned while those who followed our conversation chuckled. Under the bruises, grime, and swelling, his features were defined. He was young, unscarred. Anyone would consider him handsome with his strong jaw and straight nose. Many of the fighters had gossiped about the scout with the butter blond hair and respectful demeanor.

Now that I was on the last cage, my anxiety ratcheted up another notch. I hadn't seen Peter yet. The scout noticed how I tried to get a good look at every man there. "You're looking for the boy. Private Wilkins. I remember seeing you talking to him at your camp. Is he a friend of yours?"

"No," I lied. Shit! I hadn't thought anyone had seen me talking with Peter. "I just hate to see someone so young going into a war zone. I wanted to check with him and see if him and the others his age were okay with this shit."

The scout grunted, pulling me back to the present. "They signed up to fight."

"Yeah." I snorted. "Not the first time kids get caught up in shit that shouldn't have anything to do with them. I guess I just hoped the kid would be okay. He seemed like a nice boy." I bit my lip and hoped the tremors hadn't come through my voice.

The last lock opened and the men who could walked out. Squinting, I barely made out a shape still on the floor in the corner.

The scout jostled past me, heading to the long bundle. "Whether he'll be okay depends on what kind of care he gets," he said. The soldier flipped back the thin blanket, revealing Peter's face. He twitched, sleeping restlessly.

The ground shifted under my feet when I saw him, and I clutched the cage bars to keep from going over. "What happened to him?"

"He got shot when we were taken." The scout grunted, pulling Peter up and over his shoulders in a fireman's carry. "He's the only one who's lasted this long. Kid's a tough little bastard. He'll be fine with care."

The words "with care" snapped me out of my funk. "Right," I snapped, swinging around, raising my voice so they could hear me. "There should be another boom any—"

The ground rocked under us, then came the boom. "There they are. We've got a doctor coming, so we need to get to the meeting point. The bus will be here soon."

The scout stared at me, mouth open. "Bus?"

The sharp report of gunfire reached my ears. "Time to go! Where's that pain in the ass Hendricks?"

Their commander, a Major Hendricks, had refused assistance, been insulting, and tried to convince my fighters to walk away from me so that he could put his own second, Lieutenant French, in command. My people hadn't had any of it, but he'd still tried.

"He was executed, ma'am," another soldier reported, saluting. His left arm was crudely bandaged, and he leaned on a young giant for support, but he was up. He was a man of medium height, a little shorter than me, and slender. I reckoned the giant supporting him could carry him with one hand, but he stayed on his two feet. "His second, French, was a spy for the enemy. That's how they caught us so easily. I'm Sergeant Perry, by the way."

"Gah!" I held up my hand, as if trying to ward off a blow. "Haven't we told you we don't use names?"

He merely shrugged his good shoulder. "Doesn't matter to me." Well. It was even better that we'd moved on the moment they left our camp.

Walking quickly to the door, the men fell into a ragged formation behind me. Those who had weapons walked on the outside, the wounded and those supporting wounded in the middle.

"How many soldiers are with you, ma'am?" Perry asked.

"No soldiers," I replied, checking that my swords were loose in their sheaths. "But I've got every fighter coming in." At a ground floor door, I poked my head out, then pulled back swiftly. I held up three fingers, pointing to the left. The men readied their handguns, fingers trembling in anticipation. "Save your bullets," I whispered. "And for God's sake, don't shoot any women."

Drawing my swords, I stood poised in the doorway, the vibrations of marching feet running through the ground. As soon as they drew close enough, I spun out into the middle of the small patrol. The ecstatic agony of being extremely good at something I didn't want to be good at rolled through me. Sarge's training was...effective.

When it was done, a helmet spun gently on the ground near my foot, the chin strap neatly cut. After wiping the blades clean on the dead men's uniforms, I straightened to see the soldiers staring, mouths open. "What?" My free hand automatically went to my chest, then the hem, checking that the damn dress was in place.

"That was...fast," one pasty-faced soldier choked out.

"And bloody," another muttered.

"What it was, was efficient," the scout carrying Peter corrected. He watched me closely, faint crinkles showing at the corners of his eyes. He'd begun sagging under my brother's weight but straightened with a groan. "Which way now?"

"That way." I pointed west, away from the sounds of fighting.

"Isn't the entrance there?" Perry asked, pointing east.

"Yeah, but that's not where our ride's coming in. That's just where Steve *thinks* they are. Now, let's go."

"Move 'em out," Perry said, just loud enough to be heard, circling his uninjured hand in the air.

Peter shifted over the scout's shoulders, groaning and waking slowly. The man lowered my brother and handed him off to two other men. The men who didn't have guns quickly found things to arm themselves with, one man taking off his shoe and sock and putting half a brick in his sock.

I led the way, seventeen men in various stages of health following closely.

Roughly halfway to our destination, a ululating shriek echoed on my left. I snapped around, listening intently. Snarling, I turned to the scout, who walked next to me. "Gotta go. My people are in trouble. Keep heading that way." I pointed. "You can't miss our bus."

"Right." The scout nodded to the men. "You heard the Captain. Keep heading west. We'll see you there." I opened my mouth to tell him to go with his men, but he didn't give me time. "We've got enough men to protect them. One man more or less won't make a difference here."

Shutting my mouth with a snap, I nodded. These guys would be okay. We'd seen a couple more Steve along the way, and the soldiers had been more than eager to get a bit of their own back.

"Go," Perry said. "That's an order."

"You can't order me," the scout laughed. "I was barely in, anyway."

"Hey, Squirt." I nodded to the giant soldier supporting Perry. "Keep him in one piece. This dude's okay."

The soldier gaped at me while his buddies laughed. "How the fuck do you call a brother my size 'squirt'?"

I shrugged. "Fine. Goliath. Don't worry, at least I won't have to worry about you keeling over like Grandpa, over there." I pointed to a soldier, barely more than a boy, who hadn't managed to grow any stubble after several days without shaving. The kid walked unsupported but stumbled a bit when I pointed at him.

I headed out, closely followed by the scout. "Need a weapon?" I asked him as I headed north at a slow jog.

"Nah. I'll be fine." He managed to match my pace, but I could see he wouldn't be able to keep it up for long. Maybe just long enough.

Smoke drifted between the buildings, fresh bits of rubble scattered over the streets. Here and there, flames could be seen above the buildings. To the east, the rattle of guns moved slowly away. Seahorse was letting them drive her off. Soon, they'd disappear into the forest, getting as many soldiers as they could to chase them.

Through the general din, I could make out specific sounds of fighting. Shouts, screams, and individual gunshots cut through the air. "You go left, I'll go right." I spoke in a low voice, even though the chances we'd be noticed with the party up ahead were slim.

The scout gave me a nod and a thumb's up, then disappeared silently into the smoke.

"Huh." I stared, bemused, at the swirling smoke left in his wake. "No arguing, no 'I wanna do it my way!'" I sniggered. "I could do with more of that. Hope he survives."

ACKNOWLEDGMENTS

No book was ever written in a vacuum, and this one is certainly no exception. If Gail Noble hadn't told me to write down that one little scene that played over and over in my head, it would never have started. If Bronwen Cope hadn't challenged me to write just 1 minute a day, I'd never have finished it. My mom, Mania, and my sisters, Hanya and Raya, cheered me on even when they didn't know anything about the book. I could vent and be heard with them.

Special thanks to my cousin, Tania, for being the first person besides me to read The Rebels all the way through. She also pointed out when I used the wrong slang and gave me tons of helpful tips like "????" and "Fix this."

And finally, but certainly not least, I need to thank my editor, Dave Pasquantonio. You polished the prose, pointed out weak spots that needed to be shored up, and put so much work into this since. Publishing wouldn't have been this fun or easy without you.

ABOUT AUTHOR

Nadya Siapin is the author of The Northwest Uprising trilogy and is now moving into Arthurian myths with The Dragon Queen Cycle.

An avid traveler and story lover, she mixes what she knows with what she imagines and is always on the lookout for slightly insane, definitely chaotic quotes for some characters 2 series into the future. (Sometimes, she manages to plan ahead.)

A dual citizen of the United States and Australia, Nadya uses her travel and backpacking experience extensively in her writing. She splits her time between the US and Australia. She can (occasionally)be persuaded to wear shoes. You can check out her other work or follow her on social media here.

instagram.com/nadya_siapin/

facebook.com/nadya.siapin.author/

tiktok.com/@nadyasiapin.author